OTTO PENZLER PRESENTS
AMERICAN MYSTERY CLASSICS

THE DOOR

Mary Roberts Rinehart (1876-1958) was the most beloved and bestselling mystery writer in America in the first half of the twentieth century. Born in Pittsburgh, Rinehart trained as a nurse and married a doctor. When a stock market crash sent the young couple into debt, Rinehart leaned on her writing—previously a part-time occupation—to pay the bills. Credited with inventing the phrase, "The butler did it"—a phrase she never actually wrote—Rinehart is often called an American Agatha Christie, even though she was much more popular during her heyday.

Otto Penzler, the creator of American Mystery Classics, is also the founder of the Mysterious Press (1975); MysteriousPress.com (2011), an electronic-book publishing company; and New York City's Mysterious Bookshop (1979). He has won a Raven, the Ellery Queen Award, two Edgars (for the *Encyclopedia of Mystery and Detection*, 1977, and *The Lineup*, 2010), and lifetime achievement awards from NoirCon and *The Strand Magazine*. He has edited more than 70 anthologies and written extensively about mystery fiction.

THE DOOR

MARY ROBERTS
RINEHART

Introduction by
OTTO
PENZLER

AMERICAN
MYSTERY
CLASSICS

Penzler Publishers
New York

This is a work of fiction. Names, characters, places, and incidents either are the product of the author's imagination or are used fictitiously. Any resemblance to actual persons, living or dead, businesses, companies, events, or locales is entirely coincidental.

Published in 2024 by Penzler Publishers
58 Warren Street, New York, NY 10007
penzlerpublishers.com

Distributed by W. W. Norton

Cover image: Andy Ross
Cover design: Mauricio Diaz

Paperback ISBN 978-1-61316-590-4
Hardcover ISBN 978-1-61316-593-5

Library of Congress Control Number: 2024943989

Printed in the United States of America

9 8 7 6 5 4 3 2 1

INTRODUCTION

When she was young and her family were desperate for money, Mary Roberts Rinehart leaped into action and did the one thing she knew how to do. She wrote and became a phenomenally successful author.

During the Golden Age of mystery fiction, the years between the two World Wars, Rinehart became one of the handful of the bestselling writers in America. Not a bestselling mystery writer—a bestselling *writer*. The list of the top ten bestselling books for each year in the 1920s showed Rinehart on the list five times; only Sinclair Lewis matched that impressive feat. The only mystery titles that outsold her in those years were *Rebecca* by Daphne du Maurier and two titles by S.S. Van Dine, *The Greene Murder Case* and *The Bishop Murder Case.*

In 1929, as business in America had been booming, two of her sons, Stan, Jr., and Ted, announced that they were starting their own publishing company with John Farrar. They left their positions at Doubleday Doran and founded Farrar & Rinehart. No one anticipated the Great Depression that was just around the corner.

Deciding that she could help them by again doing the one

thing at which she excelled—writing a book—and set to work on a big book to be titled *The Door* (1930). So anxious to make it exceptionally successful, she struggled with it for months before finding her rhythm.

In a way, it has become a landmark work of mystery fiction, as it popularized a now-cliché trope of the genre—"the butler did it." The novel features Elizabeth Bell, who fills her solitary life with writing, enthusiastically reading crime stories (both fact and fiction), and a small household staff. The disappearance and subsequent murder of one of the staff disrupts her simple, quiet day-to-day life, sending her on an exciting but dangerous quest for a culprit who has been hiding in plain sight all along.

Serialization rights to *The Door* were sold to *The Saturday Evening Post* for $60,000—a staggering sum in 1929 dollars—and then Rinehart received $30,000 for the film rights, just as bankruptcies and stock market crashes wiped out innumerable fortunes. Because the mystery market managed to retain its popularity, Mary largely abandoned the serious novels that she had begun to produce and wrote eleven more suspense novels, earning more than $100,000 a year during the 1930s.

In many regards, Mary Roberts Rinehart was the American Agatha Christie, both in terms of popularity and productivity. Like her British counterpart, the prolific Rinehart wrote a large number of bestselling mysteries, short stories, straight novels, an unrevealing autobiography, and stage plays, some of which were hugely successful—*The Mousetrap* for Christie and *The Bat* for Rinehart.

Unlike Christie, however, Rinehart's popularity waned after her death in 1958. The lack of a long-running series character (although Miss Letitia Carberry, known as Tish, appeared in several books, she was not strictly a detective, and Nurse Adams, dubbed "Miss Pinkerton" by the police for her uncanny ability to become embroiled in criminal activities, had few appearances) undoubtedly hurt, but so did changing reading tastes in the United States. While Christie's detectives, notably Hercule Poirot, were reasoning creatures largely lacking in emotions, Rinehart's characters were swept up in the very human responses of romance, curiosity, fear, and tenacity.

A common element in Rinehart's mysteries was the author's penchant for moving the storyline along with foreshadowing. While this is a frequently used device in contemporary literature, Rinehart often employed a method that has become mocked by some, partially because of its simplicity as well as so much overuse that it has been defined as a cliché in her work.

Rinehart's use of this contrivance is now famously credited (or blamed, depending on your point of view) for creating the "Had-I-But-Known" school of fiction. Straightforward detection is less evident in Rinehart's mysteries than in the works of her predecessors, which generally concentrated on the methods of eccentric detectives. Rinehart's stories involve ordinary people entangled in a situation not of their making that could happen to anyone.

The heroines of these books often have poor judgment. Warned never—*never*—to enter the basement under any circumstances, for instance, they are absolutely certain to be found there within the next few pages, only to be rescued at the very last instant, generally by their lovers. These heroines often have flashes of insight—just too late to prevent another murder.

The statement (and its numerous variations) "had I but known then what I know now, this could have been avoided" often creeps into her books and has given its name to a school of fiction that has produced innumerable followers.

Born to a poor family in Pittsburgh, her father committed suicide just as she was graduating from nursing school, where she had met Dr. Stanley Marshall Rinehart, who she married in 1896 at the age of twenty; they had three sons. Because of poor investments, the young nurse and her doctor husband struggled financially so she began to write, selling forty-five stories in the first year (1903). The editor of *Munsey's Magazine* suggested that she write a novel, which he would serialize, and she quickly produced *The Man in Lower Ten*, followed immediately by *The Circular Staircase*, which was published in book form first, in 1908. After her husband died in 1932, Mary Roberts Rinehart, now a fabulously wealthy woman from the sales of her books, moved into a luxurious, eighteen-room Park Avenue apartment where she lived alone for the rest of her life.

A consistent bestseller from that point on, Rinehart's mysteries have a surprisingly violent side to them (though never graphically described), with the initial murder serving as a springboard to subsequent multiple murders. Her tales are unfailingly filled with sentimental love stories and gentle humor, both unusual elements of crime fiction in the early decades of the twentieth century.

Describing some of her books, Rinehart displayed a sly sense of humor while conceding the levels of violence and the body count are not entirely expected from an author known for her romantic, humorous, and heart-warming mystery fiction. Here are some selected titles about which she warned readers:

- *The After House* (1914): "I killed three people with one axe, raising the average number of murders per crime book to a new high level."
- *The Album* (1933): "The answer to four gruesome murders lies in a dusty album for everyone to see."

• *The Wall* (1938): "I commit three shocking murders in a fashionable New England summer colony."

• *The Great Mistake* (1940): "A murder story set in the suburbs, involving a bag of toads, a pair of trousers and some missing keys."

In her most famous work, *The Bat*, strange events permeate the Long Island manor in which most of the action occurs. *The Circular Staircase*, her first book, was adapted for a stage play titled *The Bat* (a sobriquet for a bank robber), which she wrote with Avery Hopkins. The play was then novelized under the same title as the wildly successful drama. Oddly, perhaps wary (or weary) of rewriting her plot yet again, it has been rumored that Rinehart hired Stephen Vincent Benet to write the novelization. *The Bat*, proving to be ubiquitous, was adapted for a 1926 silent movie, then a sound film in 1930 titled *The Bat Whispers*, and yet again in 1959 as *The Bat*, as well as several television adaptations.

Although some of the mores and social niceties of her time have changed, Rinehart's greatest strengths as a writer were her ability to tell a story that compelled the reader to turn the page, and to create universal characters to which all of us can relate. That ability never goes out of style and, as long as people read books, neither will Mary Roberts Rinehart, the universally beloved writer who, for two decades, was the best-paid writer in America.

—Otto Penzler

CHAPTER ONE

I HAVE wrenched my knee, and for the past two weeks my days have consisted of three trays, two of them here in the library, a nurse at ten o'clock each morning with a device of infernal origin which is supposed to bake the pain out of my leg, and my thoughts for company.

But my thinking is cloudy and chaotic. The house is too quiet. I miss Judy, busy now with affairs of her own, and perhaps I miss the excitement of the past few months. It is difficult to take an interest in beef croquettes for luncheon out of last night's roast when one's mind is definitely turned on crime. For that is what I am thinking about, crime; and major crime at that.

I am thinking about murder. What is the ultimate impulse which drives the murderer to his kill? Not the motives. One can understand motives. It is at least conceivable that a man may kill out of violent passion, or out of fear, or jealousy or revenge. Then too there are the murders by abnormals, drug addicts or mental deficients; they have their motives too, of course, although they may lie hidden in distorted minds. And as in our case, a series of crimes where the motive was hidden but perfectly real, and where extraordinary precautions had been taken against discovery.

But I am thinking of something more fundamental than motivation.

What is it that lies behind the final gesture of the killer?

Until then he has been of the race of men. In an instant he will have forfeited his brotherhood, become one of a group apart, a group of those who have destroyed human life.

Is there a profound contempt for life itself, for its value or its importance? Or is the instinct to kill stronger than thought, an atavistic memory from long past ages when laws had not induced suppressions? Is the murder impulse a natural one and are all of us potential killers, so that to save extinction men have devised the theory of the sanctity of human life? And at that last moment does this hereditary buried instinct surge triumphantly to the surface, steel the hand which holds the knife, steady the revolver, put the smile on the face of the poisoner?

There must be a something of the sort. One thing we do know; once a man has killed, his inhibitions are destroyed. He has joined the alien clan, of which no member knows the other, and has set his face against the world.

Thereafter he is alone.

But I have found no answer. In our case I have looked back, searching for some variation from the normal, or some instinct of weakening or remorse. But I have found none. We know now that there were moments of terrific danger, when the whole murderous structure was about to collapse. But if there was panic then we have no evidence of it. Each such emergency was met with diabolical ingenuity and cunning, and that cunning went even further. It provided in advance against every possible contingency of discovery.

What long hours went into that planning, that covering of every possible clue, we can only surmise; the meticulous surveying of this and that, the searching for any looseness in the whole criminal plan, the deliberate attempts to throw suspicion elsewhere.

There must have been a real satisfaction toward the end, however, a false feeling of security, a rubbing of the hands and a certain complacency.

And then suddenly the whole carefully woven fabric was destroyed. Strange and mysterious and bitter that must have been. Everything provided against, and then at the last to be destroyed by a door, a thing of wood and paint with an ordinary tarnished brass knob. Months had passed. Hundreds of hands had touched that knob in the interval; the door itself had been painted. And yet it solved our mystery and brought destruction to as diabolical and cunning a murderer as the records of crime will show.

* * * * * * *

As I have already intimated, I live alone, in the usual sense of the word. That is, I am more or less without family. A secretary, usually a young woman, and the customary servants form my household. And as the first crime occurred in this household it will be as well to outline it at once.

Outside of my secretary, Mary Martin, a young and very pretty girl, the establishment at the time of the disappearance of Sarah Gittings consisted of four servants: my butler, Joseph Holmes, who had been in my employ for many years, a respectable looking man of uncertain age, very quiet; my chauffeur, Robert White, who was not white, but a negro; the cook, Norah Moriarity, and Clara Jenkins, the housemaid. A laundress, a white woman, came in by the day, and from spring until fall a gardener named Abner Jones took care of the lawns and shrubbery.

And as my property, both houses and grounds, plays an important part in this narrative, I would better describe them also.

The house, then, sits some hundred feet back from the street. Two stone gate posts, from which the gates have been removed, mark the entrance, and the drive circles around a grass oval before the front door. Heavy old shrubbery, which I have not had the heart to thin out, shields me from the street and is spread in clumps over the grounds.

Thus the garage at the rear is partly screened from sight, although as was shown later, there is a clear view from it of the pantry window.

At the rear behind the garage lies a deep ravine which has been recently incorporated into the city park system; and at one side of me lies an acre or two of undeveloped property known as the Larimer lot.

Through this, from the street and extending sharply down the hill into the park, runs a foot-path, an unpaved cut-off. In winter when the leaves are off the trees I can see a portion of this path. Not all, for both the lot and the path are heavily bordered with old cedars.

Our first crime took place on the Larimer lot, not far from this path.

I have no near neighbors. This part of the city was country when the house was built, and the property on the other side is very large, ten acres or so. It was recently bought by a retired bootlegger and has no part in this narrative.

The house itself—my house—is old fashioned but very comfortable. But as I sit here in the library, one leg out before me and my pad on the other while I endeavor to think on paper, I realize that the house requires more description than that. Like the path, it too played its part.

I am writing in the library. Beside me on a table is the small bell which I ring to attract attention, since I cannot get to the speaking tube—I have said we are old fashioned—and a row of soft pencils like the one which later on we found on the skylight over the lavatory. There is a desk, an old Queen Anne walnut one, an open fire, chairs and books. From the side windows one commands the Larimer lot, from the front the entrance drive.

So the library has not only comfort, but a certain strategic place in the house. I can not only see my callers in advance; I can sit there and survey a large portion of my lower floor domain. It lies to the right of the front door and the hall.

Across the long center hall with its white staircase and its rear door to the service portion of the house, lies the drawing room. I can see now the forward end of it, with its ormolu cabinet, its French sofa done in old rose damask, and that painting of my father which does the Bell nose so grave an injustice.

And although I cannot see it, I know that at the end of that drawing room, opening onto a black brick wall which I have screened with arbor vitae and rhododendrons, there is a French door with steps leading out onto the grass. Also I know, by actual measurement, that it is precisely fifty feet and around a corner to the kitchen porch.

From the rear of the library double doors open into a music room, not often used nowadays, and behind that is the dining room.

This is my domain, and today in the winter sun it is very

peaceful. There has been a little snow, and the cedars at the top of the path down the hill are quite beautiful. I have a wood fire, and the dogs, Jock and Isabel—named by Judy because she had never heard of a dog called Isabel—are asleep before it.

Jock is a terrier, Isabel a corpulent and defeminized French bull. As they too played a small and not too meritorious part in our *débâcle,* it is necessary to name them.

I have listed my household as it was on the eighteenth of April of this year. Usually my secretaries do not live in the house, but come in daily for such notes, checks, bills and what not as clutter the desk of a woman who, because she has no family of her own, is supposed to expend her maternal instinct in charity.

But Mary Martin was living in the house, and due to a reason directly connected with this narrative.

During the housecleaning the previous autumn Norah had unearthed an old cane belonging to my grandfather, that Captain Bell who played so brave if unsung a part in the Mexican War.

She brought it downstairs to me, and I told her to have Joseph polish the handle. When Joseph came back with it he was smiling, an unusual thing for Joseph.

"That's a very interesting old cane, madam," he said. "It has a knife in it."

"A knife? What for?"

But Joseph did not know. It appeared that he had been polishing the knob when a blade suddenly shot out of the end. He had been greatly startled and had almost dropped the thing.

Later on I showed it to Jim Blake, my cousin, and he made the suggestion which brought Mary Martin into the house.

"Why not write the old boy's life?" he suggested. "You must

have a trunkful of letters, and this sword-stick, or sword-cane or whatever it is, is a good starting point. And by the way, if ever you want to give it away, give it to me."

"I may do that," I said. "I don't like deadly weapons around the place."

In March I gave it to him. "The Life," as Judy called it, was going on well, and Mary Martin efficient enough, although I was never fond of her.

CHAPTER TWO

THIS THEN was my household and my house on the day Sarah Gittings disappeared. The servants lived on the third floor at the rear, their portion of the floor cut off from the front by a door. A back staircase reached this upper rear hall, allowing them to come and go as they required.

Mary had the third floor front room above the library, and Sarah the one behind it and over the blue spare room. Mary's door stood open most of the time, Sarah's closed and often locked. For all her good qualities there was a suspicious streak in Sarah.

"I don't like people meddling with my things," she would say.

But Sarah was not a permanent member of the household. She was a middle-aged, rather heavy and silent woman, a graduate nurse of the old régime who had been in the family for years. In serious illness we sometimes brought in brisk young women, starchy and efficient, but in trouble we turned to Sarah.

We passed her around. My sister Laura would wire from Kansas City, "Children have measles. Please send Sarah if possible." And Sarah would pack her bag, cash one of her neat small checks and slip off. A good bit of her time was spent with my cousin Katherine Somers in New York. Katherine was devoted to her, although just why it is difficult to say. She was a taciturn woman, giving no confidences but probably receiving a great many.

Poor Sarah! I can still see her in her starched white uniform, with its skirts which just cleared the ground, moving among our various households, with us but not entirely of us; watching nervously over the stair rail while Judy, Katherine's daughter, made her début; slapping Laura's newest baby between the shoulders to make it breathe, or bending over me to give me a daily massage, her heavy body clumsy enough but her hands light and gentle.

She was not a clever woman. Or maybe I am wrong. Perhaps in a family which prides itself on a sort of superficial cleverness, she was merely silenced.

It was Wallie Somers, Katherine's stepson, who claimed that when he told her Hoover was nominated, she said:

"Really! That ought to be good business for the vacuum cleaner."

Not a romantic figure, Sarah, or a mysterious one. All of us thought of her as a fixture, growing older but more or less always to be with us. I remember Howard Somers, Katherine's husband, telling her one day that he had remembered her in his will.

"Not a lot, Sarah," he said. "But you'll never have to go to the Old Ladies' Home!"

I don't know why we were so astonished to see her burst into tears. I dare say she had been worried about the future; about getting old, and the children growing up and forgetting her. Anyhow she cried, and Howard was greatly embarrassed.

She had her peculiarities, of course. In Katherine's house,

what with guests in and out all the time, she had developed the habit of taking her meals in her room on a tray, and this habit persisted.

"I like to read while I eat," she said. "And I'm up early, and I don't like late dinners."

She had some sort of stomach trouble, poor thing.

But in my simpler household she ate with me unless there was some one there. Then, to Joseph's secret fury, she retired to her room and had her tray there.

She had come down from Katherine's a month or so before, not so much because I needed her as that Katherine thought she needed a change. Howard had had a bad heart for some time, and Sarah had been nursing him.

"Just let her putter around," Katherine wrote. "She'll want to work, being Sarah, so if you can stand a daily massage—"

And of course I could, and did.

I have drawn Sarah as well as I can, and the family rather sketchily; Howard and Katherine in their handsome duplex apartment in New York on Park Avenue, bringing out Judy at nineteen; Laura in Kansas City, raising a noisy young family; and myself in my old-fashioned house with its grounds and shrubbery, its loneliness and its memories. Dependent on a few friends, a small dinner party now and then, a little bridge; and on my servants, on Joseph and Norah and Clara and Robert, and on the Mary Martins who came and went, intelligent young women who used me as a stop-gap in their progress toward marriage or a career. A staid household, dependent for its youth on Judy's occasional visits, on secretaries whose minds were elsewhere, and on Wallie Somers, Howard's son by his first wife, whose ostensible business was bonds and whose relaxation, when he could not find some one to play with, was old furniture. Than which, as Judy once said, I have nothing else but.

As it happened, Judy was with me when Sarah disappeared that night in April of last year. She was staging her annual revolt.

"I get a trifle fed up with Katherine now and then," she would say, arriving without notice. "She's too intense. Now you are restful. You're really a frivolous person, you know, Elizabeth Jane, for all your clothes and airs."

"Frivolity is all I have left," I would say meekly. Judy has a habit of first names. Katherine had carefully taught her to call me Cousin Elizabeth, but Judy had discarded that with her stockings, which now she wore as seldom as possible and under protest. Although I doubt if she ever called her mother Katherine to her face.

Katherine was a good mother but a repressed one. Also she was still passionately in love with Howard; one of those profound absorbing loves which one finds sometimes in women who are apparently cold, and which makes them better wives than mothers. I rather think that she was even a little jealous of Judy, and that Judy knew it.

Judy would arrive, and as if by a miracle the telephone would commence to ring and shining sports cars would be parked for hours in front of the house. Joseph would assume a resigned expression, empty cigarette trays by the dozen, and report to me in his melancholy voice.

"Some one has burned a hole on the top of your Queen Anne desk, madam."

I was never anything to him but "madam." It got on my nerves sometimes.

"Never mind, Joseph. We have to pay a price for youth."

He would go out again, depressed but dignified. In his own way he was as unsocial as Sarah, as mysterious and self-obliterating as are all good servants.

So on that last night of Sarah's life, Judy was with me. She had just arrived, looking a trifle defiant, and at dinner she stated her grievance. Mary Martin was out for the evening, and the two of us were alone at the table.

"Really, Katherine is *too* outrageous," she said.

"She's probably saying the same thing about you."

"But it is silly. Truly. She wants me not to see Wallie. I don't think Wallie is anything to lie awake at night about, but after all he's my half-brother."

I said nothing. It was an old difficulty in the family, Katherine's dislike of Howard's son by his first marriage. It was a part of her jealousy of Howard, her resentment of that early unfortunate marriage of his. She loathed Wallie and all he stood for; not that he stood for a great deal. He was the usual rich man's son, rather charming in his own way but neurotic since the war. But he looked like Margaret, the first wife, and Katherine could not forgive him for that.

"You like Wallie," Judy accused me.

"Of course I do."

"And he had a wonderful war record."

"Certainly he had. What are you trying to do, Judy? Justify yourself?"

"I think he's had a rotten deal," she said. "From all of us. A bit of allowance from father, and now I'm not to see him!"

"But you are going to see him," I told her. "You're going to see him tonight. He wants to look over an old ormolu cabinet Laura has sent me."

She forgot her irritation in her delight.

"Lovely! Has it got any secret drawers? I adore looking for secret drawers," she said, and went on eating a substantial meal. These young things, with their slender waists and healthy appetites!

She had already rushed up to the third floor to greet Sarah, and while we were eating I heard Sarah on the way down. This was nothing unusual. She would go out sometimes at night, either to the movies or to take Jock and Isabel for a walk, and I could sit at my place at the table and watch her coming down the stairs. The fireplace in the music room is set at an angle, and in the mirror over it I would see Sarah; first her soft-soled low-heeled shoes, then the bottom of her white skirt, and then her gray coat, until finally all of Sarah emerged into view.

This evening however I saw that she had taken off her uniform, and I called to her.

"Going to the movies, Sarah?"

"No." She had no small amenities of speech.

"Don't you want the dogs? They haven't been out today."

She seemed to hesitate. I could see her in the mirror, and I surprised an odd expression on her face. Then the dogs themselves discovered her and began to leap about her.

"Do take them, Sarah," Judy called.

"I suppose I can," she agreed rather grudgingly. "What time is it?"

Judy looked at her wrist watch and told her.

"And do behave yourself, Sarah!" she called.

But Sarah did not answer. She snapped the leashes on the dogs and went out. That was at five minutes after seven. She went out and never came back.

Judy and I loitered over the meal, or rather I loitered; Judy ate and answered the telephone. One call was from a youth named

Dick, and there was a subtle change in Judy's voice which made me suspicious. Another, however, she answered coldly.

"I don't see why," she said. "She knew quite well where I was going ... Well, I'm all right. If I want to go wrong I don't need to come here to do it ... No, she's gone out."

I have recorded this conversation because it became highly important later on. To the best of my knowledge it came soon after Sarah left; at seven-fifteen or thereabouts.

Judy came back to the table with her head in the air.

"Uncle Jim," she said. "Wouldn't you know mother would sic him on me? The old goose!"

By which she referred not to Katherine, but to Katherine's brother, Jim Blake. Judy had chosen to affect a dislike for him, not because of any inherent qualities in Jim himself, but because Katherine was apt to make him her agent when Judy visited me.

Personally I was fond of Jim, perhaps because he paid me the small attentions a woman of my age finds gratifying, and certainly Katherine adored him.

"He asked for Sarah, but I told him she had gone out. What in the world does he want with Sarah?"

"He may have had some message from your mother for her."

"Probably to keep an eye on me," said Judy, drily.

I think all this is accurate. So many things happened that evening that I find it difficult to go back to that quiet meal. Quiet, that is, up to the time when Joseph brought in our coffee.

I know we discussed Jim, Judy and I, and Judy with the contempt of her youth for the man in his late forties who takes no active part in the world. Yet Jim had organized his life as best he could. He was a bachelor, who went everywhere for a reason which I surmised but Judy could not understand; the fear of the lonely of being alone.

"Uncle Jim and his parties!" said Judy. "How in the world does he pay for them?"

"He has a little from his mother."

"And more probably from my mother!"

Well, that might have been, so I said nothing, and as money meant nothing in Judy's lavish young life she was immediately cheerful again.

It is hard to remember Jim as he was in those days; as he must have been when he left his house that night. A tall man, still very erect, and with graying hair carefully brushed to hide its thinness, he was always urbane and well dressed. He was popular too. He had never let business, which in his case was a dilettante interest in real estate, interfere with a golf game or bridge, and by way of keeping up his social end he gave innumerable little tea parties and dinners. He had a colored servant named Amos who was a quick change artist, and so people dined with Jim on food cooked by Amos, to be served by Amos in a dinner jacket, and then went outside to find Amos in a uniform and puttees, standing by the car with the rug neatly folded over his arm.

There are some people to whom all colored men look alike, and to these no doubt Jim Blake appeared to be served by a retinue of servants.

"The Deb's delight!" was Judy's closing and scathing comment, and then Joseph brought in the coffee.

That was, according to Joseph's statement to the police and later before the Grand Jury, at seven-thirty or seven-thirty-five.

Judy had lighted a cigarette. I remember thinking how pretty she looked in the candle light, and how the house brightened when she was there. Joseph was moving about the pantry, and in the silence I could hear distant voices from the servants' hall beyond the kitchen.

Judy had lapsed into silence. The initial excitement of her arrival was over, and I thought now that she looked dispirited and rather tired. Then I happened to raise my eyes, and they fell on the mirror.

There was a man on the staircase.

CHAPTER THREE

He seemed to be crouching there. I could see only his legs, in darkish trousers, and he had no idea that I could see him at all. He was apparently listening, listening and calculating. Should he make a dash to get out, or retreat? The door from the dining room to the hall was wide open. I would surely see him; was it worth the trying?

Evidently he decided that it was not, for without turning he backed soundlessly up the stairs.

"Judy," I said quietly. "Don't move or raise your voice. There's a burglar upstairs. I've just seen him."

"What shall I do? I can close the library door and call the police."

"Do that, then, and I'll tell Joseph. He can't get out by the back stairs without going through the kitchen, and the servants would see him."

I rang for Joseph, feeling calm and rather pleased at my calmness. Such few jewels as I keep out of the bank were on me, and if he wanted my gold toilet set he was welcome. It was insured. But while I waited for Joseph I took off my rings and dropped them into the flower vase on the table.

Joseph took the news quietly. He said that Robert was still in the garage, and that he would station him at the foot of the back stairs, but that to wait for the police was nonsense.

"He'd jump out a window, madam. But if I go up, as though I didn't know he was about, I might surprise him."

"You're not armed."

"I have a revolver in the pantry, madam."

That did not surprise me. There had been some burglaries in the neighborhood recently—I believe the bootlegger had had the tables turned on him, a matter which I considered a sort of poetic justice—and I stood in the doorway watching the stairs until Joseph reappeared.

"If he gets past me," he said, "stand out of his way, madam. These cat burglars are dangerous."

He went up the front staircase, leaving me in the lower hall. I could hear Judy at the telephone, patiently explaining in a low voice, and I could hear Joseph overhead, moving about systematically: the second floor, the third, opening room doors and closet doors, moving with his dignified unhurried tread, but doing the thing thoroughly.

He was still moving majestically along the third floor hall when I heard a slight noise near at hand. I could neither describe it nor locate it. Something fairly near me had made a sound, a small sharp report. It appeared to have come from the back hallway, where there is a small lavatory. When Judy emerged I told her, and against my protests she marched back and threw open the door.

It was quite empty and soon after Joseph came down to say that he had found nobody, but that some one might be hiding on the roof, and as by that time a policeman had arrived on a motorcycle, I sent him out to look.

The officer inside and Joseph out, it seemed scarcely credible that we found nobody. But our burglar had gone; without booty too, as it turned out, for my toilet things were undisturbed.

I think the officer was rather amused than otherwise. Judy saw him out.

"If you're ever in trouble again, Miss, just send for me," he said gallantly.

"I'm always in trouble," said Judy.

"Now is that so? What sort of trouble?"

"Policemen," said Judy pleasantly, and closed the door on him.

Looking back, it seems strange how light-hearted we were that night. That loneliness which is my usual lot had gone with Judy's arrival, and when Wallie arrived at eight-thirty he found Judy insisting on my smoking a cigarette.

"You're shaken, Elizabeth Jane," she was saying. "You know darn well you're shaken."

"Shaken? About what?" said Wallie from the hall.

"She's had a burglar, poor dear," Judy explained. "A burglar in dark trousers, crouched on the staircase."

"On the stairs? Do you mean you saw him?"

"She saw his legs."

"And that's all?"

"That's enough, isn't it? The rest of him was sure to be around somewhere. The said legs then ceased crouching and went upstairs. After that they vanished."

He said nothing more, but walked back into the dining room and surveyed the mirror.

"That's a tricky arrangement you have there, Elizabeth Jane," he called. He had adopted Judy's habit. "Go up the stairs, Judy, and let me see your legs."

"Don't be shameless!" she said. "How's this?"

"All right. Yes, I see them, and very nice ones they are at that."

When he came forward again Judy insisted on examining the stair rail for fingerprints, although Wallie said that it was nonsense; that all criminals wore gloves nowadays, and that with the increasing crime wave the glove factories were running night shifts. But she departed for a candle nevertheless, and Wallie glanced up the staircase.

"Rather a blow for the divine Sarah, eh what?" he said.

"Sarah is out, fortunately. She took the dogs."

It struck me, as he stood there in the full light over his head, that he was looking even thinner then usual, and very worn. He had much of his mother's beauty, if one dare speak of beauty in a man, but he had also inherited her high-strung nervous temperament. The war must have been hell for him, for he never spoke of it. I have noticed that the men who really fought and really suffered have very little to say about it; whether because they cannot bear to recall it or because most of them are inarticulate I do not know.

While we stood there I told him about the sound I had heard, and he went back to the lavatory and looked up.

This lavatory is merely a small washroom opening from the rear portion of the hall, and lighted by an opaque glass ceiling, in the center of which a glass transom opens by a cord for ventilation. The shaft above is rather like an elevator well, and light enters through a skylight in the roof.

Onto this well there is only one opening and this the window to the housemaid's closet on the third floor. As during the tornado of 1893 the entire skylight frame and all had been lifted and dropped end-on into the shaft, crashing through the glass roof below, my father had had placed across it some iron bars. These, four in number, were firmly embedded in the walls about six feet below the window sill.

"I suppose nobody has examined the shaft?"

"I really don't know. Probably not."

He continued to gaze upward.

"He might have swung into the shaft, and stood on the bars."

"Provided he knew there were bars there," I said drily.

Suddenly he turned and shot up the stairs, and a moment later he was calling from the third floor.

"Get a ladder, somebody. There's something on top of that skylight down there."

"You mean—the man himself?"

He laughed at that.

"He'd have gone through the glass like a load of coal! No. Something small. I can see it against the light beneath."

He ran down, rushed into the library for matches, and when Robert had brought a ladder from the garage and placed it in the lavatory, he was on it and halfway through the transom in an instant.

We stood huddled in the door, Judy still holding the candle, and I—for some unknown reason—with a lighted cigarette in my hand which some one had thrust on me, and Robert and Joseph behind.

I don't know what I had expected, but I know that I felt a shock of disappointment when Wallie said:

"Hello! Here it is. A pencil!"

He found nothing else, and came down in a moment looking dirty and rather the worse for wear, but extremely pleased with himself.

"A pencil!" he said exultantly. "Now how about it? Will

Scotland Yard send for me or will it not? That's what you heard, you see."

But Judy only took one glance at it.

"Possibly," she said. "Still, as it's the sort Elizabeth Jane uses herself, with the point looking as though she'd sharpened it with her teeth, I see nothing to write home about."

That annoyed him.

"All right," he told her. "We'll see. It may have fingerprints."

"I thought you'd decided he wore gloves! Why don't you try to find how he got in? That's more to the point. And also how he got out?"

It seems strange to be writing all this; the amiable bickering between Wallie and Judy; the light-hearted experiment to find if a pencil dropped from the third floor made the sound I had heard, and my own feeling that it did not; and the final discovery of the shattered pane in the rear French door of the drawing room, and our failure to see, lying on the step outside, that broken point of a penknife which Inspector Harrison was to find the next morning.

Strange, almost frivolous.

It was Judy who found the broken pane, hidden as it was behind the casement curtains on the door, and who pointed out the ease with which our intruder had reached in and turned the key. There is another door at the back of the drawing room, a sort of service entrance which opens into the rear hall beside the servants' staircase, and it was evident that he had used this to gain access to the upper floors.

"Easy enough," said Judy. "But he couldn't get out that way. Clara was coming down to her dinner, so he hid on the front stairs."

"And I suppose he was not in the light shaft at all?" Wallie demanded.

"I don't say he wasn't," said my surprising Judy. "I only say that the pencil is not proved. I think it very likely he did hide in the shaft. He'd retreated before Joseph as far as he could go."

"But what did he want?" I demanded. "I don't suppose he broke in here to drop a pencil. If he was coming down when I saw him—"

"Well, he might have been going up," said Judy practically. "A good burglar might start at the top and work down. Like housecleaning."

Wallie had sealed the pencil in an envelope for the police, and I daresay all of this had not taken much more than half an hour. It must have been at nine o'clock or thereabouts, then, that I sent the maids to their beds and watched them as they made a nervous half-hysterical start, and nine-thirty before Joseph and Wallie had placed a padlock on the broken door in the drawing room. Then I ordered Joseph to bed, but he objected.

"Miss Sarah has not come in."

"She has a key, Joseph."

But I was uneasy. In the excitement I had forgotten Sarah.

Wallie looked up sharply from the door.

"Sarah!" he said. "Is she still out?"

"Yes. And she has the dogs. Where could she stay until this hour with two dogs? She has no friends."

I left Wallie and Judy in the drawing room, and wandered out and down the steps. It was a cold night, without a moon but with plenty of starlight, and I walked down the drive. I remembered that as I walked I whistled for the dogs. Sometimes she loosened them and they preceded her home.

It seemed to me that I heard a dog barking far off somewhere, but that was all.

I was vaguely inclined to walk in that direction. The dog seemed to be at the far end of the Larimer lot or beyond it, in the park. But at the gate I met Mary Martin, hurrying home. She had been out somewhere for dinner, and she was slightly sulky; it was a continued grievance with her that Sarah had a key to the house and she had none, but I have an old-fashioned sense of responsibility to the people in my employ, and Mary was a still young and very pretty girl.

On the way to the house I told her about our burglar, and she relaxed somewhat.

"I don't think you should be out here alone," she said. "He may still be about."

"I was looking for Sarah," I explained. "She's out with the dogs, and it's getting late."

To my intense surprise she stopped perfectly still.

"When did she go out?" she said sharply.

"At seven. That's almost three hours."

She moved on again, but in silence. The front door was open, and in the light from it I thought she looked rather pale. At that moment however Wallie appeared in the doorway, and suddenly she brightened.

"I wouldn't worry, Miss Bell. She can take care of herself. And she has a key!"

She glanced at me rather pertly, favored Wallie with a smile as she went in, greeting Judy with considerable manner—she seemed always to be afraid that Judy might patronize her—and teetered up the stairs on the high heels she affected.

Wallie gazed after her as she went up. At the turn she

paused. I saw her looking down at us intently, at Judy, at myself, at Wallie. Mostly at Wallie.

"I wouldn't worry about Miss Gittings," she said. "She's sure to be all right."

"You might see if she's in her room, Mary," Judy suggested. "She may have come in while we were in the drawing room."

We could hear her humming as she went on up the stairs, and, shortly after she called down to say that Sarah was not in her room but that it was unlocked.

"That's queer," said Judy. "She always locks it, doesn't she?"

We could hear a sort of ironic amusement in Mary's voice as she replied.

"Not so queer this evening," she said. "She knew I was out! Her key's in the door, on the outside, but she forgot to take it."

I do not remember much about the hour between ten and eleven. Wallie was not willing to go until Sarah returned, and Judy and he worked over the cabinet. The house was very still. For a time, as I sat in the library, I could hear Mary moving about on the third floor, drawing a bath—she was very fastidious in everything that pertained to herself—and finally going into her room and closing the door. But by eleven Judy had given up all hope of a secret drawer in the cabinet and was yawning, and a few moments after that Wallie left and she wandered up to bed.

But I still waited in the library. I had a queer sense of apprehension, but I laid it to the events of the evening, and after a time—I am no longer young, and I tire easily—I fell into a doze.

When I roused it was one in the morning, and Sarah had not come back. She would have roused me if she had, and she would have put out the lights. Nevertheless I went upstairs and opened her door. The room was dark. I called to her, cautiously, but there was no answer, and no stertorous breathing to show that she was asleep.

For the first time I was really alarmed about her. I went downstairs again, stopping in my room for a wrap, and in the dining room for my rings, which I had almost forgotten. Then I went out on the street.

The dog, or dogs, were still barking at intervals, and at last I started toward the sound.

CHAPTER FOUR

It is one of the inevitable results of tragedy that one is always harking back to it, wondering what could have been done to avert it. I find myself going over and over the events of that night, so simple in appearance, so dreadful in result. Suppose I had turned on Sarah's light that night? Would I have found her murderer in the room? Was the faint sound I heard the movement of her curtain in the wind, as I had thought, or something much more terrible?

Again, instead of sending Joseph upstairs to search, what if I had had the police called and the house surrounded?

Still, what could I have done for Sarah? Nothing. Nothing at all.

I was rather nervous as I walked along, going toward the Larimer lot and the park. But the occasional despairing yelps were growing more and more familiar as I advanced, and when at last I let out that feeble pipe which is my attempt at a whistle, the dogs recognized it in a sort of ecstasy of noise. I could make out Jock's shrill bark and Isabel's melancholy whine, but for some reason they did not come to me.

I stood on the pavement and called, loath to leave its dryness and security for the brush and trees and dampness of the Larimer property. Frightened too, I admit. Something was holding the dogs. I am quite certain now that when I started to run toward them I expected to find Sarah there, unconscious or dead. I ran in a sort of frenzy. Once indeed I fell over some old wire, and I was dizzy when I got up.

But Sarah was not there. Far back in the lot I found the dogs, and if I wondered that they had not come to me that mystery was soon solved.

They were tied. A piece of rope had been run through the loops of their leashes and then tied to a tree. So well tied that, what with their joyous rushes and the hard knotting of the rope, I could scarcely free them.

Asked later on about that knot, I had no clear memory of it whatever.

It was very dark. Far back on the street a lamp lighted that corner where the path took off, to pitch steeply down into the park. The Larimer lot is a triangle, of which the side of my property is the vertical, the street the base, and the ravine beyond the hypotenuse. Thus:

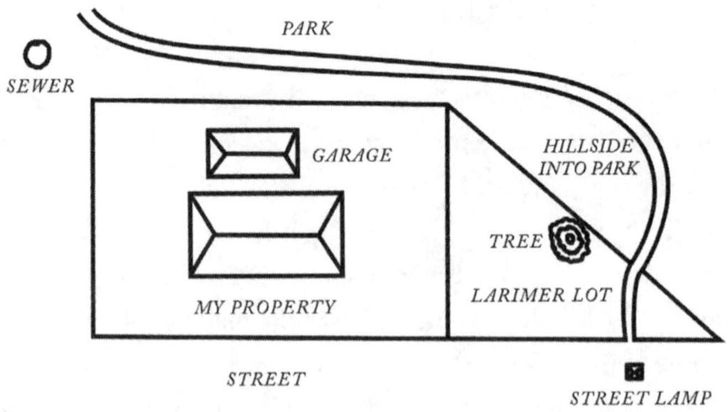

I remember calling Sarah frantically, and then telling the terrier to find her.

"Go find Sarah, Jock," I said. "Find Sarah."

He only barked, however, and an instant later both of them were racing for home.

But I still had a queer feeling that Sarah must be there. I went back to the house, to find the dogs scratching at the front door, and when I had roused Joseph I took him back with me to search the lot. He with his revolver and I with my searchlight must have been a queer clandestine sort of picture; two middle-aged folk, Joseph half clad, wandering about in the night. And so the roundsman on the beat must have believed, for when he came across to us his voice was suspicious.

"Lost anything?"

"A middle-aged woman, rather heavy set," I said half hysterically.

"Well, she oughtn't to be hard to find," he observed. "Now if it was a ring, with all this brush and stuff—"

But he was rather impressed when I told my story.

"Tied to a tree, eh? Which tree?"

"Over there; my butler's examining it. The rope's still there."

But a moment later Joseph almost stunned me.

"There is no rope here, madam," he called.

And incredible as it may sound, the rope was not there. The policeman searched, we all searched. There was no rope and no Sarah. The policeman was not so much suspicious as slightly amused.

"Better go back and get a good night's sleep, ma'am," he said soothingly. "You can come around in the morning and look all you want."

"But there *was* a rope, I could hardly untie it."

"Sure," he said indulgently. "Probably the lady you're looking for tied them up herself. She had business somewhere else and they'd be in the way. See?"

Well, it was possible, of course. I did not believe it, knowing Sarah; but then, did I know Sarah? The surface of Sarah I knew, the unruffled, rather phlegmatic faithful Sarah; but what did I really know about her? It came to me like a blow that I did not even know if she had any family, that there was no one I could notify.

"You go home now," he said, as coaxingly as he would speak to a child, "and in the morning you'll find she's back. If she isn't you can let me know."

And he said this too with an air, a certain paternalism, as though he had said: "Just leave this to me. I am the law. I'll fix it. And now just run along. I've my job to attend to."

The next morning was rainy and gray. I had slept very little, and I rang for my breakfast tray at eight o'clock. Any hope that Sarah had slipped in early in the morning was dashed by Joseph's sober face. I drank a little coffee, and at eight-thirty Judy came in yawning, in a luxurious negligee over very gaudy pajamas.

"Well, what explanation does she give?" she said. "May I have my tray here? I hate eating alone."

"Did who give?"

"Sarah."

"She hasn't come back, Judy."

"What? I heard her. From two until three she walked about over my head until I was almost crazy."

Sarah's room was over Judy's. I sat up in bed and stared at her. Then I rang the bell again.

"Joseph," I said, "have you been into Sarah's room this morning?"

"No madam. I overslept, and I hurried right down."

"Then how do you know she has not come back?"

"She hasn't been down for her breakfast. She's very early, always."

And just then we heard Mary Martin talking excitedly to Clara in the hall overhead, and then come running down the stairs. She burst into my room hysterically, to say that Sarah was not in her room and that it was all torn up. Judy was gone like a flash, and while I threw something about me I questioned Mary. She had, it seems, knocked at Sarah's door to borrow the morning paper. The morning paper, by the way, always reached me fourth hand; Joseph took it in and looked it over, Sarah got it from him, Mary Martin borrowed it from Sarah, and when I rang for it, usually at nine o'clock, it was apt to bear certain unmistakable scars; a bit of butter, a smudge of egg, or a squirt of grapefruit juice. Anyhow, receiving no answer, Mary had opened the door, and what she saw I saw when I had hurried upstairs.

Sarah's room was in complete confusion. Some one had jerked aside her mattress and pillows, thrown down the clothes in her neat closet, looked at her shoes, and turned out her bureau. Even her trunk had been broken open, and its contents lay scattered about. Those records of family illnesses, which she carted about with her as a veteran might carry his medals, had been thrown out onto the bed and apparently examined.

There was something ruthless and shameless about the room now. It had no secrets, no privacies. It was, in a way, as though some one had stripped Sarah, had bared her stout spinster body to the world.

Judy, rather white, was in the doorway.

"I wouldn't go in," she said. "Or at least I wouldn't touch anything. Not until you get the police."

Clara, the housemaid, was staring in over my shoulder.

"She'll have a fit over this," she said. "She's that tidy!"

But I had a dreadful feeling that poor Sarah would never again have a fit over anything in this world.

It was nine-fifteen when I telephoned to headquarters, and at a quarter to ten a policeman in uniform and the Assistant Superintendent of Police, Inspector Harrison, reached the house.

The two of them examined the room, and then leaving the uniformed man in charge of Sarah's room, Inspector Harrison listened to my story in the library. He was a short stocky man, very bald and with the bluest eyes I have ever seen in an adult human being.

As he talked he drew a wooden toothpick from his pocket and bit on the end of it. Later on I was to find that he had an apparently limitless supply of the things, and that they served a variety of purposes and moods. He had given up smoking, he said, and they gave him "something to think with."

He was disinclined to place any serious interpretation on Sarah's absence until it was necessary, but he was interested in the housebreaking episode; especially in Wallie's theory that the intruder on his first visit had swung himself into the light shaft, and he carefully examined it from above and below. There were, however, many scratches on the sill of Clara's pantry and little to be learned from any of them.

The Inspector stood for some time looking down into the shaft.

"He could get in all right," he decided, "but I'd hate to undertake to get myself out, once I was in. Still, it's possible."

After that he wandered around the house, sometimes alone, sometimes with Joseph. Wallie had arrived, and he and Judy and I sat there waiting, Judy very quiet, Wallie clearly anxious and for the first time alarmed. He moved about the room, picking things up and putting them down until Judy turned on him angrily.

"For heaven's sake, Wallie! Can't you keep still?"

"If I annoy you, why not go somewhere else?"

She lit a cigarette and looked at him.

"I don't get it," she said slowly. "What's Sarah to you? You never cared much for her."

"You'll know some day."

She cocked an eye at him.

"If eventually, why not now?"

But he merely turned on his heel and resumed his nervous pacing of the room.

Some time later he suggested that Sarah might have gone to New York, and that Judy telephone and find out. In the end, in order not to alarm Katherine, I called up Jim Blake and told him, and he agreed to invent a message for Katherine. Asked later about his manner over the telephone, I could remember very little. I know he seemed surprised, and that he said he was not well, but that he would dress and come around that afternoon.

When he called back it was to say that evidently Sarah had not gone there, and that he would be around at three o'clock.

The information had a curious effect on Wallie, however. As I watched him it seemed to me that he looked frightened; but that may be in view of what I know now. I do, however, recall that he looked as though he had slept badly, and that day for the first time since the early days after the war I saw him begin to twist his seal ring again.

When he was not lighting a cigarette or throwing it away he was twisting his ring, turning it around and around on his finger.

Once he left us and went upstairs to look at Sarah's room. The policeman opened the door but would not let him enter, and I believe he spoke a few words with Mary. Indeed, I know now that he did. But he was back in the library when the Inspector finally came in and selected a fresh toothpick, this time to make points with.

"First of all," he said, "it is best not to jump to any conclusions. The lady may not be dead; very probably is not dead. We are, however, sending to the Morgue and the hospitals. But there are many reasons why people occasionally choose to disappear, and sometimes to make that disappearance as mysterious as possible. For example, Miss Gittings had a key to the house. It is just possible that she herself came back last night and ransacked her own room."

"In a pair of dark trousers?" I demanded sharply.

He smiled at that.

"Perhaps! Stranger things have been done. But now about this key. It was outside the door last night?"

"My secretary said so."

"Well, it's inside now."

"I don't understand it, Inspector. Sarah always locked her door when she left the house. Locked the door and took the key."

"There isn't a second key to her door?"

"Not that I know of."

"Then we'll say that this key is hers. It may not be, but it looks like it and wherever it was last night it's on the inside of the door now. Suppose for the sake of argument that she had decided to go away; to say nothing and go away. She might have forgotten something and come back for it."

"Very probably," said Judy. "She might have forgotten her toothbrush."

He smiled at her.

"Precisely. Or something she had hidden, and forgotten where she had hidden it."

"I see," said Judy. "She forgot her toothbrush so she came back to get it, and as she didn't want Joseph to know she'd forgotten it she hung in the light shaft and dropped a pencil. It's perfectly clear."

"We have no proof yet that anybody was in the light shaft," he told her, without resentment. "Where is that pencil, I'd like to look at it."

I unlocked a drawer of my desk and took out the envelope.

"This been handled since?"

"I picked it up by the point," Wallie told him.

"Sure it wasn't there before?" to me.

"I think it is unlikely," I said. "The ceiling is glass and is regularly cleaned. It would have been seen."

He held it carefully by the eraser and examined it, whistling softly to himself. Then he dropped it back into the envelope and put it into his pocket.

"Well, that's that. Now, as to Miss Gittings herself. I suppose she had no lover?"

"Lover?" I was shocked. "She is nearly fifty."

He seemed to be amused at that.

"Still, stranger things—" he said. "Perhaps not a lover. Some man, probably younger, who might pretend to be interested for some ulterior purpose. Say money. There's more of that than you might think. I suppose she had saved something?"

"I don't know. A little, perhaps."

He turned to Judy.

"You accepted that it was Miss Gittings you heard moving in her room."

"Certainly."

"Why?"

"It was her room. And the dogs had not barked. They would bark at a stranger."

"Oh!" he said, and took a fresh toothpick. "That's interesting. So the dogs knew whoever it was! Very interesting." He sat for a moment or two, apparently thinking. Then:

"I gather she had few or no outside contacts?"

"None whatever."

"She never mentioned anybody named Florence?"

"Florence? Not to me."

He settled down in his chair.

"It is a curious thing," he said. "We think we know all about certain individuals, and then something happens, the regular order is disturbed, and we find we know nothing at all. Now let me tell you certain things about Sarah Gittings.

"She has been nervous for some time, two weeks or so. She has eaten very little and slept less. Sometimes she has walked the floor of her room at night for hours. At least twice in that time she was called up by a girl named Florence, and made an appointment to meet her. One of these was made yesterday morning at eleven o'clock. The cook was trying to call the grocer and overheard her. Unfortunately, the place of meeting had evidently been prearranged and was not mentioned.

"At a quarter to five yesterday afternoon Sarah Gittings left this house. She was back in half an hour, according to the butler. She asked for an early dinner and left the house again at five minutes after seven.

"But following that return of hers, Sarah Gittings did two peculiar things. She went down to the cellar, took a chair from the laundry there and carried it into the room where the firewood is stored; it is there now. And according to the laundress, she cut off from a new clothes line an undetermined amount of rope. The line had been neatly rolled and replaced, but she is a sharp woman, that laundress."

Wallie had been following this intently, and it seemed to me that he looked relieved. He had stopped twirling his ring.

"I see," he said. "She tied the dogs to the tree herself."

"It looks like it."

Judy was watching him. "Feeling better, Wallie?" she asked, looking more cheerful herself. "Weight off the old mind, and all that?"

But he did not even hear her. He drew a long breath and lighted a cigarette.

"I don't mind saying," he said to the detective, "that this thing is vitally important to me. I—you've relieved me more than you know."

But I had been thinking.

"If she took that piece of rope, it was not to tie the dogs up; I can assure you of that. She had not expected to take them. I don't think she wanted to take them. And as for this man on the stairs," I went on, rather tartly, "you tell me that that was Sarah Gittings, who had left the house only a half hour before, and who could get in at any time! I am to believe that Sarah went to that empty lot, tied up the dogs, put on a pair of dark trousers, broke her way in through the drawing room door, and deliberately let me see her on the staircase! Remember, she knew about that mirror."

"But that's where the man in the case comes in," said Judy, maliciously. "Sarah's lover. He met her at the lot and found she'd forgotten her toothbrush. Naturally, he refused to elope with her without her toothbrush. It's all perfectly simple."

Mr. Harrison smiled. "Still," he said, rising, "she *did* take the rope. And now we'll look at that broken door."

But with the peculiar irony of events which was to handicap all of us through the entire series of crimes, all traces of footprints in the ground near the steps—there is no walk there—had already been obliterated. The rain was over, and Abner Jones had commenced his spring cleaning up of the lawns and had carefully raked away any possible signs.

Nevertheless, Judy maintained that Mr. Harrison had found something on the steps.

"When he stooped over to tie his shoe," she said, "he stooped and picked up something very small and shiny. It looked like the point of a knife."

By noon there was still no news of Sarah. All reports had been negative, and I believe that the Inspector found no further clues. Judy reported once that he and the officer in uniform were going through the trash barrel in the service yard and taking out the glass from the broken window. But the rain must have washed it fairly clean. Clara had been told to put Sarah's room in order again, but when that had been done Inspector Harrison advised me to lock it and keep the key.

He left us at noon. It was raining hard, but some time later

I saw him, in a dripping mackintosh, moving slowly around in the Larimer property. When I looked out again, an hour later, he was still there, but he seemed to have exchanged his soft hat for a cap.

It was not until the figure had disappeared over the hillside that I decided that it was not the Inspector, but some one else.

CHAPTER FIVE

THE VAST majority of crimes, I believe, are never solved by any single method or any single individual. Complex crimes, I mean, without distinct clues and obvious motives.

Certainly in the case of Sarah Gittings, and in those which followed it, the final solution was a combination of luck and—curiously enough—the temporary physical disability of one individual.

And I am filled with shuddering horror when I think where we all might be but for this last.

That day, Tuesday, dragged on interminably. I could do no work on the biography, and Mary Martin was shut up in her room with a novel. The servants were uneasy and even the dogs seemed dejected; Joseph puttered about, looking aged and careworn, and the maids seemed to drink endless tea in the kitchen and to be reluctant to go upstairs.

At three o'clock, Jim not having arrived and Judy being out with the dogs, I decided to call Katherine once more. It seemed to me that she might have a clue of some sort. She knew Sarah better than any of us, and I felt that at least she should be told.

But all I obtained from her was a thorough scolding for harboring Judy.

"Well!" she said when she heard my voice. "It's about time! You tell Judy to come right home. It's outrageous, Elizabeth."

"What is outrageous?" I asked.

"Her chasing that idiotic youth. Now listen, Elizabeth; I want you to keep him out of the house. It's the very least you can do, if she won't come home."

"I haven't seen any youth yet," I explained mildly. "And I'm not worrying about Judy. I have something else to worry about."

Her voice was shrill when I told her.

"Missing?" she said. "Sarah missing! Haven't you any idea where she is?"

"None, except that I'm afraid it's serious. The police are working on it."

"Maybe I'd better come down."

I checked that at once. Katherine is an intense, repressed woman, who can be exceedingly charming, but who can also be exceedingly stubborn at times. As that stubbornness of hers was to work for us later on I must not decry it, but I did not want her then.

"You can't do anything," I said. "And Howard probably needs you. Judy says he's not so well."

"No," she said slowly. "No. He's not as well as he ought to be."

She said nothing more about coming down, but insisted that I see Jim at once.

"He was fond of Sarah," she said, "and he really has such a good mind. I know he will help you."

She had no other suggestions to make, however. Sarah had no family, she was certain of that. Her great fear seemed to be that she had been struck by an automobile, and as that was mild compared with what I was beginning to think I allowed it to rest at that.

I had made no promise as to Judy, which was as well, for when she came back she was accompanied by a cheerful looking blond youth who was evidently the one in question, and who was presented to me only as Dick.

"This is Dick," was what Judy said. "And he is a nice person, of poor but honest parents."

Dick merely grinned at that; he seemed to know Judy, and almost before I knew it he and I were standing in the lower hall, and Judy was dropping lead pencils down the airshaft.

"Does that sound like it, Elizabeth Jane?" she would call to me at the top of her voice. "Or this?"

To save my life I could not tell. They seemed to be less sharp, less distinct, but I was not certain. Indeed, when Mr. Carter, for that turned out to be the youth's family name, tapped with his penknife on the marble mantel in the drawing room, the effect seemed rather more like what I had heard.

"*That* for Wallie!" said Judy, coming down. "That pencil's probably been there for ages. I'd like to see his face when he finds six more there! And now let's have tea."

I liked the boy. Indeed, I wondered what Katherine could have against him. Poverty, perhaps; but then Judy would have enough and to spare when Howard died. And Howard had already had one attack of angina pectoris that I knew of, and others possibly which he had concealed.

Judy was clearly very much in love. Indeed, I felt that she could hardly keep her hands off the boy; that she wanted to touch his sleeve or rumple his hair; and that he, more shyly, less sure of himself, was quite desperately in love with her.

But he was business-like enough about the case. He wanted the story, or such part of it as he might have.

"It will leak out somehow," he said. "Probably Harrison will give it out himself; they'll give out something, anyhow. Somebody may have seen her, you know. A lot of missing people are turned up that way."

We were still arguing the matter, Judy taking Dick's side of it, of course, when Jim Blake came in.

I can recall that scene now; the tap-tap of the glazier's hammer as he repaired the broken pane in the drawing room, the lowered voices of Judy and Dick from the music room, whither they had retired with alacrity after Judy had dutifully kissed her uncle, and Jim Blake himself, sitting neatly in his chair, pale gray spats, gray tie, gray bordered silk handkerchief, and hair brushed neatly over his bald spot, explaining that he had felt ill that morning or he would have come earlier.

"Just the old trouble," he said, and I noticed that he mopped his forehead. "This wet weather—"

Some years ago he had been thrown from a borrowed hunter and had sprained his back. Judy had always maintained that his frequent retirements to his bed as a result were what she called "too much food and drink." But that day he looked really ill.

"Tell me about Sarah," he said, and lighted a cigar with hands that I thought were none too steady. He did not interrupt me until I had finished.

"You've had the police, you say?"

"I have indeed. What else could I do?"

"Katherine doesn't want it to get into the newspapers."

"Why not? There's no family disgrace in it, is there? That's idiotic."

He took out his handkerchief and mopped his forehead again.

"It's queer, any way you take it. You say Wallie was here last night? What does he think?"

"He seems to think it's mighty important to find her. As of course it is."

"And she'd tied the dogs to a tree? That's curious. Just where did you say they were?"

He sat silent for some time after that. Judy was banging the piano in the next room, and the noise seemed to bother him.

"Infernal din!" he said querulously. And after a pause: "How is Howard? What does Judy think about him?"

"I don't believe she knows very much. He's a secretive person; Katherine is worried, I know that."

He seemed to ponder that, turning his cigar in his long, well-kept fingers.

"This girl who telephoned, this Florence, she hasn't been identified yet? They haven't traced the call?"

"Not so far as I know."

Asked later on to recall Jim Blake's attitude that day, if it was that of an uneasy man, I was obliged to say that it was. Yet at the time it did not occur to me. He was an orderly soul, his life tidily and comfortably arranged, and what I felt then was that this thing with its potentialities of evil had disturbed him, his small plans, possibly for that very afternoon, the cheerful routine of his days.

"I suppose they've searched the lot next door, and the park?"

"Inspector Harrison has been over it."

He sat for some time after that, apparently thoughtful. I realize now that he was carefully framing his next question.

"Elizabeth," he said, "when was Howard here last? Has he been here recently?"

"Howard? Not for months."

"You're sure of that, I suppose?"

"He hasn't been able to get about, Jim. You know that."

He looked at me with eyes that even then seemed sunken, and drew a long breath.

"I suppose that's so," he said, and lapsed into silence.

There was, at the time, only one result to that visit of Jim Blake's. I called Dick in and told him and Judy Katherine's desire for secrecy.

"Trust mother!" said Judy. "Keep in the society columns and out of the news!"

But the story was suppressed. Not until Sarah's body was found, four days later, was there any publicity.

The discovery of the body was one of those sheer chances to which I have referred. Without any possible motive for her killing, the police still believed it possible that she had deliberately disappeared. But, as Judy pointed out, there was as little known reason for such a disappearance as for her murder.

And then on the Saturday of that week she was found, poor soul.

I have no distinct memories of those four days of nightmare, save of the increasing certainty of disaster, of Katherine's and Laura's frenzied suggestions by telephone and wire, of Judy's forced cheerfulness, and a queer sort of desperation in Wallie which I could not understand.

He had joined the police in the search, visited the Morgue, gone through her effects to find a photograph to be sent to other cities. During those days he seemed neither to eat nor sleep, and he grew perceptibly thinner. All his old nonchalance had left him, and at least once in that four-day interval he came in somewhat the worse for liquor.

It was that night—I do not remember which one—that he told me he had written me a letter and put it in his box at the bank.

"So you'll understand," he said, his tongue slightly thick. "So if anything happens to me you'll understand."

Judy looked up at him.

"You're lit," she stated coldly. "Lit and mawkish. What's going to happen to you?"

"You'll see," he said somberly. "Plenty may happen to me. If you don't believe it, look at me!"

"You're not much to look at just now," she told him. "You'd better order him some black coffee, Elizabeth Jane."

She told me later that she did not believe he had written me any letter. But he had indeed. Months later we found it where he said it would be, in his box at the bank. But by that time we needed no explanation.

The finding of Sarah's body was as extraordinary as was everything else in this strange case.

Judy had taken the dogs for their usual walk in the park, and somewhere there she met Dick, certainly not by chance. It appears that for purposes of their own they had left the main park and walked through that narrow ravine which is behind my own property, and through which a bridle path follows the wanderings of a small stream. As this ravine lies close to the lot where the dogs had been found, there had been a search of sorts. The two young people, then, were not searching. They were walking along, intent on their own affairs. In front of them a man on a gray horse was ambling quietly along.

Suddenly and without warning the horse shied violently, and the rider went off. He was not hurt, and Dick caught the horse and led it back to him.

"Not hurt, are you?" Judy asked.

"Only surprised," he told her. "Surprised and irritated! That's the second time this beast has shied at that sewer, or whatever it is. Twice this week. Yet he's seen it a hundred times."

Well, he got on again, having led the animal past the obstacle, and Judy and Dick looked at it. At some time it had evidently been intended to raise the road level there, and what they saw was a brick sewer entrance, circular, and standing about seven feet above the ground.

"Funny," said Judy. "What's happened to that thing this week?"

Dick laughed at her. Neither of them, I am sure, was thinking of poor Sarah. It was a bright cool spring day, made for lovers, and he teased her. It was a part of the game.

"I suppose that horse can see things we can't see!" he said.

"Why not? Dogs can."

And at that moment Jock, beside the base of the structure, suddenly raised his head and let out a long wail.

They were rather incoherent about what happened after that. It was Dick who finally got to the top and looked down. At first he could see nothing. Then he made out what looked like a bundle of clothing below, and Judy knew by his face.

Even then of course they were not certain it was Sarah. They did not come home; they got the park police at once, and Dick did not let Judy wait after that. He brought her back, whimpering, and I put her to bed and waited.

It was Sarah.

They never let me see her, and I was glad of that.

She had been murdered. There were indications of a heavy blow on the back of the head, not necessarily fatal; but the actual cause of death, poor creature, was two stab wounds in the chest. One had penetrated to the right ventricle of the heart, and she had died very quickly.

Only later on was I to have the full picture of that tragic discovery; the evidence that the body had been dragged along beside the bridle path for almost a quarter of a mile, a herculean task; the inexplicable fact that the shoes had been removed and thrown in after the body; the difficulty of explaining how that inert figure had been lifted seven feet in the air to the top of the sewer to be dropped as it was found, head down, into that pipe-like orifice; and strangest and most dreadful of all to me, that the very rope with which the dogs had been tied when I found them, had been fastened under her arms and used to drag the body.

The homicide squad, I believe, was early on the scene, a cordon of police thrown out, and the path closed from the Larimer lot to a point beyond the sewer. But the heavy rain and the fact that the path had been used had obliterated all traces save those broken branches down the hillside which apparently proved that Sarah had been killed on or near the Larimer property.

The body had been found at three o'clock, and the medical examination took place as soon as it could be removed. The crime detection unit, a group of specialists, had been notified before that removal, but of the seven only one found anything to do there, and that was the photographer. And a gruesome enough exhibit those pictures made; the waiting ambulance, the mounted men holding back the curious who attempted to break the line, and close-up photographs of that poor body in its incredible resting place.

Inspector Harrison, sitting gravely in my library that night, was puzzled and restless.

"It's a curious case," he said. "Apparently motiveless. She was not robbed; the purse was found with the body, although—you say she carried a key to this house?"

"Yes. Inspector, I have been wondering if she did leave her bedroom door unlocked that night when she went out. If that man on the stairs hadn't already killed her and taken both keys."

"I think not. And I'll tell you why. Now the time when you saw that figure on the stairs was at seven-thirty-five, approximately. You'd finished a seven o'clock dinner and had got to your coffee. That's near enough, anyhow. But Sarah Gittings did not die until around ten o'clock."

"I don't understand. How do you know that?"

"By the food in the stomach. It had been in the stomach for approximately four hours before she died. The autopsy showed us that. But it does not show us where Sarah Gittings was between seven o'clock and ten. Three hours between the time she left this house and the time of her death. Where was she? What was she doing during that three hours? Once we learn that, and the identity of this Florence, we will have somewhere to go."

"I have wondered if a maniac, a homicidal maniac—"

"On account of the shoes? No, I think not, although there may have been an endeavor to make us think that. No. Why did Sarah Gittings take a chair from the laundry and place it in the wood-cellar? Why did she agree to take the dogs, and at the same time take a rope with which to tie them? What was in her room that would justify breaking into this house to secure it? Those are the questions we have to ask ourselves, Miss Bell.

"About this rope," he went on thoughtfully. "You left it when you untied the dogs and went back for Joseph?"

"I left it by the tree."

"And when you got back it was not there?"

"No. We searched for it as well as we could. But a rope doesn't move itself, and it was not where I left it, or anywhere nearby."

He got up to go, and standing in the hallway stared back at the lavatory door.

"This Florence," he said, "she may try to get in touch with you. She reads the papers, and God knows they are full of it to-day. If she does, don't scare her off. Find out something. Coax her here if you can, and notify me."

He went back into the lavatory and stood looking up at the ceiling.

"A strong man," he said, "or a desperate one if he got himself out of that shaft, and he may have; and it took strength to put that body where we found it."

As an afterthought, on his way out, he turned and said:

"Strange thing. Both those stab wounds were exactly the same depth, four and a quarter inches."

Wallie and Jim had made the necessary identification, and the coroner's jury brought in the only verdict possible. After that and pending the funeral we had a brief respite, although hardly to be called a peace. Reporters rang the bell day and night, and the press published sensational stories, including photographs of the house. Camera men even lurked in the shrubbery, trying for snapshots of any of us. One they did get, of Judy.

They had caught her unawares with a cigarette in her hand, and to prevent the picture she had made a really shocking face at the camera. They published it, nevertheless, and Katherine was outraged.

Katherine came down to the funeral. She was shocked and incredulous over the whole affair.

"But why?" she repeated over and over, when we got back from the service. "She had no enemies. She really had nobody, but us."

"Is there anything phony about any of us?" Judy inquired. "Some family secret, or something she knew?"

"Judy!" said Katherine indignantly.

"But I mean it, mother. If we're all she's had for twenty years—"

Fortunately for Judy, Jim Blake came in just then, and I sent upstairs for Mary Martin, who had been left to herself for several days, and ordered tea. It seemed to me that we needed it.

We were five, then, that afternoon after Sarah's funeral when we gathered around the tea table; Katherine in her handsome black, the large square emerald which was Howard's latest gift to her on one white slim hand, saddened but controlled; Judy, with her boyish head and her girlish body; Mary, red-headed, pretty, not too sure of herself and resentful of it—it was clear that Katherine rather daunted her; Jim, well valeted and showing in relaxation some slight evidence of too many dinners and too many cocktails; and myself.

Katherine inspected Jim critically as he came in.

"You look tired, Jim."

"Well, it's been an uneasy week," he said evasively.

But she could not let it rest at that. Everything attached to Sarah had grown enormous in her eyes; already she was exalting Sarah in her mind, her virtues, her grievances.

"I didn't suppose you'd bother much. You never liked her."

"My dear girl! I hardly knew her."

"You never liked her, Jim. That's all I said. Although why you should dislike the poor dear I don't know."

It seemed to me that Jim looked annoyed. More than annoyed, indeed; alarmed. Also that Mary was staring at him with a rather singular intentness, and that Judy had noticed this. There was no particular sympathy between the two girls. Judy, assured, humorous and unself-conscious, was downright and frank to the shocking point, and her small artifices were as open as herself. But there was nothing open about Mary Martin and very little that was natural, save the color of her hair.

"Her mind's always on herself," Judy had complained once. "She poses her very fingers, if you know what I mean. She's self-conscious every minute."

And if there is one crime in the bright lexicon of modern youth it is to be self-conscious.

Katherine, upset and nervous, was gnawing on her grievance like a dog on a bone.

"But you thought Howard was foolish to remember her in his will, Jim."

"Nonsense, Katherine. Howard's money is his, to leave where he likes. Anyhow, let's hope he doesn't leave it at all for a good many years."

That silenced her. She sat very still, with her eyes slightly dilated, facing the issue she had herself brought up; Howard gone and herself alone. The years going on and she alone. And into that silence Mary Martin's voice broke, quiet but very clear.

"I have always meant to ask you, Mr. Blake. Did you receive the letter Miss Gittings wrote you on Sunday, the day before the—the thing happened?"

"A letter?" said Jim. "She wrote me a letter?"

But he was shocked. A child could have seen it. His teacup

shook in his hand, and he was obliged to rest it on his knee. I saw Judy's eyes narrow.

"She did indeed. I went in while she was writing it."

"A letter?" Katherine asked. "Did you get it, Jim?"

"I received no letter." He had recovered somewhat, however, and now he turned on Mary sharply. "How did you know it was to me? Did she say so?"

"No. She was addressing the envelope, and she put her arm over it so I could not see. That is how I know."

"Do speak up," Judy said irritably. "What's the sense in being mysterious? God knows we've got enough of that."

"Her uniform is still hanging in the closet, and Mr. Blake's name is quite clear on the sleeve. Of course you have to take a mirror to read it."

I do not think any one of us doubted that she had told the truth, unless it was Katherine. And Mary sat there, pleased at being the center of attention, the picture however of demureness, her eyes on her well-manicured hands, which were as Judy had said, carelessly but beautifully posed in her lap.

"I don't believe it," Katherine said suddenly. "Please bring it down, Miss Martin."

I saw the girl stiffen and glance at me. She was taking no orders, said her attitude, except from me.

"Will you, Mary? Please."

She went out then, leaving the four of us in a rather strained silence. Jim was staring into his teacup. Judy was watching Jim, and Katherine had put her head back and closed her eyes.

"I don't like that girl," she said. "She is malicious."

"There's nothing malicious in her giving us a clue if she's got one," said Judy with determined firmness. "We don't know that she sent the letter, but if she wrote one—"

"Well?"

"It looks as if she had had something to say to Uncle Jim which she didn't care to telephone, doesn't it?"

Mary came back then, and I daresay all of us felt rather sick when we saw Sarah's white uniform once more. There is something about the clothing of those who have died which is terribly pathetic; the familiarity, the small wrinkles left by a once warm body. And in Sarah's case the uniform spelled to most of us long years of loyal service. Katherine I know was silently crying.

Judy was the first to take the garment and examine it. I noticed that Jim did not touch it. Mary had brought a mirror, and I saw that Joseph—who was gathering the teacups—was politely dissembling an interest as keen as ours. Judy however did not help him any. She looked at the ink marks on the cuff which Mary had indicated, and then silently passed both mirror and garment to me.

There was no question of what was there. Somewhat smeared but still readable was the word "Blake," and while the house number was illegible, the street, Pine Street, was quite distinct.

No one spoke until Joseph went out. Then Jim cleared his throat and said:

"I don't care what's there. I never got a letter from her."

"She put a stamp on it," said Mary.

Judy turned on her.

"That doesn't prove that she mailed it."

But Mary shrugged her shoulders. I thought then, and I still think, that at that moment at least she was sincere enough, and also that she was enjoying the situation she had forced. For once the attention was on her and not on Katherine and Judy, with their solid place in the world, their unconscious assumption of superiority.

"You knew her," she said laconically. "She wouldn't waste a two-cent stamp."

She was unwilling to give up the center of the stage, however. She said that the uniform might or might not have importance, but that she felt the police should see it. If looks could have killed her she would never have left that room, but she had put the issue up to us and what could we do?

"Certainly," said Judy shrewishly. "You might put on your things now and take it, Mary!"

And with all eyes on her Mary merely looked at her watch and said that it was too late.

When a half hour or so later Inspector Harrison came in he found us all sitting there, manufacturing talk to cover our discomfort, and Mary blandly smiling.

We had to give the uniform to him. But from that time on there was not one of us who did not believe that Mary Martin was a potential enemy, and potentially dangerous; nor one of at least four of us who did not believe that Jim had actually received a letter from Sarah and was choosing to suppress the fact.

CHAPTER SIX

It is not easy to tell of this series of crimes in entire sequence. For one thing I kept no journal. For another, I must contend with that instinct of the human mind which attempts to forget what is painful to remember.

I do know, however, that Sarah was murdered on a Monday, the eighteenth of April, and that the death of Florence Gunther did not take place until the first of May. How she had occupied herself in that interval we cannot be certain; we know that she was terrified, that at night she must have locked herself in her room and listened for stealthy footsteps on the stairs, and that in daytime her terror was of a different order, but very real.

I can find only one bit of comfort. When death did come to her it was sudden and unexpected. She may have been smiling. She must even have been feeling a sense of relief, now that her resolution was taken. She could have had no warning, no premonition.

Yet had she had only a little courage she might have lived.

It is easy to say now what she should have done. She should have gone at once to the District Attorney and told her story. But perhaps she was afraid of that, of being discovered or followed. Then too Mr. Waite was away, and she may have been waiting for his return.

We know now that she was hysterical during most of the interval, hysterical and suspicious, that she had built up the crime to fit what she knew, and that the case as she saw it was precisely the case as the police were to see it later on. But we have no details of those terrible days through which she lived from the eighteenth of April to the first of May.

On the Tuesday following Sarah's funeral Katherine went back to New York, and on the next day the District Attorney sent for me. He had some of the papers on the case before him, and he fingered them while he interrogated me.

"You had no reason to believe she had any personal enemies? Anybody who could gain by doing away with her?"

"None whatever," I said promptly, and told him of her relations to the family. "I would have said," I finished, "that she had no outside life whatever."

"She had never married?"

"Never."

"I suppose she was in possession of a good many family facts? I'll not say secrets, but facts; relationships, differences, that sort of thing?"

"Such as they are, yes. But it is a singularly united family."

"Save, I suppose, for Mr. Somers' son by his first marriage. I understand that he is not particularly *persona grata*."

"Who told you that?"

He smiled.

"He told me himself, as a matter of fact. He seems very anxious to have the mystery solved, as of course we all are. I suppose he was fond of her?"

"I never thought so. No."

He coughed.

"In this—er—family difference, I gather that your sympathies have lain with this Walter. Is that so?"

"Yes and no," I said slowly. "Walter has never amounted to much since the war, and his father has never understood him. They are opposed temperaments. Walter is sensitive and high-strung. Mr. Somers is a silent man very successful in business—he's in Wall Street—and they haven't hit it off. Mr. Somers has financed Walter in several businesses, but he has always failed. I believe he has said that he is through, except for a trust fund in his will, a small one. But if you have any idea that Walter is concerned in Sarah's death—"

"I have no such idea. We have checked his movements that night. As a matter of fact, when he left your house he went directly to his club. He left at eleven-fifteen. He recalls your asking the time, and that your own watch was a minute or two slow. At eleven-thirty he was at his club, and joined a bridge game. That time is fixed. The man whose place he took had agreed to be at home by midnight."

He turned over the papers on his desk, and finally picked up one of them.

"Unfortunately," he said, "your own statement that Sarah Gittings had no life outside your family necessarily brings the family into this affair. Your cousin, now, Mr. Blake. How well did she know him?"

"She saw him once in a while. I don't suppose she had ever said much more than good-morning to him."

"Then you know of no reason why she should write to him?"

"None whatever."

"Yet she did write to him, Miss Bell. She wrote to him on the day before her death, and I believe that he received that letter."

He sat back in his chair and surveyed me.

"He got that letter," he repeated.

"But why would he deny it?"

"That's what I intend to find out. Actually, it appears that Sarah Gittings knew Mr. Blake much better than you believe. On at least one evening during the week before her death she went to his house. He was dining out, however, and did not see her. On Saturday night she telephoned to him, but not from your house. We have gone over your calls. Clearly this was some private matter between them. Amos, Mr. Blake's servant, says he recognized her voice; of course that's dubious, but again Mr. Blake was out. Then on Sunday she wrote, and I have every reason to believe that he got the letter on Monday."

"Why?"

"Because he went out that night to meet her."

I think, recalling that interview, that he was deliberately telling me these things in order to get my reaction to them, to watch for those reactions. Later on I believe he attempted to convey something of this system of his to the Grand Jury; that he said, in effect:

"You are to remember that guilt or innocence is not always solved or otherwise by the sworn statements of witnesses. People have perjured themselves before this. The reaction to a question is an important one; there is a subtle difference between the honest man and the most subtle liar."

So now he watched me.

"Did you know, when she left your house that night, that she was going out to meet Mr. Blake?"

"No. And I don't believe it now."

"You saw the writing on her cuff. Was that hers?"

"It looked like it. I daresay it was."

"Yet no such envelope was found in her room the next day, when the police searched it. Nor among the trash which Inspector Harrison examined. She wrote and sent that letter, Miss Bell, and he received it. Unless some one in your house found it and deliberately destroyed it."

"If you think I did that, I did not."

"No," he said. "I am sure you did not. That is why I know he got it. But why should he deny it? Remember, I am bringing no accusation against Mr. Blake, but I want him to come clean on this story. He knows something. You might suggest to him that it would be better for him to tell what he knows than to have us find it out for ourselves."

I was slightly dazed as I left, and sitting back in the car I was puzzled. How little, after all, we know of people! Sarah, moving quietly about my house, massaging me each morning with quiet efficiency; her life an open book, not too interesting. And yet Sarah had had a secret, a secret which she had withheld from me and had given or tried to give to Jim Blake.

I decided to see Jim at once and give him the District Attorney's message. But Jim had had a return of his old trouble and was in bed. And as it happened, something occurred that night which took my mind away from Jim for the time, and from everything else except Judy.

She had been in a fever of anger and resentment ever since Sarah's death. After all, Sarah had helped to bring her into the world, and she was outraged. I daresay under other conditions I might have found her determination to solve a crime amusing rather than otherwise, but there was a set to her small jaw, a feverish look in her eyes, that commanded my respect. And in the end, like Katherine, she did make her small contribution.

To Dick of course she was wonderful, no matter what she did.

So she and Dick were working on the case; she in a fury of indignation, Dick largely because of her. I know that they had gone over every inch of the lot where the dogs had been tied, but that they had found nothing. I think, however, that they were afraid I could not give their efforts sympathetic attention, for except for their lack of success they did not confide in me.

On that night, Wednesday, they had been making a sketch of the lot and the park, but Judy looked very tired, and at ten o'clock I sent Dick away. Judy started up for bed, but in the hall she must have thought of something and changed her mind. She went back through the pantry, where Joseph was reading the evening paper, and asked if he had a flashlight. Joseph had none there, and she went into the kitchen, got some matches and the garage key from its nail and proceeded to the garage.

Shortly after she came back to the kitchen door and called in to him:

"Where's the ladder, Joseph? The ladder Mr. Walter used in the lavatory that night?"

"It's in the tool room, Miss Judy. Shall I bring it in?"

"Never mind," she said, and went out again.

At half past ten I heard him making his round of the windows and doors, before going to bed. At the front door he stopped, and then came to me in the library.

"I suppose Miss Judy came in by the front door, madam?"

"Miss Judy! Has she been out?"

"She went out through the kitchen, a little after ten. She said she wanted the ladder; she didn't say why."

I was uneasy rather than alarmed, until I saw that the garage was dark.

"She's not there, Joseph!"

"Maybe she took the car and went out, madam."

"She'd have told me, I'm sure."

I was starting out at once, but he held me back.

"I'd better get my revolver," he said. "If there's anything wrong—"

That sent a shiver of fear down my spine.

"Judy!" I called. "Judy!"

There was no answer, and together Joseph and I started out, he slightly in the lead and his revolver in his hand. It was a black night and starless; just such a night as when poor Sarah met her death, and the very silence was terrifying. Halfway along the path Joseph wheeled suddenly.

"Who's there?" he said sharply.

"What did you hear, Joseph?"

"I thought somebody moved in the bushes."

We listened, but everything was quiet, and we went on.

In the garage itself, when we switched on the lights, everything was in order, and the key Judy had used was still in the small door which gave entrance from the side. This door was closed but not locked. The first ominous thing was when we discovered that the door into the tool room was locked and that the key was missing from its nail. I rattled the knob and called Judy, but received no reply, and Joseph in the meantime was searching for the key.

"She's in here, Joseph."

"Not necessarily, madam. Robert hides the key sometimes. He says that Abner takes his tools."

But Judy was in there. Not until Joseph had broken a window

and crawled in did we find her, poor child, senseless and bleeding from a cut on the head.

Joseph carried her into the house, and into the library. She was already stirring when he placed her on the couch there, and she was quite conscious, although dizzy and nauseated, in a short time. Enough indeed to protest against my calling a doctor.

"We don't want any more fuss," she said, and tried to smile. "Remember mother, Elizabeth Jane! Always in the society columns but never in the news."

But as she was violently nauseated almost immediately I got Joseph to telephone to Doctor Simonds, and he came very soon afterwards.

She had, he said, been struck on the head, and Joseph suggested that the ladder itself had fallen on her. As a matter of fact, later investigation showed the ladder lying on the floor, and as Judy said it was against the wall when she saw it, there was a possibility of truth in this. But one thing was certain; however she was hurt, she had been definitely locked in the tool room. She had used the key and left it in the door. Some one had locked her in and taken the key. It was nowhere to be found.

We got her up to bed, and the diagnosis was a mild concussion and a lucky escape. The doctor was inclined to be humorous about it.

"You have a hard head, Judy. A hard head but a soft heart, eh?"

Well, he ordered ice to what she called her bump and heat to her feet, and while Joseph was cracking the ice below she told her story. But although Joseph maintained that she had asked him about the ladder, she gave an entirely different reason herself.

"Abner has a foot rule in the tool room," was her story to me. "I wanted to measure the cabinet. Sometimes you find a secret drawer that way. So I got the key to the garage and went out. I thought I heard something in the shrubbery behind me once, but it might have been a rabbit, I don't know.

"The tool room light had burned out, so I lighted a match when I went in. The door was not locked, but the key was in it. There was nobody in the tool room, unless they were behind the door when I opened it. I lighted a fresh match, and just then the door slammed behind me and blew out the match. I said 'damn,' and—that's all I remember."

To add to our bewilderment and my own secret anxiety, Joseph brought forth something when he carried up the ice; something which was odd, to say the least. This was that just before ten o'clock, when he let the dogs out the back door, he heard them barking in the shrubbery. This barking, however, ceased abruptly.

"As though they'd recognized the party," said Joseph, who now and then lapsed into colloquial English. "Jock now, he'd never let up if it was a stranger."

But there was something horrible in that thought; that any one who knew us would attack Judy, and the situation was not improved by Norah's declaration the next day that, at two o'clock in the morning, four hours after the attack on Judy, she had seen some one with a flashlight in the shrubbery near the garage. The night had been cool and she had got out of bed to close her window. Then she saw the light, and because it was rather ghostly and the *morale* of the household none too good, she had simply got back into bed and drawn the covers over her head.

Inspector Harrison had come early at my request, and Norah repeated the story to him.

The flashlight, she said, was close to the ground, and almost as soon as she saw it, it went out.

Up to that moment I think he had been inclined to lay Judy's condition to accident, the more so as she refused to explain why she had been in the garage.

"Come now, Miss Judy. You had a reason, hadn't you?"

"I've told you. I wanted to get the foot rule."

"Did you tell Joseph you wanted to see the ladder?"

"I may have," she said airily. "Just to make conversation."

"This ladder," he persisted. "It is the one Walter Somers used in the lavatory?"

Judy yawned.

"Sorry," she said. "I lost some sleep last night. Is it the same ladder, Elizabeth Jane? You tell him."

"It is," I said flatly, "and you know it perfectly well, Judy. You're being silly."

But she had no more to say, and the Inspector stamped down the stairs in no pleasant mood and inclined to discredit her whole story. For which I did not blame him.

He did however believe Norah. She was looking pale and demoralized, and she said something about witch lights and then crossed herself. The result was that he at once commenced an investigation of the shrubbery, and that his men almost immediately discovered footprints in the soft ground to the right of the path and where Norah had seen the light.

There were four, two rights and two lefts, and when I went out to look at them the Inspector was standing near them, surveying them with his head on one side.

"Very neat," he said. "Very pretty. See anything queer about them, Simmons?"

"They're kind of small, if that's it."

"What about the heels?"

"Very good, sir. Clear as a bell."

The Inspector drew a long breath.

"And that's all you see, is it?" he demanded violently. "What the hell's the use of my trying to teach you fellows anything? Look at those heels! A kangaroo couldn't have left those prints. They've been planted."

He left the discomfited Simmons to mount guard over the prints and to keep the dogs away from them, and not unlike a terrier himself, set to work to examine the nearby ground and bushes.

"The fellow, whoever he was, stepped off the path there when Miss Judy came along. But he left footprints, and later on he remembered them. He came back, smoothed them over and planted false ones. If he's overlooked one now—"

He was carefully turning over dead leaves with a stick he carried, and now he stooped suddenly and picked up something.

"Look at this!" he said. "The key to the tool room, isn't it? I thought so. Threw it here as he ran."

He was examining the key, which is the flat key of the usual Yale lock, and now he gave an exclamation of disgust.

"Clean as a whistle," he said. "Pretty cagey, this chap. Must have been in a devil of a hurry, but he wiped it first; or he wore gloves."

He stood there for some time, staring at the key.

"Well," he said finally, "we have just two guesses, Miss Bell. Either he wanted to do away with Miss Judy, which is unlikely; or he did not like her going into that tool room."

"But he let her go in, and he locked her there."

"Not in shape to do much looking about, however," he said grimly. "Now which was it?"

He glared at me as though he expected an answer.

"I'm sure I don't know," I said meekly.

Later on I stood by while his men measured the distance between the footprints and made molds of them. They sprayed the marks with something first, and then poured in plaster of Paris which the Inspector reinforced with the inevitable toothpicks. The result was a pair of rather ghastly white shoes, which he surveyed with satisfaction.

"How do I know they were planted?" he said. "Well, the stride was too long for the foot, for one thing. Here's a small foot and a long stride. Then the ground's soft; they weren't deep enough. And there's another point. When a man walks there's a back thrust to his foot, and the weight's likely to be more on the outside and back of the heel. Look at me; I walk in this earth. What happens? I break the earth at the rear as I lift my foot."

"You might try that, Simmons," he called. "Maybe the next time you won't let somebody put something over on you."

He left soon after that, greatly pleased with himself but considerably puzzled, and carrying the two molds carefully wrapped in a newspaper.

His examination of the garage and of the ladder had yielded nothing whatever.

CHAPTER SEVEN

JUDY HAD been hurt on Wednesday, the twenty-seventh of April, and Florence Gunther was not killed until the first of May, which was the Sunday following.

On either Tuesday or Friday of that week, then, Wallie came in to see me.

I remember being shocked at his appearance, and still more shocked at the way he received the news that Judy had been hurt.

"Good God!" he said. "I'll stop this thing if I have to—" He hesitated. "If I have to kill somebody with my own hands."

But he would not explain that. He called Joseph and went out to the garage, leaving me to make what I could out of that speech of his, and of his conduct generally since Sarah had been killed.

He had searched far more assiduously than had the police, had shown more anxiety than any of us. His gaiety had gone, and he had a hollow-eyed and somber look during those days which I could not account for.

Nor did the discovery of the body afford him any apparent relief. To the rest of us, grieved as we were, it at least ended that tragic search. After all, it was over. We could not help Sarah, and the rest was for the police. But Wallie had not appeared to share this relief.

Yet Wallie had not liked Sarah. She was not a part of that early régime of which Joseph was the lone survival; of Margaret and the noisy, gay, extravagant days before she left Howard and a young son both of whom had passionately loved her, to run away with a man who abandoned her within six months.

I found myself thinking of those days. I had known Howard even then. Indeed, it was through me that he met Katherine. Margaret had had a brief unhappy year somewhere in Europe; then she died. And Wallie had needed a mother. But Katherine had not proved to be a mother to him.

He had resented her, and she had resented him. She had never liked him, and after Judy was born this dislike greatly increased.

It accentuated her jealousy of Margaret that Margaret had borne Howard a son, and that she had not; for Katherine was passionately in love with her husband. And she had kept nothing of Margaret's that she could avoid. Even Joseph had had to go, and so I took him. Not unusual, I daresay, this jealousy of second wives for the women they have followed, even when that woman is dead. But it worked badly for Wallie.

Certainly Wallie was not blameless for his alienation from his father, but also certainly Katherine never raised a finger to restore the peace between them. Wallie was too reminiscent of his mother, fiery, passionate, undisciplined, handsome. When he had learned that Margaret was dying in Biarritz, abandoned by the man for whom she had left Howard, he had demanded permission to go to her. But he was refused on the score of his age—he was only fourteen at the time—and in desperation he had taken out of Howard's wallet the money for a second-class passage there.

He was too late, at that, but Howard never forgave him the theft, and he had made the mistake of telling Katherine.

After her marriage, when Wallie was in the house, she kept her purse locked away. And he knew it and hated her for it. But he was not there very often. First at school and later at college, Katherine kept him away as much as possible. And after that had come the war.

Naturally then the relationship between Judy and Wallie was almost as remote as the relationship between Wallie and Sarah. To have him grow morose and exhausted when Sarah disappeared was surprising enough, but to see him grow pale and furious over the attack on Judy was actually startling.

He was quieter, however, when he came back from the garage. He planted himself in front of me, like a man who had made a resolution.

"See here," he said. "How fond are you of Jim Blake?"

"I like him. I don't know that it's any more than that."

"What time was it when he telephoned here that night?"

"About a quarter past seven."

"And he asked for Sarah?"

"Yes."

"Why did he do that? Was he in the habit of calling Sarah? Of course he wasn't. How do you know that when she left the house that night it wasn't to see Jim Blake? To meet him somewhere?"

"I don't believe it," I said sharply. "Why would she meet him? I don't believe they've exchanged two dozen words in twenty years."

"She went out to meet him," he insisted. "I know that. I've

made it my business to know it. I've been talking to that darky of his. You know his habits; you know he dines late and dresses for dinner. Well, that night he didn't. He dined early and he put on a golf suit. And he left the house at seven o'clock."

"Good heavens, Wallie! If a man may not eat when he's hungry and dress as he likes—"

"Listen," he said doggedly. "That's not all. He carried with him that sword-stick you gave him."

"Even then—"

"Let me finish, Elizabeth Jane. That cane or stick or whatever you call it, has disappeared. It's not in the house. It stood in the hall with his other sticks until Sarah's body was found. Then it went."

He was looking at me with his tired sunken eyes, but there was no doubting his earnestness or his conviction.

"What does that look like?" he demanded. "He has an appointment with Sarah. He goes to meet her, armed. And then—"

"Wallie, I implore you not to give that to the police."

"No," he said somberly. "Not yet. But some day I may have to."

This then was our situation, during the few days which remained before the first of May. Sarah was dead; dead of two stab wounds four and a quarter inches deep, inflicted after she had been stunned by a blow on the back of the head. Judy had been attacked by the same method, a blow on the head from the rear, but no further attempt on her life had been made. Wallie suspected Jim Blake, apparently only because the sword-cane was missing, and my household was in a state of nerves so extreme that the backfiring of automobiles as they coasted down the long hill which terminates at my drive was enough to make the women turn pale.

Of clues we had none whatever.

Because of the sensational nature of the crime the press was clamoring for an arrest, and the Inspector was annoyed and irritated.

"What do they want, anyhow?" he said. "I can't make clues, can I? And if you'd listen to the District Attorney's office you'd think all I had to do was to walk out and arrest the first man I met on the street. Lot of old women, getting nervous the minute the papers begin to yap at them!"

He must have broken up hundreds of toothpicks that week. We would find small scattered bits of wood all over the place.

By Sunday, the first of May, Judy was still in bed, but fully convalescent. She had ordered a number of books on crime to read, and flanked by those on one side and her cigarettes on the other, managed to put in the days comfortably enough.

The evenings were reserved for Dick. Their first meeting after Judy's injury had defined the situation between them with entire clarity. He was on his knees beside the bed in an instant.

"My darling! My poor little darling!" he said.

She lay there, looking perfectly happy, with one hand on his head.

"Your poor little darling has made a damned fool of herself," she said sweetly. "And you'll give me hell when you hear about it. Go on out, Elizabeth Jane; he wants to kiss me."

Which, Katherine or no Katherine, I promptly did.

It was then on Sunday afternoon that there occurred another of those apparently small matters on which later such grave events were to depend. Already there were a number of them: Sarah's poor body found by the coincidence of Judy being near when a horse shied; the coolness of an April night so that Norah must go to her window to close it; Mary Martin happening to open Sarah's door while she was writing a letter, so that Sarah had made that damning record on her white sleeve; Jim Blake's deviation from his custom of dressing for dinner and its results; Judy's sudden and still mysterious desire to visit the garage at night; even my own impulsive gift to Jim Blake of my grandfather's sword-stick.

On that Sunday afternoon, at five o'clock, Florence Gunther came to see me and was turned away. I had gone upstairs to rest, and she was turned away.

Why had she not come sooner? She was frightened, of course. We know that now. Afraid for her very life. The nights must have been pure terror, locked away in there in the upper room of that shabby house on Halkett Street. But she knew she held the key to the mystery. One can figure her reading the papers, searching for some news, and all the time holding the key and wondering what she ought to do.

If she had gone to the police with her story, she might have saved her life. But if all of us behaved rationally under stress there would be no mysteries, and the dread of the police and of publicity is very strong in many people. And in addition she herself had something to hide, a small matter but vital to her. How could she tell her story and not reveal that?

She must have thought of all those things, sitting alone at night in that none too comfortable room of hers with its daybed covered with an imitation Navajo rug, its dull curtains and duller carpet, its book from the circulating library, and perhaps on the dresser when she went to bed at night, the gold bridge with its two teeth which was later to identify her.

Yet in the end she reached a decision and came to me. And Joseph, who was to identify her as my visitor later on by a photograph, answered the bell and turned her away! I was asleep, he said, and could not be disturbed. So she went off, poor creature, walking down my path to the pavement and to her doom; a thin colorless girl in a dark blue coat and a checked dress.

She had left no name, and Joseph did not tell me until I went down to dinner.

Even then it meant nothing to me.

"What was she like, Joseph? A reporter?"

"I think not, madam. A thinnish person, very quiet."

Dick was having an early Sunday night supper with me, early so that the servants might go out. That, too, is a custom of my mother's, the original purpose having been that they might go to church. Now, I believe, they go to the movies.

But I thought no more of the matter. Mary Martin had rather upset me. She had come in from a walk to tell me that she was leaving as soon as I could spare her, and had suddenly burst into tears.

"I just want to get away," she said, through her handkerchief. "I'm nervous here. I'm—I guess I'm frightened."

"That's silly, Mary. Where would you go?"

"I may go to New York. Mrs. Somers has said she may find something for me."

Judy's comment on that conversation, when I stopped in her room to tell her, was characteristic.

"Mother's idea of keeping Mary's mouth shut," she said. "And polite blackmail on the part of the lady!"

So Mary had not come down to dinner, and Dick and I were alone. He talked, I remember, about crime; that Scotland Yard seized on one dominant clue and followed it through, but that the expert American detective used the Continental method and followed every possible clue. And he stated as a corollary to this that the experts connected with the homicide squad had some clues in connection with Sarah's murder that they were not giving out.

"They've got something, and I think it puzzles them."

"You don't know what it is?"

But he only shook his head, and proceeded to eat a substantial meal. I remember wondering if that clue involved Jim, and harking back again, as I had ever since, to Wallie's suspicion of him.

Why had he telephoned to Sarah that night? Could it be that he was, in case of emergency, registering the fact that, at seven-fifteen or thereabouts, he was safely at home? But we had the word of Amos that he was not at home at that time; that, God help us, he was out somewhere, with a deadly weapon in his hand and who knew what was in his heart.

He was still shut away, in bed. What did he think about as he lay in that bed?

"Dick," I said. "You and Judy have something in your minds about this awful thing, haven't you?"

"We've been talking about it. Who hasn't?"

"But something concrete," I insisted. "Why on earth did Judy want that ladder?"

He hesitated.

"I don't know," he said slowly. "I don't think she wanted the ladder; I think she must have intended to look at it."

Upon this cryptic speech, which he refused to elaborate, I took him upstairs.

That evening is marked in my memory by two things. One was, about nine o'clock, a hysterical crying fit by Mary Martin. Clara came down to the library to tell me that Mary was locked in her room and crying; she could hear her through the door.

As Mary was one of those self-contained young women who seem amply able to take care of themselves, the news was almost shocking.

To add to my bewilderment, when I had got the smelling salts and hurried up to her, she refused at first to let me in.

"Go away," she said. "Please go away."

"Let me give you the salts. I needn't come in."

A moment later, however, she threw the door wide open and faced me, half defiantly.

"It's nothing," she said. "I was low in my mind, that's all." She forced a smile. "I have a fit like this every so often. They're not serious."

"Has anything happened, Mary?"

"Nothing. I'm just silly. You know, or maybe you don't; living around in other people's houses, having nothing. It gets me sometimes."

I came nearer to liking her then than I ever had, and I wondered if the sight of Dick, intent on Judy and Judy's safety, had not precipitated the thing. After all, she was pretty and she was young. I patted her on the arm.

"Maybe I've done less than my duty, Mary," I said. "I'm a selfish woman and lately, with all this tragedy—"

And then she began to cry again. Softly, however, and rather hopelessly. When I went downstairs again I wondered if she was not frightened, too; after all, her loneliness was nothing new to her.

I can look back on Mary now, as I can look back on all the other actors in our drama. But she still remains mysterious to me, a queer arrogant creature, self-conscious and sex-conscious, yet with her own hours of weakness and despair.

The other incident was when Dick received a telephone call, rather late in the evening.

That must have been around eleven o'clock. Judy and he had spent the intervening hours together, the door open out of deference to my old-fashioned ideas, but with Dick curled up comfortably on her bed in deference to their own! He came leisurely down to the telephone when I called him, but the next moment he was galvanized into action, rushed into the hall, caught up his overcoat and hat, and shouted up the stairs to Judy.

"Got to run, honey. Something's happened, and the star reporter is required."

"Come right up here and say good-night!"

"This is business," he called back, grinning. "I can kiss you any time."

And with that he was out of the house and starting the engine of his dilapidated Ford. I could hear him rattling and bumping down the drive while Judy was still calling to him from above.

CHAPTER EIGHT

I WAS astonished the next morning to have Clara announce Inspector Harrison before I was dressed. I looked at the clock, and it was only half past eight. Clara plainly considered the call ill-timed.

"I can ask him to come back, ma'am."

"Not at all. You have no idea what he wants, I suppose?"

"Joseph let him in. If you'd like some coffee first."

But I wanted no coffee. I threw on some clothing—Judy was still asleep—and when I got down Mr. Harrison was standing in the lavatory doorway, thoughtfully gazing up at the skylight. He looked tired and untidy, and his eyes were blood-shot.

"I've taken the liberty of asking your butler for a cup of coffee. I've been up all night."

"Why not have breakfast?"

"I'm not hungry. I don't think I could eat anything."

But he did eat a fair meal when it appeared, talking meanwhile of unimportant matters. Not until we were in the library with the door closed did he mention the real object of his visit.

"Miss Bell, did you ever hear of a young woman named Gunther?"

"I think not. Why?"

"Florence Gunther?"

"Florence! The Florence who telephoned to Sarah?"

"I think it's possible. I'm not certain."

"Well," I said, "I'm glad you've found her. She must know something."

"Yes," he said. "Yes, I think she did know something. But she will never be able to tell it. She was shot and killed last night."

Later on I was to wonder why he did not tell me then the details of that killing. Perhaps he was still rather sick; perhaps he had reasons of his own. But what he told me then was only that the girl had been shot and that there was some evidence that her room had been gone through, like Sarah's. The body had been taken to the Morgue.

"There are certain points of resemblance," he said, "although this girl was shot, not stabbed. For instance—I don't want to harrow you—but the shoes had been removed. And although her room is not in the condition of Sarah Gittings', it had been searched. I'll take my oath to that. She seems to have been an orderly person, very quiet, and—"

But that phrase, very quiet, recalled something to me. Quiet. A quiet person. I remembered then; Joseph's description of the young woman who had tried to see me the day before.

"I wonder," I said, "if she could have been here yesterday."

"Yesterday?"

"How was she dressed? What did she look like? Joseph turned away a young woman while I was resting. It just might have been—"

He was in the hall in a moment, calling Joseph, and what I had feared turned out to be correct. Joseph not only identified a cabinet photograph of her, but recalled that she had worn a blue coat, and "a sort of plaid dress, sir; checked, it might have been."

When he had excused Joseph, who looked shaken over the whole business, the Inspector gave me such facts as he had.

Florence Gunther had been shot and killed; the bullet had gone into her brain and out again. But the murderer had also tried to burn her body, and had largely succeeded. A farmer named Hawkins, out on the Warrenville road, had gone out at ten o'clock the night before to look after a sick cow, and in a gully beside the road, not two hundred yards from his front gate, had seen a fire blazing.

Thinking that a passing motorist had ignited the brush with a lighted cigarette, he went back into the house and got an old blanket and a broom with which to beat out the flames. He had actually commenced this when he realized what lay before him. He smothered the fire with the blanket and called the police. But for the incident of the sick cow the body would have been destroyed, as the family had already retired.

As it was, identification would have been a slow matter, had it not been for the one thing which Mr. Harrison had said every criminal overlooks, and this was that where the body had been placed a small spring, a mere thread of water really—I saw it later—effectually soaked the ground at this point. Such garments as were in contact with the earth, then, were not destroyed, and they revealed the fact that the unfortunate woman had worn a checked dress and a dark blue coat.

There must have been footprints in that soft ground, the heavy marks of a man carrying a substantial burden; but a passing car with a group of curious and horrified motorists, Hawkins himself extinguishing the fire, the police and police reporters when they arrived, had thoroughly erased them. The three detectives from the homicide squad reached the spot to find the body, a crowd of curious onlookers, and not a discoverable clue to the murder.

At four in the morning Harrison went home and threw himself, fully clothed, on his bed. There was nothing then to connect this crime with Sarah, or with us; nor was there until seven-ten the following morning. The body had been taken to the Morgue, Mr. Harrison was peacefully asleep, and Dick Carter had written his story of the murder and gone to bed, a blue-beaded bag in his coat pocket and forgotten. At seven-ten, however, an excited telephone message was received at a local police station from a woman named Sanderson, a boarder in a house in an unfashionable part of the city, on Halkett Street.

She reported that one of the roomers, a young woman named Florence Gunther, was not in her room, and that as she never spent the night out she was certain that something was wrong.

In view of the crime the night before the call was turned over to the Inspector. Breakfastless and without changing his clothing, he got into his car—always kept at his door—and started for Halkett Street. The Sanderson woman, greatly excited, was waiting at the front door.

Her story was simple and direct.

She had not slept well, and some time in the night she had been annoyed by movements overhead, in Florence Gunther's room.

"She seemed to be moving the furniture about," she said, "and I made up my mind to talk to her about it in the morning. So I got up at seven and went up, but she wasn't there. She hadn't slept there. And when I found all her clothes except what she had on I got worried."

He told her nothing of the crime, but he examined the room with her. The landlady, a woman named Bassett, had been ill for some time and did not appear. It was clear to both of them that the room had been searched, although there had been an attempt to conceal the fact. But the important fact was that Florence Gunther when last seen the evening before had worn a checked dress and blue coat.

He knew then what he had found. He locked the room, put Simmons on guard at the door, sent word by a colored servant to Mrs. Bassett that the room and the officer were to be undisturbed, and with a photograph of the dead woman in his pocket had come to me.

"The point seems to be this," he said. "If this is the Florence who was in touch with Sarah, the same motive which led to the one crime has led to the other. The possession of some dangerous knowledge, possibly certain papers—it's hard to say. The one thing apparently certain is that there was something, some physical property for which in each case a search was made. Whether it was found or not—"

He broke the end from a toothpick with great violence.

"Curious thing to think of, isn't it?" he went on. "If you'd seen this girl yesterday she might be living today. She knew the answer to Sarah Gittings' murder, and so she had to go. Now, if we knew how friendly they were, how they met, what brought them together, we'd have something."

And, although we have learned many things, that association of theirs remains a mystery. By what tragic accident they were thrown together we shall never know; two lonely women in a city of over half a million, they had drifted together somehow, perhaps during their aimless evening walks, or in a moving picture theater. We have no reason to believe that there was any particular friendship between them. One thing, discovered by accident, held them together and in the end destroyed them.

The Inspector got up to go.

"I'm going down to headquarters," he said. "Then I'm going back to that room of hers. Whether the same hand killed both women or not, I imagine the same individual searched both rooms. There's a technique about such matters."

"Still, I should think that a man who had just killed—"

"Not this one. He's got no heart and he's got no nerves. But there's always a chance. If he goes on killing, he'll slip up some time, and then we'll get him."

With which optimistic words he left me!

Later on in the day I heard from him by telephone.

"Just to cheer you up," he said. "We have a clear slate for Walter Somers last night. He played bridge from eight until three this morning, and won two hundred dollars."

He hung up abruptly. It was the first time I had known that the police were watching Wallie.

From the papers, ringing with another "shoe" murder, and from various sources then and later, I gained a fair idea of the unfortunate young woman.

She was about thirty years of age, a quiet but not unfriendly woman. Shy. She seldom joined the others in the parlor of the Halkett Street house; in the evenings she took a walk or went to the movies. She had apparently no family, and received no mail of any importance.

She had been an expert stenographer in the law office of Waite and Henderson, well-known attorneys, and was highly thought of there. Recently, however, she had shown signs of nervousness, and her work had suffered somewhat.

Her life had been apparently an open book.

In the morning she was called at seven. She dressed slowly, ate her breakfast, and reported at nine at the office. She had not been interested in men, or they in her; but she had had one caller, a gentleman, about two weeks before. His identity was unknown, but he seemed to have been a well-dressed man, not young. He had arrived, according to the colored woman servant, about eight o'clock and stayed until nine-thirty. She had had only a glimpse of him and could not describe him.

On the day of her death, which was Sunday, she had spent the morning doing some small washing and mending. In the afternoon, however, she had put on the blue coat and started out. She was back in less than an hour, and had seemed low-spirited.

No one had seen her leave the house that night. It was thought that she had left the house about eight, and the police believed that she had been killed at or near that ditch on the Warrenville road where the body was found.

But on Monday afternoon we were to learn where she had been shot.

My property lies at the foot of a longish hill. As a result of this, and an annoying one it is, a certain number of cars come down in gear but with the switch off, and by and large a very considerable amount of backfiring takes place directly outside of my drive. The result is that when, quite recently, a bootlegger fired a number of shots at a policeman and finally wounded him in the leg, the poor wretch lay untended for some little time.

All of which bears directly on the killing of Florence Gunther.

Dick had telephoned me during the day, when the identity of

Florence Gunther had been given out by the police, and begged me to send Judy away.

"She's not safe," he said, worried. "Until we know what's behind this nobody's safe."

I agreed to do what I could, and when he came in at six o'clock looking rather the worse for wear, he was more cheerful. I had kept the news of the murder from Judy until then, thinking she might hear it better from him, and she greeted him with a great coolness.

"Don't come near me," she said. "And don't ask him to dinner, Elizabeth Jane. He walked out on me last night."

"Listen to her! If I don't work I don't eat, my child. These millionaire's daughters!" he said to me. "They think honest toil is cutting coupons. Money's nothing to them."

Then he remembered something, and put his hand in his pocket.

"Speaking of money," he said, "hanged if I didn't forget I'd had a windfall. Look what I found!"

He drew out of his pocket a blue beaded bag, and Judy snatched it from him.

"I suppose you've advertised it?" she said severely.

"Darling, I am this moment out of my bath. Of course I shall," he added virtuously. "'Found: bag.' Vague but honest, eh what? It's got ten dollars in it!"

"Where did you find it?"

"I just drove out from the Bell estate in my Rolls-Royce, and there it was."

"On the street?"

"On the street. Right outside your gates, oh daughter of Eve. I said to myself: 'What's that?' Then I replied: 'It's a pocketbook.' Then I shouted 'whoa,' leaped from my trusty steed and—"

It was then that Judy found the typed slip and drew it out. "You won't have to advertise. Here's her name; Florence Gunther."

"Florence Gunther?" I said. "My God!"

It was then that Dick told her of the murder the night before. He was as careful as he could be not to horrify her, but the bare facts were dreadful enough. She went very pale, but she watched him steadily, and somehow I got the impression that he was telling her more than appeared on the surface, that between them there was some understanding, some secret theory against which they were checking these new facts.

"On the Warrenville road? Then she was taken there in a car?"

"Presumably, yes."

"Did anybody see the car?"

"The police are working on that. Apparently not."

"And you've checked up on—things?"

"They seem all right. Absolutely O. K."

Still with this mysterious bond between them they took me out to where Dick had found the bag, and standing there he pointed out where he had found it; not near the pavement, but almost in the center of the street. It had shown up plainly; at first he had thought it was a bird, and veered to avoid it. Then he saw what it was.

"You might figure it like this," he said. "She's coming again to see you. She suspects something, and she's got to tell it. Now, there are two ways for that bag to have been where I found it. Either she saw somebody and ducked out into the street; or she was in a car already, was shot while in the car, and the bag dropped out. I think she was in a car. You see there's no blood," he ended awkwardly.

Judy looked a little sick, but she spoke practically enough.

"Couldn't he have shot her there, dragged her quickly into the shrubbery, and then got a car? She must have been here at eight-thirty or so, and the body wasn't found until after ten."

Well, it was possible; but a careful search of the hedge, and the lilacs, forsythia and syringa bushes inside of it—some of them in leaf, for the spring had been early—revealed nothing whatever.

I find myself dwelling on that question of time, which Judy brought up. It puzzled the police for a long time, but now we know about it; the driving about, with that dead woman lolling on the seat; the decision to use the river, and the bridge crowded and no hope there; the purchase of oil at some remote spot, leaving the car and its grisly contents at a safe distance; and finally the Warrenville road and the sleeping farmhouse. And the sick cow.

The sick cow! Everything safe, another perfect crime. And then, of all possible mischances, a sick cow.

CHAPTER NINE

THAT WAS on Monday. Tuesday morning, Jim being still in bed and incommunicado by the doctor's orders, the District Attorney sent again for Amos, Jim's servant, and terrified him into a number of damaging statements. That early dinner of Jim's, the fact that he had left the house immediately after it, and that he had carried the sword-stick, all of these came out. And finally the frightened wretch told that the stick had disappeared.

That was enough, more than enough. After that Jim was under surveillance day and night, one of those apparently casual affairs, but sufficient to report his movements. He made no movements, however. He lay in his bed, and if he knew the significance of the men who moved back and forward along Pine Street, or that his telephone and mail were both under espionage, he made no sign.

But, although suspicion was now directed at Jim, it was only suspicion.

On Tuesday night Inspector Harrison came again to see me. I was growing to like the man. He was to oppose me and all of us for a long time, but he was at least sturdily honest with me, and he was to try later on to be helpful.

He was very grave that night. He sent Judy away, to her annoyance, closed the library door, and then turned to me.

"I came here tonight with a purpose, Miss Bell," he said at last. "I want you to think, and think hard. Is there anything at all, however remote—I don't care how absurd—which would provide a motive for the killing of Sarah Gittings? For this second crime is subsidiary to that. That I know. Think, now; some remote family trouble, some secret she knew, even some scene at which she happened to be present."

"We don't have family scenes, Inspector."

"Nonsense! Every family has them."

"There is nothing, I assure you. Walter Somers doesn't hit it off with his stepmother, but they don't quarrel. They simply keep apart."

"And Mr. Blake?"

"Why should he quarrel with them? They have been very good to him. I think Mrs. Somers even makes him a small allowance, and a man doesn't quarrel with his bread and butter."

"Tell me something about the Somers family. I know they are wealthy. What else?"

"Howard has been married twice. His first wife eloped with another man, and died in Europe many years ago. After her death he married my cousin, Katherine. They have one child, Judy, who is here. And they are very happy."

"And that's the whole story?"

"Yes, except that Howard Somers is in bad health. He has had at least one attack of angina pectoris. He had that here last year, while I was abroad with his family. He almost died, and I suppose the end is only a question of time."

"I see. How old a man is he?"

"Almost sixty. Quite a handsome man."

"Now, about this sick spell. When you say he was sick here, do you mean in this house?"

"No. The house was closed. He was at a hotel, the Imperial. Sarah Gittings came down to take care of him."

"And Mr. Blake? Was he here at that time?"

"He was in Maine. He has a small cottage there."

I believe now that certain of these interrogations were purely idle, designed to put me off my guard. For the next instant, in the same tone, he asked me a question so unexpected that it found me totally unprepared for it.

"And when did you give Mr. Blake the walking stick which belonged to your grandfather?"

I must have showed my agitation, for he smiled.

"Come, come," he said. "You're a poor witness for the defense, Miss Bell! I see Amos has told the truth. Show a darky a police badge and he'll come clean. How long has Mr. Blake had that cane?"

"Since some time in the early spring. In March."

"You have no idea where it is now?"

"Not the faintest. He certainly didn't bring it back here."

He bent toward me, wary and intent.

"Ah," he said. "So you know it has disappeared! Now that's interesting. I call that very interesting. Who told you that it had disappeared? Not Amos. He was warned. Mr. Blake himself, perhaps?"

"No. It was Walter Somers. Amos told him."

He sat back.

"By and large," he said, "we have too many detectives on these crimes. And the family seems to be curiously interested, doesn't it? For a family with nothing to conceal. Now, I would like a description of that stick, if you don't mind."

There was nothing else to do. Much as I loathed the idea I was obliged to describe the thing, the heavy knob, the knife concealed in the shaft.

"This blade now, was it sharp?"

"Absolutely not. But I daresay Jim had it sharpened. He would have had to, if he had meant to commit a murder."

But my sarcasm was a boomerang.

"It may interest you to know that he did just that, Miss Bell. About a week after he got it."

He gave me little time to worry about that, however.

"There is something else I want to verify. On the night Sarah Gittings was murdered, Mr. Blake telephoned here, I believe; to Miss Judy. At what time was that?"

"Shortly after seven. A quarter past, possibly."

"That was a message from Miss Judy's mother, I gather?"

"Yes, but he—"

I checked myself, too late. He was bending forward again, watching me. "But what?"

"I have just remembered. He asked if Sarah was here; but that is in his favor, naturally. If he had known he need not have asked."

"Or if he did know, and wished to give the impression that he did not."

He sat there looking at me, and for the first time I realized that he was potentially dangerous to me and mine. His china blue eyes were cold and searching; under his bald head his face was determined, almost belligerent. And he was intelligent, shrewd and intelligent. Later on I was to try to circumvent him; to pit my own wits against his. Always he thwarted me, and often he frightened me. In his way, almost to the very end, he remained as mysterious as Sarah, as aloof as Florence Gunther, as implacable as fate itself.

Yet he treated me always with friendliness and often with deference, and now his voice was almost casual.

"Did he say where he was when he called up?"

"No. At home, probably."

"Don't you know better than that, Miss Bell?" he inquired pointedly. "If you don't, let me tell you. On that night Jim Blake dined early, and left the house at seven, or a few minutes after. He did no telephoning before he left. We have a list of his calls out for that night. Wherever he was when he telephoned—and we are trying to locate that—he was not at home."

And I felt again that this communicativeness of his was deliberate, that he was watching for its effect on me.

"But why? Why would Jim Blake kill Sarah?" I demanded. "What would be his motive?"

He was getting ready to go, and he stopped by the door.

"Now and then, in criminal work," he said, "we find the criminal before we learn the motive. I make no accusation against Mr. Blake. I merely say that his movements that night require explanation, and that until he makes that explanation we have to use our own interpretation. If that's unfavorable to him that's his fault."

One comfort at least we had at that time. The reporters, the camera men and the crowds of inquisitive sightseers had abandoned us, and out on the Warrenville road Hawkins had thriftily piled brush about the site of the crime, and was letting in the morbid minded at a price until the county police stopped him.

The cow had died.

But in my own household demoralization was almost complete. The women were in a state of hysteria, afraid to leave the house and almost as terrified to stay in it. On Tuesday morning the laundress had come upstairs pale and trembling, to say that the chair had been taken from the laundry again, and was once more in the room where the wood was stored. And on that night, at something after twelve o'clock, Clara ran down to my room, pounding on the door and shouting that there was a man under her bed.

It required Joseph with the revolver and myself with all my courage to discover Jock there, neatly curled up and asleep.

The matter of the chair, however, puzzled me. I took Judy and went down. It was a plain wooden chair, and it had been left where it was found. Judy mounted it and examined the joists above, for this portion of the basement is not ceiled. But there was nothing there except a large black spider, at which she got down in a hurry.

I don't know what I had expected to find. The sword-stick, perhaps.

It was on Wednesday that I determined to see Jim. I had not seen him for over a week, not indeed since the day of Sarah's funeral, and if Wallie's state had bewildered me Jim's frankly shocked me.

I had been fond of Jim, but with no particular approval. The very fact that he was still idling through his late forties; that he was content to live modestly because extravagance meant work; that he could still put in weeks of preparation on the Bachelors' Ball, given each year for the débutantes; that his food and drink were important to him, and his clothes—all these things had annoyed me.

Nor had I ever quite believed in his feeble health; certainly he was a stronger man than Howard, who had always worked and who was still working in the very shadow of death. Certainly Jim was able to play golf, to sit up all night at bridge, to eat and drink what he wanted, and to dance with a young generation which liked his cocktails and the flowers he sent them.

But this was the surface of Jim Blake. Of the real man, buried under that slightly bulging waistline, that air of frivolity, those impeccable garments, I doubt if even Katherine knew anything. He went his way, apparently a cheerful idler, with his present assured, and his future undoubtedly cared for in the case of Howard's death.

There was, however, nothing cheerful about the Jim I found on Wednesday night, lying in his handsome bed and nursed and valeted by Amos. I have often wondered since just what were his thoughts as he lay there day after day, watching Amos moving deftly about the room; Amos who knew so much and yet not enough.

The two watching each other, the black man and the white, and yet all serene between them on the surface.

"I've ordered sweetbreads for luncheon, sir."

"That's right. Put them on a little ham, Amos."

And Amos going out, efficient and potentially dangerous, to order sweetbreads.

Jim must have had his bad hours, his own temptations. He could have escaped even then; could have slipped out the rear door to his car and gone somewhere, anywhere, for his illness was certainly not acute. But he did not. He lay there in his bed and waited for the inevitable.

He was glad to see me, I thought. He was propped up in bed in a pair of mauve silk pyjamas, and with a dressing gown of dark brocade hanging over a chair beside him. The room was masculine enough, but a trifle too carefully done, as though Jim had taken pains to place the jewel which was himself in a perfect setting. There was something incongruous in the contrast between that soft interior, shaded and carefully lighted, with Jim as the central figure, the star of its stage, and the man I had seen across the street as I walked to the house. I had walked. I felt that it was not necessary to take my household into my confidence in this particular matter.

"Well," he said, "this is a kindly and Christian act! Sit down. That's a good chair."

He was nervous. I saw for the first time, that night, the slight twitching about the mouth which was never afterwards to leave him, and as I told him my story it grew more and more marked. Yet save for that twitching he heard me through quietly enough.

"What do you want me to say?" he said. "Or to do? If the police want a scapegoat—innocent men have been arrested before this for the sake of the sensational press—what am I to do about it? Run away?"

"You can tell them the truth."

"What truth?" he said irritably.

"Tell them where you were the night Sarah was killed. Surely you can do that, Jim."

"I have already told them. I live the usual life of a bachelor. I'm neither better nor worse than others. I decline to drag a woman into this; any woman. They can all go to hell first."

I felt my heart sink. His indignation was not real. He spoke like a man who has rehearsed a speech. And from under his eyebrows he was watching me, intently, furtively. For the first time I realized how badly frightened he was.

"I see," I said, quietly. "And I daresay that's where you left the cane. Naturally you would not care to speak about it."

"The cane? What cane?"

"The one I gave you, Jim. It's missing, apparently."

He said nothing for a full minute. It must have been a terrible shock to him. Perhaps he was going back, in his mind; who knew about the cane? Amos, of course. And Amos had been talking. His distrust and anger at Amos must have been a devastating thing just then. But he rallied himself.

"What's that got to do with it? Anybody can lose a stick. I've lost dozens, hundreds."

"You carried it out with you that night, you know."

"And I suppose that proves that I killed Sarah Gittings! And that I got up out of a sick bed the other night, put a can of kerosene in my car and shot this Florence Gunther! There's no case there. I carry a stick out one night and forget it somewhere. Well, they can't hang me for that. And I wasn't out of this house last Sunday night."

What could I say? Tell him Wallie's story, that the sword-cane had not disappeared until Sarah's body was found? That he had brought it back, and that the police knew he had brought it back? He hated Wallie, and I was in no condition to face an outburst of anger from him, especially since I felt that that too might have been prepared in advance; the careful defense of a frightened man.

One thing I was certain of when I left. He was a frightened man, but not a sick man. The loose sleeve of his pyjama coat revealed a muscular and well-nourished arm, and when Amos came in reply to the summons he carried a night tray with a substantial supper and a siphon and bottle.

Jim scowled when he saw it.

"You can leave that, and I want you to drive Miss Bell home, Amos. She walked over."

"Yes, sir."

I had a flash then of the strange relationship between the two of them, shut in there together; of suspicion and anger on

Jim's part, and on the negro's of fear and something else. Not hostility. Uneasiness, perhaps.

"Can I shake up your pillows, sir?"

"No. Don't bother."

I felt baffled as I went down the stairs.

I daresay it is always difficult to face civilized human beings and to try to realize that they have joined the lost brotherhood of those who have willfully taken human lives. There appears to be no gulf; they breathe, eat, talk, even on occasion laugh. There is no mark on their foreheads. But the gulf is there, never to be bridged; less broad perhaps for those who have killed in passion, but wider than eternity itself for those who have planned, plotted, schemed, that a living being shall cease to live.

All hope that Jim Blake would clear himself, at least in my eyes, was gone. And at the foot of the stairs Amos was waiting, enigmatic, the perfect servant, to help me into my wrap.

"I'll bring the car around at once, ma'am."

"I'll go back with you, Amos. It will save time."

"The yard's pretty dark, Miss Bell."

"Haven't you a flashlight?"

He produced one at once from a drawer of the hall table, and I followed him, through his neat pantry and kitchen and out into the yard. Here in mild weather Jim sometimes served coffee after dinner, and he had planted it rather prettily. I remember the scent of the spring night as I followed Amos, and seeing the faint outlines of Jim's garden furniture, a bench, a few chairs, a table.

"I see you have your things out already, Amos."

"Yes'm. I painted them a few days ago. We'll be having warm weather soon."

I took the light while he unlocked the small door and backed the car into the alley beyond. It occurred to me that the watcher out front would hear the noise and come to investigate, but the alley was lined with garages. One car more or less would make little difference.

I have wondered about that surveillance since. Clearly it would always have been possible for Jim to come and go by the alley way if he so desired. Probably the intention was not that, but rather to see what visitors he received, and for all I know there may have been some arrangement with Amos, to warn the watcher if Jim left his bed and dressed for any purpose.

However that may be, we were not molested, and I still carried the flashlight when I got into the rear of the car. I knew the car well. I had sold it to Jim a year or so ago when I had bought a new one. It was a dark blue limousine, the driving seat covered with leather, the interior upholstered in a pale gray.

"Car doing all right, Amos?"

"Very well, ma'am."

Idly I switched on the flashlight and surveyed the interior. Undoubtedly the car had begun to show wear. There were scars on the seat cushions from cigarette burns, and one or two on the carpet. I think now that these movements of mine were a sort of automatism, or perhaps the instinct of the uneasy mind to seek refuge in the trivial. The car was of no importance to me. Let them burn it, these people who shared the "usual life of a bachelor," these men for whom Amos painted the garden furniture, these women who must be protected, not dragged in.

And then I saw something.

There was a ring-shaped stain on the carpet near my feet, well defined, dark. It was perhaps seven inches across, and I lowered the flashlight and inspected it. It looked like oil, and woman-fashion I ran my finger over it and then sniffed the finger. It was oil. It was kerosene oil.

I put out the flashlight and sat back. There were a dozen possible explanations for that stain, but only one occurred to me. Sitting there in the dark, I pondered the matter of eliminating it before Amos found it. Or had he already found it? Was he sitting there beyond the glass partition, driving as perfectly as he did everything else, and all the time aware of my movements, knowing what I had found? Did the police know, too?

Suppose I were to say to Amos:

"Amos, this carpet is dirty. I'm taking it to have it cleaned, while Mr. Blake is not using the car."

Perhaps that in itself would rouse his suspicion. He might say: "Don't bother, Miss Bell. I'll see to it." And then Amos and I would be bickering over the carpet; it would grow important to him, and if he conquered he would take it to the police.

I did the best thing I could think of at the moment. I stooped down and loosened the carpet, rolled it up carefully, and then hid it as best I could underneath my long cape.

If I looked strange to Joseph when he admitted me, he said nothing. Once Judy had said that Joseph had no capacity for astonishment, and the thought supported me that night as, certainly nervous and probably bulging, I entered my own house.

Judy called to me from the library, but I passed the door with as much expedition as I dared. She and Dick were settled there over a card table, with a sheet of paper before them. I saw that, and that Dick was apparently making a sketch of some sort. As I went up the stairs he was saying:

"Now get this. Here's the daybed. The closet door is there—"

Then I was in my room, the door bolted, and that incriminating carpet on a table under a good light. There was no question about it. A jug or can containing kerosene oil had rested on it, probably quite recently.

CHAPTER TEN

A LONE woman who has lived in a house for many years grows to know her house. It is like a live thing to her; it has its moods, its contrary days, and it has its little eccentricities. This stair creaks, that window rattles, that door sticks.

Especially, if she is not a good sleeper, she grows to know her house at night. All houses are strange at night. It is as though, after the darkness and silence have fallen, they stir and waken to some mysterious life of their own. In my house, some of these movements I can account for. When the windows are raised the old beams creak, as though the house is cracking its knuckles, and when we have a north wind the skylight wails and whines. A metal weatherstrip that is, vibrating like a string.

Then, too, a breeze from the west will set the ivy outside my window to whispering, little sibilant voices which have roused me more than once, convinced that I was called; and an open window in the drawing room beside the speaking tube there will send on windy days a fine thin whistle through the house.

But I do not like my cellar. Perhaps this is a throwback to my childhood; I do not know. The fact remains that I go into it at night under protest, and that I have had installed in the back hall a switch by which a light below is turned on before any one need descend. A bit of precaution for which I could have shrieked with rage before that night had passed.

It was eleven o'clock when I returned, and soon afterwards I heard Dick leave the house. His paper is an afternoon one, and so he has to rise fairly early. Judy wandered in to say good-night, but I had locked the carpet in my closet, and she merely lighted a cigarette and stood inside the door.

"When is Mary going?" she asked.

"She hasn't said. Why?"

"She's been packing tonight. Dick helped Joseph to bring her trunk down from the storeroom. She doesn't seem too keen to go."

"It's her own choice," I said, rather acidly.

"Well, I hope to heaven mother doesn't wish her on us! She may. To shut her mouth about Uncle Jim."

But she did not go away at once. She stood there, smoking fast and apparently thinking.

"Don't you think Wallie's been rather queer over all this?" she said. "'So if anything happens to me you'll understand,'" she mimicked him. "If he knows anything now is the time to tell it. And if he doesn't, why don't he keep out? Where does he come in, anyhow? What's he worried about?"

"I do wish *you'd* keep out of all this, Judy."

"Why? It's the day of the young, isn't it? Everybody says so."

"It's the hour for the young to be in bed."

"All right, I'm going right now. But just to show you why I'm not going back to New York, in spite of you and Dick—Wallie didn't find that pencil on top of the skylight. He took it up with him and put it there."

With which she went away, whistling softly, and left me to my thoughts, which were nothing to boast about.

I did not go to bed. I sat shut in my bedroom, with the carpet from the car rolled in my closet, waiting for the house to quiet down for the night. My mind was a welter of confusion; Jim's evasions and half truths, the possible significance of the oil stain, and Judy's strange statement as to Wallie and the pencil.

And to add to my discomfort Joseph tapped at my door after letting Dick out and locking up, and told me that the women in the house had started a tale that poor Sarah was "walking," and were scaring themselves into a fit over it. I am not a superstitious woman, but there is something of the mystic in every Christian, and I must confess that when, at something after one, the speaking tube in my room set up a thin whistle, my hair seemed to stand on end.

Ever since the night of Sarah's death Joseph had been instructed to leave a light burning in the lower hall, and it was burning then. I opened my door carefully and slipping out, leaned over the banister. Save that Jock had apparently been asleep there, and had now risen and was stretching himself drowsily, there was no sign of anything unusual. If there was a window or a door open in the drawing room I felt that it could stay open for a while.

I had other business to attend to first.

Jock's attitude had given me confidence, and at something after one, wearing a dressing gown and my felt-soled bedroom slippers, I took the rug and a bottle of patent cleaner and made my way gingerly to the basement laundry, stopping in the kitchen to pick up the poker from the range. I was minded to have a weapon of some sort at hand.

I had a plan, of sorts. If the stain came out I could return the rug to Amos, and he could think what he might; lay my high-handed proceeding to the eccentricities of a middle-aged female if it pleased him. If it did not come out, I could burn the thing in the furnace.

But I was very nervous, and the basement itself daunted me; the long vistas of blackness forward, to the furnace and the coal and wood cellars, the darkness of the laundry and the drying room. The small light at the foot of the stairs, which turned on from the back hall above, made little impression on the gloom, and as I stood there it seemed to me that something crawled over the wood in the wood cellar. A rat, possibly, but it did not help my morale.

The laundry was dark, and to light it one must enter the room, and turn on the hanging globe in the center. I went in, shivering, and directly in the center of the room I struck violently against something. It was a chair, and it upset with a clatter that echoed and re-echoed in that cavernous place.

What was the chair doing there? It belonged under a window, and here it was, out of place again. What was it that moved that chair? And Joseph's somber statement came back to me, to complete my demoralization. After all, chairs did move. They moved in séances. Chairs and tables, without being touched.

I was badly frightened, I confess. A dozen stories of phantasms, discredited at the time, rose in my mind. The place seemed peopled with moving shadows, sinister and threatening, and from somewhere I seemed to hear footsteps, spectral, felt rather than heard. And when I finally found courage to try the laundry light, it had burned out.

Such efforts as I could make then to remove the stain were of no practical value, and I decided once and for all to burn the rug and take the consequences.

I did one of the hardest things I have ever done in my life when I went forward to the furnace cellar, carrying the rug. Once the light there was on, however, I felt better. I built a small fire of paper and kindling, and thrust in the rug. It began to blaze, although not as rapidly as I had hoped. I stood there watching and wondering about the dampers; like most women, I know nothing about a furnace.

I wandered about, waiting for that slow combustion to become effectual, examined the windows and the door to the area way, and was retracing my steps forward to the furnace again, when I stopped suddenly.

Some one was moving about over my head.

I pulled myself together. The dogs had not barked. It must be Joseph, Joseph who had heard the whining in the speaking tubes and come down to investigate. But to have Joseph discover me burning that rug would have been disastrous. I turned out the furnace light at once, and went back toward the foot of the stairs, where the small light still burned. To my horror, I saw that light go out, and heard the bolt slipped in the door above.

"Joseph!" I called. *"Joseph!"*

It was not Joseph. The footsteps had ceased, but there was no answering call. Somebody, something, was lurking there overhead, listening. The thought was horrible beyond words.

I was crouched on the foot of the staircase, and there I remained in that haunted darkness until daylight. At dawn I crept up the stairs and half sat, half lay, on the narrow landing. Perhaps I slept, perhaps I fainted. I shall never forget Joseph's face when, at seven o'clock, he unlocked the door and found me there.

"Good heavens, madam!" he said.

"Help me up, Joseph. I can't move."

"You're not hurt, are you?"

"No. You locked me in, Joseph. I've had a terrible night. You—or somebody."

"I locked you in, madam? At what time?"

"About two o'clock, I think."

"I was not downstairs after midnight," he said, and helped me to my feet.

He got me into the pantry and made me some coffee. Norah was not yet down; my household slept badly those days, and therefore late. He had had a shock, however. His hands shook and his face was set. I can still see him moving about, his dignity less majestic than usual, making the coffee, laying a doily on the pantry table, fetching a cup and saucer from the dining room. While he waited for the coffee to boil he made a tour of the first floor, but reported everything in order. The drawing room door and windows were locked.

"But I would suggest, madam," he said, "that we change the lock on the front door. Since Miss Sarah's key is missing it is hardly safe."

Norah came in as I finished my coffee, and she gave me a queer look. But I did not explain. I went up and crawled into my bed, and I did not waken until Joseph came up with a tray of luncheon.

He came in, closed the door, drew a table beside the bed, opened my napkin and gave it to me. Then he straightened and looked at me.

"I have taken the liberty of destroying the rug, madam."

My heart sank, but he spoke as calmly as though he had been reporting that the butter was bad.

"The dampers were wrong," he said. "It's a peculiar furnace. You have to understand it."

He looked at me, and I looked back at him. Our relations had subtly changed, although his manner had not. We shared a secret; in effect, Joseph and I were accomplices. Between us we had compounded a felony, destroyed evidence, and Joseph knew it. Whether he had seen the stain or not, he knew that carpet.

"You should not have tried to do that, madam," he said. "In the future, if you need any help, you can always call on me."

Then he went out; strange inscrutable Joseph, living the vicarious life of all upper class servants. Somewhere he had a wife, but he never mentioned her. His room at night, the pantry and the newspapers by day, apparently comprised his life and satisfied him.

It was when he came to remove the tray that he told me, very quietly, that his revolver was missing.

"I have been keeping it in my bedroom lately, under my pillow," he said. "Now it is gone. Taken by some one who knew the habits of the house, madam."

CHAPTER ELEVEN

WHATEVER WAS the meaning of that unpleasant episode, it was impossible to go to the police with it. I was seeing rather less of the Inspector now; he and the entire homicide squad were working on the Gunther case; the crime detection unit of photographer, chemist, microscopist and gun expert were at work, but I believe their conclusions were unimportant. The bullet was missing. From the size of the wounds in the skull and the fact that it had passed entirely through the head, they believed that it had been a large caliber bullet fired at close range, and that the time of her death had been about eight or eight-thirty.

The bag, then, had lain in the street for almost three hours.

Outside of these facts the murder remained a complete and utter mystery. She appeared to have been without friends or family, one of these curious beings who from all appearances have sprung sporadically into being, without any past whatever. She had had no ability for friendship, unless that odd acquaintance of hers with Sarah could be called friendship.

Strange that two such reserved women should have found each other, have somehow broken down their repressions, have walked, talked, maybe even laughed together. For it seems now that during the month or so before the murders, they had met a number of times. One pictures them walking together, maybe sitting together in a moving picture theater, and then one day something said; a bit of confidence, and both were doomed.

The day passed without incident, save that Mary Martin took her departure. She even cried a little when she left, although she had shown no affection for any of us.

Judy seemed relieved to have her gone.

"Thank heaven," she said. "I don't have to whisper any more. She was always listening, Elizabeth Jane. I've caught her at it, leaning over the banisters. I'll bet my hat she knows something. And I'll bet two dollars, which is all I have in the world at the moment, that she took Joseph's gun."

"Why would she take Joseph's gun? That's silly."

"Is it? Well, ask Norah. She knows."

And ask Norah I did, with curious results.

It appeared that on the day before Joseph had missed his revolver, Norah had gone upstairs to her room to change her uniform before she prepared luncheon. She wears rubber-soled shoes in the kitchen, as it has a tiled floor, and so she moved quietly.

Joseph, it seems, was downstairs. The door at the top of the back stairs is a swinging one, as otherwise the maids forget to close it, and it swings noiselessly. She pushed it open, and there was Mary Martin, down the hall and just coming out of Joseph's room. She stepped back when she saw Norah, and then reconsidered and came out again.

"I was looking for some matches," she said.

According to Norah she had no matches in her hands, however, and she looked so pale that Norah was curious. When Mary had shut herself in her room Norah glanced inside Joseph's door. There were no matches on his bureau, and his revolver lay on top of the bed.

But with Mary gone, and the house quiet again and with no "snooping," as Judy called it, I went into the library that night to find Dick grinning and Judy with her mouth set hard.

"Well, tell her, if you think it's so funny."

"Tell her yourself, lady of my heart. Do your own dirty work."

"Don't be such an ass. It's a perfectly simple thing I want, Elizabeth Jane. I want to get into Florence Gunther's room."

"The answer is just as simple, Judy," I said shortly. "You'll do nothing of the sort."

But she was argumentative and a trifle sulky.

"Oh well, if you must have it. I want to look for something. That's all."

"For what?"

"I don't know. But now listen to this; I don't know why poor Sarah was killed, or Florence either. But I do know why their shoes were taken off. One or the other of them had something; I don't know what, but she had. It might have been a paper—"

"Give me the papers and take the child!" said Dick.

She ignored that.

"Now Dick has struck up an acquaintance with a blonde out there at the house on Halkett Street. She's named Lily, and he's quite fond of her; he's even had her out to lunch."

Dick groaned, and she grinned maliciously.

"Her name is Sanderson, Lily Sanderson, and she's rather a mess. But she likes to talk, and she's got something she hasn't told the police. She won't even tell him, but she might tell us."

"Who are 'us'?"

"You and I, Elizabeth Jane; you to give staidness and respectability to the excursion, I to use my little wiles to wheedle her if necessary. Dick says she's afraid of the police, but once she sets eyes on you she'll open up like a flower."

I declined at once, but she has her own methods, has Judy, and so in the end I reluctantly consented to go.

The appointment was made for the next night, Friday. Evidently Miss Sanderson was uneasy, for she made it Friday because the colored woman would be off for her afternoon out. And it was she herself who admitted us when, having left the car at the corner, Judy and I presented ourselves on the following evening.

She opened the door with her finger to her lips.

"Now how nice!" she said, in a loud clear tone. "Here I was, afraid I was to have an evening alone, and this happens!"

All the time she was urging us in with little gestures, and Judy's face was a study. Miss Sanderson was a large blonde woman with a slight limp, and she was evidently prepared for company. She was slightly overdressed, and her room when she took us up to it was very tidy. Suspiciously tidy, Judy said later, as if she had just finished with it.

When she had closed the door she lowered her voice.

"You never know who's around in a place like this. It's all ears. And since poor Miss Gunther's awful end—" She looked at me with her pale blue eyes, and they were childish and filled with terror. "I haven't slept much since. If there is a homicidal maniac loose, nobody can tell who'll be next."

"I wouldn't worry," said Judy. "There's no maniac loose. Whoever killed her knew what he was doing."

That seemed to relieve her. She was, for all her clothes, a singularly simple woman, and I am glad here to pay my bit of tribute to Lily Sanderson. She had her own small part in the solving of the mystery, and of the four major crimes which it involved.

She liked Judy at once, I think. There is something direct about Judy, for all her talk about using her wiles; and Judy, I think, felt the compassion of youth for her, for the narrow life that one room typified, for the loneliness of soul which was feeding on this one great excitement. I saw her looking about at the dreadful reach at beauty which the room revealed, the tea table at which nobody obviously ever had tea, at the silk shawl draped over the bed, at the imitation shell toilet set, the gaudily painted scrap basket, and at the screen which concealed the washstand in its corner, and behind which, I had no doubt, Miss Sanderson had dumped a clutter of odds and ends.

"You are very comfortable here, aren't you? It's quite homelike."

Miss Sanderson smiled her childlike smile.

"It's all the home I have," she said. "And Mrs. Bassett likes everything to be nice. She's very clean, really."

Before she settled to her story she opened her door, looked out, closed it again.

"I'm only talking because you were friends of poor Florence," she said. "And I don't know if what I have to tell you is important, or not. I won't have to go to the police, will I?"

"Certainly not," said Judy sturdily.

"You know I told them that I'd heard her moving things about, that night? Well, I did. I didn't like to say what I really thought." She lowered her voice. "I thought she had a man up there. That's what I went up in the morning to speak to her about."

"A man?" I asked. "Could you hear him?"

"A man and a woman," she said. "I could hear them both."

Her story amounted to this:

She was a light sleeper, and she was wakened some time after midnight by movements in the room above. As Florence never stirred about in the night, this puzzled her. Especially as the movements continued.

"Somebody seemed to be moving the furniture," she said. "Very carefully, but you can't move a bureau in a house built like this without it making some noise. Even then I might have gone to sleep again, but there were two people. One walked heavier than the other."

She was curious, rather than alarmed. She got up and opened her door, and at last she crept up the stairs and—she seemed to apologize for this—put her ear to the door. There was a man talking in a low tone in the room.

That scandalized her. She went downstairs "with her head whirling," and stood there, uncertain what to do. She seems to have been in a state of shock and indignation, imagining all sorts of things. And the sounds went on, only now she could hear a woman crying. She was outraged. She thought Florence Gunther had a man in her room and that they were quarreling.

Finally she took her haircurler and rapped vigorously on the chandelier. The noises ceased at once, but although she set her door open and waited inside in the dark, nobody came down. Whoever they were, they must have escaped down the rear staircase.

But she could not sleep. A sort of virtuous fury possessed her, and half an hour later she threw something on and went up valiantly to Florence's room.

"I was going to give her a good talking to," she said. "It makes me sick now to think of it, but this is a respectable house, and—well, you know what I mean. If she was carrying on with anybody—"

The door was closed but not locked, and she spoke to Florence and got no answer. She turned on the switch inside the door, and there was the room; in chaos. She seemed unable to describe it. She made a gesture.

"Even her shoes," she said. "Her poor shoes were on the floor. But she hadn't been robbed. Her dime bank was still on her dresser, and she had an old-fashioned watch for a clock, beside the daybed on a table. It was still there."

She shot downstairs after that, trembling, and got into bed. Even then she was not certain that Florence was not concerned in it somehow. She knew that one of the two in that room had been a woman. Then too she "didn't want to be mixed up in any trouble." She might lose her position, and in addition she had a childish fear of the police.

"If they knew I'd been up there—"

She went to sleep finally, but at seven she went up the stairs again and opened the door. The room had been straightened. It looked better.

"Not just right, you know. But things were put away. The way the police found it."

"And what do you think now?" Judy inquired. She had lighted a cigarette and was offering one to "Lily."

"Oh, may I? I'd love to. We aren't supposed to smoke here, but every now and then I open a window and—It rests one, I think."

"Yes, it does rest one," said Judy politely. "And now what were those people after? Have you any idea?"

"Not really. But she was in a lawyer's office, and they get some queer things sometimes. Letters, you know, and so on. If she had something like that it might explain a lot. It had to be something small, or they'd have found it. But I'm sure I don't know where it is, if it's there."

"Oh, you've looked?" said Judy.

"Yes. The room's kept locked, but my key fits it. I suppose it's hardly the correct thing, but she was a friend of mine—"

Her eyes filled with tears, and Judy patted her heavy shoulder.

"Of course it was the correct thing. Perfectly correct. As a matter of fact I'd like to go up myself and look around. You don't mind, do you?"

Miss Sanderson not only did not mind, but looked rather gratified.

"I'll wait down here with the curler," she said with a conspiratorial air, "and if I hear anything I'll rap on the chandelier."

I was all for waiting below, but Judy took me with her, maintaining that the very sight of me would remove her from the sneak thief class if we were discovered, and at last I consented. Nevertheless, I was frankly trembling when we started up the stairs. Miss Sanderson had preceded us, creeping up with a stealth which gave the entire procedure a clandestine appearance which was disquieting, to say the least. After unlocking the door, however, she left us as noiselessly as we had come, and Judy moved the key from the outside to the inside of the door.

As we stood there in the darkness I think even Judy was uneasy, and I know that I felt like a criminal. The house was exceedingly quiet. Mrs. Bassett, Miss Sanderson had said, slept at the rear of the floor, but she was ill, had been for some time. And whatever was the mysterious life of the women behind the closed doors around us, it was conducted in silence.

Judy drew the shades before she turned on the light, and

then the two of us gazed at this strange room, from which Florence Gunther had started out in a checked frock and a blue coat and with a blue bag on her arm, to a sudden and unaccountable death.

It was neat now, very orderly, the daybed covered with the imitation Indian rug, her clothing still in its closet, her shoes in a row underneath. Practical shoes, flat heeled, without coquetry, each with its wooden tree. Judy looked depressed and angry.

"She had so little," she said. "Why not have let her alone?"

But she was businesslike, too.

"No use looking in the obvious places," she announced. "They'll have seen to that. Something small. I suppose the police took it for granted that they got it, whatever it was. But if Lily is right—! If I wanted to hide a paper here, where would I put it? I hid a love letter once from mother, in my can of tooth powder."

Poor Florence's tooth powder was on her washstand, but although with much difficulty and a pair of scissors Judy finally worked the top off, she found nothing there. Then she examined the bottles on the dresser; one dark blue one interested her, but it contained an eye lotion and nothing else. The wall paper—"she might have loosened the paper and then glued it back again"—showed no signs of being tampered with, and the baseboard was close to the wall.

She reached the clothes closet, then, by elimination, and with small hope.

"They'll have done that first," she said.

Apparently she was right. No pocket, no lining, no hem of any garment revealed so much as a hint. Save one thing, which at first looked as though our search was useless. There was an old pocketbook in the closet, and she brought it out and examined it.

"Look here!" she said. "She's carried something in this pocketbook, hidden. See where she's cut the lining and sewed it up again?"

"It's not sewed now."

"No," she said slowly. "Of course, if she transferred it to the blue bag—!"

But time was passing, and I was growing impatient. The whole excursion seemed to me to be an impertinent meddling, and so I was about to say to Judy, when there came a sharp rap from the chandelier beneath our feet.

Neither one of us moved, and I know I hardly breathed. Some one was coming up the stairs, moving very quietly. The steps halted just outside the door, and I motioned wildly to Judy to turn out the light. But in a moment they moved on again, toward the rear of the house, and I breathed again.

After that we locked the door, and Judy matter-of-factly went on with her search. She was on the floor now, carefully inspecting Florence's shoes.

"I used to hide my cigarettes in my slippers," she stated. "Mother raised hell about my smoking. I'll just look these over and then we'll go."

"And the sooner the better," I retorted testily. "If you think I'm enjoying this, I'm not. I've never spent a night I enjoyed less."

But she was paying no attention. She had found, in a pair of flat black shoes, leather insoles designed to support the arches. Glanced at casually each was a part of the shoe, but Judy's sensitive well-manicured fingers were digging at one of them diligently.

"Flat feet, poor dear," she said, and jerked out the insole.

It was, I believe a quite common affair of its sort, although I had never seen one before. In the forward portion was a pocket, into which fitted a small pad of wood, designed to raise the forward arch.

Behind this Judy dug but a small scrap of paper, neatly folded.

I think we were both trembling when she drew it out and held it up. But without opening it she dropped it inside the neck of her frock and finding a pin, fastened it there. She wears so little underneath that this precaution was necessary.

"No time now to be curious, Elizabeth Jane," she said. "We have to get out of here, and to stall off Lily."

Everything was still quiet as we relocked the door and went down. Miss Sanderson was peering out of her door and beckoned us in, but Judy shook her head.

"They made a pretty clean sweep," she said, "but thank you anyhow. You've been very sweet to us."

"He didn't try to get in, did he?"

"Somebody stopped outside the door and then went on. Who was it?"

"I couldn't see. It was a man though. It might have been the doctor," she added doubtfully. "I just thought I'd better warn you. Won't you come in again?"

She was clearly disappointed when we refused. She must have had many lonely evenings, poor soul, and to entertain Judy would have been a real thrill; Judy Somers, whose pictures were often in the New York evening papers and in the smarter magazines.

"I've got some sandwiches," she said.

"Thanks, no. I never eat at night."

She saw us out, rather forlornly.

"If anything turns up, I'll let you know."

"Please do. You've been wonderful."

She brightened at that, and the last we saw of her she was peering around the half-closed front door, loath to go back to her untasted sandwiches, to her loneliness and her wakeful nights.

We found the car around the corner where we had left it, but not until we were in my bedroom with the door locked did Judy produce that scrap of paper. And then it turned out to be completely unintelligible. Neatly typed, on thin copy paper was this: "Clock dial. Five o'clock right. Seven o'clock left. Press on six."

"Clock dial!" said Judy. "What clock? There's something in a clock somewhere, but that's as far as I go. It wasn't her clock. She didn't have one. As far as I can make out, we're exactly where we started!"

Which turned out to be very nearly a precise statement of the situation.

CHAPTER TWELVE

Just when Amos discovered that his carpet was missing from the car I do not know. With Jim in bed the car was not in use, and it may have been a couple of days before he missed it, or even more. I hardly think he suspected me, although he may have.

But some time before Sunday he saw Wallie and told him. Just why he should have told him I do not know. Certainly he believed Jim Blake to be the guiltiest wretch unhung, but we also know that he had a queer affection for him. Maybe Wallie questioned him; Wallie had his own problem to solve, and he may have gone to Amos.

The result, however, was an extremely unpleasant interview between Wallie and myself a day or two after Judy had found the paper. I know now that he was frightened, terrified beyond any power of mine to imagine, and with Wallie as with other nervous persons anxiety took the form of anger.

He stalked into the house then late on Sunday afternoon, looking so strange that at first I thought he had been drinking again.

"Do you mind if I close the door?" he demanded. "I've got some things to say that you may not want overheard."

"Then I'd better leave it open. I don't care for any more secrets, or any scenes."

"Very well," he said savagely. "It's you I'm trying to protect."

But he slammed the door shut, nevertheless, and then confronted me.

"I've got to know something. Of all the damnable, outrageous messes—! Did you or did you not take the rug out of Jim Blake's car the other night?"

"Why? Is it missing?"

"You know damned well it's missing."

"I don't like your tone, Wallie."

He pulled himself together then, and took another turn about the room.

"Sorry," he muttered. "I get excited. God, who wouldn't be excited? I'll ask you in a different way. Was the carpet in the car the other night when Amos drove you back here?"

"It was."

"And you left it there?"

"Why shouldn't I?"

"That's not an answer."

"Now see here, Wallie," I said. "I won't be bullied. There is no reason why I should answer any questions you put to me. Go to the police, if you like. Then if they choose to come to me—"

"The police. I'm trying my very best to keep the police out of this. But that darky of Jim Blake's blabs everything he knows. They'll get it out of him yet. All I want to find out is why the carpet was taken. What was on it? It told something. What did it tell?"

I eyed him.

"Wallie," I said, "do you believe that Jim Blake committed these crimes? You've insinuated that, and that there was a reason."

"I could think of a reason, but this Gunther thing—No, I don't believe he's got the guts."

"If you could think of a reason, it's your business to tell it. Tell me, at least. If I'm to work in the dark—"

"Ah, so you have been working! Now look here, what was on that carpet? Oil? Blood? You took it, didn't you? Amos says you did."

"Why should he say that?"

"He says that if you got in the car and it was missing, you'd have asked about it."

I made up my mind then to make a clean breast of it.

"I did take it, Wallie, I took it out and burned it in the furnace. There was oil on it; a ring of oil. Something containing kerosene oil had been carried in it."

"My God!" he said, and seemed to sag lower in his chair.

He had aged in the past few days. That is the only way I can describe the change in him. That buoyancy and gaiety which had made him likable, with all his faults, had deserted him. But I could not feel sorry for him. He knew something; I rather thought that he knew a great deal.

"Do you think Amos knew what was on that carpet?" he asked.

"I haven't an idea. If he did, the police may know it too; but I think, if they do know it, they would have taken it away for safekeeping. No, I think you and I, and Joseph, are the only ones so far."

"Joseph? What's Joseph got to do with it?"

He listened intently while I told him of my attempt to burn the carpet, and of my being locked in the cellar. I could not gather from his face what he made of the incident. He had had time to recover, and the fact that the carpet had been actually destroyed seemed to reassure him. But when I finished he remained sunk in a silence which was more like brooding than anything else. I finally broke in on this.

"Isn't it time you told what you know, Wallie? If this thing is to go on, none of us are safe. Even Judy."

"Judy's all right," he said roughly. "And I don't know anything."

"That's not entirely true, is it?"

"You'll know all I know, when the time comes." He got up, looked at me furtively, and then began to finger the pens and pencils on my desk. "I suppose," he said, with an attempt at casualness, "that you are one of the uncorruptibles, eh? A lie's a lie, and all that?"

"I will assuredly not perjure myself, if that's what you mean."

"Why put a label on everything? What's perjury anyhow? What's the difference except the label between your pretending you have a headache and making a statement that might save a life?"

"Perjury is a lie before God."

"Every lie is a lie before God, if you believe in God. All I want you to do is to say, if it becomes necessary to say anything, that that carpet was not in the car the other night. Wait a minute," he said, as I started to speak, "your own position isn't any too comfortable is it? You've destroyed valuable evidence. And what do you do to Jim Blake if you tell the truth? I tell you, there's more behind this than you know. There are worse sins than lies, if you insist on talking about lies. I give you my word, if you tell about that carpet, Harrison will arrest Jim. Arrest him immediately."

"I'm not going to volunteer anything, Wallie."

"You've got to do more than that. You've got to stick it out.

There are always thieves about, and what's to have hindered some one crawling over Jim's fence and getting in by the garage window? The car hadn't been out, according to Amos, from the day Jim took sick; or went to bed, rather. He's not sick. That carpet might have been gone for a week."

I was in a state of greater confusion than ever when he had gone. Judy and Dick were out; on the hillside of the Larimer lot, I suspected, and after Wallie's departure I sat down at my desk and made an outline of the possible case against Jim Blake. I still have it, and it is before me now.

(a) Sarah had tried to communicate with him by call and telephone.

(b) She had finally written him a letter, which he had probably received, but had denied receiving.

(c) On the night she was murdered he did not dress for dinner, but dined early and went out, carrying the sword-cane.

(d) From some place, not his house, he telephoned to Judy, offering her mother's anxiety as an excuse, and asking for Sarah.

(e) He was out that night for some time. He offered no alibi for those hours, intimating that to do so would affect a woman's reputation.

(f) When he returned he still carried the sword-cane, but on the discovery of Sarah's body it had disappeared.

(g) Also, shortly after that discovery, he had taken to his bed, although actually not ill.

From that it was not difficult to go on to the second crime.

(h) Sarah and Florence Gunther knew each other, probably shared some secret knowledge. The paper Judy had found might or might not refer to that knowledge. Certainly one or the other of them possessed some knowledge or some physical property, or both, which had been desperately sought for in each case.

(i) According to Inspector Harrison, the two rooms had been searched by the same individual.

(j) The oil stain on the carpet of Jim's car may not be suspicious in itself, but coupled with the above is highly evidential.

To this list I added certain queries:

(a) Would Jim, under any conceivable circumstances, have attacked Judy?

(b) Was he capable of such sustained cunning as had been shown throughout? The planted footprints, for example?

(c) Had Jim actually worn golf clothes on the night of Sarah's murder? If not, had he had time after his telephone message to break into my house? Fifteen minutes, or at most twenty, was all he had had.

(d) Was Sarah in Jim's house for the three hours still unaccounted for?

And under the heading "Florence Gunther":

(a) Did Jim know her?

(b) Was Jim the visitor testified to by the colored woman at the Bassett house?

(c) Why had so cunning a murderer overlooked the oil stain in the car?

I studied this last.

Surely were Jim guilty, lying there in his bed he would have gone over inch by inch the ground he had covered; have thought of every detail, have followed his every act, searched for the possible loose thread in his fabric.

He knew he was under suspicion. He had only to raise himself in his bed to see that figure across the street. Then why would he have left that stain in the car? Why not have burned the carpet? Burned the car?

There was more than that. He was definitely under suspicion, and there had been a city-wide search for the "death car," as the press called it. But either the police had not found that stain, or they had chosen deliberately to ignore it. Why? Jim Blake and a box of matches could at any time destroy that evidence.

It was too much for me. And to add to my anxieties Joseph told me that day that the maids were talking of leaving. Ever since Norah had found the kitchen poker in the laundry the haunting of the house had been an accepted matter, and it was finally getting on their nerves.

Yet the remainder of the day was quiet enough, on the surface. Since Wednesday night Judy and Dick had been working over the house clocks at intervals, and that Sunday was no exception. I have no doubt that the servants thought them slightly mad.

One by one the clocks were taken into the library, and there investigated. By and large, I had quite a collection of odd springs and wheels, and Dick would sit there over his wreckage, his hair rumpled, and try to reassort what Judy called "the innards."

"Now where the devil does that go?"

"Don't be such an ass! Right there."

"It doesn't fit. Try it yourself, since you know so much."

And with this very wrangling, which was the cloak to hide their deeper feelings—after the fashion of youth today—they would be making love to each other. They would jeer at each other, their mouths hard and their eyes soft.

"Keep quiet! How can I do anything if you jerk my arm?"

"Well, you're so damned clumsy."

The final result, even the servants' alarm clocks having been investigated, was that the establishment ran rather erratically. Meals were at queer hours, and I remember that on that very

Sunday, with nobody the wiser, we found that we had breakfasted at eleven o'clock and lunched at half past three.

Then that Sunday night at eleven o'clock, or as near that as our ruined time system allowed me to judge, Katherine called up from New York.

Howard had had another attack. He was better, but she wanted Judy at home.

Judy left the next morning. Dick was working and so I took her to the station, and on the way there I gathered that she and Dick had reached an *impasse* in their love affair. She stated it quite flatly, after her fashion.

"He's crazy about me," she said, "but I'm a child of the rich! If he condescends to marry me I'm to live on his salary, and a bit he has outside! It's absurd! It's sublime! It's perfectly barbaric these days for a man to insist on supporting a wife. It's childish vanity; the great male 'I am.'"

It was quite characteristic of her that she should be crying at the moment. But she wanted no sympathy, and I gave her none.

"If you'd rather have things than have Dick—"

"Oh, to the devil with things. It's the principle of the thing. He'd deprive me to nurse his own vanity."

Well, it is a problem which is confronting a good many young people today, both of them right and both of them wrong. I had no solution, and whatever their troubles it had not affected Dick's feeling toward her, for he came in to see me that night, out of sheer habit.

"Tried to pass by," he said, "but the old bus just naturally headed in and stuck its head over the hitching post."

I was glad to see him. I had been very lonely; missing Judy, even missing—to tell the truth—the Inspector, with his blue eyes and his toothpicks and his general air of competence. He had deserted me almost completely for several days.

And in the expansiveness of that hour, then and there, I told Dick about the carpet. He was incredulous.

"But see here: the first car the police would examine would be that car."

"So I think. But they may know about it, at that."

"You're sure Amos hasn't been carrying oil in it?"

That had not occurred to me. I felt rather foolish, and the net result of the talk was that Dick saw Amos the next day and learned certain things.

On the night of Florence's death, being a Sunday, he had been out and Jim was alone. But he could not have taken the car out, for Amos carried the key to the small door of the garage from the garden. The main doors to the alley were bolted on the inside.

Not that Dick asked these direct questions. He asked Amos where he was on Sunday night, and if any one could have got at the car.

But Dick was not satisfied. He watched the negro leave the house on an errand, and then climbed the rear wall into Jim's yard. There he found two interesting facts; the side window into the garage had a broken pane, and it was possible to reach in and unlock the sash. And there were marks on one of the newly painted garden chairs.

He got into the building and examined the car. The driving seat and the one next to it were leather and could be washed, but there were no blood stains.

"Amos doesn't watch the mileage," he said, "so he doesn't know whether the car was out or not. But he does suspect that the gas is lower than it ought to be."

He did, however, discover that Amos had carried no oil in the rear of the car. He had said to him:

"What's all this about the carpet being missing? You've done away with it yourself, haven't you? Spilled something on it?"

"No, sir!" said Amos. "I never carry nothing back there. Mr. Blake's mighty particular about that car, sir."

All of which, important as it was, did not help us at all. Nothing was clearer than that Jim himself, locked out of the garage, might have placed a garden chair under the window, broken the pane, and taken his car out himself, on Sunday night.

That was on Tuesday, the tenth of May. Sarah had been dead for three weeks, and Florence Gunther for ten days. Apparently the police had found nothing whatever, and we ourselves had nothing but that cryptic cipher, which was not a cipher at all but a key.

I daresay I should have shown it to the police; but already I had done a reckless thing with the carpet and I was uneasy. Then too the Inspector had ceased his almost daily visits, although I saw him once on the Larimer lot, poking about with a stick and the faithful Simmons trotting at his heels. But he did not come to the house, and soon—on Wednesday morning, to be exact—I was to receive a message which made me forget it entirely for the time.

Howard Somers was dead.

CHAPTER THIRTEEN

So far I am aware that I have painted a small canvas of the family; only Judy, Wallie and myself, with a bit of Katherine. As Laura was never involved, it is unnecessary to enlarge on her. She remained in Kansas City, busy with her children, mildly regretful over Sarah but not actively grieved.

The one figure I have not touched is Howard Somers. Perhaps this is because I never understood him particularly, never greatly liked him. Katherine's passion for him had always mystified me.

But Howard was to add his own contribution to our mystery, and that by the simple act of dying. It was not unexpected, although Katherine had sturdily refused to accept it, or to face its possibility. I fancy that there must have been times after that almost fatal attack the summer before when she was abroad, when he must have wanted to talk to her. There are many things in the heart and mind of a man facing death which must long for expression.

But I know from Judy that her mother never let him speak. It was as though, by admitting the fact, she would bring it closer.

"We really ought to paint the place at Southampton, before we go up next summer," she would say.

And her eyes would defy him, dare him to intimate that there might be no next summer for him.

All this I was to learn from Judy later on, trying perplexedly to understand the situation among the three of them, and that strange silence of Howard's about matters which concerned them all.

"Probably he wanted to tell her, poor darling," she said. "But how could he? She wouldn't let him. It was like Wallie, only worse. She wouldn't speak about Wallie, you know."

"Do you think he was seeing Wallie?"

She shrugged her shoulders.

"He must have been, but he never said anything. He never even told her that Wallie had been with him when he took sick last summer. I suppose he didn't want to hurt her."

And, without being aware of it, she had drawn a picture for me which was profoundly to affect my judgment later on; of the barrier Katherine had for years been erecting between Howard and his son, and of a relationship there perhaps closer than she imagined. The two driven to meetings practically clandestine, and Wallie with Margaret's charm, her eyes, much of her beauty, making his definite claim on his father's affection.

A conversation I was to have with Doctor Simonds later on was to confirm this.

"Whatever their trouble had been," he said, "they had patched it up. Wallie was there every day. For a night or two he slept there, in the suite. Later on he relieved the nurse for a daily walk. He was Johnny on the spot all through."

He had insisted on knowing his father's condition, and had gone rather pale when he learned it.

"How long?"

"A year. Two years. Nobody can say. It might even be longer."

But that was some time later.

Howard had died on Tuesday night, or rather some time early on Wednesday morning. A footman called me to the telephone, but it was, of all people in the world, Mary Martin who spoke to me.

"I am sorry to have bad news for you," she began, and went on to tell me. Mr. Somers had seemed fairly well during the evening. Miss Judy had sat with him until after eleven. At eleven Evans, his valet, had brought a whisky and soda and placed it in his bedroom, and a short time after that Judy had gone to bed.

Katherine had found him in the morning, in his dressing gown and slippers, lying across the bed as he had fallen.

I took the eleven o'clock train and was at the apartment at something after two that afternoon. Mary was in the hall when I was admitted, her red head flaming over her decorous black frock. She was talking competently and quietly with what I gathered was an undertaker's assistant, and she greeted me with considerable manner.

"Mrs. Somers is trying to get some rest," she said. "Have you lunched, or shall I order something for you?"

"I have lunched, Mary. When did it happen?"

"The doctors think between three and four this morning. It was his heart."

"Then there will be no inquest?"

"Inquest?" I thought she looked at me strangely, as though I had shocked her. "No. It was not unexpected."

She went on, as she led me to my room. The doctors had not been surprised. He had died very quietly, that was one comforting thing. And she had notified the family. She had called up Mr. Blake, and had telegraphed Laura. Also—she hoped this was all right—she had sent a wire to Mr. Walter.

"Why not?" I said rather sharply. "He is his son. And is Mr. Blake coming?"

"He will try to be here for the funeral."

Judy was shut away with Katherine, who seemed to be dazed and entirely unprepared. In my room I had time to think. Mary was there, apparently at home; and as Judy had predicted, Maude Palmer was gone. She had worked fast, I reflected, had Mary Martin. She had been out of my house less than a week, and there she was.

I know now what happened, how it came about. Katherine has told me.

On the Friday before Mary had called at the apartment and asked for Katherine. Katherine was dictating letters in that small room off the great drawing room which she likes to call her study. She went out and Mary was waiting in the hall, soft voiced and assured. Within the next half hour she had told her things we had never dreamed she knew, about the sword-cane, for example, and Jim's refusal to alibi himself the night of Sarah's murder. She knew—or guessed—that he was not ill but hiding, and then, bending forward and speaking cautiously, she told her that the carpet was missing from Jim's car.

Katherine was stunned.

"How do you know that?" she demanded sharply. "Amos, I suppose."

"Partly Amos. Partly my own eyes. Miss Bell tried to burn it, but it didn't burn. When I went down to breakfast the cook told me the poker was missing, and I found it in the cellar. So I looked about, and the carpet was there. It was in the furnace."

"You'd swear to that?"

"Not necessarily," said Mary, and sat waiting for Katherine to comprehend that.

Within an hour Katherine had dismissed poor Maude Palmer, who had been her secretary for five years, giving her two months' salary in advance, and the next morning Mary Martin was threading a new ribbon into the machine in that small neat room where Katherine attended to the various duties of a woman of wealth and position.

What were her thoughts as she sat there? Was she exultant or depressed? She may have been frightened. Indeed, I think now that she was, for some time during that day she asked Katherine not to tell me she was there.

"Why?" Katherine asked. "Miss Bell would be glad to know that you are in a good position."

"She would think I had used what I know, to my own advantage."

Katherine gave that faint cold smile of hers, and the girl flushed. But in the end she agreed to say nothing, for a time at least.

"Of course, when Miss Judy comes back—" she said.

"It may be all right then," Mary said quietly, and turned back to her machine.

Incomprehensible, that girl, now as I look back; hiding as definitely and more safely than Jim was hiding. She never gave even Katherine the address of her room downtown. She must have felt safe too for the first time, for on that night, as we know now, the night of the day she was engaged, she walked out on the Brooklyn Bridge and dropped something into the water. She had not tied a string around it, and as it fell the paper blew away.

Then she walked uptown to a branch post office, bought a stamped envelope and sent a note to Wallie. Not giving him her address; just a line or two. After that she went to her room and "slept very well."

Anyhow there she was, established, settled in that handsome Park Avenue apartment where a dozen servants moved quietly about in the early hours of the day, later on to disappear and only emerge on the ringing of bells or the ritual of the table. What she felt I have no idea. She adapted herself, I fancy. She had learned a good bit while with me. But she was there for a definite purpose. That over she moved on. Vanished. A queer girl, I think now; not entirely explicable, even by the light of what we now know.

I settled down, then, to the hushed routine of a house in mourning. Katherine did not appear. People called, spoke in low voices, went away. Flowers began to arrive, and Mary entered the names of the senders, neatly in a small book. She was to stay there at night now, until after the funeral.

I thought she looked changed, not so pretty and rather worn. Once, carrying some cards into her room to be entered, I found her with her head on her desk, and I thought that she was crying. But she was not crying. Her eyes were defiant and rather hard.

I had not the faintest idea that there was any mystery about Howard's death until I talked to Judy. Then I was fairly stunned.

And as the apartment itself figures in that story of hers, I must begin by describing it.

It is of the duplex type; on the lower floor are the large drawing room, a small living room, a library, and Katherine's study. Behind these, along a corridor, lie the long dining room, the pantry, kitchen and servants' rooms, and above, connecting by a front and rear staircase, are the family rooms; Katherine's boudoir connecting with her bedroom, Howard's study opening from his. Judy's room, guest chambers, a room for Katherine's maid and a small sewing and pressing room opening from it, constitute the remainder of that floor.

On that Tuesday evening, then, Judy met Mary in the lower hall preparing to go. Judy was resentful of her presence in the house and inclined to be short with her, but Mary detained her.

"I don't think your father ought to be alone at night," she said.

Judy eyed her.

"And why?"

"Because he's a very sick man. If he—if he should take sick in the night, he mightn't be able to call for help."

"We have no intention of neglecting him," said Judy shortly, and turned away.

But she was worried nevertheless, and she spent that evening with Howard in the study off his bedroom. He had a heavy cold and was rather uncomfortable. Mostly he read, and when at eleven o'clock Evans, his valet, brought the highball and placed it beside the bed in the bedroom, she prepared to leave him.

What followed she had not yet told her mother.

The telephone rang, and Judy herself answered it. It was for Howard, apparently a long distance call, and he appeared rather surprised when he answered it.

"Tonight?" he said. "Where are you? It's pretty late. You'll be a couple of hours yet."

But in the end he agreed, and Judy said he seemed thoughtful as he hung up the receiver.

"Your Uncle Jim," he said. "He's motoring up. I thought he was ill."

"He has been," said Judy, thinking hard. "I wish you wouldn't see him, father. He'll upset you."

"Why?"

"I don't know. He's in trouble, father. Of course it's silly, but the police are trying to connect him with Sarah, and all that."

"Nonsense! Why should he want to do away with Sarah? It's an outrage."

She wanted to wait up, but he said Jim had been very urgent that his visit be kept a secret. He proposed to come in by the service entrance and up the stairs, and she was to unlock that door on the floor below. He called up the night watchman while she was still there and asked him to admit a visitor there, or better still, to open the door onto the alley and go away. He was smiling when he hung up the receiver.

"Probably thinks I'm receiving my bootlegger," he said.

"Or a lady, father!" said Judy. "I think I'll tell mother!"

"Your mother is not to know. He's very insistent about that."

She persuaded him to go to bed and see Jim there, and after he was settled she went in and herself gave him a book and fixed his light.

"Door unlocked?" he asked.

"All fixed."

He had not touched the whisky in the glass at that time. She remembered that.

She kissed him good-night and went to her own room. But she was very uneasy. How Jim had escaped surveillance did not interest her, but she was fearful for Howard; Jim bursting in on him with that whole hideous story, perhaps begging for help to escape, perhaps—she says this entered her mind—perhaps even confessing.

She heard no footsteps by two o'clock, and she dozed off. At three she wakened suddenly, sat up and finally got up. She went along the corridor to her father's door, and listened. She could hear voices, one low and quiet, her father's louder and irritated.

Shortly after that she had heard a sort of thud, "Like somebody falling," she said with a shiver. She had sat up and listened, but it was not repeated, and soon after that she heard Jim come out and close the door.

She went to sleep after that.

At nine o'clock the next morning she was wakened by a shriek and the sound of a chair being overturned. Quick as she had been to throw on a dressing gown and run out, Mary Martin was before her. She was standing staring into Howard's room, where Katherine lay in a faint on the floor, and Howard was quite peacefully dead across his bed.

He was in his dressing gown, a thing of heavy dark brocade, and his face according to Judy was very quiet and very peaceful. Whatever his last thoughts had been, if indeed he had any, they were wiped clean.

Some weeks afterward Inspector Harrison was to give me a little talk on just such things.

"There is no expression on a dead face," he said. "In two minutes it's wiped clean, like a slate. All this stuff about expressions of horror on murdered people is pure nonsense. I've seen a fellow beaten to death, and he looked as peaceful as though he'd died in his bed."

Judy called for help, and the servants flocked in. Katherine's maid, a hysterical Frenchwoman, was entirely helpless, and it was Mary Martin who threw up the windows and ran into Howard's bedroom for water.

"But she dropped the glass," said Judy, gazing at me with reddened eyes. "She took the highball glass from beside the bed and dropped it on the bathroom floor. It broke into bits. I want to know why she did that. There were glasses in the bathroom."

I tried to reassure her. After all, her father had been a dying man for some time. And any one might drop a glass. But she was not satisfied.

"How did she get there so quickly?" she demanded. "It's as though she was waiting for it."

I advised her to say nothing, especially to Katherine in her grief. But she only made a small gesture.

"She'll know soon enough that Uncle Jim was here," she said. "The night watchman saw him. And he told Evans this morning when he heard that father was—gone. All the servants know it, probably."

"He recognized your Uncle Jim?"

"I don't know. He knows somebody was here."

"And the doctors? They think everything is all right? I mean, that it was his heart?"

"Why would they think anything else?" she said drearily. "If it was poison—"

"Hush, Judy."

I got through the remainder of the day somehow; not for years had we faced an emergency without Sarah, and I missed her now.

Sarah would have taken hold; would have put Katherine to bed matter-of-factly and with authority, have driven out that hysterical Frenchwoman who was wringing her hands in the servants' hall, have given us all sedatives or got the doctor to order them, and then flat-footedly and as if death were as normal as living, have read a book until we were all safely asleep.

But Sarah was gone. Florence Gunther was gone. And now Howard.

CHAPTER FOURTEEN

WALLIE ARRIVED that evening. Katherine was still shut in her room. Now and then Judy would wander in, but Katherine was absorbed in her grief, alone with it. She would kiss Judy and then forget she was there.

But she made a ghastly mistake when she refused to see Wallie. One gesture from her then, one bit of recognition of their common grief, their common loss, and things would have been different.

Whatever might be his weaknesses, Wallie had cared about his father, and he looked stricken when I went in to see him. His face was blank and expressionless, and he had little to say. He sat slumped in his chair, and for the first time I saw a hint of gray in his hair. He was only in his middle thirties, but he might have been fifty as he sat there.

"It was the heart, of course?"

"Yes. It was bound to come before long, anyhow, Wallie."

He seemed to hesitate, to bring his next question out with an effort.

"Then there was no post-mortem?"

"No."

"I asked for *her,* but I suppose she won't see me."

"She's not seeing any one, Wallie. I haven't seen her myself."

"Does she know I'm here?" he insisted.

"I told her, yes. Through the door. She's quite shut away, Wallie."

But I did not tell him that I had urged her and had been refused. It had seemed to me that death ought to wipe out old angers, old jealousies. But she had been coldly stubborn, would not even unlock her door.

"I have no intention of seeing him, Elizabeth. Do go away."

"Shall I tell him you will see him later? He seems to think it is important."

"Nothing is important, and I never want to see him again.

Of course that was pure hysteria, but no man has ever understood a woman's hysteria.

Mary Martin came in just then with a number of telegrams, but he did not so much as look at her. She glanced at him, waited a moment, then put down the telegrams and went quietly away.

"Give her a little time, Wallie," I begged him.

"No," he said. "She's had her chance. I'm through."

His face had hardened. It was as though he had come with some overture of peace, and the impulse had died as I looked at him. He was standing in the big drawing room, with its tapestries, its famous paintings, its well-known collection of eighteenth century French furniture, and I saw him look around as if appraising it. Then he smiled unpleasantly.

"She has good taste," he said. "Good taste but bad judgment. I daresay I can see *him*? After all, he was my father."

I asked no one's permission for that, and he had had about five minutes alone with Howard before he left. Judy took him to the door and left him there. It must have been five minutes of pure agony, knowing what we know now, but he came out quietly enough.

When he left I thought I saw Mary waiting in the hall, but she disappeared when she saw me. She was staying for the night, working late in order to attend to all the details, and I could still hear her at her desk when at last I went up to bed.

But I did not sleep. I had taken two cups of coffee, and my mind was racing like a mill stream. The news that Jim Blake had been with Howard, that for all his pretended illness he had driven his car the night before to New York, arriving stealthily after that long distance call, had been a profound shock.

True, that might have been explicable. He was in great trouble. He might have felt the need of Howard, of some balanced judgment. But suppose that the shock of his story had destroyed Howard? Suppose he had died before Jim left?

Suppose the thud Judy had heard had been his body as it fell? Then why had Jim slipped away like a thief in the night? His own sister in a room beyond, with only her boudoir intervening, and he had not called her.

It seemed monstrous, inhuman.

Then of course Judy's suspicions played their part. We would probably never know the truth. Unless we told Katherine the whole story she would never permit an examination of the body, and to tell her the story was to involve her own brother.

So I turned and re-turned. How long could this visit be kept under cover? Not long. The servants knew, and from the servants to Mary Martin was only a step. Then, when it was known, what? How would the police argue? That Jim had made a confession to Howard, and that the shock had killed him? Certainly they could argue that this secret visit of Jim's was not the act of a consciously innocent man.

But what did any of them know, after all? That Howard had had a visitor, but not necessarily that visitor's identity. Or did Mary suspect who that visitor had been? Moving in her mysterious way among us all, never of us but among us, unfathomable, shrewd, unscrupulous when she chose to be, she had her own methods, her own purposes.

Suppose then that she made inquiries, downstairs? Suppose she had talked to the night watchman, got a description of the visitor, was proposing to give that description to Wallie?

And Wallie perhaps already suspicious, asking about a post-mortem, maybe about to demand one.

Still, she had broken the glass. Why should she do that? What picture had been in her mind? Did she suspect or did she know of something—a powder perhaps—shaken into that glass beside the bed, and Howard drinking it? Sitting there, talking maybe, and drinking it.

Where was the glass now? She had broken it, but the pieces would be somewhere about. Suppose they were, and Wallie was suspicious? Suppose he had gone to the police that night, and early morning would find the trash-can examined, and Jim's guilt proved beyond a doubt?

I thought that it would kill Katherine.

Outside it was raining, a heavy spring shower. I got out of bed and paced the floor in my bare feet, to the accompaniment of heavy thunder and the beating of the rain on neighboring roofs. Suppose I got those pieces of glass and disposed of them? Hid them and then carried them off? Dropped them in a river or out of the window of a railway carriage? Innocent or guilty, they would be gone.

Looking back, I know that I was not entirely normal that night, but I was on the verge of desperation. I was ready to pay any price for peace. It did not even seem to be important that Jim Blake might be a cold-blooded and deadly killer; what mattered was that it should not be known, that we be allowed to go back to our quiet lives once more, that no scandal break to involve us all.

So, thinking or not thinking, I put on a dressing gown and went quietly down the stairs.

As I have said, the dining room, kitchen, pantries and so on are at the rear of a long hall. One passes from the dining room through a butler's pantry into the kitchen, and beyond the kitchen, opening from a rear hallway, is a small cement-floored room in which is the dumb-waiter by which refuse cans and so on are lowered to the basement, there to be collected. This room I knew well. During the day it was there that the boxes had been taken as the flowers were unwrapped, and when last I saw it that day it had been waist deep in paper.

To this room, therefore, I went. Save the dumb-waiter, there is no access to it other than by the one door, and I felt my way along in the darkness, fearful of rousing the servants. But outside the door I stopped, almost paralyzed with amazement. Some one was in the room. There was the stealthy movement of paper, the sound of a lid being fitted cautiously onto a can.

It took all my courage to fling that door open, and for a moment, after the darkness, the blaze of light almost blinded me. Then I saw, sitting calmly on the floor, Mary Martin. She was looking at me with a half smile, and the light on her red hair was positively dazzling.

"Good heavens, how you scared me!" she said.

"What on earth are you doing here?"

"I couldn't sleep," she said, "and I got to worrying about a card. That bunch of orchids and lilies of the valley—the card's been thrown away."

She had emptied one of the trash-cans onto a paper before her. Now she ran her fingers through the debris, the flotsam and jetsam of the day; a chipped cup, bits of string, old envelopes, even sweepings from the floors. And suddenly she picked something up and waved it before me.

"Here it is," she said. "Now I can sleep in peace."

I do not know why I felt that she was acting. Perhaps the open window had something to do with it; the rain driving in and blowing over her, and that assumption of hers that this was as it should be; that she liked sitting in that chaos and allowing the rain to wet one of those alluring negligees which she affected.

"Why don't you close that window?"

She drew her kimono about her, and got up.

"I will," she said. "Not that I suppose it matters here."

And then, at the window with her back to me, I saw her release her clutch on the kimono, so that it blew out into the room, and I saw her lower the window with one hand. I knew then that she had dropped something over the sill.

And I saw another thing. There were no bits of glass among the trash on that paper. If she had thrown them out, as I suspected, the rain would wash them clean of evidence. They were gone.

But lying in bed later on I was bewildered beyond thought. Had this unfathomable girl lain awake as I had, reached the same conclusion, acted on the same impulse? Or was there something more sinister there, some knowledge I did not possess which she did? And once again I was back in my house at home, hearing that desperate weeping of hers.

"It's nothing. I was low in my mind. That's all."

I have rather a confused memory of the next two days. I recall that early the next morning I made an excursion into the courtyard of the building, but without much result. It was still raining, and although here and there I could see very small pieces of glass, there was nothing large enough to be worth salvage. Which was not surprising, considering that if I was right they had had a sheer drop of twelve stories.

Dick Carter appeared on Thursday. I did not know he had come until I saw him in the library with Judy. I happened to walk in on them, and I saw at once that things were not well between them. He was standing at a window, staring out, and Judy was huddled in a chair.

"I don't see what difference it makes," she was saying.

"Don't you? Well, I do."

Nevertheless, it was from Dick that I got the first intimation that some one besides myself was suspicious of Howard's death. Judy had disappeared, but the boy stayed around after she had gone, uncomfortable but apparently determined.

"I suppose it's all right?" he said to me. "No chance of anything queer, eh?"

"What do you think?"

"I don't know. Suppose Blake told him something and the shock killed him; that's not murder. That is, supposing it *was* Blake."

"Good heavens! Do you think it was some one else?"

"Well, figure it out for yourself. Blake's sick, or he says he is. But he comes here in the middle of the night, driving his own car for ninety-odd miles, sees Mr. Somers and gets back, presumably, at daylight or thereabouts. That's some drive for a sick man. Then all this secrecy. Why? The police couldn't have stopped him if he'd wanted to take a train and come here. They've got nothing on him yet. All he had to do was to pack a bag and come. Or hire an ambulance! He's coming for the funeral, isn't he?"

I sat down. My knees were shaking. Dick looked at his watch.

"What time does the night watchman come on duty?"

"I haven't an idea."

"Well, he's the boy to see."

I made up my mind then to tell him about Mary and the glass, and I did so. He listened attentively, but when I told him she had actually found the card, and that I was not certain she had thrown anything from the window, he made rather light of it.

"Wait a minute," he said. "Now either we've got another crime or we haven't. In the first place, who would want to kill a man who had only a few months to live anyhow? But grant that. Grant that there was poison in the glass. Something quick, like cyanide. First we have to admit that Howard Somers, drinking a highball, is talking to some one he knows, and trusts. He's not scared. He's drinking a highball. But you've got to go further; you've got to figure that Mary Martin knew he was going to be murdered, and how. Yet she warns Judy that he's not to be left alone at night. Only did she do that?"

"I haven't an idea," I said dismally.

"I suppose there's no chance of a post-mortem?"

"Not unless we told Mrs. Somers; and not then. It's her brother who is involved."

Naturally we said nothing to Judy of all this, and the day passed quietly enough, people coming and going, more flowers, and Mary keeping her neat entries and moving decorously about. Once I caught her eyes on me, a curious speculative look in them, and I thought she was depressed all of that day.

Late in the afternoon she asked to be allowed to go home for the night, and I told her to go. She remained to dinner and left at nine o'clock, and at nine-fifteen Dick called me on the telephone.

"Listen," he said, "I'm at a drug store around the corner. I wanted to tell you; there may be something in what we discussed today."

"Yes?"

"The lady in question—do you get that?"

"Yes. All right."

"She's been interviewing the night watchman. Interesting, isn't it? Just thought I'd tell you, so you can keep an eye on things."

He hung up the receiver, and I was left to make of that what I could.

I remember that Alex Davis was there that night. Howard's attorney. He was settled comfortably in the library with a glass of old port at his elbow, and what with the port and probably an excellent dinner tucked away, he was unusually talkative. A fat man, Alex Davis, with small sharp black eyes set in a broad expanse of face.

"I suppose you know," he said, "that there will be a great deal of money. More, I fancy, than any one realizes. Poor Howard was a secretive man."

"I suppose he left a will?"

"Yes. A very fair one, I think. He's taken care of the servants and certain charities, and there is provision too for Mrs. Somers' brother."

"And Wallie?" I asked.

He cleared his throat.

"He has already done a good bit for Wallie. Certain businesses which failed, and last summer certain notes to be paid. But there is a very fair arrangement; a trust fund with a substantial income. Not large. Substantial. Of course this is in confidence. I am one of the executors."

And I saw that this last pleased him; that it was a vote of confidence, as well as providing certain emoluments; that already he saw his name in the press everywhere; the size of the estate, the inheritance tax royalty calculated. "Mr. Alexander Davis and the Guaranty Trust Company, executors."

He leaned back and patted his substantial abdomen.

"Howard was a money maker," he said. "A lot of people are going to be surprised."

I was not listening very attentively. I was thinking of Mary and of that conversation with the night watchman, and after Alex Davis had taken his complacent departure I wandered into Katherine's study and looked about me.

The desk was cleared. There was no sign of those small personal belongings which she was wont to keep by her. Nor were they in the drawers of the desk, or any place else.

It came to me with a shock of surprise that Mary Martin had gone, and gone for good.

Jim arrived at noon the next day, for the funeral. Save for a certain pallor—he had been in the house for over three weeks—he seemed much as usual; impeccably dressed, with a black tie and a black band on the left sleeve of his coat.

I had no chance whatever to talk to him. He went at once to Katherine's room, and their luncheon was served to them there.

Only during the solemn process of carrying Howard's body downstairs was he seen at all until after the services. But that seems to have been sufficient. Some time in that slow and affecting progress Jim came face to face with an individual whom I was later to know as Charles Parrott, a man of middle age, with a cap drawn low over his face. This Parrott was carrying in the chairs usually provided for such occasions, and was opening them and placing them in rows, and as Jim passed him he gave him a long steady look. Jim did not notice him, apparently.

I was not there at the time. The name Charles Parrott meant nothing to me. But in due time Charles Parrott was to play his own part in our tragedy, to make his own contribution to the tragic *dénouement* which was to follow. For Charles Parrott, introduced by Dick by methods of which I have no knowledge, was the night watchman of the building. And he identified Jim Blake as being of the same build and general appearance as that visitor to Howard whom he had admitted two nights before.

True, he stubbornly refused under oath to make a positive statement.

"He's the same build. He looks like him. But that's as far as I go."

So Jim moved about, unsuspicious, changing the flowers, softening the lights, and Parrott watched him. He disappeared when Jim had gone upstairs again, to remain with Katherine and Judy during the services. Wallie was not asked to join them. He was left to sit alone, where he chose. A cruel thing, perhaps; a stupid thing certainly. Katherine had taken the strongest affection he had ever felt, the deepest grief, and flung them back in his face.

So he sat alone, rigid and cold during the services, and stood alone at his father's grave. However he had wavered before, some time then he made his decision. He went that night to call on Alex Davis, sitting complacent and smug in his library, and slammed out only a half hour later, leaving Alex in a state bordering on apoplexy.

Half an hour later Alex Davis was frenziedly ringing the bell of the apartment and demanding to see Katherine. He was admitted and taken up to her, but Judy and I knew nothing of all this until later.

Judy had determined to talk to Jim, and asked me to be present in the library.

"I can't stand it any longer," she said. "He was here. Why doesn't he speak up? He must know that watchman saw him. Even if father was—was alive when he left, why doesn't he say something?"

But Jim's reaction to her first question was a surprise to both of us. He denied, immediately, categorically, and almost violently, that he had made any visit to Howard Somers on the night of his death.

"Here?" he said. "Why, it's madness. Why should I have come like that? You've lost your good common sense, Judy."

"Some one was here and used your name. He telephoned on the way, from somewhere in the country."

When she had told her story, however, he looked ghastly. Not only was there the implication that Howard had been murdered, but there was the terrible possibility which the situation held for himself. What was he to do, where to turn? To go to Katherine and demand that the body be exhumed? And that with the police watching him, and maybe poison to be found? All that he must have thought of, sitting there so neat and dapper in his chair.

"It's terrible," he said. "It's all terrible. And this night watchman? He says he recognized me?"

"He says the man was your height and build."

Suddenly he was savagely angry. "And so this fellow, this Parrott—he's in the secret, is he? He's been brought here to look me over! Good God, Judy, do you want to send me to the chair? I wasn't here. How the hell could I get here? I've been sick for weeks. If somebody came here that night, using my name and impersonating me, he was a liar and an impostor, and before God I believe he was a murderer too. Why should I have come here in the night? I could come at any time."

Then he quieted, although he was still shaking.

"Does your mother know anything of all this?"

"Nothing."

"Then keep it from her. You can do that much. She is in great trouble."

"So am I in great trouble," said Judy bitterly. "But I suppose that doesn't matter."

He looked at her.

"You believed it, did you? Do you still believe it?"

"I don't know. No, of course not."

"Judy," he said, more gently, "what motive could I have? What possible reason? Your father was my friend. To put the thing boldly, what could I possibly gain by his death? By any of these deaths?"

And as if in answer to his question a footman knocked at the door and said that Katherine wanted to see him in her room.

I have no picture of that scene, but I can see it: Katherine frozen in her chair and Alex Davis walking the floor, and after a habit of his snapping his fingers as he walked. Into that scene Jim was projected, and in the forcible language he was told what Wallie had said.

Briefly, Wallie had claimed that, during his illness the summer before, his father had made a second will. That this will was in Howard's safe deposit box at the bank in New York, and the copy in the hands of Waite and Henderson, Mr. Waite having personally drawn it, here in my own city.

By this will, Wallie received no trust fund and no annuity, but a full half of the estate, and the previous will had been revoked. The new will made no provision whatever, either for Sarah or for Jim.

"He may be lying," said Jim, still apparently confused.

But Alex Davis snapped his fingers with excitement, and said that if so it was fairly circumstantial lying.

"He's even got the names of the witnesses," he said, and drawing a slip of paper from his pocket he read them aloud. "Sarah Gittings and Florence Gunther."

I believe it was then that Jim collapsed.

Naturally I knew nothing of this at the time, nor did Judy. Both Katherine and Jim were still shut in their rooms when I left early the next morning.

But I was sufficiently dismayed and confused. If we were to believe Jim—and I did—then the possibility of a third murder was very real. And once more, sitting in the train, I endeavored to fit together the fragments of that puzzle. I saw Howard, that night, waiting in his room, settled in his bed, the highball beside him, a book in his hand. Getting up to admit his visitor, finding it was not Jim, but making no outcry. Still calm, putting on his dressing gown and slippers, talking. Judy had heard them talking.

Some one he knew, then; knew and trusted. Was it Wallie? Wallie was not unlike Jim in build, although taller and slimmer. Might not that be the answer, and no poison, no third murder. A talk between father and son, and then Wallie going and the heart attack after he had gone.

I admit that this comforted me. I sat back and tried to read.

Shortly before the train drew in to the station Dick Carter came through the car. He looked depressed, but he forced a smile when he saw me.

"Well," he said, "I'm back on the job! Even funerals can't last forever."

He sat down in the empty chair next to mine, and said that Judy had telephoned him of Jim's denial.

"She believes him," he said. "In that case—this Martin girl seems to be fairly vital. It begins to look as though she's the key, doesn't it? Take that glass, for instance. She thought fast that morning and she was still thinking that night. It's not coincidence, all that glass stuff. Get why she did that, and we've got somewhere. Where does she come in in all this, anyhow?"

"I wish I knew."

"Tell me something about her," he said, leaning forward. "Who is she? What do you know about her?"

"Nothing, really. She answered an advertisement last fall. I tried her out, and she was efficient. Very. She had no local references."

"And on that you took her into the house? To live?"

"Not at first. But she was really very capable, and sometimes I work at night. I rather drifted into it."

He was silent for some time. Then he made a circle on a piece of paper and marked it around with perhaps a dozen dots. It bore a rough relation to a clock-face, but without the hands, when he held it out to me.

"This dial thing," he said. "It may not refer to a clock, you know. It might be a safe. You haven't a safe in the house, have you?"

"No."

"A safe, or something resembling a clock, but not necessarily a clock. Something round. Would that mean anything to you? A picture, maybe? Have you any round pictures, with nails at the back?"

"One or two. I can examine them."

The train was drawing in. He helped me into my wraps, and we sat down again while we were being slowly moved into the station.

"I suppose," he said, not looking directly at me, "that you realize what all this has done to me?"

"To you!"

"About Judy. I'll be nobody's kept husband, and Judy's got a couple of millions or so. I fade, that's all."

"Judy has a right to a vote on that, hasn't she?"

"She's voted. She'll keep the money."

"I don't believe it."

"Well, the equivalent of that. She says I'm a poor mean-spirited creature to refuse to let her support me in luxury. She says it takes a strong man to marry money, and I'm weak or I'd do it."

Then the train stopped.

I was glad to get home, to find Robert at the station and Joseph at the open door. I like my servants; I have to live with them, and so when I do not like them they must go. And the house was cool and quiet, after New York. I relaxed at once under Joseph's care; the well-laid tea table, the small hot rolls, the very smoothness and greenness of the lawns outside the windows. For the first time since Sarah's death I felt secure. Surely now it was over; we had had our three tragedies, according to the old superstition.

I leaned back and looked at Joseph, and for the first time, I realized that he was pale, almost waxy.

"Have you been ill, Joseph?"

"No, madam. I have had an accident."

"An accident? What sort of an accident?"

But as it turned out, Joseph had had no accident. Dragged out of him, and later corroborated by the maids, came the story of an attack in broad daylight so mysterious and so brutal that it made my blood run cold.

The story was this: on the afternoon of the day I left for New York, he had allowed the women servants to go out. He often did this in my absence, getting himself a supper of sorts, and apparently glad to have his pantry to himself.

The house was locked and Robert was washing the car in the garage. According to Robert, and this was later found to be true, the first knowledge he had of any trouble was at four o'clock that afternoon, when he heard a faint rapping on the pantry window and looking toward the house, saw a bloody head, wavering with weakness, inside.

Robert was frightened. He made no effort to get into the house alone, but summoned a white chauffeur from the garage of my bootlegger neighbor, and the two of them broke open the basement door and rushed up the stairs.

They found Joseph unconscious on the pantry floor, his head bleeding profusely from a bad cut, and as Doctor Simonds later discovered, his body a mass of bruises. It was two hours before he recovered consciousness, and then he could give no description of his assailant.

"I saw and heard nobody," he told me. "I was on the second floor. It looked like rain and I was closing the windows. I had finished that and was about to go down the back staircase when I felt that some one was behind me. But I never saw who it was.

The next thing I remember, madam, I was at the foot of the stairs, trying to crawl to the pantry."

And this story of his was borne out by the fact that the maids later found blood on the stairs and a small pool at the bottom.

Doctor Simonds however did not place too much confidence in the story of the attack, when he came in that night to see me.

"Sure he was hurt," he said, with that cheerful descent into the colloquial with which the medical profession soothes its fearful patients and its nervous women. "Surest thing I ever saw. It took four stitches to sew him up! But why assault? Why didn't Joseph catch his rubber heel on something and pitch down those stairs of yours? There are twenty odd metal-edged steps there, and every one got in a bit of work."

"He says he felt that there was some one behind him."

"Exactly. He was stepping off as he turned to look; and why he didn't break that stiff neck of his I don't know. It's a marvel to me that he's up and about."

But Joseph stuck to his story. He had been attacked by some one from the rear, armed either with a club or a chair. And as we know now, he was right. Joseph had indeed been murderously assaulted, and very possibly left for dead.

As it happened, it was during that call of Doctor Simonds' that I first learned of the possibility that Howard had left a second will. He had attended Howard during his illness at the Imperial the summer before, and expressed regret over his death.

"Of course it was bound to come," he said. "He knew it. He was not a man you could deceive, and that attack he had here was a pretty bad one. By the way, did he alter his will at that time? Or do you know?"

"Alter it? I don't know, I'm sure."

"He was thinking of it. Walter had been very attentive to him, and they'd patched up a peace between them. It was rather amusing, in a way. Poor Miss Gittings hated Walter, and she would have kept him out if she could."

"I hope he did change the will," I said, thoughtfully. "After all, his only son—"

"He may, and he may not. I talked it over with Walter, and he said there would be hell to pay if it did happen. He wasn't sure, of course. But he got me to give him a letter, to the effect that his father was capable of drawing such a document; 'not under drugs, or mentally enfeebled.'" He laughed a little. "Mentally enfeebled," he said. "If Howard Somers was mentally enfeebled I wish I had arterio-sclerosis!"

But Joseph's injury had made me most uneasy. What was the motive? What had been gained by it? I must confess that once again I considered the possibility of a killer who killed for the sheer lust of murder.

That day I bought a new revolver for Joseph, and moved him to a guest room on the second floor. Before he retired I made the round of the house with him, and even of the garage and the cellars. Then, with my own door locked, I was able to pass a quiet if not an easy night.

But again I did not sleep. I lay in bed with a pencil and a sheet of paper, and tried that night to put together what we knew about this unknown. I wrote down that he was crafty and physically strong; that he had no scruples about taking human life; that he knew my house even to the detail of the airshaft and its window; that he was—at least probably—of the same height and build as Jim Blake; that my dogs knew him; that, although since Sarah's death the front door lock had been changed, he was still able—if Joseph's story were accurate—to enter my house at will; and that his motive, still hidden, had somehow already involved and destroyed Sarah and Florence Gunther and possibly Howard, and might in the end affect others, God only knew who.

I was badly frightened by that time, and when just as I had finished the list I heard the stealthy padding of feet in the hall, I was in a cold sweat of terror. It was only Jock, however, moving restlessly about, with the call of the spring night in his blood and a closed and double-locked front door between him and his kind.

CHAPTER FIFTEEN

THE NEXT day I went through my house, acting on Dick's suggestion. I imagine that the servants thought that our recent tragedies had slightly unbalanced me, as I took down one circular object after another and examined it. One or two old daguerreotypes in round frames I literally ripped open, but at the end of these acts of vandalism I was no wiser than before.

It was that afternoon that I was sent for by the District Attorney; a disquieting interview, with accusation and suppressed anger on his part, and sheer dismay on my own.

"This is a curious case, Miss Bell," he said. "Two horrible crimes have been committed by the same hand, and two attacks, one of them certain; the other, on your butler, at least possible. We have either a maniac loose in the community, or we have a motive so carefully concealed that so far we have not found it. I think there is a motive. Of the two women killed, one was apparently negligible, without background. The other had no background save a certain family, to which she had been loyal and from which she had certainly received a considerable measure of confidence. These two women became friends; the secret of one became the secret of the other. Therefore, granting there was some detrimental knowledge, when one died the other must die. That's simple. But the family in question has done nothing to help the law. It has even withheld certain matters from the police."

"I deny that, absolutely."

"Do you? Is that entirely wise, Miss Bell? If this case comes to trial, and you are put under oath on the witness stand—"

"How can it come to trial? You have made no arrest." But he ignored that.

"I want to urge you to tell what you know, Miss Bell, as a public duty. You owe that to the community. If there is a man of this description loose, a wholesale murderer, shrewd, without conscience or scruple, defeating justice to serve his own ends, then your obligation lies plain before you."

"I know nothing. If you think you are describing Jim Blake, I do not. He is as innocent as you are."

He bent forward.

"Then why did you burn the carpet from his car? You need not answer that. We know that you did. We are not guessing."

"If you are going to try to convict a man on purely circumstantial evidence—"

"What *is* circumstantial evidence? It is the evidence on which we rely every day of our lives. Your door bell rings; you have not seen anybody at the door, but you know that somebody is there, ringing that bell. That's circumstantial evidence."

He leaned back and spoke more quietly.

"This cane," he said, "the one with the hidden blade. How wide was that blade?"

"It was very narrow; perhaps a half inch at the widest part. It tapered."

"And it had a double cutting edge?"

"I don't remember."

"You haven't seen it since you gave it to Jim Blake?"

"Not since."

"And when did you give it to him?"

"I've already told you that; last March. He had admired it."

"Did he ask for it?"

"Hardly that. He said if I ever wanted to get rid of it, he would take it."

"He dropped in to see you rather often?"

"Not so often. Once a month or so."

"And where did you sit, when he called?"

"In my library, usually."

On my way out I saw Mr. Henderson, of Waite and Henderson, and bowed to him. It seemed to me that he looked worried and upset, but I laid this to the death of Florence and its continuing mystery, and thought no more of it.

That was on Saturday, May the fourteenth, and that night Inspector Harrison came in. He looked tired and rather untidy, and when he took off his overcoat a flashlight fell to the floor.

For some reason he brought it into the library with him, and sat snapping it on and off as he talked. Perhaps he was out of his customary ammunition. He began rather apologetically.

"I've got the habit of dropping in here," he said. "I suppose it's because I like to talk and you're willing to listen."

"I daresay," I observed, "although I had hoped it was due to my personal charm."

That embarrassed him. He smiled rather dubiously, gave me a quick glance, and then proceeded quite calmly to focus the flashlight on my feet.

"You see," he said. "I've been studying those molds I took. It's my belief that they were made with a woman's shoe. Not *that* sort; a big woman's shoe. Flat heeled and sensible, and considerably worn. A woman who walked on the outsides of her feet; maybe bandy legged."

"I assure you, Inspector—"

"No need of it," he said politely. "But before I go I'd like to look over the closets here. Somebody appears to have pretty free access to this house, and it's just possible we'll locate that pair of shoes."

He made no immediate move, however. He surveyed himself rather ruefully.

"I've been tramping about," he explained. "It's a curious thing, but things can be seen at night that can't be seen in daytime. Take blood on furniture. In the daylight it looks like varnish, but in a good electric light it often shows up. Then take marks in the ground. Look at what your car headlights do! I've slowed down for a rut no deeper than my finger."

"And now you have found something?"

"Well, I have," he said. "It's bad news for you, Miss Bell. It's like this; I went to the museum and looked at one of those sword sticks they have there. They look like other sticks, but there's one difference. The ferrule is open at the bottom. When you put it down on the ground it makes a circle, not a hole. I took it out and tried it. You get the idea, don't you? A ring is what it makes. In the one in the museum the blade is loose, so it makes a ring with a dot in the center. That's the tip of the knife. In yours the blade is hung better. There's only the ring."

I could hardly speak.

"And you've found such rings?"

"A dozen of them. Maybe two dozen. I've got them marked and covered, and tomorrow we'll lift them. I thought I'd better tell you."

"Then Jim—"

"He was there, all right. There are a half dozen of the things in the bridle path between the sewer and the foot of the hill; and there are others on the side of the hill. What's more, I think I have found what stunned Sarah Gittings before she died."

It appears, then, that the examination of poor Sarah's body had shown more than we had known. The wound at the back of her head had been made with a blunt instrument, as we had been told; but the nature of that instrument was unknown. However, inspection had shown in her hair and in the wound itself numerous small fragments of bark from a tree.

"Of course the body had been dragged, and that would account for some of it. But there was bark deeply buried in the tissues. And there was another thing: the blow had been struck from above. The lower side of the wound was torn. Either she had been struck by a very tall man, or she was sitting down. I had to argue like this; we'll leave out the tall man for the minute, and say she was sitting down. Now where does a woman like that sit, if she's out in the open? She's a neat woman, very orderly, and she isn't young. She doesn't sit on the ground. She finds a tree stump, or a fallen tree or a stone, and she sits on that."

But he had been some time in coming to that, and Florence's death had interfered. There had been rain, too, and sunlight. Sunlight, it appeared, faded blood. That night, however, he had started out, and he had found what he was looking for. Near a fallen tree at the top of the hill, and perhaps forty feet from where the dogs had been tied, he had turned his flashlight on the broken branch of a tree, about four feet long, and both heavy and solid. When he turned it over, on the side protected from rain and weather, he had found stains and one or two hairs.

He had wrapped it up carefully and sent it back to headquarters.

I felt sick.

"And you found the marks of the sword-stick there, too?"

"Well, no. But that's not surprising. A man doesn't walk up to commit a murder swinging a stick. He crept up behind her. I doubt if she knew anything until it was all over."

I was thinking desperately.

"This sword-stick in the museum, would the blade of such a stick have made the other wounds?"

"They would," he said promptly. "But we have to be careful there, Miss Bell. All stab wounds look alike. You can't tell whether a blade has had two cutting edges or one. You see, every knife has two cutting edges at the point. Take this knife here." He drew a substantial one from his pocket. "It cuts both ways for half an inch. No. Taken by itself, the fact that Jim Blake carried that stick that night doesn't prove that he used it, or that it's the weapon that was used. It's the rest of the case—"

He had said what he came to say. There had been no new developments in the death of Florence Gunther. The bullet had been fired at close range, and from the left. The point of entry was a neat hole, but on the other side there had been some destruction. He was inclined to believe with Dick that she had been shot while in a car, and in front of or near my property.

"Even a head wound bleeds some," he explained, "and that sort of wound is generally pretty—well, pretty messy. Of course that may be wrong. She may have been stunned first like Sarah Gittings; and killed in the country somewhere."

He got up to go, and as he stood there with the light shining down on his bald head, I saw that like the rest of us he looked tired and depressed.

"There are times," he said, "when I don't like this job of mine. And this is one of them. Take you. Take little Miss Judy. She's got troubles enough just now, and the chances are that in a day or two we're going to add to them."

"You're going to arrest Jim Blake?"

"I'm going to do just that, Miss Bell. I don't mind telling you that we think we've got the motive. Maybe you know about it, maybe you don't. But we've got the motive now, and we know he was on that hillside that night. Only I'd like to find that sword-stick first."

He was on his way to the door when I stopped him.

"How did you know I had burned that carpet, Inspector?"

"Well, somebody had burned it, and it looked as though you might be the guilty party."

"But how did you know?"

He gave me a whimsical glance.

"Did you ever examine one of those things, Miss Bell? Well, I'll tell you something maybe you don't know. That carpet had snaps—or buttons—on it to fasten it to the floor; and those snaps are metal. They won't burn. A smart man now, going carefully through certain ashcans, can find them without any trouble."

He turned, his hand on the door knob.

"But I'll say this to you Miss Bell, in confidence. I'd like to know why you burned that carpet. I'd been over that car myself with a magnifying glass the day after Florence Gunther was killed. If you found anything in it, you're smarter than I am."

I could only stare at him in silent stupefaction.

"Never mind, then," he said. "You think it over. There's no hurry." And with that he left.

It was only after he had gone that I remembered the shoes he had meant to examine.

I had two days in which to think that over, although thinking did me no good whatever. I had burned the carpet and thus put a weapon against Jim in the hands of the District Attorney, and no statement by the Inspector that he had found nothing suspicious on or about it would alter that.

They would believe, as he believed, that I had found something incriminating there which they had overlooked.

But mingled with this was a sense of relief. If they had not found the oil stains on the day after Florence's murder it was because they were not there.

Those two days, however, were all I could bear. I saw nobody, heard nothing. It was as though there had been no murder of our poor Sarah, or of Florence; as though there had been no mysterious unknown, able to enter my house at will on some equally mysterious errand. But by the third day, Tuesday, I began to relax. Nobody had been arrested. Life was once more a quiet round of breakfast tray, lunch and dinner. I even prepared to go over my notes on my father's biography, as a matter of *morale*; that poor endeavor we all make in trouble to provide some sort of protective mechanism for the mind.

So I got out the material. Mary's neatly typed pages, my own illegible jottings, and those ruled notebooks in which Mary had taken down my dictation. Their queer symbols meant nothing to me; they were as unfathomable as the girl herself. And it occurred to me, sitting there, that these books written in her hand, were all that remained to any of us of Mary Martin. She had come, played her strange part, and departed. A queer girl, with her poses, her defiant beauty, and her faculty of being around where there was trouble; or of carrying it with her. Who could say which?

I turned over the pages, but although here and there I found notes in longhand—"Send to Laura for daguerreotypes" I recall was one of them, and another "Have Joseph find out about terrapin for dinner party"—there was nothing of any value until I reached what appeared to be the latest book.

Not on the pages, but inside the cover in ink, she had written: "New number, East 16."

Now I happen to have a peculiar faculty, one born of necessity, for I frequently forget my glasses. I have a flair for remembering telephone numbers. And this number ran familiarly in my mind.

It did not come at once. I sat back and closed my eyes, and at last it came. I saw Dick Carter sitting at my desk, with Judy beside him, and he was calling East 16. Then I knew. Dick had called East 16 the night he was arranging for Judy and myself to visit Lily Sanderson.

New number, East 16. That meant that there had been another number, an old one, and that Mary had known it. But it seemed to me that it meant much more; that Mary had known some one in that house, possibly Florence Gunther herself. What that would explain I did not trouble to contemplate. It seemed to me that I must see Lily Sanderson again, see if she had met Mary about the house or with Florence, and that then we must find Mary herself. Find her and make her talk.

When I called East 16, however, Miss Sanderson was at work. And then that afternoon, as though she had caught my mental message, Lily Sanderson herself came to see me.

It was fortunate that Joseph was taking his afternoon out, or he might not have admitted her. He had his own methods of discriminating between people making social calls and people who came for purposes of their own. Indeed, I have seen him; the swift glance at car or taxicab, the rapid appraisal, gloves, shoes, garments. And then the quick decision.

"Madam is not at home."

Or a widening of the door, a bow; taking the cards, rather in the grand manner, and through it all a suggestion—merely a suggestion—of welcome.

But as it is Clara's rule to admit all comers Lily Sanderson gained access without trouble, and I found her in the drawing room, rather stiff and formal.

"I hope you don't mind my coming," she said. "I just had a feeling I had to see you."

"I am glad you came. Would you like a cup of tea?"

"If it isn't too much trouble. I came from the store, and I've had a hard day. I didn't take time to go home and change."

She watched with interest while I rang for Clara and ordered tea, and the long drawing room seemed to fascinate her.

"Such a lovely place," she said. "I was looking at your bushes, as I came in. And this room! That's a lovely cabinet over there."

"It is lovely," I agreed. "It is very old."

And as I sat there looking at this big blue-eyed woman with her faint limp, her almost childlike assumption of sophistication, her queer clothes, I felt that I liked her. Liked her and trusted her.

She did not come immediately to the reason for her visit, and I did not urge her. It was after the tea had come and Clara had gone that she finally brought up the subject.

"I don't know whether it's valuable or not," she said. "But as a friend of Florence's you ought to know. She was seen getting into a car, the night she was killed. Two people saw her."

"What kind of a car?"

"A large one; a limousine."

"Did they notice the color?"

"They don't agree about that. They're the Italians who keep the fruit stand at the corner. I don't know their names. We call him Tony. They knew Florence well; she often bought apples there. Tony says it was black, but Mrs. Tony says it was blue."

The story was as follows: on the night of Florence Gunther's murder both the Italians at the fruit stand saw her coming along the street. She shook her head, to say she wanted nothing, and then waited for a street car. Both of them saw her distinctly. She seemed restless, walking a few steps each way, then back again.

Before a car arrived, however, an automobile drew up before her; a closed car with a man at the wheel. Owing to the fact that the street light was directly overhead, neither of the Italians saw him clearly, except that he wore a soft hat.

There was some conversation. The man and woman at the fruit stand were interested. They had known her for a long time, and she was always alone. She seemed to demur at something, the man appeared to insist. Finally he opened the door and she got in beside him.

But—and here was the curious part—the woman at the fruit stand maintained that this same car had been standing halfway down the block in the shadow for some time. That she had seen it there, and that the man driving it had been working at something about it; front and rear.

"She thought he was rubbing dirt over the license plates," Miss Sanderson said. "And they had been held up a month or so before, so she watched him. She says now that he got into the car the moment he saw Florence. Then he drove up rather fast, and threw on the brakes in front of her, as though he had just seen her. But Mrs. Tony was interested in the license plates, and she went out and looked at the rear one. He had blacked it. She couldn't read it, at all."

But that visit of Lily Sanderson's was disappointing in one way at least. I asked her point blank if she knew a young woman named Mary Martin, and it produced no effect whatever.

"Mary Martin?" she said thoughtfully. "No, I can't say that I do."

"I think she knew Florence Gunther. If not, she certainly knew some one at the house."

"I can ask, if you like," she said. "I've only been there since last fall, and most of the rest are new too. You know how it is, everything's fine at first. Then you're caught doing a bit of washing or having a gentleman friend more than one night a week, and there's trouble. And that reminds me. I've got something to tell you about the man who called on Florence Gunther. Clarissa saw him."

"Clarissa?"

"The colored woman at the house. And a surly creature she is, at that. I gave her a dress the other day, and she talked. He was a thin man, rather tall; she thinks about fifty. Well dressed, she says. He had a cane with him, and he wore a sport suit. Out our way that means something!"

CHAPTER SIXTEEN

It was that evening, Tuesday the seventeenth, at dinner, that I received one of Katherine's characteristic terse telegrams.

"Arriving tonight eleven o'clock train."

The telegram was not only unexpected but ominous. That Katherine, sunk in grief as she was, should leave her house and come to me at that time seemed almost incredible. I could think of only two things; either that Jim had told her of the danger in which he stood, or that something had aroused her suspicions as to Howard's death.

In any event her coming was certainly significant, and I am not ashamed to say that I took a small glass of sherry before I left for the station. Nor did the sight of Katherine in her widow's weeds, with that white cold face of hers set like a mask, improve matters. She offered me her cheek, and as I offered mine at the same moment, what resulted was rather like the nose rubbing of the Africans, or whoever it is.

Not then, nor later when I showed her her room and the Frenchwoman, Elise, began to lay out her toilet things, did she offer any explanation of her visit. Judy, she said, was all right and would come with Jim the next morning. She herself had come on business. And then very politely she put me out and left me to lie awake most of the night, wondering.

It was not until ten the next morning that I got my explanation, and then it was clear enough, and worrying enough, in all conscience. At ten o'clock the door bell rang, and it was Jim, accompanied by Judy and, to my intense surprise, Alex Davis.

Judy looked odd and uncomfortable, but she was irrepressible, as always.

"It's not a convention," she said. "It's merely a delegation."

She went upstairs to Katherine and the two men waited in the library, Jim moving about restlessly, Alex Davis glancing over some notes in his hand. In five minutes or so the bell rang again, and Joseph announced Mr. Waite.

I was practically beyond speech by that time. I listened dumbly while Mr. Waite made his apologies; he had just got off the train; he had been taking the sun cure in Arizona for his arthritis and was much better, thanks. Then his eyes fell on the black band on Jim's sleeve, and he said something polite about Howard's death.

But it all seemed unreal to me, and when Joseph ushered in Doctor Simonds I was not surprised to see Alex Davis rise and clear his throat, as though he were about to address a meeting.

"I believe that completes us," he said, as though he had announced that there was a quorum present. "And now, if Joseph will notify Mrs. Somers—"

Bewildered as I was, I had to admire Katherine as she came in, in her long black gown and with her fine head high in the air. There was a superb dignity about her, a refusal to make any concessions to the expected, so unlike my own fluttering as to make me self-conscious.

She shook hands with no one, smiled at no one. She simply sat down and looked at Alex Davis.

"Very well," she said. "I believe we are all ready."

And then Alex Davis did indeed make a speech. He referred to his late dear friend, Howard Somers, and to the grieving woman who sat there, finding herself in a position which it was difficult for her to accept.

"In all their conversations together, this husband and this wife, she was led to believe that the bulk of his fortune would come to her. Now she is confronted with a new will, a will she cannot explain and does not accept." I saw Mr. Waite frown slightly. "A will in which a wastrel son receives one half of this large estate. It is to discuss, not the validity of this will"—he glanced at Mr. Waite—"but the circumstances under which it was drawn, that she has asked you to meet her here today."

He sat down, and Mr. Waite took off his glasses and polished them with his handkerchief.

"Am I to speak?" he inquired. "I presume, since the integrity of the document is not in question, that it is really up to the doctor."

Urbane as he was, I saw that he was irritated. Under Alex's fine words he must have seen, as I did, that it was the will itself which was under fire.

"I actually know nothing," the doctor said. "Walter Somers told me, during his father's illness here last summer, that he was thinking of changing his will. He asked my opinion of his father's mental condition, and I said I wished mine were as good. Later on he asked me to give him a note to that effect, and I did so."

He sat back, smoothing a small Van Dyke beard with a hand deeply stained from cigarettes. Katherine eyed him and spoke for the first time.

"You had given him no drugs, Doctor?"

"Drugs?" he said rather testily. "I gave him drugs, of course. That's my profession. But I gave him nothing that could by any stretch of the imagination affect his mind."

Mr. Waite's story was given circumstantially and directly.

On the twelfth of the previous August he had received a telephone call from Walter Somers, asking him to see his father that afternoon at the Imperial Hotel and to draw up a will for him. As he knew that Mr. Somers had been very ill and was still a sick man, he took the precaution of calling up the doctor here, who was attending him, and inquiring as to his mental condition. Doctor Simonds said that he knew Mr. Somers was contemplating a new will, and that he was entirely competent to make one. The result was that he had drawn up the draft late that afternoon, and took back the finished document at something after four o'clock the next day. It was signed in duplicate.

Katherine listened with slowly rising color.

"Do you mean to say that you would draw up a will as vital as that, as—revolutionary, without question? What about undue influence being brought to bear? A man may appear to be normal, but after a severe illness, when he is weak and broken—"

"There was certainly no influence evident at the time. The manager of the hotel took me up, and Walter Somers met me at the door and took me in. Then he went out and I did not see him again, either that day or the next."

"Was Sarah Gittings present?"

"She left the room. She was there when I first went in, and she came in on the second day to witness the signatures. And I may add this. There was some discussion of the terms of the will. Mr. Somers himself knew that it was what you have called revolutionary, but he said that Walter had reached years of discretion, and that he felt that there was plenty for all."

"That is not the question," said Katherine sharply. "The money's nothing. What does money matter? What does matter is that at the end he should have repudiated me. What brought that about, Mr. Waite? What happened here last summer to change his entire attitude toward me? Why did he put that will in his box, endorsed in his own hand 'to be given to my son Walter in the event of my death'? That is very serious, Mr. Waite. Had he ceased to trust me? And that fund of fifty thousand dollars to be administered by Walter at his discretion! What did he say about that? What secret was he covering?"

"He said that Walter understood."

"And that is all he said?"

"That is all."

She leaned back in her chair, apparently exhausted, and there was a short silence broken at last by Alex Davis.

"Have you the duplicate of the will with you, Mr. Waite?"

And then some of Mr. Waite's air of offended dignity left him. He stirred in his chair.

"I was coming to that. As a matter of fact, a very strange thing has happened to that copy, Mr. Davis. It has disappeared from our files. Mr. Henderson has been searching for several days, ever since Mr. Somers' death, in fact. He has a theory as to its disappearance, but as it is not a pleasant one—"

I happened to glance at Jim and his mouth was twitching crazily.

"I think we must hear it, nevertheless."

"It's like this. On the day of Sarah Gittings' murder—that afternoon in fact—a clerk in our office opened the safe at Florence Gunther's request, and left her there to secure certain documents. Later on she returned these papers, and he closed and locked the safe. She was a trusted employee, and everything apparently was all right.

"When Mr. Somers died, however, in my absence Mr. Henderson, who knew about the will, went to the safe for the duplicate and found that it was gone.

"No suspicion attached itself to Florence Gunther, who had herself gone with me on both days to the hotel and who had later witnessed the will. But during the intervening time she had been murdered, and naturally everything pertaining to her had become a matter of great interest.

"Four days ago Mr. Henderson telegraphed me that the will was missing, and to come back. When he met me at the train this morning he told me that one of our clerks, a man named Lowrie, had remembered that on the afternoon of the day Sarah Gittings was killed he had seen Florence Gunther on the street; that he saw her meet a heavy-set woman whom he believes now, from the published photographs, to have been Sarah Gittings, and there on the street pass to her a long envelope of the legal type.

"If that is true, it is at least possible that the duplicate of the will was in that envelope."

Jim spoke for the first time, trying to control his mouth.

"Why would she have done that?"

Mr. Waite considered.

"She was a reliable woman," he said. "If she did that at all, and I am only telling you the office talk, she meant to show that will to Miss Gittings and then to put it back in the safe. But things happened and—Mr. Henderson has been to the police, and it was not found among her effects. The effects of either of the two women."

"But why have shown it to Sarah?" Jim insisted. "She knew about it. She'd witnessed it."

"She had no idea of the contents."

"Florence Gunther knew the terms, I suppose?"

"Naturally. She had typed it. I have had very little time to think, but it strikes me that these two women met, and that the will came up for discussion. One of our strictest rules is that such matters are kept absolutely secret so far as our office force is concerned, and Florence Gunther was no talker. Besides, in this case there had been particular instructions that the existence of this document remain confidential, so I cannot understand—"

"Who gave you those instructions?" Katherine interrupted.

"Mr. Somers himself."

"Now about this fund, this fifty thousand dollars," Alex Davis said. "He merely said that Walter Somers would understand?"

"That is all. Naturally I wondered, but it was not my affair. He was not a man to explain why he was doing certain things. I rather thought that the family understood."

Katherine looked at him.

"Understood? With the entire proceeding to be secret and confidential!"

"I didn't think of it in that light. It might, of course, refer to charity."

"Charity! And given to Walter Somers to disburse! I'm not an idiot, Mr. Waite, and I give you credit for more intelligence than that."

"Perhaps if you talk to Walter?"

"What good would that do? He's as secretive as his father, and not so honest. I know what you think, Mr. Waite; I know what you thought when you were drawing that will. You thought Howard Somers had been leading a secret life, and that this provision was to provide for somebody. Well, I do not believe that, and I'll fight that clause, and this will in court if it ruins me."

That was all. Katherine rose, and the men scrambled to their feet. She gave to each of them a steady look, said, "Thank you, you have been very good to come," and then turned and went out.

I did not see her again until dinner.

During the afternoon however, I heard Judy telephoning Wallie, and he came at six o'clock. From six until almost seven he was closeted with Katherine in her room, and the very fact that their voices were never raised seemed to me an indication of the tenseness of that meeting.

There was no compromise in either of them. Only suspicion and jealousy on Katherine's part, and a fury of hatred and revenge in Wallie. I know now that a little gentleness, some remorse for that tragic youth of his, and he would have weakened. But poor Katherine was as she was; she made no play for sympathy. She sat perfectly still and interrogated him.

"You refuse to say what this secret fund was for? Or for whom?"

"Absolutely."

"You know what you are doing, of course. You are allowing your father's memory to be besmirched. For I warn you I shall take this will into court."

"Then it will be you who are doing the soiling," he said, and stood turning the ring around his finger.

Just before seven he went down the stairs and out the front door. I was sitting in the library, but he did not turn his head.

In the meantime other things were happening of which we

had no knowledge at the time. We knew of course that Mr. Henderson had been to the District Attorney, and that the police had learned that the two murdered women had been the witnesses to the second will.

But we knew nothing of the activities of the night watchman in New York, Charles Parrott.

He was shrewd enough, this Parrott, but even a stupid man might have been suspicious. Here was Howard receiving a secret visitor at two in the morning, a man who ducked in past him, with his cap drawn down over his head, a large ulster overcoat and a muffler about the lower part of his face. And in the morning Howard was dead.

That apparently roused no suspicion in itself. But two things followed it. One was that fatal attempt of Mary Martin's to bribe him to say nothing of the night visitor. That had failed, and so she had vanished. Then there was that early morning search of mine. He was still on duty, and the sight of a woman of my age wandering in that courtyard in the rain and carefully inspecting the ground must have been unusual, to say the least.

And then came that fatal move by Dick Carter the day of the funeral.

"Which one is it?" Parrott had asked.

"Dark coat and striped trousers," said Dick.

"Well, he's the same build. I didn't see much of his face."

He read the papers, and he knew Sarah Gittings; knew about her murder too, and Florence's, the "Shoe" murders.

He went to Evans, the valet, a day or so later.

"Did you see Mr. Somers when he died? I mean before he'd been moved?"

"I did," said Evans with dignity.

"How about his feet? Did he have anything on them?"

"I believe he was in his stockings," said Evans, and through the simple and fortuitous circumstance that poor Howard had dropped his slippers before he picked up his highball, Parrott went to the police!

The rest is shrouded in mystery. Some time toward the end of that week a lieutenant from the homicide squad in New York took a train and saw Inspector Harrison and the District Attorney. On Monday an order was obtained to disinter Howard's body, and a secret examination made. Nothing was given out, even Katherine did not know.

But it was discovered that Howard Somers had died, not of an acute heart attack, but of cyanide of potassium, "probably administered in whisky."

Cyanide of potassium! And Howard had had a cold, and could not detect its peculiar and unmistakable odor; and Mary Martin had opened the windows, so that no one else might notice it. Opened the windows and broken the glass.

They kept their secret well, did the authorities. After all, murder had not been proved; men with hopelessly broken health had killed themselves before this. And our own local authorities were not minded to let go of Jim, anyhow. They had Jim, and now they had the motive.

Mr. Waite saw the District Attorney that afternoon, Tuesday, the seventeenth. I think myself that he was frightened. And small wonder. Of the three who had met in that room at the Imperial Hotel only he himself was left.

He must have been worried; he must have wondered how long he had left for those little vacations to cure his arthritis, for the pleasant routine of his office, for his golf and bridge, for the little dinners with good wines and his friends about him.

So it is not extraordinary that he went to the District Attorney that morning after he left us, and asked for police protection. Or that in doing so he virtually signed Jim Blake's death warrant. The District Attorney listening absorbedly and Mr. Waite telling that story.

"And what do you make out of it, Waite? There was still a valid copy of the will among Somers' papers."

"Wills have been destroyed before this."

"You think the Gittings woman got the copy to show Blake, and then he killed her?"

"He may have, hoping to get hold of the original later."

"And later on the Gunther girl got troublesome and had to be put out of the way?"

"Something like that, perhaps. I don't know. It's damned sordid. Only I don't want to be the next to go!"

"You're all right. As for its being sordid, almost all motives for crimes are sordid; cupidity, sex, jealousy. Sordid, all of them, but actuating motives just the same. Well, you don't need a policeman; we'll get this bird now, thank God. The press has been yelling for weeks, and I've had a few letters myself."

That was on Tuesday afternoon, May the seventeenth.

That night the District Attorney sent for Jim to question him for the second time, and in Jim's absence they searched his house; issuing a search warrant on a trumped-up charge against Amos for bootlegging.

For the sake of form two Federal officers ostensibly conducted the search, but Inspector Harrison actually did so. Amos opened the door, and protested violently that he knew nothing of any liquor. But they pushed past him and went upstairs, taking him along. In Jim's room they found the golf suit and the shoes which Amos admitted Jim had worn the night of Sarah's death, and later they smuggled them out. Also they discovered that Jim had recently burned some letters, and Inspector Harrison spent some time on his knees examining the fireplace.

But they still had that pretense of bootlegged liquor to carry out, and they had not found the sword-stick. So they went over the house. Amos was calmer by that time. It was only when they got to the door of the cellar that he showed excitement.

"Nothing down there but the furnace, sir," he said to the Inspector.

That made them suspicious, so they went down and turned on the lights. At first glance it was unsatisfactory; a cement floor, a white-washed brick wall. They went over that wall carefully for loose bricks, but there were none. They were quite sure by that time that Amos was uneasy. Indeed, one of the Federal officers drew a notebook from his pocket and pretended to write down a memorandum. When he had finished he passed the note to the Inspector.

"I guess that's correct, Inspector?"

"I believe so," said the Inspector.

But what he had read was this:

"Watch the darky. He's scared."

They started to search again.

CHAPTER SEVENTEEN

THERE IS no record of that scene in the District Attorney's office, but from what we know now, and from what was brought out at the trial, I can measurably reconstruct it. Jim, wary and uneasy, holding one of his eternal cigars in a mouth that twitched steadily, taking the opportunity they offered of lighting them, the careful bestowal of their ashes, to think; and the District Attorney, firing questions at him, endlessly, interminably.

"You knew nothing whatever of this will, then?"

"I never heard of it until Alex Davis told me, in New York."

"He told you you had been disinherited?"

"Yes. That didn't bother me. What worried me was my sister."

"Why?"

"That's evident, isn't it? She was devoted to her husband. She had to learn that without her knowledge he had done a thing which affected her child as well as herself."

"And in favor of her stepson."

"Yes."

"What were her relations to this stepson? Friendly?"

And Jim pausing, lighting a fresh cigar, or pulling on the one he had.

"Not entirely. The usual difficulty. He resented her."

"And she resented him?"

"Probably. Somewhat."

"You're fond of your sister, Mr. Blake?"

"Very. She is all I have."

"You saw this second will in New York?"

"I did."

"Do you remember how the envelope was marked?"

"Yes. Perfectly."

"It was endorsed in Mr. Somers' own writing, 'To be handed to my son Walter in the event of my death.' Is that right?"

"Yes."

"Why was that, Mr. Blake?"

"I don't know."

"Doesn't it show that Mr. Somers wanted to be certain that this will reached his son's hands? That there would be no—interference?"

"You can construe it that way if you like."

"You had no knowledge of this will when you made that night visit to Howard Somers?"

"I never made such a visit. How could I? You've had men watching me for weeks."

"Now, on the night of Sarah Gittings' death, I want you to describe your movements."

"I have said all I intend to say. I went out for a walk. After I had started I remembered that my sister, calling from New York, had given me a message for Sarah. I went to a drugstore and telephoned, but she had gone out."

"What was this message from your sister to Sarah Gittings?"

"I've told you that. She wanted her to look after my niece, Judy. There was a young man here she was fond of. My sister didn't approve."

"After you telephoned, where did you go?"

"I walked on. I went to see a woman. I don't intend to say more. Then I started back."

"That would have been when?"

"Perhaps nine o'clock. I don't know exactly."

The District Attorney bent forward.

"And you still decline to give the direction you took?"

"I do. I have done nothing wrong. I decline to be put on the offensive."

"But suppose I show you the route you took that night, Mr. Blake? Suppose I tell you that from that drugstore you went to the path through the Larimer lot, and down that path to the park? And that later you returned by the same route? I warn you, Mr. Blake, that we know a great deal, and that you are only damaging yourself by these evasions."

And still Jim obstinately silent, and the District Attorney leaning back in his chair and watching him.

"You carried the sword-stick that night?"

"I told you before that I did."

"Did you see Sarah Gittings during that walk?"

"No. Absolutely not."

"Yet you were on that path that night, Mr. Blake. We know that. You went down that path into the park, and later on you went up again. At one point you stopped for some time. You either sat or stood on that hillside, and you smoked a cigar. You were not alone at that time. A man does not pause on a dark hillside on a cool spring night to look at nature."

And then Jim made his unconscious admission.

"I was alone. Absolutely alone."

"Ah! you admit then that you were there?"

"I was there, yes."

"You met nobody? Talked to nobody?"

"I did not."

"At what time were you there?"

And again that almost infinitesimal pause, and Jim mopping his forehead.

"I went down about half past seven."

"And you came back?"

"Something after nine."

"And reached your house a little after ten? Come, come, Mr. Blake, that's childish."

"I don't know the time."

"What route did you follow, coming back?"

"I cut across the park, coming up by the bridle path near Miss Bell's house. From there I walked along the Avenue."

"That would take you past the Larimer lot where the dogs were tied at about what time?"

"Possibly a quarter past nine."

"And you carried the sword-stick?"

"Yes."

"Why?"

"There had been some hold-ups around the park. I don't own a revolver, so I carried the stick."

"You saw or heard nothing suspicious? Near the lot, I mean?"

"I heard some dogs barking."

"Where?"

"Back on the Larimer lot."

"You knew Miss Bell's dogs well, didn't you?"

"Yes."

"Well enough to recognize the noise they made? A dog's bark is as individual as a man's voice, Mr. Blake."

"I didn't recognize them, no."

"Where did you put the sword-stick, on your return?"

"In the hall, with my others."

"And it disappeared from there?"

There must have been a slight delay, a slower reaction to that question.

"It disappeared. Yes."

"Just when?"

"I don't know. I was ill at the time."

"How did you learn that it was gone?"

"I had gone into the hall to call Amos. I looked down, and it was not there."

"You didn't ask Amos about it?"

"I don't recall. I think possibly I did."

"And he said it was missing?"

"That's the way I remember it."

"Now, Mr. Blake, I am going to the night of the twenty-seventh of April. Where were you that night?"

"The twenty-seventh of April?"

"The night Judy Somers was struck down in the Bell garage."

Jim stared across the desk.

"You are not intimating that I attacked my own niece, are you?"

"I have asked you a question."

"I was at home. So far as I can recall, I have not been out of the house at night since Sarah Gittings was killed. And I certainly never struck Judy. That's—that's ridiculous."

The District Attorney glanced at the paper in front of him.

"Do you recall the night when Miss Bell went to see you, after Florence Gunther's body was found?"

"Perfectly."

"Had you sent for her?"

"No."

"Not telephoned, or sent any message?"

"None whatever."

"She walked over?"

"Yes."

"But you sent her home in your car?"

"I did."

"During the course of that visit, were the two crimes discussed?"

"Somewhat."

"Did you make any suggestion to Miss Bell about your car?"

"I don't know what you mean. It had been her car. I bought it from her."

"There was nothing said about the carpet of that car?"

"Nothing."

"Do you keep the mileage of this car, Mr. Blake?"

"No. Amos may. I don't know."

"Who carries the key to the garage?"

"Amos. I don't drive myself."

"You don't know how to drive?"

"I can drive, but I dislike it."

"Is the window of the garage kept locked?"

"Usually. Not necessarily."

"If some one entered the garage by a window, could he take the car out?"

"Yes. The doors to the alley are bolted. The key is to the small door into the garden."

"That is, some one who wished to take out the car could climb through the window, providing it was not locked, and take the car out?"

"Probably. The window is rather high."

"But if he took a chair from the garden it would be easy?"

"I imagine so. I hadn't thought of it."

"So that if Amos had the key, it would still be possible to take the car out?"

"I never crawled through a window and took that car out. If that's what you mean."

"Do you know Miss Bell's garage?"

"I've been in it once or twice."

"It overlooks the ravine in the park, doesn't it?"

"Yes."

"Do you know the tool room?"

"I've never been in it."

"But you know she keeps a ladder there?"

"I know she has a ladder. I don't know where she keeps it."

This, or something very like it, went on for hours. And some time in that long interrogation they brought in the man Parrott. He came in on some excuse or other, looked Jim over and went out again. Jim was not suspicious.

But by midnight he was showing signs of exhaustion, and even the District Attorney showed strain. It was a warm spring night. The men who came and went had taken off their coats, but Jim still sat there in his hard chair, neat and tidy, and twitching, and faced them all down.

"You still decline to account for the time between seven o'clock and ten-thirty, on the night of April eighteenth?"

"I shall do that if necessary. Not before."

"What were your relations with Sarah Gittings?"

"Relations? I knew her, of course. Had known her for years."

"In case of distress she might come to you?"

"She might, yes."

"Then this letter to you would not be unusual."

"I never received a letter from her. Why should she write me? She could have seen me at any time."

"We have absolute proof that she did write to you, Mr. Blake. And we believe that you received the letter."

"You can't prove that."

"Perhaps not, but I can damned well try. Some one made an appointment to meet Sarah Gittings on the night she was killed; to meet her and see with his own eyes this copy of Howard Somers' will which the Gunther girl had abstracted from the files. From that appointment Sarah Gittings never returned, and during that evening the copy of the will disappeared."

"Why should I destroy it? Or her? The original document was safe in New York."

"Did you know Florence Gunther?"

"No."

"Never saw her?"

"No."

"Never waited for her on Halkett Street, near a fruit stand, with a car?"

"Absolutely no."

And, if the two previous denials had lacked force, this last was impressive enough.

But the heat and the tension were telling on them both. Hours had passed, putting a fine edge on Jim's nerves. He had exhausted his cigars, and no one offered him any. He asked for water, and after a long delay it came.

And then, on top of his exhaustion he was told that Howard

Somers had been poisoned. He very nearly collapsed, but if they had hoped to wear him into confession they were disappointed. He was still fighting. But he said a curious thing.

"How do you know he was poisoned? How do you know he didn't take the stuff himself?"

"I'm not answering questions. I'm asking them."

Jim was angry now, however, and he braced himself for one last effort.

"I never went to New York to see Howard Somers the night he died. Some one else used my name, that's all. And the more I think over this case—and God knows it's all I do think of—the more I am convinced that a definite attempt is being made to put the guilt on me.

"Why would I have killed him? I stood to lose by his death, not to gain. He was my sister's husband and my friend. If you are trying to show that I escaped the watch on my house, climbed the window of my garage and drove my car to New York that night, I swear before God that I never did it, or thought of it. As for this will, I had never heard of a second will until Alex Davis revealed its existence in New York.

"I swear before God that I have never killed any one, have never thought of killing any one. And I protest against your methods. You are wearing me out. But you can't wear me into confession. I'm innocent."

They had worn him out, however. His face was gray with exhaustion, and sweat was running down his face. Now and then he ran his finger under his collar, as though it choked him. The whirring of an electric fan, the tick of a clock on the wall, and the District Attorney never relaxing; watching him, firing at him his staccato questions, deliberately trying to torture him until confession would be sheer relief.

Some time in that last half hour a memorandum was placed on the desk, and the District Attorney nodded his head.

"Send him in when he comes."

Jim had listened, with an impassive face. But he felt—perhaps his exhaustion had sharpened his faculties—that something vital had happened. The questions began again, sharper, a little excitement in them.

"You have admitted that on the night Sarah Gittings was killed, you carried with you this sword-stick, and that later on it disappeared. You had no theories about that disappearance?"

"None whatever."

"You left it in the hall and it disappeared?"

"Yes."

"And when did you notice that it had disappeared?"

"It was several days later. I don't know exactly."

"I think you do know exactly, Mr. Blake. It disappeared on the day Sarah Gittings' body was found."

"Possibly. I'm not certain."

"What is your explanation of that disappearance?"

"I've told you that before. I think it was stolen."

"As a part of the plot against you?"

"Possibly."

"You did not conceal it yourself? I mean, you did not feel that its presence was a dangerous thing in your house?"

"I thought of that, naturally. Yes."

"But you did not hide it."

Jim made an effort, moistened his dry lips.

"Not exactly. I put it in a closet."

"What closet?"

"The liquor closet, in the hall."

"And you locked it there?"

"Yes."

"Then the story that it was missing from the hall was not true?"

"Not entirely. But it is true that it disappeared. It was taken from there."

"You had the key to that closet?"

"Yes."

"Was there more than one key?"

"No. I have wondered since if Amos took it. I was in bed. He could have taken the key."

"And why would Amos do that?"

He was utterly confused by that time, faint, sagged in his chair and gray of face.

"He may have known—he may have thought—"

"What did Amos know?"

And then Inspector Harrison walked into the room, and laid something on the table. Jim took one look at it, and fainted dead away.

CHAPTER EIGHTEEN

IN THE cellar Inspector Harrison had renewed his prowling about, the Federal officers mildly interested, and Amos watching his movements with a sort of fascinated terror.

He rapped on the cement walls again, inspected the ceiling. Now and then, furtively, he looked at the negro, and it seemed to him that the negro was increasingly alarmed each time he neared the coal cellar. But the coal cellar was full of coal. It had overflowed into the main cellar, and lay about. And suddenly Inspector Harrison remembered that it was spring.

"Plenty of coal, for the summer?" he said to Amos. "Cook with coal?"

"No sir. With gas," said Amos.

"And when did you get in all this coal?"

"I don't rightly remember, sir. Seems to me it was in May some time."

Inspector Harrison stooped down, and cleared a few lumps from the margin of the heap.

"What's under here? Cement?"

"I don't rightly know, sir."

But it was not cement.

There was a shovel on the coal, and at first they put Amos to work on it. He was terrified. He made noisy protests, but there were three of them, grim and determined. They were not inhuman, however, for as the negro began to play out they took the shovel from him. One after the other, they dug into the coal, throwing it out into the clean cemented floor, scrutinizing it, and then falling to work again. It required more than two hours to clear the place, but at last they reached the end and they had found nothing.

There was the hard-pounded black earth, glistening with black dust under their flashlights, and no sign that it had been disturbed. One of the men laughed.

"Well, that's that," he said, "and now I want a bath and a bed. Let's go."

But the Inspector was not listening. He was watching Amos, and Amos was smiling again.

"If that's all you gentlemen want," he said, "you all can go up and I'll put out the light."

The Inspector was wiping his face, which was streaming.

"What's the hurry, Amos?" he said gently.

"There's no liquor here, sir. You've seen for yourself."

"Have I? Well, maybe that's so. Now, Amos, if you'll go wherever you have to go to get a bucket of water, and will bring it here—"

"There's a lavatory on the first floor, sir."

"Do what you're told," the Inspector said sharply. "And be quick about it."

The Federal officers were examining their hands for blisters and swearing at the dust. Amos went cheerfully up the cellar stairs, and came back in a moment with his pail. He carried soap and a towel also, and his face was a study when the Inspector passed them back to him.

The next procedure, however, astounded the negro. With one of the officers holding a light close to the surface of the ground, the Inspector went over it carefully. He would pour a little water on the earth and watch it, then move on, repeating the performance.

Suddenly he muttered something and asked for the shovel. Amos gave it to him, his eyes fixed on the earth, his color the peculiar gray of the terrified negro.

And there, not more than a foot beneath the surface, Inspector Harrison came across the sword-stick.

I can still see the rather smug complacence of his manner at the trial.

"I then sent Amos for a pail of water."

"Perhaps you would better explain to the jury your purpose in sending for that water."

"In case of buried objects the surface of the ground may not appear to have been disturbed. In case however that it has been recently dug up, small bubbles of air will appear when water has been poured over it."

"And were there such bubbles?"

"Plenty of them."

So there they stood in that cellar, the four of them. One of the Federal officers whistled softly. Amos was staring at the thing, pop-eyed with terror. It must have savored to him of witchcraft, that discovery; this detective, this policeman, muttering incantations to himself and then turning out that weapon into the cruel light.

"My Gawd Amighty!" said Amos, and turning, ran up the stairs.

They did not bother to follow him. The Inspector carefully wrapped the thing in paper, and some one telephoned to the District Attorney's office. They had been holding poor Jim for the message.

But they held him after the message also. Jim Blake was placed under arrest that night, and within three days he had been indicted by the Grand Jury for the murder of Sarah Gittings.

He was to be tried only for the murder of poor Sarah, but in the opinion of the public at that time Jim Blake was guilty of two, and in the minds of the police, of a third one.

Press comment was universally approving. That the police would not have taken this drastic step "without good and sufficient reason"; that "murder is murder, whether committed by the gangster or by the individual in high place in the community"; that "the District Attorney's office is to be congratulated in having at last taken steps to solve these crimes," these were some of the comments.

Jim had been arrested after one o'clock Tuesday night, or rather early Wednesday morning, the eighteenth. Sarah had been dead for precisely a month.

We were stunned with horror. It came as less of a surprise to me than to the others, but it was a shock for all that.

We did little or nothing that first day. Jim was in a cell in the jail and had sent for his lawyer, Godfrey Lowell. Late in the day Godfrey came in to see me, and his face was very grave. Jim's cell was damp and the food terrible, but these things he passed by with a gesture.

"He's not telling all he knows," he said. "He says he's innocent, and I believe he is. But he isn't frank. He's holding something back."

Nevertheless, Jim's story as Godfrey told it to us that afternoon in the library, was sufficiently damning. Katherine hardly spoke during that recital. Dick sat holding Judy's hand, but I doubt if Katherine noticed it.

Briefly, Jim admitted having had an appointment to meet Sarah that night, but not in the park or by letter. She had, he maintained, telephoned him. "I have never received a letter from her, then, or at any time." In this message, evidently sent after she had met Florence Gunther on the street and received the envelope, she had asked him to meet her that night on a very urgent matter.

The address she gave was a house on Halkett Street, and he determined to walk, going by way of the park.

On the way, however, he found that he had left the house number in his other clothing—he had changed to a walking suit—and he stopped at a drugstore to call her up. She had started, however; he talked to Judy for a moment and then went on, taking the short cut through the corner of the Larimer lot.

He remembered that the house was in the seventeen hundred block on Halkett Street, and that he was to ask for a Miss Gunther. When he reached the block in question he had walked along slowly, and at one of the houses a youngish woman was waiting on the steps.

He asked if she knew of a Miss Gunther in the vicinity, and she said that that was her name, and that Sarah had not yet arrived.

They went together into the house and waited in the parlor. It was a boarding house, but although the door into the hall was open, he saw no one except a colored woman who passed by shortly before he left.

The Gunther woman had been silent and very nervous. As

time went on and Sarah did not arrive she seemed almost hysterical, and at twenty minutes to ten he had gone away, still in the dark as to why he had been there at all.

"Florence Gunther apparently refused to tell him," Godfrey said. "He came home by the same route, mystified over the whole business. He reached the path up the hill at or about ten o'clock, stopped to rest halfway up and then went on. He maintains that he knew nothing about Sarah until he got your word that she was missing, and that he never saw her that night at all."

"And the sword-stick?" Judy asked. "What does he say about that?"

"That he hid it in the closet, but he did not bury it."

Katherine spoke, after a long silence.

"When they found the stick, I suppose they had searched the house?"

"I understand that they did, and that they found certain things which they believe strengthen the case."

"His letters? Everything?"

"He had burned his letters. He had felt that this was coming, and yesterday he more or less got ready. Nothing important, he says, but he didn't care to have them going through his papers."

I thought that Katherine looked relieved.

I have re-read that paragraph. I know now that she was relieved. But I do not know even now what she had thought of that frantic inquiry of his, and his warning to send the reply by hand. It was burned, anyhow. She must have found some comfort in that.

How could she know that after that scene in the District Attorney's office Inspector Harrison had gone back to Jim's house, armed with a small box and a delicate pair of tweezers, and had taken from the grate in that handsome room of Jim's certain charred and blackened fragments of paper ash.

Some time, that day or the next, he must have spent a painful hour over them. They had to be steamed and softened, and then they had to be laid out on a gummed paper and carefully pressed down. But he had his reward in the end. He had one sentence of nine words.

It must have puzzled him, however.

Late that evening the Inspector came in to see me, but he made no mention of his discovery in the fireplace. He seemed indeed to be rather apologetic, and he broke numberless toothpicks into fragments and strewed the floor with them.

He had to tell me that Howard had been poisoned, and he plainly hated doing it.

"No need of telling Mrs. Somers or Miss Judy," he said. "After all, he may have done it himself, although that would be small comfort to them." He looked at me. "Everything all right with them?" he asked. "Happy married life, and so on?"

"Absolutely. He never killed himself, Inspector."

"Maybe not. Cyanide of potassium," he said reflectively. "Quick and sure, but no imagination in it. No real imagination in any of these murders, for that matter. Now Walter has imagination; Blake hasn't."

"Walter?" I said sharply.

"He didn't commit them, of course. Why should he? Leave out his affection for his father, and still he wouldn't. The copy of the will is missing. To kill the witnesses wouldn't get him anywhere. No, Walter Somers is out. I don't have too much faith in alibis, but he didn't do it."

Before he left he told me that the Grand Jury would have the case by Friday, and that it would undoubtedly bring in a true bill. But he did not seem particularly happy over it.

"The more I study crime," he said, "the less I know about the criminal. Take this case: these three murders were cold and audacious. They were committed by a man without fear and without scruple. They were fiendishly clever.

"Yet we run into this situation; we find and arrest the criminal, because he has not been clever at all. He has buried his weapon in his house, although if he killed Somers he could have dropped it into a dozen streams on that trip of his. He has absolute nerve, a thing few men possess, and he faints when he is confronted with it. He is strong enough to get into that airshaft and to pull himself out later—a thing I couldn't do, and I'm a strong man for my age—and here's his doctor swearing he's a sick man, has been sick for several years.

"I've built this case. I've got evidence enough to convict Jim Blake and still have some left over. But I'm not satisfied. Not yet anyhow."

He broke three toothpicks in rapid succession.

"Personally, I don't believe we have scratched the surface of this thing. Go back to the night Miss Judy was hurt. And, by the way, has she ever told you why she went to the garage that night?"

"She said she wanted a foot rule."

"But she asked Joseph where the ladder was kept, didn't she?"

"Yes."

"Now what did she want with that ladder? To look at it or to use it?"

"I haven't an idea, Inspector."

"Curious," he said. "She had something in her mind. She's shrewd. Now let's go over that night."

"Joseph has heard the dogs barking in the shrubbery; they stop suddenly, as though they had recognized the intruder. You and Joseph start to the garage, and Joseph hears something. He calls 'What's that?' There is no answer, and you both go on. Some one is in the shrubbery, or has passed through it. The next day I find footprints there; not the original ones. Planted. And by the way, those prints were made by a woman's shoe. I've done some work on them! Not shoes from this house, however. Joseph and I have seen to that.

"But here's the point. Miss Judy was hurt at ten o'clock, and it was two when Norah saw this figure in the grounds.

"And here is what I want to know. Where would Jim Blake go, between ten and two o'clock at night, to get a pair of shoes belonging to a heavy woman who walked on the outsides of her feet? He has no women in his house. Even his laundry goes out.

"And why would Jim Blake cover those footprints as skillfully as he did, and then bury that cane in his cellar? The act of a fool or a lunatic, and the man who made those prints was neither."

"Have you told the District Attorney all this, Inspector?"

"He wants an indictment. That's his business." And he added: "A man who's been indicted by the Grand Jury has a pretty hard time of it. His trial may prove him innocent, but he's got the stigma anyhow."

He picked up a pencil from my desk, examined it, laid it down.

"Let's go back still farther," he said, "to when Blake first talked to you about Sarah Gittings' disappearance. When was that, and where?"

"In this room, the next day. When she did not come back I sent for him. He was uneasy, but that was all."

"You recall nothing else?"

"Nothing important. I remember now that he asked about Howard."

"What did he ask?"

"It was something about his health, and if he was able to travel; if he had been here lately."

The Inspector slid forward on his chair.

"That's an interesting point. Now why would he ask such a question? The talk, I gather, had been about Sarah Gittings?"

"Entirely."

"And he knew Mr. Somers' condition, of course. Did you understand from that that he had reasons for thinking that Somers had been in town?"

"Yes. I remember that it surprised me. He asked me if I was certain that Howard had not been in town. I thought it unlikely, myself."

"I suppose you have no reason to think that he had been here?" And when I shook my head, "Don't answer that too quickly. Think it over, Miss Bell. Sometimes we think we know all about certain individuals, only to find that we know nothing at all. Why did Howard Somers secretly alter his will last summer while he was here? What is this secret fund of fifty thousand dollars? And what made Mr. Blake ask if he had been here recently?"

"I don't believe Howard was here. He was ill, and his wife seldom left him."

"But it would be possible? Some night when his wife had retired early? Or was out to dinner? He had a fast car, of course, and a dependable chauffeur."

"Possibly? Yes, I daresay. But why?"

"That's the point, exactly. If you can induce Mr. Blake to tell his attorneys why he asked you that question it might be helpful." He moved impatiently.

"If people only told all they knew, there would be no miscarriages of justice. But out of fear or self-interest or the idea of protecting somebody they keep their mouths shut, and so we have these mysteries. Look at you yourself; you burn that carpet, and produce evidence against Jim Blake that to the average jury is enough to send him to the chair! Why did you burn it? What did you find that we'd overlooked? I'd been over that carpet with a fine tooth comb."

"And there was no oil on it?"

"Oil! You found oil on that carpet?"

"I did indeed. A ring of oil."

He got up and reached for his hat.

"It may interest you to know," he said, "that there was no oil on that carpet when I examined it, the morning after Florence Gunther's murder."

But whatever conclusion he drew from that, his last speech that night was small comfort to me.

"Well, I don't see how that will help with a jury," he said, rather heavily. "On the surface it's a water-tight case, Miss Bell. He had the weapon and the motive. The only thing he didn't have—and you'll have to excuse the word—was the guts. Mind you," he added, "I'm not saying that Blake is innocent. He looks as guilty as hell. But I am saying that there are discrepancies, and I've got to have an explanation of some of them."

CHAPTER NINETEEN

THAT WAS on Wednesday the eighteenth, a month after Sarah's death and about six weeks before Joseph was shot.

I went upstairs that night exhausted both mentally and physically, to find Judy curled on my bed and very despondent.

"Let me stay awhile," she pleaded. "Until mother comes in, anyhow. I want to talk."

"I didn't know she had gone out," I said in surprise.

"She took Robert and the car. I think she went to Uncle Jim's. To Pine Street."

That surprised me, but Judy explained that it was to select some clothing to be sent to the jail.

"Only why would it take her all this time—" she added, almost pettishly.

"I didn't hear the car."

"You're a little deaf, you know, Elizabeth Jane. I wouldn't be surprised if a lot goes on that you don't hear. Or hear about."

"What goes on that I don't hear about?"

"You didn't hear Elise scream last night."

"I had taken a sleeping tablet," I said with dignity. "And what did Elise scream about?"

"She saw the ghost," said Judy.

And when I came to examine that story, and to talk to Elise, I had to admit that she had seen something.

The Frenchwoman was still pale when I saw her. It appears that she had wanted to tell me the story, but that Joseph had sternly ordered her to keep quiet. Also that she was under no circumstances to tell the women servants, or she might "have the cooking and housework on her hands." That seems to have been sufficient, but she had told Judy, talking in her rapid gesticulating French.

But her story gained credibility by the fact that she spoke no English, although she had understood Joseph well enough. She could have had no knowledge of the talk in the kitchen and servants' hall, and indeed Joseph had told me later that he had warned both women to keep their mouths closed over the whole business.

Her story, punctuated by dramatic pauses where Judy saw that my French was inadequate, was as follows:

She was occupying Mary Martin's room, and the night as I have said was sultry and like midsummer. She went to bed leaving her door open, but the breeze was from the opposite side of the house. She got up and opened the door across, thinking that it belonged to a room there.

It was, however, the door to the attic staircase which she had opened, and she was surprised to find not only the steps but that a faint light was going somewhere above.

She was curious rather than alarmed. In her bare feet and night dress she went on up quietly, but not thinking of caution. However, near the top she must have made some sound. She had only an instant to see a white figure bending over something. The next moment she was stumbling down the staircase.

But she was not quick enough. The thing, and she shuddered when she said it, the thing overtook her and passed her. She felt the brushing of its spectral garments, as she put it, and it was then that she screamed.

When Joseph found her—the women would not stir out of their rooms—she was locked in her room and was still screaming. It was some time before he could induce her to open her door.

When I talked to her, which was that night, she was still sitting in Katherine's room and obstinately refusing to go to bed.

"I think you dreamed it, Elise," said Judy. "What's the use of being a fool? There is no such thing as a ghost."

"I saw it. I touched it, mademoiselle."

"Well, you can't touch a ghost. And mind you, nothing of this nonsense to mother. Go to bed and say your prayers. That ought to help."

We had to take her up ourselves finally, and wait until she was safely locked in. Then and only then did Judy look directly at me.

"Now," she said. "She saw something, or somebody. She may be an idiot, but I'll say this for her. It takes a lot to keep her out of her bed."

Together we went up to the attic, but although it was rather ghastly at that hour of the night, I could not find that anything had been disturbed. Judy, it appeared, had been up before, and had found nothing.

It was from Joseph, still waiting in the pantry to admit Katherine, that I secured what looked like a partial explanation.

"The sewing room window on the second floor was open," he said. "I think he got out there, madam. He could drop to the roof of the kitchen porch."

He had, it seems, instructed Elise to say that she had seen a mouse! Which, as Judy said, was from the sublime to the ridiculous.

Katherine came in very late, and I thought she looked rather better.

She had been going over Jim's house, she said, and she had decided to move over there.

"It looks as though I shall be here for some time, Elizabeth," she said. "At least until they have cleared Jim of this ridiculous trumped-up charge. And there are three of us. I don't like to crowd you. I can get the servants from New York, and be quite comfortable."

I made no demur. I saw that she was determined, although Judy looked rather unhappy over it.

"What will you do with Amos?"

"I shall let him go," she said with decision. "I don't like him and I don't trust him."

The net result of which was that Amos gave his damaging testimony before the Grand Jury and then disappeared.

That was on Friday, May the twentieth.

I daresay some such system must exist, but the whole proceeding drove me almost to madness. And it was sheer farce from beginning to end. The result was a foregone conclusion, with, as Godfrey Lowell says, the indictment typed and ready to sign before it began.

There was no chance from the first; from that sonorous opening by the District Attorney: "Gentlemen of the Grand Jury, it becomes my duty this morning to bring to your attention a most serious case. On the night of the eighteenth of April last, when most of us were peacefully asleep in our beds, a human life was ended under circumstances so brutal that they stun the normal mind. A woman named Sarah Gittings, a nurse, devoted solely to a career of service, was atrociously murdered." There followed certain details, dramatically presented, and after that: "Through the efforts of the police department an array of facts has been discovered, which point to a certain individual as the guilty man. These facts will now be presented to you by certain witnesses, and it is for you to decide whether a true bill shall be presented against this prisoner, or not.

"Shall we proceed, Mr. Foreman?"

From that until the end the mounting testimony against Jim was appalling. The District Attorney grew more and more unctuous, and his secret satisfaction was evident. When all was over he made, I believe, a dramatic gesture with his hands, and standing by the table, ran his eyes along the half circle of chairs.

"Gentlemen," he said, in a low voice. "I have done my duty. Now must you do yours."

As he closed the door behind him and stepped into the hall, Dick says that he was still acting for the benefit of the press men and the crowd. He stood still, half leaning against the door like an exhausted man, and mopped his forehead with a fine handkerchief, faintly scented. Then he drew himself up, justice personified, and marched along the corridor.

But in between those two dramatic moments were two days of sheer horror for us.

The secrecy of the procedure, the oaths of silence, the occasional cheerful amusement of the twenty-three men who sat in that semicircle of chairs, the terrified or determined faces of the witnesses, the avid crowd of reporters outside studying these faces as they came and went, and then rushing to their typewriters: "It is reported that Miss Bell stated—"

Building a case that might send a man to the chair, out of

staircase gossip, a look, a gesture, or such information as was refused by the District Attorney but managed somehow to reach them *via* his office.

Experts came and went. The heap of exhibits on the long table grew; poor Sarah's stained and pierced clothing, the ghastly fragments of Florence Gunther's checked dress and blue coat, for although Jim was only charged with Sarah's murder, there were no legal limits, no laws of testimony, to be considered before the Grand Jury.

The sword-stick was brought in, its ancient mechanism arousing a sort of childlike interest among the jurymen; and small boxes of earth, each duly ticketed and bearing the impress of the stick as Jim had touched the ground with it. And Dick telephoned once to say that there was a story among the newspaper men that something had been carried in, carefully covered with a cloth, and that the story was that a letter Jim had burned had been restored, and had been introduced as incriminating.

We were all in the library, and I thought Katherine started when Judy repeated this. But she said nothing. She sat staring at her emerald ring, and made no comment.

The list of exhibits grew. Sarah's uniform, with a mirror so that the writing on the sleeve might be read; the plaster casts of the foot marks Inspector Harrison had made in my garden; the snaps from the carpet which had been rescued from my furnace; even the pencil which Wallie had found in the airshaft, the fragments of broken glass from my drawing room door, the rope which had once tied the dogs, and had later on been used to drag poor Sarah's body down the hill; and certain pages in Sarah's own hand of her sick-room records, designed to show that the reversed writing on Sarah's sleeve was authentic.

There were photographs, also. Showing the sewer structure,

showing poor Sarah within it, showing the well-marked spot where the body had lain near the tree, and that room of hers as it was discovered the next day. Florence's room was there too, and Sarah's, in the disorder in which we had found it on the morning of the nineteenth of April.

It must have been like sitting through a crime play to those jurymen, lifted out of their humdrum lives into that welter of crime and clues and blood.

And against all that, what had we? My own testimony, received with evident scepticism, that the man on my stairs the night of Sarah's murder had not worn light golf knickers, but conventional trousers! At no time was it brought out that the stains in Jim's car had been put there later; were not there when the police examined it the following day. It was sufficient that I had burned the carpet. And when I suggested that any juryman over forty was welcome to try to hang in the light shaft by his hands, and then to try to pull himself out of it, there was general laughter.

There was also one other development which left us in little doubt of the final outcome. This was the introduction on the second day of the colored woman, Clarissa, from the Bassett house on Halkett Street.

It was Dick too who reported this to us. He had seen her taken in, uneasy and yet somehow deadly. A big woman, powerful and determined but frightened. When she came out her relief was manifest, and Dick took advantage of that relief. He followed her, caught her at a corner, and brought us what he had learned.

Briefly this woman, Clarissa, having positively identified Jim at the jail, stated that on the night of Sarah's murder he had spent some time at the Halkett Street house with Florence

Gunther. He had sat in the parlor with her for an hour or more, and she remembered that he had a stick.

That we already knew. But she had further testified that, going forward to lock the front door before leaving for the night, she had heard Jim speaking and that she remembered distinctly what he had said.

"He said: 'I'd better start, then. I may meet her on the way back.'"

Some little hope however we had on the second day. The jury sent out for copies of the two wills, and they were duly produced. It looked for a time as though they might be looking for a larger picture; that the clause referring to the fifty thousand dollars might lead elsewhere.

But to offset that the District Attorney produced those two exhibits which he had held for the psychological moment. He brought in Jim's walking suit and his golf shoes, to prove that by laboratory test there was blood in minute quantities on both. And he re-introduced the sword-stick.

The blade of the weapon had been carefully washed, but from inside the sheath, when it had been soaked in the laboratory, there had come a pine needle of the same variety as had been found on Sarah's clothing; and unmistakable traces of blood. Human blood.

It was after that that the District Attorney made his dramatic gesture.

"Gentlemen, I have done my duty. Now must you do yours."

I daresay none of us was greatly surprised at the outcome. Certainly at least twenty-two out of the twenty-three men on the Grand Jury believed Jim guilty, and the indictment was signed, late on the second day.

Katherine received the news better than I had expected.

"An indictment is not a verdict," she said, quoting Godfrey Lowell, no doubt.

Judy, however, took it very hard and as for Wallie, the effect on him seemed devastating. Newspaper extras had announced the result, and he came in while Judy and I were at dinner. Katherine had retired to her bed, and to tea and toast on a tray.

"The damned fools!" he said. "The—damned fools!"

Judy looked at him out of eyes that were red and swollen.

"Since when have you changed your mind? You were sure enough."

"Well, I was a damned fool myself. That's all. He didn't do it. And he'll never suffer for it; I promise you that, Judy. Nothing is going to happen to him."

"Even if you have to tell all you know? Why don't you do that now and save time? You might die or get run over, and then where is he?"

He said nothing. I had had a good look at him by that time and I must confess that his appearance shocked me. His clothes were unpressed; his eyes were congested, as from sleepless nights, and he had developed a curious *tic*; now and again, by some involuntary contraction of the muscles, his left shoulder lifted and his head jerked to the right. I saw that he tried to control it by keeping his left hand in his coat pocket, but in spite of him up would go the shoulder. It was pitiful.

I saw, too, that he had not wanted to come; that he had dreaded the visit, and that to reinforce his courage he had taken a drink or two before he started. Not that he showed any effect, but that the room was full of it.

Judy eyed him.

"You look terrible," she said. "And stop jerking. You'll have me doing it. Stop jerking and tell us where Mary Martin is."

He said he did not know, and sat in silence until we had finished. It was not until Judy had gone up to her mother and we had moved into the library that he spoke again.

"Look here," he said. "How soon are you going away for the summer?"

"How soon are they going to release Jim Blake?"

"That's ridiculous," he said sharply. "He's well enough where he is. He'll get some of the cocktails and food out of his system, that's all. They'll never send him to the chair. They can't send him to the chair. It's absurd."

But it seemed to me that he was listening to his own words, trying to believe them; and that when he looked at me his bloodshot eyes were pleading with me. "You believe that too, don't you?" they said. "They'll never send him to the chair. They can't send him to the chair. It's absurd."

"When I'm certain of that I shall go away. Not before, Wallie."

He jerked again, rather dreadfully.

"Not if I ask you to go?" he said.

"Why should you ask me to go?"

"Because I don't think you are safe here."

"Who could have any design against me? I have no enemies; no actively murderous ones anyhow. I mind my own business and my conscience is as clear as the ordinary run of consciences. Why should I run away?"

"I'm telling you. That's all. Get away, and get Judy away."

"Then you know something I don't know, and it is your business to tell me what it is."

He refused to be drawn, however, and with all the questions I had in mind, managed to get away before I could ask him any of them. Save one, and that had a curious effect on him.

"Can you tell me," I said, "why Mary Martin suggested to Judy that your father should not be left alone at night?"

"Because he was sick. That's enough, isn't it? Why try to read into this case something that isn't there? And why drag her in? She has nothing to do with the case. Absolutely nothing. She's as innocent as—as Judy."

I made my decision then, to tell him the facts as to his father's death. I told him as gently as I could, with my hand on his arm. But he showed no surprise and pretended none. Save that he grew a shade paler he kept himself well in hand.

I felt then that he had been certain of it from the day Howard died.

Jim was arraigned a day or so later. It was a hideous ordeal for him, and for the rest of us; the courtroom crowded, and the crowd hostile. It seemed to me that the concentrated hatred in that room was a menace in itself, that if thought is a force, as I believe that it is, there was enough malignancy there to have destroyed a man.

They had brought him from the jail in the Black Maria; very carefully dressed, he was, and holding his head high. He had not come alone. There were criminals with him, black and white and even one yellow man. He had to wait while they entered their pleas, and he fixed his eyes on Katherine. I saw her smile at him, and her whole face warmed. A queer woman, Katherine, filled with surprises.

He listened gravely to the reading of the indictment, and nodded a sort of mute thank-you to the clerk when he had finished. I saw him draw a long breath, and I fancy he had meant that his "Not guilty" was to be a full-bodied and manly thing, a ringing assertion of his innocence. But he failed. At the last moment he looked at the crowd, and its concentrated hatred struck him like a blow in the chest. I saw his spirit fall under it and lie there, a broken thing, and Judy moaned a little. His "Not guilty" was not heard beyond the front benches, and he knew it.

Some hysterical woman somewhere giggled, and he heard it. I have never seen such torture in a man's face. When they took him out he stopped at the prisoners' door, as though he would come back and face them down, but Godfrey Lowell put a hand on his arm, and he went out to face again the battery of news photographers waiting outside.

I have one of those pictures now. It shows him handcuffed to another prisoner and with his head bent. The other man is smiling.

CHAPTER TWENTY

So we entered into that period of dreadful waiting between the indictment and the trial. Not that the waiting was to be long. The prosecution was doing everything possible to get the case on the docket before court closed in June, and the press was urging haste.

On the twenty-fourth of May, Tuesday, Katherine moved into Jim's house, and took Judy with her. Apparently she paid no attention to the curious looks of the neighbors, or to the cars which halted in the street to survey the house. She was like a woman set apart, not so much hardened as isolated.

As Laura wrote: "She seems superhuman to me. I'd come on if she wanted me, but quite frankly she doesn't. And what is this mysterious fund, anyhow? Poor dear Howard leading a double life seems rather incredible, at his age and with that heart of his. As for the rest of it, I don't see why Wallie shouldn't have his share. No matter what you think about Margaret, she stood by Howard in the early days, and he was certainly crazy enough about her; although I wouldn't care to tell Katherine that."

She said she would be on for the trial, and to be sure to get the best men to defend Jim; and she ended by saying that the whole thing was preposterous, and that the Grand Jury must be insane. "Collective insanity," she put it.

Dick was rather at a loose end after the move. There could be no informal dropping in at any house of Katherine's. Amos was gone, and a part of her own staff from New York had taken his place. Just how they found houseroom I do not know, but somehow they managed. Judy reported to me daily, and so matters went on for a week or so; Jim in jail, I alone once more in my house, and Katherine moving silently and austerely about that little house, sipping her after-dinner coffee in the back garden and passing, in order to reach it, the door to the liquor closet, and the passage to the cellar stairs.

Then one day Judy told me that her mother wished to see the manager of the Imperial Hotel, and wanted me to go with her.

"But why, Judy?"

"She didn't say. She thinks something must have happened here last summer; I know that."

"The hotel wouldn't know about it."

"They might know if father had had any visitors."

She glanced at me, then looked away. I think she felt that there was something shameful in this prying into a dead man's past, and that she had herself refused to go.

I agreed, however. It seemed the least I could do, although I do not frequent hotels. I had never been inside the Imperial in my life. I daresay I belong to a generation which is absurd to the present one, but it has always seemed to me that well-bred folk should use hotels as necessities, not for pleasure.

But the hotel manager, a short ruddy man, swollen somewhat with good living, was unable to help us.

"I knew Mr. Somers well, of course," he said, "and I gave him the suite he usually occupied. I remember asking him if he wanted so much space, for he came alone. Usually he brought his valet. He said he did, and I went up with him myself.

"I thought he looked tired, and I suggested he have dinner in his sitting room. He said he would, and that his son would dine with him.

"The attack came on just after dinner. I was in the lobby when the word came, and I went up. The hotel doctor was there, and we got Doctor Simonds also. He—it looked pretty serious for a while."

"Walter Somers was there when it occurred?"

"Yes. He telephoned for help."

As to visitors, he did not know. The floor clerk might remember. From her desk near the elevator she could see the doors of the suite clearly, and of course Mr. Somers was an important guest. It was a chance, anyhow. She had known Mr. Somers for years, and naturally his grave illness had been a matter of interest and solicitude.

A pleasant enough little man, if rather unctuous. He took us to the sixth floor and left us with the floor clerk. I imagine he had wanted to remain, but Katherine's "thank you" was a dismissal. He turned and went away.

The clerk at the desk on the sixth floor turned out to be a middle-aged woman, with keen eyes and a shrewd mouth. Long ago, I daresay, she had lost any illusions as to the men and women whose comings and goings it was her business to watch. They came and went, intent on their own affairs, hardly aware of her at all. But she saw them and studied them; their tragedies, their serio-comedies. A thousand small dramas were played about her, and sometimes she was audience, and occasionally she was God.

I saw that Katherine had impressed her, even before she

heard her name; her air of breeding, the heavy handsome black she wore. But Katherine was intent on herself and her problem; her eyes were on that long corridor, with its mirrors and heavy jars, its chairs and its rows of doors.

"You were here, I believe, while my husband was ill last summer?"

"Yes, Mrs. Somers. He was in six-ten, the corner suite down there."

But Katherine did not look, although I did.

"And I suppose that you know we are in trouble. Very great trouble."

"I do indeed. I am so sorry."

But the interview, at the time at least, appeared to develop very little. Miss Todd, the floor clerk, was on duty from four o'clock in the afternoon until midnight, when she turned in her keys to the main office and went home.

She knew of no visitors to Howard during those hours.

"His son came and went," she said. "At first, when Mr. Somers was critically ill he stayed all night, getting such sleep as he could, and there was a day nurse and a night nurse. When Miss Gittings came she replaced the day nurse, and after he began to gain strength she took the case herself. The night nurse was dismissed. She wanted it that way."

"The evening he was taken sick, do you remember anything unusual about that?"

"Well, I do; in a way. Mr. Walter Somers came out about ten minutes before the attack. He had his hat, and I remember thinking he had eaten his dinner in a hurry. He came along to about that third door there, then he turned right around and went back again."

"And it was after that that he telephoned for help?"

"About ten minutes. Yes."

Katherine hesitated. She was a proud woman, and only desperation could have forced the next question.

"You don't know if there had been a quarrel? Some excitement, to bring on the attack?"

It was Miss Todd's turn to look embarrassed.

"Well, I hardly like to say. The waiter, William, said there were some words while he served dinner, and that Mr. Walter looked upset. But these waiters talk a good bit."

"He had no idea what the trouble was? Did he hear anything? I am sorry," Katherine interrupted herself, "but this may be more vital than you realize. What was said? What did this William hear?"

"William's gone now, but he said Mr. Somers had accused Mr. Walter of lying about something. And he said: 'You can't put that over on me. I know. I've got the facts, and if you think you are going to hold that over me you can think again.' Those are not the exact words, but after he took sick William came here and told me."

Katherine sat very still, thinking that over. It must have satisfied that furious jealousy of hers that Howard and Wallie had quarreled. But it must have puzzled her, too, as it was certainly puzzling me. She drew off her gloves, sat smoothing them absently.

"But of course that was nothing serious," Miss Todd went on brightly. "Things were all right after that, and Mr. Walter was devotion itself. He came in every day. He was nice to everybody. We all liked him."

Katherine moved in her chair.

"Did Mr. Somers have any other visitors?"

"Well, it was summer and his friends were all away. There

were the doctors, of course; Doctor Simonds had called in several. But I remember no callers."

"Were you on duty when Mr. Waite came in?"

"Yes. Both days. The manager, Mr. Hendrickson, brought him up himself. He had only the stenographer with him; she sat here until Mr. Waite opened the door and signaled to her. A quiet person. They came back again the second day, and I think they called up the notary from downstairs. Mr. Walter brought him up, I believe, but I was at my supper at the time."

"Was his son—was Walter Somers with his father at these times?"

"On the first day he met Mr. Waite in the hall and took him in. But he did not stay. He came out and rang for the elevator. I remember that, because he brought me some flowers from the sickroom. He said his father had suggested it. He had just received a large box."

I saw a quick flicker of suspicion in Katherine's eyes, and I knew that her quick jealousy had been again aroused. Flowers to her meant a woman, and with some justification, at that. Men do not ordinarily send boxes of flowers to other men. And this had been in midsummer, when practically all the few people Howard Somers knew in the city would be out of town.

"Flowers?" Katherine said. "I suppose you have no idea who sent these flowers?"

"I haven't an idea," said Miss Todd, looking slightly surprised. "Mr. Walter Somers would know, of course. He came out and got some vases for them."

Katherine's face set, as it always did when Walter was mentioned. Nevertheless, she was calm enough on the surface.

"And who brought these flowers, Miss Todd? Walter Somers?"

"No. They were delivered by the florist. At least I suppose so. An elderly man brought them. Usually such parcels are left here at the desk, but he said he had been told to get a receipt for them, and I let him take them in himself." She stopped suddenly. "That's curious," she said. "I don't remember his coming back this way, now that I think of it."

"He delivered the flowers and did not come back?"

"He may have, of course. I was pretty busy that day. I just don't remember seeing him again. But there is a service staircase near the suite. He could have walked down. I remember him," she added, "because it was a rainy day and he was soaking wet. He seemed old and feeble to be out and working."

She remembered nothing else of value. The messenger with the flowers she had seen only once; a shabby man, elderly and with longish white hair, and considerably stooped. Several times, during the illness, a squat heavy-set woman had come to give Howard a massage. She had reported at the desk the first time. After that she had merely nodded and passed by.

Visitors were forbidden. Walter came and went, getting little sleep at the beginning but later on in better spirits. It was evident that Miss Todd had liked Walter. Sarah Gittings had gone her efficient way. "Very particular about his food she was, too!" As Howard improved he had insisted that Sarah take a walk in the afternoons, and she did so. At such times Walter often stayed with his father and read to him. Sarah would wait until Walter would come, after office hours, and then dutifully go out.

There was no fuel there for Katherine's jealousy and suspicion to feed on; the record of a normal illness, with no women visitors save a muscular *masseuse.* No men, even, save Walter and the doctors, this messenger from a florist, the elderly man with stooped shoulders and a box of flowers, and Mr. Waite himself, sole survivor now of that little group of three which had stood by a bed in that hotel suite and watched a wavering hand sign a will which was to send four people to their deaths and three others into danger and injury.

Before we left Miss Todd asked if we would care to see the suite. Katherine refused, but I agreed. It seemed to me that the secret, whatever it was, might lie there; that if the florist's messenger could depart by a rear staircase, it would be possible for others who wished to avoid scrutiny to arrive by the same method. Something had happened to Howard Somers in those rooms, I felt; something which had altered his attitude toward his family and toward Walter, and which Jim had indicated in his defense.

And—strange how things will come to one at the most unusual times!—it was while walking down that corridor, with its Chinese vases on pedestals, its gilt mirrors here and there over console tables, that I thought of Margaret Somers.

Suppose Margaret were still alive? And suppose that Walter knew this, had secured that fund of fifty thousand dollars for her? No wonder, in that case, that he had refused to explain it! He had shown a real fondness for Judy, and detest Katherine as he certainly did, he would certainly never willingly invalidate his father's second marriage at the cost of exposure of Margaret's deception.

So perfectly did this theory fit the facts that I found myself stopping in the hall and turning to look back at Katherine, secure in the dignity of her grief, handsome and immobile in her chair.

The suite was a four-roomed one. Each of the rooms opened onto the hall, and the sitting room occupied a corner. To the right was the room which Howard had occupied, and beyond it a small one for maid or valet. Opening from the sitting room on the left was another bedroom, and just beyond it lay the service staircase.

Miss Todd was explaining.

"The small bedroom was used by the nurses, as it connected with the sickroom. The one beyond was kept for Mr. Walter, and for several nights he slept there."

But whatever their secret, the rooms yielded nothing.

I was still thinking of Margaret, and I wondered then if Katherine suspected what I did; if behind her strangeness during these last weeks there had been such a suspicion; a terror in which she saw her wifehood not only stultified but destroyed, and Judy nameless. And I know now that she had suspected, had feared just that. Why had Howard come, almost stealthily, to the city, light of luggage and without his valet, prearranging to meet Walter and dining upstairs so that they might talk undisturbed, unless it was that Walter had some shocking and terrible thing to tell him? Something which Howard refused to believe, and later had believed.

When I went out into the hall again she had not moved in her chair.

Miss Todd glanced toward her.

"She looks very sad."

"She is in great grief, naturally."

She was locking the door. Now she turned to me swiftly, and lowered her voice.

"He was a fine man, Mr. Somers," she said. "No nonsense about him; you know what I mean. If you sat where I do—! So you'll understand me when I tell you this: there was a young woman who tried to see him, after he began to improve. I think myself that she had waited below in the lobby until she saw Miss Gittings go for her walk, and then came up. She didn't come to the desk. She got out of the elevator somewhere below and came up the service stairs. I happened to see her, or she'd have been inside. She had tried the bedroom door, but it was locked, and I caught her before she got to the sitting room door."

"What excuse did she give?"

"She said she must be on the wrong floor. She was looking for a Mrs. Stewart, from St. Louis. But I took the trouble to find that there was no Mrs. Stewart from St. Louis or anywhere else, in the house." We were close to Katherine now, so she lowered her voice still further. "She was a pretty girl," she added hurriedly, "with bright red hair. And she went as white as a sheet when I spoke to her."

CHAPTER TWENTY-ONE

I HAD plenty to think of that day, and plenty of time in which to think.

It is a strange fact that death or sickness brings friends in numbers. They call, send flowers, telephone. But real trouble, a trouble like ours with its accompaniment of tragedy and shame, embarrasses them. The kindest thing apparently is to stay away.

I did not miss them, but I did miss the Inspector. I had grown fond of him, and his visits had been breaks in what were long and not too cheerful days. But he too, perhaps out of some mistaken sense of delicacy, was absenting himself, and I was much alone.

I needed him badly that day. Elise's discovery of a "ghost" in the trunk room, the possibility that Mary Martin as long ago as last summer had tried to see Howard, and that angry statement of Howard's to Wallie, "if you think you are going to hold that over me you can think again"; all these must have some bearing on our mystery.

And he was friendly to us. I knew that. Friendly and not too certain of Jim's guilt. I was resolved that from now on there would be no reservations on my part. I would show him the clock dial paper and tell him of that quarrel in the hotel. But before I did that I would go over Sarah's record of Howard's illness. She had a habit of scrawling on them odd facts, not always relating to the patient.

"Set mouse trap," I recall seeing on one of them long ago.

It was with a certain amount of hope then that I went up to Sarah's room that afternoon.

The records I had placed in the lower drawer of her wardrobe trunk, and I got them out and laid them on the bed. They were all there; Judy's diphtheria, the measles among Laura's children, the time I fell downstairs and broke my collar bone, and Katherine's periodic quinsy.

At last I found what I wanted. I sat back and went over it carefully. The early days of that sickness at the hotel had been active ones; the records showed treatments, hypodermics, careful comments on the patient's pulse, his weakness, his depression. It was clear that he had been depressed.

Then came improvement. "Patient more cheerful." "Appetite better." "Sitting up in bed today." On the eighth day came an entry at four o'clock. "Mr. Walter with patient from four to six while I took walk. Reports him more cheerful." After that, not regularly, but often, came the entry, "Out for walk. Patient comfortable."

It was not until I reached the date when Mr. Waite had made the rough draft of the will, August 12th, that I found anything of importance. The page for that date, and the one for the day following, were missing!

I could not believe it at first. I went over the record again and again; I even searched the other records, neatly clamped together and docketed. But it was not until I reexamined the page dated August 11th that I found anything, and what I found was more surprising than helpful.

At the bottom of the column marked Notes, Sarah had written in pencil "August 12th and 13th withdrawn for safekeeping." And beneath that: "Clock dial. Five o'clock right. Seven o'clock left. Press on six."

"Withdrawn for safekeeping." Then Sarah had known that she had written something on those two pages which was of grave importance; I only prayed that she had not known how grave. What visitors had she entered in that column on the 12th? Or what had happened to make Howard Somers, on that very day, decide to make a new will and leave Wallie a half of his estate plus a secret fund?

It was beyond me. I locked the room, went downstairs and telephoned for the Inspector.

He came that night, looking sheepish and uncomfortable.

"Didn't know you'd care to see me," he said.

"You know well enough that you don't believe Jim Blake is guilty, Inspector."

To my alarm he shook his head.

"I'm not so sure. He was with the Gunther girl that night, according to the colored woman. He knew about the will all right. Mind you, I'm not saying he'd planned the thing. He got excited and angry, and Sarah Gittings wouldn't give up the will. Maybe he knocked her down first. Then he went crazy, and he finished the job."

My heart sank.

"After that he'd have to do away with Florence. She knew too much."

"And Howard?"

"Murder's not proved there."

However, when I told him of what we had learned at the hotel, and about Mary Martin, he seemed less certain.

"Funny thing about that girl," he said. "We can't locate her. You'd think she'd be looking for work, but she hasn't. The District Attorney isn't interested, but I am. She knows a lot, if you ask me."

"Do you always find what you are looking for, Inspector?"

"Pretty often."

And then I laid out on the desk that page from Sarah's record, and the clock dial Judy had found in Florence's shoe. His face was a study when I explained the latter.

"So Judy found it, eh?" he said, and poked it with the end of a toothpick. "Intelligent girl, Miss Judy. And what does she think it means?"

"In view of the record, I think it indicates the place where Sarah hid the two missing pages."

He placed the two clock dial directions side by side, and fell to studying them.

"They are not ciphers," he said. "They are perfectly clear directions, if one only—I suppose you've tried all your clocks?"

"The young people have," I said resignedly.

"The chances are that it doesn't refer to a clock at all. Something which might be described in clock fashion; that's all. And something to which one or both the women had access. Not a safe, either."

"You think I'm correct as to the records?"

"It's probably so. What happened is this: until Sarah learned the terms of the new will those records lay in her room. They had no importance, no value. But she learned the terms of the will, and then for some reason they were important. So she hid them. She may have hidden them first in the wood cellar; that would account for the chair.

"But before she went out that last night she hid them again. Now let's see. She didn't leave the house between her return at five-fifteen and seven, when she left again?"

"I don't know. I don't think so."

"Still, that means nothing. She didn't die until ten o'clock. Between seven and ten she was somewhere, and according to the colored woman she was not at the house on Halkett Street."

I was tempted then to tell him Jim's story to Godfrey Lowell of that evening. But I did not.

"She went somewhere, and she hid those records," he said. "Find where she went and we find them, and perhaps some other things I'd like to know. Why, for instance, with these two women dead, does the search for those records go on? What did Sarah Gittings record on at least one of those two days which is vital to the killer? Here's Jim Blake under indictment, and they're apparently still important."

"Still very important," I said, and then I told him about Elise and her ghost.

He asked at once to see the window, and later on he talked with Elise, while I interpreted as best I could. It was not until he was with us in the hall on the way out that he asked me if I suspected any of the servants.

"They could be bribed, you know," he said. "Are you sure all this fright is genuine?"

"I have almost to put the women to bed myself, Inspector. As to Joseph, he puts up a good front, but I notice that he draws the window shades before dark now, and I'm terrified to walk suddenly into his pantry at night, for fear he shoots me."

"He still maintains that he was attacked?"

"He's sure of it."

I went out to the drive with him. It was a warm spring night with plenty of stars, and he stopped and looked up at them.

"Mighty nice," he said. "I like the stars. I like nature, too. And I'm in this sort of business!" But a moment later he was advising me to get back into the house.

"Either Jim Blake's guilty, or whoever is guilty is still free. And that's not a nice thought, Miss Bell. It's somebody who can think faster than the police, and see every angle and every emergency. A dangerous mind, Miss Bell, prepared to go to any length to attain its end. Big men in business often have it, professional gamblers have it; some traders on the Exchange have it. Lombroso says there's a criminal type. There may be. But there is a criminal mind, and this fellow has it."

He waited to see that I got safely back into the house, and then went on.

That was the evening of the 27th of May, and long shall I remember it.

At half past nine Judy and Dick came in. Katherine had made it clear that Dick was not welcome at the Pine Street house, and so now and then the two of them met in my library. On such occasions I would discreetly retire, but I think even Katherine would have found these meetings harmless enough. Early and late the two were on the crime. On one never to be forgotten night, for example, Dick had lowered himself into the light shaft by his hands, and found that it was just possible to obtain a precarious foothold on the iron bar beneath.

But getting him out had been a different matter, and when at last he hung panting on the sill, both Judy and I were exhausted.

"Well," he said. "If Jim Blake did that by himself, he's a better man than I am, Rudyard Kipling."

On this particular night they came in filled with suppressed excitement.

Amos had emerged from hiding long enough to see Dick that day, and he had told him certain details which he had withheld before the Grand Jury.

Dick did the talking, while Judy watched him.

"In the first place," he said, "do you believe Jim Blake is guilty?"

"I do not."

"Well, neither do we. But I've got something to tell you that will make you think. Amos went into his room the next morning, and he found some blood on Jim Blake's clothes, and a handkerchief pretty well soaked with it. He showed it to Blake, and Blake said he'd cut his hand the night before. The hand was tied up, all right, and there was a cut. Amos saw it later. Of course he might have done that himself to explain the blood, but we don't believe it. Amos is hiding because he doesn't want to tell that at the trial. He cleaned the clothes as best he could, but when he sent the laundry out some time later he found that Jim had washed the handkerchief.

"But there's something else. The next day, after Sarah was missing, at noon and after you had telephoned to him, Jim Blake got out of bed, dressed in some old clothes and went out. It was raining, and when he came back he was wet and his shoes were muddy.

"Now; I'll admit that all that looks queer. I believe he was on that hillside the next day, looking for something. What? Either he'd killed Sarah and was afraid he'd dropped something incriminating, or he knew something had happened there the night before.

"He was there. He saw somebody, or something, but he isn't saying what or who. Now why?

"Why has he done the things he has done? Why leave that sword-stick around until the body is found, and then only put it in a closet? That's foolish.

"And why go to bed? Guilt? The normal thing would have been to go around as though nothing had happened. But he goes to bed, like a baby. Now what puts him to bed; if he wasn't guilty he wasn't scared. So what's the answer? He's shocked. He's had an awful jolt of some sort. He's either happened on the body or on the murderer with the body. If he saw only the body he'd have notified the police. But if he saw the murderer—"

"I daresay I'm stupid, Dick. If he'd seen either of them, why not call the police?"

Judy turned to me.

"Dick believes," she said patiently, "that Uncle Jim recognized somebody on the hillside that night, and that he is either afraid to tell who it was, or that he has—other reasons."

"For not telling?"

"For not telling."

"Reasons so strong that he is willing to go to the chair rather than tell them? That's ridiculous."

"Not if he recognized the person he saw on that hillside, or wherever it was."

And I saw between them once more that practically wordless exchange which I found so irritating; Judy staring at Dick, and Dick making a gesture, at once protesting and protective.

"But who could that be? Not Wallie. We know that."

Judy looked at me, and I have never seen so tragic a look in a child's eyes.

"Dick thinks it might have been father."

I do not blame them, poor young things. Indeed, thinking that over later, I was not so sure that they were not right. Here was Jim, asking the day after Sarah's death about Howard, and if I was certain he had not been down recently; and burning his papers later on, as though some such inquiry might have been made by letter and answered.

And there was the whole situation; a secret will, to be kept from Howard's family, and even embodying a further secret clause. Howard might have had reason in his own mind for desperate measures to prevent Katherine learning of that will. And then, unable to bear that weight of guilt, or confronted with Jim the night of his death, he had resorted to suicide.

I was, however, profoundly shocked at the time, so much so that Judy rang for some sherry for me.

"I know," she said, "I feel like that too. But if Uncle Jim's innocent he's not going to the chair. And it will be the chair unless something is done, and done soon."

Apparently there was something to be done, simple enough on the face of it. We were to go, the three of us, to the path into the park, and there conduct an experiment as to the possibility of recognizing each other.

"It's the same sort of night," Dick said. "Stars but no moon. You two can go down to where Uncle Jim said he rested"—even then I noted the Uncle Jim—"and I'll cut across the hillside. I'll stop when you can see me enough to recognize me."

And this we did. That end of the park was deserted, and we saw no one. Dick left us at the Larimer lot, and cut across directly to the hillside. We could hear him working his way through the brush for some time, then we lost him. Judy and I followed the street to the path, and then down the hill.

Halfway down we stopped and Judy lighted a cigarette. She had not spoken at all until then. An unusual thing for her, and by the light of the match I thought she was crying.

"It's a crazy idea," she said. "We're all crazy. And why the devil doesn't he come?"

It did seem to be taking Dick a long time. Judy sat down finally, her hands clasped about her knees.

"There's more light than I thought," she said. "That street lamp up there helps. I can see you plainly, Elizabeth Jane."

But stare as we might we could not see Dick, and at last Judy got up.

"I'd better go over," she said. "He may have fallen."

I had a queer feeling even then that something was not right. The silence was appalling, and I remember wishing we had brought the dogs. Judy was ahead, hard to follow in her black dress, and so we progressed for some two hundred feet along the steep hillside.

But we did not find Dick at all. Judy was frantically calling him by that time, and I remember looking up to see my own garage towering above me, and so excited was I that I hardly recognized it. And then hearing Judy's voice Joseph came on the run, and in no time at all we had the police there.

They found Dick unconscious in a deep wash beneath the Larimer lot. Whether he had fallen or had been struck we did not know, but he had a deep wound on the back of his head.

They took him to the hospital at once, and up to the operating room. There was no fracture, however, but a bad concussion of the brain, and both Judy and I spent the night in his room.

Some time during that endless night, with Judy sitting beside the bed where Dick's long figure never moved and nurses came and went in that silence which is as ominous as death, a thought came to me, who seemed not to be thinking at all. This thought was that here was a crime which could not be laid to Jim; which might even help him. Whether Dick lived or died—and I prayed God that he live—the unknown killer was still at large.

And, now that Dick was to live, something of that relief, and more, was in Judy's mind.

Toward morning she got stiffly out of her chair and coming over to me put her hand on my shoulder.

"You see, we were wrong," she said, rather childishly. "We were both wrong, Elizabeth."

At dawn Dick became conscious and reached out for Judy's hand. But it was not until evening of that day that he told his story.

He had reached the edge of the lot, and was climbing down the hillside. When he reached the gully he stopped, hesitating whether to cross or go around it, and at that moment he heard a sound above him.

There was at this point no direct light from the street lamp, but a faint reflected radiance. The crest of the hill, however, with the lamp behind it, stood out clearly silhouetted against the night. And against that outline something was moving; an indistinguishable mass, close to the ground.

It was perhaps eight feet above him, and he had thought at first that it was a dog. He decided to go up the hill and around the head of the wash, and then the thing came at him. That was all he remembered, and even now that is all we know.

It is probable that nothing more than surveillance of our movements was intended. But Dick altered his course, recognition was imminent, and the reaction was quick and violent.

CHAPTER TWENTY-TWO

WITH THE surprising recuperative power of youth Dick was out again in a few days. But although preparations for Jim's trial were going on rapidly, that attack had not only completely undermined the *morale* of my household, it was causing Inspector Harrison some sleepless nights also.

He had examined the hillside again but without result. The weather had been dry as well as warm, and there were no footprints. He was completely baffled, and he did not hesitate to say so.

"I don't want any miscarriage of justice," he said. "I'm not like the District Attorney. I do my work and my job goes on, convictions or no convictions; and I don't give a particular damn for the press. What I want is the guilty man. And I'm not so sure we've got him."

Dick had been hurt the twenty-seventh of May, Friday. On Monday morning I came downstairs to find the Inspector having a comfortable cup of coffee in the pantry. He was not at all abashed, put down the kitchen clock which he had been examining, said briefly that it needed cleaning, and followed me into the front hall.

After his habit, he stopped at the lavatory and looked inside.

"Has it ever occurred to you," he said, "that that pencil Walter Somers produced was not what he found in that airshaft?"

"I think Judy—"

"Ha!" he said. "Trust Miss Judy. She knows. Well, it wasn't. Now, here are the facts about that pencil, Miss Bell. In the first place, I believe that it was yours; to be truthful about it, we found your fingerprints on it. Yours and Walter Somers'. No others. In the second place, I believe it was taken from your desk that night, and deliberately placed on that skylight. I have not said that it was taken for that purpose, although it might have been. Do you recall Walter Somers using a pencil that night? Before he started the investigation?"

"I don't think he did. He may have."

"He didn't look into the skylight, get down and go on some errand into the library?"

"He went in for some matches."

"Matches, eh? Well, he's a smoker, and the average cigarette smoker carries them. I think he got that pencil, and let's see if I'm right. We have to remember, of course, that Walter Somers knows something he's not telling. Now, he looks down that airshaft, and he sees something there which he recognizes; a key, maybe; or a watch charm, or a fountain pen, or a false tooth! Anyhow, something that he knows at sight, or suspects. He comes down, goes into the library for matches and picks up a pencil and slips it in his pocket. He climbs the ladder, gets this object, shows you the pencil instead, and there you are.

"Being afraid of nothing, he seals it up for the police. Clever, wasn't it? Only it was a bit too clever."

"He fooled us all, then."

"Not quite all of us," said the Inspector cheerfully. "You're not a smoker, I take it?"

"I don't smoke. No."

"Don't carry pencils around in your pockets?"

"Women have no pockets nowadays."

"All right. And what sort of clothing did Walter Somers wear that night?"

"His dinner jacket."

"Black. Now here's what the microscope showed, Miss Bell. That pencil had been carried in the pocket of a black suit; in the side pocket, where a man often carries a package of cigarettes. There were bits of tobacco from cigarettes caught around the eraser, along with black filaments from the pocket. Now, I've watched Walter Somers. He doesn't use a cigarette case; he carries his cigarettes in a paper packet in his right hand coat pocket. And I don't mind telling you that I've had that coat, and that this pocket bears out the facts. He had that pencil there before he climbed that ladder."

"Walter!" I gasped. "But I thought you said—"

"Not so fast," he warned me. "No, he didn't kill Sarah Gittings, if your alibi for him is correct. Although alibis are tricky things. Still, three alibis are good and sufficient for anybody. But look at the case against him!

"He gets his father to change his will in his favor. The news leaks out, and he's afraid it will get to Mrs. Somers and the good work will be undone. So he kills Sarah Gittings for fear she'll talk, and Florence Gunther because she's trying to see you and tell you what she knows. Then, later on—"

"He would never have lifted a hand against his father."

"No? Well, I daresay not. Anyhow, he didn't. We have him

checked for that night too. But it's a pity. It's a perfect case otherwise. But to get back to this pencil. We have only two guesses; either he had had it in his pocket for some time, and substituted it for what he found on the skylight. Or he already suspected or knew what was there, took the pencil from your desk, and used the ladder to remove something which was damaging."

"To him?"

"Not necessarily; but to some one." He sat back, thoughtfully. "I've already said that this is a family matter, Miss Bell. I've never seen a family more apparently united to frustrate justice and protect a criminal! It's disunited every other way, but when it comes to these murders it turns a solid front to the world. Now, what was the purpose of that little drama on the hillside the other night?"

"To see if poor Jim Blake could have recognized somebody there," I said defiantly.

"Precisely! And Jim Blake keeping his mouth shut and ready to take what comes! Who is he protecting? Who is Joseph protecting? He helps somebody out of that shaft, or at least to get out of the house. He finishes your job in the cellar and burns the carpet, and later on he gets knocked on the head for his trouble. How far can the police go, in a case like that?"

They had not found Mary Martin. That is strange, when I think back over it. She was not trying to hide; not then, at least. She was indeed, as the Inspector was to admit disgustedly later on, "under their noses."

Nor were any of us seeing much of Wallie. Judy suggested that he was trying, like the police, to locate Mary.

"But why?"

"Because he's crazy about her."

"I don't believe it."

"Don't you? I found her in his arms the day he came to New York, after father died. He had gone out, but he came back."

"Judy!"

"Well, I did. She was crying, and he was smoothing her hair and whispering to her. I just backed out and let them be miserable."

"She may have broken down, and he was trying to quiet her."

But she only smiled, as from the depths of some secret knowledge which she knew well enough I did not possess.

I thought over that after Judy had gone. I thought back to the night of Sarah's death, and Mary's sudden pause in the drive when she learned that Sarah was still out. Wallie had been nervous too, I seemed to remember. At some time in the evening he had asked about Sarah.

"And where was Sarah, while all this was going on?"

"She was out."

"And she's still out?"

"Yes."

It seemed to me now that he had looked slightly surprised and rather thoughtful; but how much of this impression was due to what had followed I was not certain.

But what did Mary Martin know? What possible business could she have had with Howard? A business so furtive that she must wait until Sarah was out, and so urgent that she had gone as white as a sheet when she was stopped.

She had not gone to Walter. Her errand—providing there was an errand—was one she was apparently concealing from Walter. It was a part of that same motive which had lain behind that strange procedure of hers when she had walked into Katherine's New York apartment and by sheer audacity superseded poor Maude Palmer.

According to Katherine she had not wanted me to know that she was there.

"Why?" Katherine had asked.

"She would think I had used what I know, to my own advantage."

Frightened, beyond a doubt; pale, as she had been pale that day at the hotel. But quietly determined. Hiding herself away in a little room downtown, going out at night to throw something into the river, and then—going to bed and "sleeping well." As though some weight was off her mind, as though now at last all was well, and safe. Poor Mary!

I had had my talk with the Inspector on Monday morning, and on Tuesday he asked permission to go over the house once more. Never have I seen a more exhausting search, or less result from it, unless I except the bewildered indignation of the servants. But at the last I did a thing I shall regret to the end of my life. I locked the ormolu cabinet and put the key away.

Simmons was in charge, and he came to me about it. But I explained that it had been examined, and that my mother's Chelsea figures inside were very precious and not to be handled. He was satisfied, and so it was not opened.

Nothing else escaped them; the chair and sofa cushions, the mattresses, even the kitchen utensils and the washing machine in the laundry were closely examined; and the unfortunate Simmons spent some warm hours in the wood cellar, carefully moving the wood. But they found no papers, nor anything resembling a clock dial save on the clocks themselves.

The mere fact of the search, however, had greatly unnerved both Clara and Norah, and had a result beyond any of our expectations.

Norah asked that night to be allowed to keep Jock in her

room, and Clara took Isabel. The total result of which was that I was awakened at three o'clock in the morning by a most horrible scream. It seemed to come from the back of the house, and was both prolonged and agonized.

I leaped out of bed and threw open my door. Joseph had similarly opened his, and I heard his voice.

"Who is it? What is wrong?"

There was a moan, and turning on the lights Joseph and I ran to the back stairs. Norah in her night dress was crouched there on the landing, her hands over her eyes.

"I've seen her!" she wailed. "I've seen her!"

"Stop that noise," said Joseph sternly. "You're scaring the whole neighborhood. Who have you seen?"

"Miss Sarah. I saw her, right at the foot of those stairs. She was standing there looking at me. In her uniform, too. All white."

And to this absurd story she adhered with the dogged persistency of her type.

It appeared that Jock had wakened and had demanded to be taken out. He had whimpered and scratched at the door, and at last, none too happily, Norah had started down with him.

At the top of the back stairs, however, he had stopped and given a low growl. Norah had looked down. There is a lamp on the garage, and since our trouble I had ordered it left burning all night. Through the pantry window it sends a moderate amount of light into the pantry, and in that doorway Norah claimed to have seen her figure.

"And after that, what?" I demanded.

"I don't know. I shut my eyes."

Only one thing struck me as curious in all this. So far as I know, Elise, terrified by Judy's dire threats, had said nothing of the figure in the attic and was now at a safe and discreet distance.

The next day I went over the house again with Joseph. New locks had been placed wherever possible and bolts supplemented them at the doors, and in the basement I had had placed over the windows gratings of stout iron well set into the bricks.

"What is it, Joseph?" I asked. "Do these women imagine these things? Or is somebody getting into the house?"

"They're very nervous, madam. And nothing has been taken."

I looked at him. It seemed to me that he stood not so erect as formerly; that he looked older and very tired. And lately I had noticed that he was less certain in his movements, slightly inco-ordinate. I put my hand on his arm.

"This is wearing on you, Joseph," I said. "Would you like a vacation? I daresay we could manage."

But he shook his head.

"Thank you, madam, but I'd prefer to stay. I've been a bit shaken since the attack; that's all."

"And you still have no idea who struck you?"

I thought that he hesitated. Certainly the arm under my hand perceptibly tightened. But although I know now that Joseph knew perfectly well who had struck him and that his very soul was seething with anger, it shows the almost incredible self-control of the man that his voice was as impassive as ever.

"Not the slightest, madam."

He must have been intensely curious. That searching of the house by the police, what did it mean? But he said nothing, asked no questions. A perfect upper servant, Joseph. A very perfect servant.

The incident did not add to my peace of mind. I would lie in my bed at night and imagine that I heard stealthy movements, faint stirrings. Nor were these limited to the lower floor; sometimes they were over my head, and once indeed in my very boudoir, next to my bedroom. When I called out sharply they ceased and were not renewed.

It was on the second day after Norah's experience, and sitting alone in my study that evening, that I decided to spy on my house; to lock myself securely in my room and listen to it. And this was less difficult than may appear.

The old speaking tubes in the house are simple of operation. To use them one opens them and drawing a long breath, expels it into the tube. The result is a wail of no mean calibre, wherever the tube may lead. But, once opened, these tubes are excellent conductors of sound, and as during a long invalidism my dear mother had managed her household from her bedroom, some four of these tubes led to the chamber which I now occupy, practically forgotten but still serviceable.

Joseph was out, but Clara was in the pantry. I shall never forget her face when I told her to go to the wood cellar and to bring me a small piece of wood to the library.

"And a knife, Clara. A very sharp knife."

"A knife, ma'am? A butcher knife?"

"The sharpest one you can find, Clara."

She was still staring at me as I turned and went out, and it shows the state of nerves in the household that after she had brought me the knife she turned and ran like a scared rabbit.

I cut my wood—and also my finger—and in the end I managed to prop open all the tubes except that in the pantry. After I had sent Clara to bed I opened that one also, and by midnight I was safely locked in my room with the lights out, and ready for my vigil.

For the first hour nothing happened. I heard Joseph come in

the back door, apparently pick up the knife, mutter something and put it away. I heard the sound of the refrigerator opening and closing, and gathered that he was taking a little refreshment up to bed with him. And then, until one o'clock, there was a complete silence.

At that time I began to hear a faint sound. It came from the drawing room, and was too far away to identify, but it was unmistakable. Now and then it stopped, only to resume again. It was a stealthy scraping, rather like that of a mouse nibbling at a board. And indeed, as it went on interminably, I believed that that was what it was. The tube ran through the old walls, and we are liable to onsets of mice, as are all old houses.

I do not know how long it lasted, or when it ceased. It stopped abruptly, and although I listened intently there was nothing further. No stealthy footsteps followed it. The silence was complete.

I was up early the next morning, a trifle ashamed of the whole proceeding, to remove the strips of wood. The drawing room was undisturbed, as was the rest of the lower floor.

But Joseph was to interpret those sounds for me that very morning, and with my breakfast tray.

"I think we will not be troubled again, madam."

"Troubled?"

"At night. I have found the means by which the person entered."

And so indeed he had. According to his story he had gone into the drawing room to open it, and had set the rear door open. On the upper step he noticed some bits of putty, and on examining it he found that it was soft.

The device had apparently been a simple one. The old putty around one of the panes had been carefully dug out and fresh soft putty substituted. To gain access to the house it was only necessary to remove this, a matter of a moment, and with some adhesive material fastened to the pane, to draw it carefully out.

Inspector Harrison, examining the pane, decided that adhesive tape had been used for this purpose.

As there is no path there, the steps leading directly onto the grass, there were no footprints. But as a result of this discovery the Inspector himself that day placed a heavy iron bar across the door, and personally examined the doors and windows.

He was not entirely satisfied, however.

"That bolt on the door," he said to me, "it's beyond a normal man's reach from that pane. Now it's conceivable that Joseph might forget that bolt once, and on the night that somebody had planned to get in. But twice, or a half dozen times! I don't believe it."

"He might have pushed it back with something. The man outside, I mean."

"Well, he might," he admitted grudgingly.

CHAPTER TWENTY-THREE

THE IMMEDIATE result of that discovery was my decision to tell Katherine all I knew. Partly to save her in her trouble and partly because I did not trust her discretion at that time, I had never told her about the missing sheets from Sarah's records.

She listened attentively while I told her of that excursion of Judy's and mine to Florence Gunther's room, and of what we had found there, and I showed her Sarah's record of the eleventh of August.

"Have you told Godfrey Lowell that?"

"Not yet. I've been trying to locate the missing pages."

She got up, rang the bell and ordered the car.

"It is hard to forgive you for this, Elizabeth," she said. "To hold that back, with Jim's very life hanging on it!"

"I don't see how it helps Jim."

"Don't you? Don't you know what was on those records? That Howard never made a will at all, or that he was drugged when he did it. One of those two things."

She had not waited for Elise. She was dragging out her outdoor garments, hurrying about—strange to see Katherine hurry—with two purplish spots of excitement high on her cheeks. Judy came in and stood by helplessly.

"It's been clear to me from the start. That man Waite has forged this will, and Walter Somers bribed him to do it."

"With what?" Judy demanded.

"On his prospects. How do you know that fifty thousand dollars wasn't the bribe?"

She was still talking when we got into the car, still feverishly excited. Judy begged her to be calm, not to say anything disastrous, but I doubt if she heard her. But when she made that flat statement to Godfrey Lowell, he sat upright in his chair, stiff and angry.

"I have the utmost confidence in Mr. Waite," he said. "An accusation of that sort necessarily involves his probity, Mrs. Somers."

"How do you know how honest he is?" she said sharply. "Men have been bought before this."

"The will was witnessed. I can have those signatures examined if you like. But—"

"What good would that do? The witnesses are dead. Maybe that's the reason why they are dead."

But Godfrey shook his head.

"No," he said. "I understand and I sympathize with you, Mrs. Somers. But that will was made by Mr. Somers, properly drawn by a man above reproach and signed and witnessed by two persons in Mr. Waite's presence before a notary. He has already sworn to that before the Grand Jury. He will so testify at the trial."

"Then why did Sarah hide the records of the two days when the will was drawn?"

"She did that?"

"She did. What was on those records, Mr. Lowell? Did she show that some pressure was brought to bear on Howard, or that he had been drugged?"

"Doctor Simonds says he was not drugged."

"What does he know? He wasn't there, was he?"

"Barring evidence to the contrary we shall have to take his word. He was there that night, and Mr. Somers was normal then."

Before we left he referred again to Katherine's statement about Mr. Waite.

"I know that you have had a great burden to bear, Mrs. Somers, and that naturally it is difficult for you to accept certain things. But some facts we must accept. During that illness all unpleasant feeling between Walter Somers and his father had been wiped out. In his conversation with Mr. Waite, Mr. Somers mentioned this. He was feeble, but quite clear as to his wishes. He felt that perhaps an injustice had been done to his son, and he wished to rectify it. That is why the will was drawn as it stands, and—as it will stand before any court, Mrs. Somers."

"Have you examined the signature?"

"I have, at Mr. Waite's own request. We have even had an expert on it. A forged signature under the microscope shows halts and jerks; the hand works slowly, and there are tremors."

"And this shows none of these?"

"Mr. Somers was not allowed to sit up. It shows the weakness of a sick man, writing in a constrained position. That's all."

She sat there, smoothing her gloves after that habit of hers, and her face looked drawn in the glare from the wide-open windows. Her anger was gone, and something disquieting had taken its place.

"Then this secret fund is beyond question?"

"Beyond question."

She said nothing more until we had got into the car. Then she spoke, looking ahead of her and with her face a white mask.

"So she is living, after all!"

"Who is living, Katherine?"

"Margaret."

Just how long she had been brooding over that possibility I do not know, but I think it explains much that had almost alienated me at the time; her refusal to accept the will, her frozen attitude even to Judy, the hours she spent locked away in her room, inaccessible even to her maid.

"I don't believe it, Katherine."

"I do," she said with stiff lips. "It would be like her, wouldn't it? To hide away for all these years, and then when she knows Howard is ill and dying, to let him know. She told Walter, and Walter told him."

Nothing I could say could shake that conviction. And here again we had grazed the cheek of truth, touched it and gone on. For Margaret was not living, as we were to learn at the end.

Certainly one of the most astounding things about our series of crimes—and perhaps about all baffling crimes—is the narrow margin by which, again and again, the solution evaded us. Despite the extraordinary precautions taken by the criminal, on at least a half dozen occasions safety was a matter of seconds only. One such incident was the sound outside Florence Gunther's room, the night Judy and I were there. Another, for example, was Clara's failure to identify the figure in the pantry door. Again, had the intruder on my staircase the night of Sarah's murder happened to have crept a few steps lower, the entire situation would have been changed. That I was resting when Florence came to see me resulted in her death before she had told her story.

There were others, also.

Had Judy turned that night in the garage she might have seen who it was who struck at her. And Dick, deciding by the merest chance to retrace his steps around the wash, confronted that crouching figure and was violently flung into the gully.

These and a dozen other instances which I was to recall later, had given me an almost superstitious attitude toward the case. Clearly it was not meant that we were to know until the deadly roster was complete, the whole sanguinary business finished. Then, when it was all over, Katherine with her deadly pertinacity was to step in, and the door was to play its part.

The next incident was a fair example of the narrow margins to which I have referred.

I have said little about reporters, but of course life had been made miserable by them for weeks; masculine and feminine, they had more or less invaded us. Dick's injury had resulted in a fresh influx, and so I had instructed the servants to inspect all callers from the library bay window before opening the doors.

A day or two after the visit to Godfrey Lowell the bell rang and Joseph tiptoed upstairs to say that a suspicious looking woman was on the doorstep. By that I knew he meant probably a reporter, but something made me ask what she looked like.

"A big woman," he said. "Rather flashy, madam."

"Humph," I said. "Big? All the ladies of the press so far have been small, Joseph. Small and young."

The bell rang again, almost fiercely, and suddenly a curious thing happened to me. I had a vision of Florence Gunther standing there, ringing the bell and being turned away. It came and went while the bell was still ringing.

"Let her in, Joseph. I'll see her."

He disapproved, I knew. It was in every line of his back. But in the end he admitted her, and it developed that my caller was Lily Sanderson.

She looked tired, I thought, too tired even to be self-conscious.

"I guess you have enough bother without my adding to it," she said. "But I had to come. I had really."

She sat down and put her hands to her hat.

"I guess I look something dreadful. I've been losing a lot of sleep, and what with being on my feet all day—"

"Would you like some tea?"

"No, thanks. I feel too mussy. I want to get home and get my shoes off. My feet swell something dreadful these days. Not getting to bed properly, you know."

"Can't you slip them off now? Your shoes?"

But the idea seemed to outrage her sense of the proprieties. She shook her head.

"I'll just give you my message and be getting on. It's about Mrs. Bassett. She's sick. She's got—" She lowered her voice, as always will women of a certain age when mentioning cancer. "She's got a cancer, and it's too late to operate. She's living on morphia. Her daughter's there now, but I relieve her at night. That is, I sleep on a sofa, and if she gets bad she calls me."

But the point of the matter was this: after Mrs. Bassett had had morphia she would grow talkative, "what with the pain stopping, and anyhow I guess morphia does loosen the tongue." And Miss Sanderson would listen.

"It's really awful," she said. "Me working all day and trying to sleep, and her talking on and on. Sometimes she'll say: 'You're not listening.' And I'll wake up and tell her I am. But what I'm coming to, she's talked a lot about Florence. She's got her on her mind. And she knows something, Miss Bell. She knows something about that murder."

"What makes you think that?"

"She's as much as said so. The other night she called me in the middle of the night and told me to get somebody from headquarters; she wanted to make a statement about something. So I got the telephone book, but I didn't know what to look for, and then I heard her calling like a crazy woman. I went in, and she was running her tongue over her lips—morphia makes them dry, you know—and looking at me with a queer sly look. 'I haven't anything to tell the police,' she said. 'It's this stuff they give me. I guess I was dreaming.' But I didn't believe her then and I don't now. She meant to tell the police something, and then she got frightened."

"It might not have been about Florence, at that."

"Listen!" She leaned forward. "I told you I heard two people in that room the night Florence was killed, didn't I? And that one of them was a woman and she was crying? Well, why wasn't that Mrs. Bassett?"

She sat back, having made her effect, and gazed at me triumphantly.

"Mind you," she said. "I'm not saying she had anything to do with the murder. She's a decent sort of woman, and she's had a hard time; roomers at the house, and going out to give body massage into the bargain. She knows something, that's all I say. And I stick to it."

"Would she talk to the police if they went there?"

"I doubt it. She's thought it over, and she's made up her mind. She's afraid; afraid of somebody."

She had, however, no more idea as to this somebody's identity than I had. She knew no more of Mrs. Bassett than the average roomer knows of her landlady. She believed that there was a husband living, but she had never seen him. The daughter had given up a good position to take care of her, she understood. She rambled on while I thought. Only one thing struck me as being significant in all this, and that was that Mrs. Bassett had given massage.

"What does she look like?" I asked. "I mean, in build? Is she tall?"

"She's medium height, and stocky. Very muscular. Even now she isn't as weak as you'd expect."

I sat up. Was it possible that Mrs. Bassett was the heavy-set woman who had given Howard Somers massage at the hotel? And if so, what would that mean? What did she know? What had she learned in those rooms, during those mysterious days of the illness, that might be valuable now? That, it seemed to me, was the important thing, and not Lily Sanderson's guess that she had been in Florence's room the night she was killed.

One could imagine her, her sleeves showing her strong arms as she bent over the bed, working mechanically. And then, something being said, some quarrel going on or some name being mentioned which had registered in her mind. Then, lying in her bed, the impulse to tell what she knew, and the second impulse, more profound, to be allowed to die in peace.

"Did she ever mention any of her patients?"

"I think not. She isn't what you would call talkative."

"I wondered. We know that a woman answering that description gave massage a few times to Mr. Howard Somers here last year. But I daresay Doctor Simonds would know."

That, however, did not interest Miss Sanderson. What she wanted, and finally brought out, was that I should myself see Mrs. Bassett and talk to her. That night if possible.

"Her heart's bad, and she may go any time like *that.*" She snapped her fingers. "If you could work on her she might talk. Tell her all the trouble and sorrow that's going on. She's kind enough. I could have yelped myself when I saw that picture of Mr. Blake with the handcuffs."

Here the feeling that she had committed an indelicacy caused her to get up suddenly and prepare to go.

"That's fixed, is it? You'll come? Say about nine o'clock? I'll be watching for you. She'll have had her hypo at eight, and the daughter's going out. I've promised to relieve her early. I can smuggle you in." But she seemed loath to go. "I don't know why," she said, "but I get a funny feeling in that house at night. She thinks she hears things, and she lies and listens."

I let her out myself, and watched her go down the drive to the street. It occurred to me then that she was frightened, that she had been frightened all along; that she knew that to meddle in this matter might be deadly; that the same fear which had turned Mrs. Bassett stubbornly silent was in her. There was pathos in that. These two women, one worn with watching, one dying, and no peace for either of them. Shut in those two upper rooms, awake in the long night, and the sick woman "hearing things."

Doctor Simonds did not remember the Bassett woman. He had suggested massage, and either Sarah or Wallie had found some one. He himself had never seen her. He had two or three *masseuses* on his list, but they were all Danes or Swedes, there was no one named Bassett.

CHAPTER TWENTY-FOUR

I DID not take the car that night. I had no desire to let Robert know of that visit. But I took Joseph, out of sheer panic, to see me safely down the hill and into the lighted portion of the park. There he turned back, and I went on alone.

A week of June had passed. The trees were in full leaf, and the scent of flowering shrubbery was in the air. I remember thinking that it would soon be two months since Sarah had been murdered, and that Florence had been dead for more than a month. And what did we know now, more than we knew then? Almost nothing. That Sarah had known Florence, that they had shared the knowledge of the will, and that Sarah had hidden two pages of a record which were being diligently sought by some one unknown!

Cleared of all extraneous matter, that was our case. We might suspect that Howard had been murdered, but we did not know it. We might believe Judy had been attacked, but had the ladder possibly fallen, after all? Had Joseph tumbled down the stairs? And had Dick surprised some venial malefactor who had simply pushed him out of the way?

And was the answer of the Grand Jury the correct one? Was

it, after all, as simple as that, that Jim had killed Sarah to get the duplicate will, trusting to luck—and possibly Katherine—to get hold of the other?

I daresay I walked slowly, for it was after nine o'clock when I rang the door bell.

Almost at once it was opened and Lily Sanderson slid out on the step, closing the door behind her.

"Well, wouldn't you know it?" she said. "The husband's come to see her! He's up there now, and the daughter too, and there's been all sorts of a row. She'll be upset, and it's bad for her. It might even kill her."

I saw that she was crying, and I realized that her tears were not for me and my disappointment; that for a little time she had fed her starved womanhood on service, and that she had developed an affection for this unfortunate woman who had become for the time at least her child.

"You need sleep," I said. "Let the daughter stay tonight, and go to bed."

But she shook her head. She had stepped into the vestibule and drawn me in with her. "Look here," she said in a low voice, "what do you suppose the fuss is about? She's sick, and he knows it. Why is he jawing her? Is he afraid she'll tell something?"

"Who is he? What does he look like?"

"I never saw him, and I don't want to."

But she caught something in my face—we were in the vestibule, and there was a little light—and she turned swiftly and went into the house. She was back again almost immediately, her finger on her lips.

"He's coming down," she whispered. "Don't move."

She had partially closed the door behind her, and we stood there waiting, while the man slowly descended to the second floor. Still as it was on that by-street, his movements were amazingly quiet. Indeed, had I not been told that some one was descending that staircase, I would not have believed it. A creak now and then, the indescribable faint sounds of a moving body, were all I could hear.

Then, part way down the second flight he stopped. Evidently he had seen the partly opened door, and was looking at it. Lily Sanderson's face was curious in that half light. It was as though that descent, harmless enough until then, had become sinister. She stared at me, her mouth partly open, and thus we stood for an absurd time, waiting for the man on the stairs to make the first move.

Suddenly the tension became too much for her. She made an odd little sound and threw open the door. There was no man on the stairs, nobody in sight. She looked profoundly shocked, and she gave a sort of hysterical giggle.

"Can you beat that?" she whispered. "He went back!"

"Back where?"

"He went up to the second floor and down the back stairs. That is, if he's gone." Some rather awful thought evidently came into her mind at that moment, for she left me and ran up the stairs, her heavy legs and ridiculous heels moving with incredible rapidity. She went all the way to the third floor, and I could hear voices there; the daughter's, I imagined, and her own. She came down more quietly.

"It just occurred to me," she said breathlessly, "that—but she's all right. The daughter is with her."

"What in the world did you think?"

But she seemed rather ashamed.

"It was funny, his slipping out like that, wasn't it?" she asked. "Maybe Clarissa saw him."

As it turned out, however, Clarissa had already gone home. Her kitchen was dark, and I think it took some courage on Lily's part to go in and turn on the lights. But it was empty, and she turned her attention to the door. She looked around at me with a startled face.

"I forgot! He couldn't get out here. Clarissa takes the key with her. It's locked now, and the key's gone."

It was then that we both heard a sound from the pantry, and the swinging door into it opened and closed a few inches. It was an uncanny thing, and I can still see poor Lily, leaning on the kitchen table and staring at it, and admire the courage with which she raised her quavering voice.

"Who's there?"

In the silence which followed we both heard the front door softly close.

Evidently Mrs. Bassett's husband, or whoever the stealthy visitor might be, had found himself locked in the kitchen, and when we went there had taken refuge in the pantry. There were two swinging doors, and the opening of the one, as we found by experiment, caused the other to move. As he escaped by the simple expedient of going forward through the dining room, this had happened.

But as Lily said, now blind to the proprieties and sitting weakly in a chair with her slippers in her hand, why escape at all?

"I don't believe it was her husband, Miss Bell," she said. "Anybody could come here and say that. That's why I went upstairs."

"To see if it was her husband?"

"To see if he had murdered her," she said, and somehow my blood ran cold.

I took a taxicab home that night, and I did not feel safe until

I was in my own house once more, with Joseph double barring the door and the dogs, as usual in my absences, settled on the best library chairs.

I told the Inspector the next day of that experience in the Halkett Street house, but he pooh-poohed the idea of its having any connection with the crimes.

"Why make so much of it?" he said. "Most men tiptoe out of a sickroom. They may raise the devil inside but they tiptoe out. Watch that some time. And as for his hiding, well, maybe he did and maybe he didn't. How do you know he hadn't been crying? He'd rather be caught without his clothes than crying."

He was not so certain, however, after he had seen Mrs. Bassett that night. He had arranged with Lily Sanderson as I had, and this time the daughter was out. He stopped by on his way home.

"Not that I got anything," he said. "But there's something peculiar there."

She had absolutely refused to talk. Asked about her request for the police some time before, she denied having made it.

"I get queer ideas when I've had the dope they give me," she said, and lay there quietly, looking at something he could not see.

When he tried to discuss the murder of Florence Gunther she said nothing whatever. Nor was she much more communicative about her husband.

"My daughter's a good girl, but the least said of him the better."

Then she had said she was in pain and had called sharply for Lily, and he had come away.

"But she knows something," he told me. "Not necessarily that the husband has anything to do with it. She knows something. She had a queer look about her. I've seen it before."

"What sort of look?"

"I saw it once before in the face of a man just before he jumped out of a tenth story window."

And so, like everything else which might have helped in the defense, that too had come to nothing. I believe the Inspector made at least one other attempt to see her, but either she was frightened, or more likely she had been warned, for she told him nothing. And before our mystery was cleared up she was dead.

By the tenth of June Jim's trial began. Public opinion and the prosecution had done everything possible to expedite the proceedings, and the defense was equally anxious. Jim was not bearing the confinement well. The jail was dark and airless, and the general feeling against him so strong and so infuriated that the authorities could do nothing to ameliorate his situation.

There had been leaks of various sorts. It was known that Jim's clothing had shown minute blood stains in spite of Amos, and that he had been on the hillside the night of Sarah's death at ten o'clock. Two persons, a man and a woman, had come forward to state that they were coming up the path that night, and that they had seen a man in light golf clothing, standing beside the path and wiping something from his hands with a handkerchief.

The man, named Francis X. Dennis, made his statement unwillingly enough.

"I didn't want to be mixed up in this," he told the reporters, "but my wife thinks we'd better speak up. We'd been taking a walk, and we came along to the foot of the hill about five minutes to ten.

"My wife's hearing is better than mine, and she stopped and said there was somebody scrambling through the bushes overhead. We listened, and it seemed like somebody was running along the hillside. We didn't start up until it got quiet again, and my wife was kind of nervous.

"Well, when we'd got about halfway up there was a man. He was about ten feet off the path on our right and I saw that he had on a light golf suit and cap. He didn't pay any attention to us. He seemed to be busy with his hands, wiping them.

"After we'd got up the hill my wife said: 'He's cut himself. He's tying up his hand.' I said maybe he'd slipped and fallen when he was running, and—well, I guess that's about all."

It was a body blow for the defense, coming when it did and with a detail the more convincing because it was unstudied. Both these people believed that it was Jim they had heard running along the hillside below the Larimer lot toward the path, and Godfrey Lowell threw up his hands in despair.

"This case is being tried in the press," he said. "We'll have a verdict before we even get into court!"

But I have thought about Godfrey since, sitting in his office and talking to the imposing array of counsel who were to help him, and going home at night to lie awake for hours, studying the darkness for some weakness to attack, some point to be made:

"And I say to you, gentlemen of the jury—"

What? What could he say? That Jim was a good fellow who gave good dinners and played excellent bridge? That he was a decent citizen, who had spent that evening conversing harmlessly with another woman who had since been murdered? And that he was given to nosebleed, which would account for the blood on his clothes?

Jim still stubbornly silent, and Godfrey lying there and wondering. Was Jim innocent, after all?

I believe that until the day before the trial he was uncertain.

Then I was able to give him a little, a very little help. Small as it was it heartened him, and on it he hung his defense, but even then he was not sure.

It was an odd conversation I had with the Inspector that second evening before Jim's trial. He marched in like a man with a purpose, and I saw that whatever that purpose might be he had dressed for it. He was always neat enough, but that night he was resplendent.

"This is a social call," he said. "I'm not a policeman now; I'll ask you to remember that."

And he added, not without embarrassment, that he felt very friendly toward all of us; that he had enjoyed his talks with me, and that he liked Judy. Then he sat still and stared at his well-polished boots.

"In that case," I suggested, "out of office hours, so to speak, and the whisky being some my father put away years ago, would you like a highball?"

Which he would, and did.

Perhaps it warmed him; perhaps he had come for the purpose. The upshot of it was that he said he did not want any miscarriage of justice the next few days, and that things were looking pretty black.

"The prosecution's going to get a conviction. It's out for one, and it'll get it. Mind you, the District Attorney thinks he's right. I've talked it over with him, and he had God with him, as he sees it. But there are one or two little points they're not likely to bring up, and I thought I'd talk them over with you."

And then and there, categorically, he outlined the defense for us. As I wrote it down for Godfrey Lowell at the time, I have it before me now.

(a) Jim was being tried for Sarah's murder, but the story of

Florence Gunther's would inevitably enter the case. Why was it that there was no oil in Jim's car the morning after Florence's death, although I found it later? "Tell Lowell to bring that out. The prosecution won't."

(b) Find Amos, and get him on the stand. "He buried that sword-stick. His prints were thick on it."

(c) Ask the microscopist who examined Sarah Gittings' clothing if he found anything wrapped around a button. "I may lose my job over this, but he did. He found a longish white hair."

(d) Ask him—the microscopist—if that hair was living or dead? If it came from a head or a wig. "I think it came from a wig, myself. Make them produce that hair in court. They've got it."

(e) Ask the microscopist what he found on that piece of wood from the Larimer lot. "He found something besides blood and that dead woman's hair. He found some fibers from cloth on the end of it. Black cloth, or grayish black. They've got those, too."

(f) Put a lot of emphasis on that three hours from seven to ten. Where was she? "I'm not so sure myself that the whole solution doesn't lie there."

And

(g) Why were both those stab wounds the same depth?

He leaned back, like a man well satisfied with himself.

"Now here's the situation, to my mind," he explained. "And Lowell's welcome to use it if he likes. Here's a man who has worked himself into a mood to kill. He's out to kill. And he's got a sword in his hand; a rapier, rather. It's got a blade a foot and a half long, and it's as sharp as a dagger. What does he do? He drives it home with all his strength, and this man who did this had strength, plenty of it. If your grandfather ever fought a duel with that weapon, he'd have run his man through, wouldn't he? Providing he got the chance, of course!

"But here are two stab wounds, and both of them short. That's not accident, that's necessity. That's a short knife, to my mind anyhow. He might have gone short the first time, but not the second. Never the second."

I was re-reading my notes.

"What do you mean by the wig?" I asked.

"Well, that hair was peculiar. It had no root, for one thing. A hair that's torn out usually has a root; and there was no dust on it, nothing that ought to be on hair in active service! Nothing but a lot of brilliantine. Mind you, that's only a chance. Still, it has its points. A man old enough to have white hair and wear it long is too old to have put that body in the sewer."

"You mean that whoever it was was disguised?"

"I say there's a possibility of it. You see, men often disguise themselves to commit crimes. That and to make an escape are practically the only times any criminal uses disguise at all. In other words a murderer is seen at or near the scene of the crime, and identified by certain marks; hair, eyebrows, clothes or what not. But in his own proper person he has none of those marks."

"And they won't bring that out at the trial?"

"Well, why should they?" he said reasonably. "It wouldn't help Blake any. How do we know he didn't wear a wig that night?"

"Then why bring it in?"

He smiled.

"For the effect on the jury," he said. "Nobody has shown that Jim Blake wore such a wig, or even owned a wig. As a matter of fact I don't believe he did. But get Lowell to work that three hours and the unknown in a white wig, and dress clothes, and at least he's got a talking point."

CHAPTER TWENTY-FIVE

I TOOK those notes to Godfrey the next day, and by the eagerness with which he seized on them I realized his desperation.

"Where on earth did you get all this?"

"Never mind, Godfrey. It's our case; that's all."

And that was the situation the day before Jim's trial opened; Laura arriving in the early morning, having left her children for once, and outraged over the whole situation. But not for a moment taking the outcome seriously; coming in from the car, smartly dressed and vocative, followed by that mass of hand luggage which she requires for a twenty-four-hour journey.

"Don't look at me. I'm a mess, but of course I had to come. Of all the ridiculous and pointless accusations! How are you, Joseph? How d'you do, Clara! Charles told me to see that I had an extra bolt on my door! Isn't that like him? That cabinet looks well in there."

Nor did she once consider a possible unfortunate outcome for Jim until the trail began. Then the dignity of the court, the gravity of the counsel for both sides, all the panoply of a trial in which a sovereign state with all its resources is opposed to a single individual in a prisoner's box, began to impress her.

Our faces, too, must have told her something of our doubts; Judy pale and thin, and Katherine as if she had been chiseled out of marble.

"Oh, the poor dears!" said Laura. "Somehow I didn't realize it had been like this."

But it was Jim who struck her dumb; Jim, so carefully dressed, so drawn, so isolated. She reached out and caught my hand, and for once she was silent. Silent she remained, through that ghastly impaneling of a jury which required days, and until the opening speech of the State's Attorney. During that speech, however, her color rose and her eyes flashed.

"How dare they?" she muttered. "How *dare* they?"

I have no space here for that trial, for its heartbreaks and its insufferable dragging hours and days. Witnesses came and went. The audience, those who had won the daily battle for admission, sat and fanned themselves with hats, handkerchiefs, newspapers. To such few points as told in Jim's favor they were cold; they were united against him, a seething mob of hatred, waiting and furiously hoping for revenge.

Laura said they were like the market women who knitted around the guillotine while the French aristocracy was being executed, and so I felt that they were.

In vain Godfrey Lowell fought, cross-examined, almost wept out of his exhaustion and anxiety; in vain he made the Inspector's points, from "a" to "g." The jury was hot and growing weary. Sarah's blood-stained clothing and the sword-cane were on the table. They reasoned from cause to effect.

He had had the cane, she had threatened his easy-going life, he had been seen where she was killed, he killed her.

Judy's eyes were sunk in her head by the end of the third day, but she remained throughout the trial, from that sonorous opening speech of the District Attorney, of which I reproduce only a paragraph or two:

"We will show, gentlemen of the jury, that this unfortunate woman, on the day before she was killed, wrote to this defendant and asked him to meet her, on urgent business. A reconstruction of a portion of this letter as shown on her blotter will be produced in due time. And we will show that she sent this letter. She not only wrote it but she addressed an envelope, and the imprint of this envelope, left on the cuff of that uniform of service which she wore, has been examined by experts and pronounced to be her own handwriting. It has been compared, as the law requires, with valid examples of her handwriting; samples easy to obtain, for this good and faithful friend to this family for years kept a record of all their illnesses, day by day.

"We will show that on the night of the crime, this defendant varied from his ordinary procedure; that he dined early and without dressing, which in this case means that he did not put on a dinner jacket. That is more important than it may sound. There are certain individuals, gentlemen, to whom a dinner without a dinner jacket approaches the unthinkable. It is cataclysmic. And so revolutionary was it in the habit of this defendant that his servant made a mental note of it.

"Following this early meal, and he ate very little, he went out. He had put on a light golf suit and a pair of heavy shoes, and this suit and these shoes will be shown to you later on, stained with blood; the blood, we fully believe of this dead woman.

"But there was another and even more terrible, more sinister object in that house that next morning. The sword-stick stood once more in the hall, where it had stood before. But this sword-stick, or sword-cane, gentlemen, had become a matter of intense importance to this defendant.

"Either on his return the night before, or during that day, or even following the discovery of Sarah Gittings' body, this defendant proceeded furtively and secretly to wash the sword-cane.

"But he could not clean the interior of the sheath. That remained for the experts of our department. They have found human blood in that sheath, and also another object.

"The age of human blood, after a certain period of time, is difficult to determine. My friends of the defense may urge that this blood may be from some ancient duel long since forgotten. But of this other object discovered the age is unquestioned. Adherent to this sheath was a needle from a pine tree, and this needle was fresh, gentlemen of the jury. It came from a particular variety of evergreen to be found only on that slope of the city park down which this unfortunate woman had been dragged.

"Numbers of similar needles, from similar trees, were found clinging to her clothing on the recovery of the body. And I may add that in the opinion of the experts for the state, this blood inside the sheath was similarly fresh."

Why go on? Bit by bit he built his case, and bit by bit Jim sagged in his chair. When he reached the question of motive, and named Florence Gunther, there was such a stir in the courtroom that it had to be called to order.

"Now, gentlemen of the jury, it is not our purpose here, directly or indirectly, to try this defendant for the murder of Florence Gunther; but here and there this girl's name will have to enter the record.

"On the day of this murder Florence Gunther took from the safe of her employers a certain document, sealed in a brown manila envelope and duly endorsed. This document has disappeared, but its identity has been established."

And with the description of the will which followed, the supplying of the motive, the case was indeed as Godfrey had predicted; over before it commenced.

He fought on doggedly, but what were such things as hairs and fibers to a jury which had already reached its verdict? And we had a blow or two which were unexpected, at that.

One was the proof that Sarah had indeed written the letter to Jim, as claimed by the state. A photograph had been made of her blotter and greatly enlarged, and certain words had come out clearly enough. So far as they could put the words together, allowing for certain undecipherable places, she had written somewhat as follows:

"Dear Mr. Blake: I must see you as soon as possible on a very urgent matter. When I tell you that I believe that there is a—"

The first page had ended there, or she had used less pressure, for that was all. And even in this only certain words were at all clear; "urgent" and "possible" and "believe," for example. But the "Dear Mr. Blake" was beyond dispute.

Katherine, too, had her own particular shock to face. This was the reconstruction of that charred fragment of a letter from her to Jim, which had been found in his fireplace.

"Your message alarms—What am I not to say?"

She had no warning. She had not expected to be called, and I am sure she had not the slightest idea of what was to confront her on the stand.

"Can you identify this?"

"I don't even know what it is."

She put up her lorgnette, stared down at that flat board, then lifted her head slightly.

"Do you recognize it now?"

"I think it is something I have written."

"To the defendant?"

"Yes."

"Do you remember when you wrote that?"

"No."

"Or how you sent it? By mail?"

She was under oath, and she would not lie.

"By hand."

"By whose hand?"

"By my chauffeur. I was sending certain things to my brother by car, and the letter went with them."

We know now that that was true, that she had had no idea then that Jim's mail was being watched. But on the face of it the admission was fatal, and when later on she was asked to explain that sentence and refused, there was little more to be done.

In the eyes of the jury and of the audience that day Katherine had as much as admitted that she knew something about the crime which she was "not to say." And the next question, ruled not competent by the court, was not only designed to show that, but had a sinister purpose not lost on the jury or the crowd.

"Did you see your brother the night he went to New York?"

"What night was that?"

"The night of your husband's death."

"I did not," said Katherine haughtily. "He was not in New York that night."

But the effect had been made. The introduction of Charles Parrott was likewise fought, but on the District Attorney's statement that he was important to their case he was put on the stand, and he made his semi-identification.

"He's the same height and the same build," he said, "but he was pretty well covered. It looks like him, but that's as far as I go."

The purpose of the prosecution was then revealed. Judy was unwillingly obliged to say that the telephone call had been apparently from Jim, and Howard's checkbook was introduced.

It was shown that on the day, or night, of his death he had drawn a check to cash for a thousand dollars. The book was found on his desk in the morning, with the stub so marked. This check had not been presented, but evidence was introduced to show that two days before Jim had called up a local steamship agency and inquired about sailings.

And underlying all this, brought out again and again, was the sinister reference that when Jim had left the apartment in New York that night, or just before he left, Howard was dead.

Judy made a fine witness, and she got over more than the prosecution allowed to enter the record; she deliberately talked until they stopped her, and I think the jury found her a bright spot in a long day.

"Why hasn't Mr. Waite been murdered?" she asked once, out of a clear sky. "Why wasn't he the first to go?"

And again, relative to the finding of the cipher, she brought a laugh.

"Why did you search that room?"

"I thought the police needed a little help." And after the laugh, and before she could be brought to order: "Why on earth would Sarah hide whatever she did hide, if she was going to tell Uncle Jim about it? She trusted him. She wasn't hiding it from *him*. Find who she was afraid of and—"

They stopped her then, and under pretense of getting her

handkerchief I saw her looking at a card in her bag. Evidently she had made some notes on it.

When they took her back to the night of Sarah's death, and the intruder in the house, she was ready for them.

"You didn't see him?"

"No, nor since. He's been breaking in ever since, while Uncle Jim has been locked up. He didn't find what he wanted on Sarah, so he—"

She was making a valiant effort, but I heard none of her testimony after Godfrey Lowell had read aloud the cipher itself. Laura suddenly caught my arm.

"For God's sake, Elizabeth!" she whispered. "Didn't Sarah tell you about the cabinet?"

"What about it?"

"Let's get out of here. We've got to get home."

It took us some time, however, to escape from that crowded courtroom. The very doorways and the halls outside them were filled, and when we finally reached the street, Robert had left his car and joined the morbid throng inside the building. Laura was exasperated and almost tearful, and I was not much better.

It was Wallie who finally found him for us, and who went with us to the house.

I had my key, for all the servants were at the courthouse, and at first glance everything appeared to be as it should be.

On the way Laura made her explanation.

"I meant to write you," she said, "but I had some buying for Sarah to do, and so I wrote her. She was to tell you. Why didn't you tell me she had hidden something? It's in the cabinet, of course."

It must have been forty minutes from the reading of the cipher to the time we turned into the drive. Save for a natural urgency to get into the house and find the key to the mystery, I think none of us except Wallie realized the necessity for any haste. And he had his own reasons for not stressing that.

He said very little during the drive. I remember now that he was very white, and that he jerked his shoulder and head even more than usual. But when I had unlocked the front door and opened it everything seemed quiet and in order. The dogs came to meet us, Isabel with corpulent dignity, Jock effusively. The servants were all at the courthouse, and the house was very still.

Laura turned at once to the drawing room on the left, and as I had restored the key to the cabinet some time before, she unlocked the center door without difficulty.

The cabinet is a fine example of Louis Fourteenth, of satinwood and kingswood. It is really a small secretary; that is, a shelf draws out and forms a writing desk, and above are three doors. The two outer doors are of glass, and behind this glass are my mother's old Chelsea figures. The center door, however, is solid, and on this is fastened a very handsome oval piece of ormolu.

It was the center door which Laura opened, and I then noticed for the first time that this ormolu was fastened to the walnut lining of the door inside by some dozen very small bronze rosettes, ostensibly covering the heads of the screws. There was one in the center also, and thus they formed what might be interpreted as a clock dial.

"Five o'clock right, seven o'clock left, press on six," said Laura, and did so. "Give me your knife, Wallie."

But Wallie's knife had a broken point. I remember that now, although it meant nothing to me at the time; I remember that, and that his hands were shaking when he tried to open it. In the end I had to get my own penknife from my desk, and Laura inserted the blade along the metal binding of the door.

It sprang open, revealing between the inner lining and the front of the door a flat space, the size of the door in area but hardly more than half inch in depth.

But that space was empty.

We stared at each other. My disappointment was more than I could bear, and Laura was almost in tears. What Wallie felt I can only surmise. He bent over and examined it, and I saw then that there the lining was badly scratched. Laura saw it too.

"Those weren't there when you got it, were they?"

"I don't think so."

Wallie spoke then, for the first time.

"Why should anything be there?" he said. "Somebody was quicker than we were, that's all."

"You mean that this has been done recently."

"Since those directions were read out in court," he replied grimly. "You'll find a window broken somewhere, or a door left unlocked."

He was right. With all of us out of the house there had been no one to put in place the chain which now supplemented the lock of the kitchen door. The key of that door lay on the floor, as though it had been pushed out from outside and a duplicate or skeleton key had been used. And the door now stood open.

It was that night that Wallie disappeared.

I was less surprised than I should have been, perhaps, when he was not in the courtroom the next morning. On the evening before, at seven o'clock, he had telephoned Judy and told her not to worry.

"I'm going on the stand tomorrow," he said, "and everything will be all right, Judy."

"What do you mean, all right? If everything isn't as wrong as it can be, I don't know what it is."

But he said that he was going to testify, and that he had plenty to say. That she was to be ready for a shock, but not to think badly of him. He had got himself into this mess, and he would "take his medicine."

"Go to bed and get a decent sleep," he said. "Let me do the staying awake. And don't worry. Jim Blake isn't going to the chair."

She said later that he was not drunk, she was certain, but that his voice sounded queer.

"I've made up my mind," he finished, "and I feel better for it. It's a clean slate and to hell with what happens, for me."

But he did not appear.

I was bitterly disappointed, and Judy looked puzzled and anxious.

"He lost his nerve," she said. "He'll never tell now, whatever it is that he knows."

But the trial went on, although the papers commented unpleasantly on his absence, and Godfrey Lowell was upset. Still, on the surface at least, Wallie's testimony could neither damn Jim nor save him. Whatever the true story of that pencil in the shaft, the fact remained that Wallie was in my house at ten o'clock, and Jim was in the park.

Things went badly for Jim that day. Amos had not been located, but there was his damaging testimony before the Grand Jury; and now read into the record, over protest, that the cane had been in the hall until Sarah's body was found and then disappeared; and that further and damning fact that he had found a bloody handkerchief of Jim's the morning after Sarah's murder and placed it with the soiled clothes; that on listing the laundry the following Monday he had found this handkerchief, but that in the interval it had been washed clean and dried.

The accumulated mass of testimony was overwhelming. Nothing could shake the opinion of the experts that Sarah's letter to Jim was in her own hand, or that the drops of blood here and there on his clothing and inside the sword-stick were human blood.

"How do you know they are human blood?"

"By the shape and size of the corpuscles. Also by their numbers and groupings."

Indeed, so badly did things go that on the day following Godfrey Lowell at last put Jim himself on the stand. Jim had asked to testify and so he did, although how he thought it would help him nobody can say.

CHAPTER TWENTY-SIX

I HAVE before me now that statement of Jim's. Given much of it in question and answer, and broken by cross-examination and objections here and there, it takes many pages of the stenographic report.

As I have also, however, that document which Jim himself prepared later as the basis of an appeal, I shall use that instead.

I give it word for word.

"I had nothing whatever to do with the death of Sarah Gittings, or of Florence Gunther. I am willing to swear that before God. If I had kept back part of what little I know, it has been partly because I saw that things looked pretty hopeless for me, and partly because of my sister, who has been and is in deep trouble.

"I did not see Sarah Gittings on the night of the eighteenth of April. I had expected to see her. She had made two previous attempts to get in touch with me, both of which had failed. But on that day, a Monday, I received a telephone message from her, in which she mentioned a letter she had sent me. She seemed disturbed when I said that I had not received such a letter.

"I examined my desk, but there was no such letter. Then she asked me to meet her that night on a matter of vital importance.

"I agreed to do this, and I started rather early, intending to walk to the address she had given, which was at 1737 Halkett Street. I was to ask for a Miss Gunther. I wrote down the address, but on the way I found that I had left it in my other clothing, so I stopped at a drugstore and telephoned to the Bell house, hoping to catch Sarah before she started.

"She had gone, but I remembered that the address was in the seventeen hundred block, and rather than go back I decided to make inquiries in that block.

"I walked across the park and out. I walk rather slowly, and it was fully eight when I reached the block, and possibly eight-fifteen when I had located the house. Miss Gunther was waiting on the steps, and she took me into the house. I had never seen her before. She seemed very nervous, and had very little to say. When I asked her why I had been sent for, she said that Miss Gittings would tell me.

"We sat there until perhaps twenty minutes to ten. I asked her repeatedly to give me an idea of what it was all about, but she would not. It was not her affair, she said. But she asked me to keep my visit a secret. She made me promise it, as a matter of fact. She said she 'didn't want to be mixed up' in anything. And I did so promise.

"She seemed unduly uneasy about Sarah Gittings. I could not understand it, and as time went on she was more and more uneasy. She said she was sure something terrible had happened, and at last she began to cry. I tried to reassure her, but she said I didn't understand, and at nine-forty her condition was such that I advised her to go to bed, and myself started for home.

"In my statement to the District Attorney I said that I had

reached the path to the Larimer lot at nine-thirty. This was not true. I saw that I was under suspicion, and so I changed the time. I was on the path, or beside it, at or about ten o'clock.

"I took the same route on my return, but when about halfway up the hill toward the Larimer lot I sat down to rest. I left the path and moved some feet to the right; that is, in the direction of the Bell house. I lighted a cigar there and rested. I may have been there five minutes, when I heard some one moving on the hillside to my left, and some distance away.

"At first I thought it was a dog. I had heard dogs barking a few minutes before. I had thrown away my cigar, and I believe that against the hillside where I sat I was practically invisible to any one at that distance. But I was not certain that it was a dog, and as that part of the park has been the scene of several hold-ups, I pressed the spring which released the knife in the cane, and then waited.

"There were two people in the park below. I could hear them talking, and it occurred to me that somebody on my left was hiding there, possibly with the idea of attacking and robbing them. But this was not the case, and I believe now that this man on my left was the one who killed Sarah Gittings, and that he was dragging her body down the hillside for later disposal.

"With the two people, Mr. and Mrs. Dennis as I now know, at the foot of the hill, and myself more or less hidden above, something alarmed this man. Possibly a park policeman. I believe that this end of the park had been watched at night for some time.

"He ran toward me. I could hear him coming, and he was breathing very hard. I had the general impression of a tall man, in evening dress or dinner clothes, and wearing a soft cap drawn down over his face. That was my impression of him. I may be wrong.

"But I swear that this man was there, that he ran toward me, and that he almost ran over me. So close was he that in passing he struck my stick with his foot and knocked it to a considerable distance. He ran past me and disappeared along the hillside beyond, taking a slanting direction down into the park.

"When I had recovered I felt around for my stick, and unfortunately it was the blade which I found. I cut my hand, and I bear a small scar from that cut to this day.

"I have not invented this. The blood on my clothing and on my handkerchief that night was my own blood. Mrs. Dennis saw me tying up my hand. I went home and went to bed.

"The next morning I was not well. My servant, Amos, brought me some coffee, and laid out my fresh clothing. He picked up the handkerchief I had used the night before, and asked me if I had hurt myself. I told him I had cut my hand but that it was nothing of any importance.

"I never thought of Sarah Gittings in connection with all this until I learned that day that she was missing.

"I began to worry then. I had had an appointment to meet her, and I was uneasy. I called up Florence Gunther at her office, but she was not there, and I had no knowledge of the house where she lived save the street number. That is, I could not call her on the telephone.

"But in view of what had happened on the hillside the night before, I felt anxious. Some time around noon of that day I went back to the Larimer lot and walked over it. I also examined the hillside. But I found nothing suspicious.

"I went to the Bell house that afternoon, but Sarah was still missing, and in addition the house had been entered the night before and Sarah's room had been searched. In leaving the Bell house I again went back to the hillside. I located the spot where I had rested, and went to the left of it along the hill for a considerable distance. I found nothing suspicious and no trace of Sarah Gittings.

"The next day I had a desperate letter from Florence Gunther. She had seen in the papers that Sarah was still missing, and she was certain that she had been killed. She begged me not to bring her name into it; that it meant the loss of her position, and maybe physical danger also. Also she asked me to destroy the letter, and I did. I should have acted anyhow; as it turned out, my silence did not save her.

"But in that interval several things had happened. While I was debating what to do Sarah's body had been found, and she had been stabbed. Not only that, but I had been on the spot, or close to it, at the very time the reports said she had been killed.

"Walter Somers and I made the identification that day together, and Walter drove me home. I let myself into the house through the garden, and I found Amos in the front hall with the sword-stick in his hands. He was trying to get the blade back when I found him.

"I knew then that he suspected me. Later on I sent him out and examined the stick. There was a little dried blood on the blade, and some bits of grass and earth. That frightened me. I took it to the lavatory downstairs and washed it, and then I hid it. I put it in my liquor closet in the lower hall, and locked it there.

"But things grew worse. Mary Martin had produced the uniform, and it was evident that Sarah Gittings had written to me, as she had claimed. I was frantic, and that night I made an attempt to see Florence Gunther. She was not at home, but I found her walking on the street, near an Italian fruit stand. But I was horrified to see her go white when she saw me.

"She refused to speak to me, and when I insisted she said that I had killed Sarah; that she knew it and knew why, and that if I didn't leave her she would call an officer. On the way home I worked that out. I remembered that on the night when I saw her, while we waited for Sarah, I had idly shown her the mechanism of the sword-stick. I am not surprised that she believed that I had killed Sarah Gittings. It is easy to see why, now. She believed that Sarah Gittings had come to me with that copy of a will which disinherited me, and that to get possession of it I had killed her.

"I made no more overtures. I was afraid I would drive her to the police.

"I went home that night a sick man, and took to my bed. Some time during that week, however, I crawled downstairs. It seemed to me that if she told the police and they found the stick hidden, it would damn me. I decided to put it back in the hall, where it had stood before.

"I unlocked the door, but the stick had disappeared. I do not yet know how it disappeared, or why it was found in the cellar. My personal belief is that my servant Amos was alarmed at the situation in which I found myself, and that he buried it himself.

"It is also my belief that Amos has been either killed or bribed to leave the city, for fear that he may make this confession and thus help to clear me.

"In a similar manner, I believe that a ring of oil was planted in my car, so that I might be suspected of having killed Florence Gunther. The police know that this ring was not in the car the day after her murder.

"During this trial, much has been made of the fact that by a new will made by my brother-in-law, Howard Somers, I lost a bequest originally devised to me. In reply to that I say most solemnly that I never knew that Howard Somers had made a new will until Mr. Alexander Davis told me in New York, following Mr. Somers' death. Even had I known of it, the murder of these two unfortunate women could certainly not benefit me. The will itself was safe among Mr. Somers' papers in a New York bank vault and Mr. Waite could testify to its existence and its authenticity.

"I know nothing whatever of Florence Gunther's death. When I found that she suspected me of Sarah Gittings' murder I made no further attempt to see her, and I solemnly swear that I never did see her. Nor did I make any visit to Howard Somers on the night of his death. Whoever saw him that night deliberately used my name to gain access to him. Nor did I receive a check from him for one thousand dollars.

"As to leaving the country, I had such a thought at one time. My position was unbearable, and I was helpless. I did nothing further about the matter, nor have I attempted to escape.

"I have not invented this story since my arrest, or preceding it. I have told the absolute truth, under oath. I have never killed any human being. I am innocent of this charge. If I suffer for it I suffer for another man's crime."

Much of this was in the story he told on the stand. I believe that outside of ourselves hardly a soul in that crowded courtroom believed it. And against it was that mass of accumulated testimony, including our own unwilling appearances on the stand.

It should have helped him that on that very day the body of poor Amos was found floating down the river, but it did not. He had been drowned, poor wretch, and although we have our own suspicions we do not know to this day that he was murdered.

But I think I can reconstruct that scene; Amos confiding and amiable, flattered at being consulted. On a bridge, maybe, or on the river bank somewhere; and then a sudden thrust of a muscular arm, and the muddy swirling water closing over his head.

Jim was found guilty after only three hours' deliberation by the jury. Guilty of murder in the first degree.

CHAPTER TWENTY-SEVEN

Jim was sentenced to the chair on the twenty-fifth of June. One and all the newspapers were gratified by the verdict, and not a few kind words were said of the acumen of the police and the fairness of the trial.

Godfrey Lowell at once moved for an appeal, but he warned us that lacking fresh developments there was little to be hoped from a new trial, if it was granted.

We were stunned. Katherine took to her bed, not as a refuge but out of sheer necessity, and Doctor Simonds saw her daily. Judy went about, a thin and pale little ghost of herself, thinking eternally of the mystery, as convinced as ever of Jim's innocence.

"He's protecting somebody," she said. "He *saw* that man on the hillside. He was twenty feet from the path, and that precious Dennis pair saw him well enough to know he had on a golf suit and was wiping his hands. And this man he tells about; he almost ran over him. Uncle Jim saw him, and he knows who it was. He knows and he won't tell. And Wallie knows. Wallie ran away so he wouldn't have to tell."

She looked as though she had not slept for days, and I myself took a sleeping tablet every night and then lay awake until morning. I was alone once more, for Laura had had to go back to her children. She had wept noisily on the way to the train, and had promised to come back as soon as possible.

Of our small family group then only Katherine, Judy and I remained, for Wallie was missing. That defection of his had angered me almost beyond words. He had known something which might have saved Jim, and he had gone away. Somewhere he was hiding until everything was over.

And then, on the twenty-eighth of June, the steward called up from Wallie's club. Wallie had not been seen since the night of Wednesday, the twenty-second, and this was on the following Tuesday.

"We would like to know where he can be found," he said. "We have a number of messages for him, and one that seems to be urgent."

"Urgent?"

"Yes. A lady had been telephoning every day. Today she made me go up and look at his room. She seems to think there's something queer about his absence. She asked me to call you and tell you."

"Queer?" I said, with that now familiar tightening around my chest. "What did she think? Did she give any name?"

"No. A young woman, I imagine. I don't want to alarm you, but she seemed very nervous. As a matter of fact, she said something about notifying the police."

"She gave no reason for that?"

"No, but I've just been up to his room. It doesn't look to me as though he had meant to be gone for any length of time. His clothes are all there. And his car's missing. Still, I don't think you need to be particularly alarmed; he was erratic at times, as you probably know. If this girl hadn't seemed so excited—"

"His car is gone?"

"It's out of the garage. Yes. Has been since last Wednesday night."

It was Tuesday then, and he had been gone for six days. Of course that might merely bear out Judy's theory that he had simply "beat it," as she put it, but I myself was not so certain. It was hardly conceivable that he had taken himself off for an indefinite stay without extra clothing, or even a toothbrush.

The thing worried me. Who was it who had telephoned? Was it Mary Martin, and if so why had she suggested the police? My entire experience with Mary convinced me that she regarded the police with fear, if not with horror. Yet who else? With all his faults Wallie had apparently steered clear of the type of underworld woman who might naturally think of the police.

In the end I called the club again and got the steward.

"This young woman who telephoned, Mr. Ellis—did she give any name?"

"No. She called from a pay station. I thought she was crying, as a matter of fact, but she hung up before I could find out anything."

"Why do you say she was young?"

"Well, her voice was young, if you know what I mean."

I was sure then that it was Mary, and the fact that she had been crying convinced me that something was terribly wrong. I left the telephone and went into the library and there I had as bad an attack of palpitation of the heart as I have ever had in my life.

Joseph found me there and hurried for some bicarbonate, and when I felt a little better I told him the story. It upset him greatly. The hand holding the glass shook until the spoon clattered, and he had to steady himself by a chair.

"The police, madam? Then this young person thinks he has met with real trouble?"

"She was crying, Joseph."

In the end I called up Dick Carter, and that evening he and Joseph went to Wallie's room at the club. They examined everything there, but without result, and the story they brought back was ominous, to say the least.

On that previous Wednesday night Wallie had eaten no dinner. Instead he had gone into the writing room and there had written for a long time, until eight or after. The boy on duty there "thought he was writing a book." When he finished he had asked for a long manila envelope, put into it what he had written, taken his hat and a light overcoat from the man in the hall and gone out.

He stood on the outside steps for a moment, and then he came back. He seemed nervous and irritable, and he went into the telephone booth and talked to some one for a considerable time. Then he started out again, and so far as was known he had never come back.

Dick and Joseph examined his room carefully. Joseph, who occasionally went there to go over his clothing and to put things in order for him, said that he found nothing missing.

"But you must remember, madam," he said, "that Mr. Walter has been under a great strain lately, and it is not unusual for him to start out on an evening ride in his car and then to keep on. I have known him to do that a number of times."

"For six days, Joseph? And when he was to testify at a murder trial the next day? That's ridiculous."

"That is probably the reason, madam."

"Nonsense, Joseph! Nobody believes that Mr. Walter had anything to do with it."

From the club they went to the garage. The night man remembered clearly his coming there, and that he must have meant to return, for he had ordered the car washed that night.

"I'll be in about eleven," he had said. "I want it properly washed, too. The last time it looked worse than before you started."

He had seemed to be in a bad humor. It was about a quarter after eight when he reached there, and he ordered the car filled with gas and oil. He said he was going into the country, and he stood by watching while this was done. He seemed to "be in a hurry to be off."

But after he was in the car something happened of which the mere telling made my hands cold and sent despair into my very soul.

To quote the man at the garage:

"He had an overcoat—it's still here—and at the last moment he threw it out to me. It was a warm night. Then he asked for it again and he took a revolver out of it. He tried to slip it out so I wouldn't see it. But I saw it all right. He put it in the pocket of the car."

To me that night that revolver meant only one thing. Wallie had killed himself. Somewhere he had stopped his car on a lonely road and ended a life which had ceased to be endurable.

But why? What did he know? What had he done? Was it possible after all that those three alibis of his were wrong? Had he slipped out of my house that night of the eighteenth of April and killed poor Sarah? I went over that night once more, and I was certain that he had not.

Late as it was by that time, almost midnight, I called up Inspector Harrison. I had evidently wakened him from a sound sleep, but he said he would come as soon as he could, and while I sat there waiting my mind fairly seethed.

If Wallie was innocent, then what did he know that he would rather die than tell, and for which he would let Jim suffer? And once more I harked back to Judy and that strange suspicion of hers about her father. Were we all wrong, after all? Was Howard being blackmailed, and that will with its ambiguous clause his final price for silence? Was Katherine right and was Margaret living? And were Sarah and Florence Howard's desperate last attempt to keep that secret under cover?

Wallie and Jim both silent, the one ready to go to the chair if necessary before he would speak, and the other perhaps dead by his own hand; what did that look like?

And when the Inspector came I told him all that was in my mind, my fears for Wallie, my suspicions about Howard. He listened attentively, biting hard on the end of a toothpick and silent for some time after I had finished.

"It's ingenious," he said at last. "It's even possible. Funny thing Miss Judy would think of that, isn't it, and the rest of us would miss it? Sure he might have recognized this fellow if he was there; especially if he knew him. There's more to recognition than features. There's the outline and the clothes and the way a person moves. And here's a thing that struck me at the trial. If he was inventing that man, why put him in evening clothes? It was plausible enough up to that minute. Then the jury just sat back and yawned. Now, Mr. Somers had white hair, I think, and he wore it fairly long?"

"Yes."

"Queer case, isn't it?" he said. "Unless Blake invented the evening coat to fit the black fibers on that log. Well, let's get to this other matter."

When he left it was to go to the garage and secure a description of Wallie's car, and I believe it was almost morning before he got to his bed again. He had started the entire machinery of the city and county on the search by that time, and the only reason he did not extend that search over the country was because he felt certain, as he confessed later, that Wallie was dead by his own hand, and not too far away.

That was on Tuesday, and on Wednesday morning the papers were filled with his disappearance. "Young Millionaire Missing." "Police Hunting Walter Somers."

And on Thursday afternoon, the last day of June, we had some news.

Wallie's car had been found on the Warrenville road, not far from the end of the street car line, and about two miles nearer the city than the Hawkins farm. Some boy scouts, out for a hike, had selected for lunch a gully with a small stream flowing through it, and a half dozen had wandered up this ravine for a half mile or so.

The car had been driven over the hill, and was upside down and badly demolished. A local deputy constable had notified the police and kept the boys away. They had been anxious to turn it over.

When Inspector Harrison arrived on the scene with Simmons and four or five others, the ground had not been disturbed. They found no footprints, however, save the smaller and unmistakable ones of the boys, and they were forced to the conclusion either that the car had been empty when it started on its wild journey, or that Wallie had been thrown out somewhere on the hill.

But they found no Wallie, and nothing further to help them.

The Inspector, reporting the matter, had his own opinion of it.

"He deliberately got rid of that car," he said. "It might have lain there for a year, if those youngsters hadn't happened on it."

There was no sign of the revolver, and although inside it—it was a roadster, with one seat and a rumble—there were certain scratches, and a leather seat cushion torn in one place, these were probably the result of the terrific impact after it had shot down the hill.

There was however an unexpected result to the discovery and description of the car in the press. A woman named Wiggins came forward to say that she had seen such a car as she was leaving the street car at the end of the line at something before nine on the evening of Wednesday, June the twenty-second. She fixed the date absolutely, as she had gone to town to see her daughter off on a train, also she remembered the car distinctly, because it had almost run over her.

And she stated positively that there had been two men in it at the time.

The Inspector was very sober when he told me that.

"It looks now," he said, "as though somebody knew that Walter Somers meant to go on the stand that next day and tell all he knew. And that he was—prevented."

"Murdered is what you meant, isn't it?"

He cleared his throat.

"It's possible. It's very possible. And I suppose Walter could swim and Amos couldn't!"

Which was what he left me with, to make of it what I might.

Those few days had told terribly on Joseph. The maids reported that he walked the floor at night until they were almost crazy, and for the first time in my service he was forgetful and absent. I was startled one day to have him pour ice water into my soup, and his hands were so uncertain that he broke a piece of my mother's Lowestoft china, a thing he had not done in all his years of dusting and washing it. On the plea that he knew Wallie's habits I loaned him my car, and he took his afternoons and joined the search. That he went to the club I know, but I have no other knowledge of his movements save one.

Dick had taken Judy out to the road above the gully, and they were surprised to find my car there. When they got to the edge they saw Joseph below; he was sitting on a rock, his head on his breast, and when they called to him he jumped and then came toiling up the slope.

"What on earth are you doing?" Judy demanded.

He looked down sheepishly at his muddy clothes.

"I was looking for the revolver. Mr. Walter never killed himself, Miss."

"Joseph," said Judy impulsively, "why don't you tell what you know? You know something."

"What little I know is Mr. Walter's secret, Miss." And that was all he would say.

CHAPTER TWENTY-EIGHT

THAT NIGHT Joseph was shot. Not killed, but painfully injured. The bullet struck his collar bone and broke it, near the shoulder. But fired from only five or six feet the impact was terrific, and at first I thought that he was dead.

The two children had come in about eight-thirty, and Judy was very low. The appeal was still pending, and unless we secured a new trial Jim would go to the chair early in September. There was strong pressure being brought against a re-trial.

"James Blake has had every opportunity to prove his innocence, and has failed. A jury of thoughtful men and women found him guilty and sentenced him to death as the penalty of at least one crime. There is no question but that an acquittal would have found him at once accused of at least one other murder, and possibly two.

"There is however more at issue than this. In the past the murderer with wealth at his command has found it possible to evade punishment for almost indefinite periods, with the result that the sacredness of human life—"

It is not surprising then that our group of three was silent that night.

Judy I remember had gone back to the night of Sarah's death, as though she was desperately attempting to prove something to herself.

"Why wasn't it Wallie after all?" she said. "He was in dinner clothes that night. Suppose he broke into the house here at night? Why hadn't he stunned Sarah with that piece of wood, and then come here to get whatever it was, the records or the will? She may have lain unconscious for those three hours. Then later on he could have gone back to her."

Well, that too was possible, although Dick thought the question of time entered into it.

"He'd have had to work pretty fast," he said. "It takes time to get old putty out of a window. When I was a housebreaker—"

"He didn't finish. He broke the pane."

I recall that they wrangled about it, and that finally they decided to go out and experiment a bit. Dick's idea I think was to get Judy's mind away from Jim's tragic situation, and as I needed the same thing myself rather badly, I trailed along. It was a steaming July night, for it had rained during the day. Somewhere in the grounds next door the ex-bootlegger's children were exploding a few premature firecrackers, and on the street a steady procession of cars was passing, the riders not so much seeking a breeze as producing one.

We went out by the pantry and kitchen. Joseph was reading the paper in the pantry, and I remember that as we passed through the pantry Judy asked him the time.

"Ten o'clock, Miss."

"Aren't you hot in here, Joseph?" I asked. All the windows were down and the shades drawn.

"It's safer like this, madam."

I remember too that when we went outside, Dick carrying a

flashlight, the dogs went with us; and that Jock saw a rabbit or something of the sort in the shrubbery by the garage and made a dash for it. I whistled him back, and he came reluctantly.

We made our way slowly about. Dick turning the flash alternately on the trees, one or two of which grow close to the house, and onto windows and doors. At last we reached the back drawing room door and Dick turned the light full on it.

"Now for the knife," he said. "Durn you, I'll learn you, Miss Judy."

"Knife? What knife?"

"I gave you a pocket knife, oh love of my life. What the hell did you do with it? I put it on the desk for you."

Judy maintained that he had done nothing of the sort, and after a momentary squabble Dick went back by the kitchen to get it. As I have said somewhere, it is exactly fifty feet around the corner from this door to the kitchen porch, and as he was running he made it very quickly. It could not have been more than three minutes from the time he left us until he rejoined us.

Jock, I recall, was restless, and Judy was obliged, to hold him. She was slightly querulous. In his excitement Dick had carried the flashlight with him, and she grumbled.

"He might have left us the light, anyhow. I feel creepy."

And indeed she did, for when Dick unexpectedly turned the corner, having left the house by the front door and emerging from behind us, she jumped and screamed.

As I sit here, recalling that night, I am again obsessed with that peculiar fatality which seemed to attend all our actions during those months of terror. Here again was an instance of it. Dick goes into the house by the kitchen door and departs by the front door, leaving both wide open, and as a result we have not only another crime, but no clue whatever to the identity of its perpetrator. And in that night's tragedy lay the whole story. A matter of deadly reasoning; deadly inevitable, and as coldly and recklessly carried out.

Dick came back, as I say, and began working with the knife on the hard putty around one of the panes.

"It's hard," he said. "Look at this. Like cement. No, lady love, Wallie hadn't time to meet Sarah and knock her senseless, get here, dig out as much of this as he did dig, and then be seen on the stairs apparently on his way out, when he was seen. All those little things took time."

They wrangled about it, Judy sticking to her point. Wallie had taken the pencil up the ladder with him, because he had dropped something of his own down the shaft. Later on having to dispose of the body, he used the same ladder to reach the top of the sewer. That was why she had wanted to look at it. There was red clay around the sewer.

But we were not there more than fifteen minutes in all, perhaps less. And next door the firecrackers were popping, and the cars on the street were backfiring after coasting down the hill. What was one report more or less to us, as we stood there? When we started back toward the kitchen Judy and Dick lagged behind me, like the lovers they were, and as I was leading Jock by the collar, it so happened that I was still in this stooped position when I reached the pantry door.

Joseph was still there, in his chair. But he did not rise when I entered, and I released the dog and straightened up, rather surprised. I saw then that a thin stream of blood was slowly spreading over his shirt front, and as I stared at him his body relaxed and he slid out of the chair and onto the floor.

His eyes were open, and he seemed to be looking at me. It was as though we gazed at each other, Joseph and I, and as though he said: "You see what has happened to me. It is incredible, but here I am."

He was not conscious. Just when that look of shocked surprise left him I do not know. One moment it was there, the next it was as though a hand had been passed over his face and left it smooth. I dropped down on my knees beside him, stricken with grief. I caught his hand, which had served me for so many years. Strange, in all that time, how seldom I had touched his hand.

I felt a deep remorse, an overwhelming pity. There, under the light, still shone beneath his thin iron-gray hair the scar from that mysterious attack which might have killed him. I put my hand up and touched it, and with that I remember that I began to cry.

I realize now that some time in those shocked first seconds I heard the front door slam, but it no more than registered on my dazed brain. On the kitchen porch Dick and Judy were still talking, and the red spot on Joseph's shirt front spread a little, but very little.

I got up and went into the kitchen.

"Judy," I said, "will you go around by the front door? Joseph is—not well."

"Not well? You don't mean that he's been drinking?"

"No. Please do what I tell you."

I left them and went back to the pantry. There was no indication there of any visitor. The evening paper lay on the table, and Joseph's reading glasses beside it. Apparently he had stopped reading, and perhaps had dozed.

I had noticed lately that he dozed rather often; a sort of half-sleep, like that of a very old man. Although Joseph was not that. He was perhaps in his late fifties.

Of a weapon there was no sign whatever.

I was apparently calm enough by that time. I knew that we had probably heard the shot, but that we had laid it to the customary explosions in the street. I knew that Jock had not seen a rabbit, but something infinitely more sinister, and even to an extent I was able to reconstruct the crime; Dick had left open the door to the kitchen, and Joseph had not closed it, or certainly not locked it.

There had been ten minutes after Dick had passed through the pantry, and a shot required but a second of time. I think it was then that I remembered the slamming door, and I realized that while I stared at Joseph the murderer was still in the house, working his way forward.

The sharp ringing of the door bell over my head at that moment sent a chill over me. But it was only Dick and Judy, to report that the front door had been closed, although Dick had recklessly left it standing open, and to stare at me with curious eyes.

"Look here," Judy said. "Something's happened to Joseph, hasn't it?"

"He's hurt."

"Who hurt him?"

"I don't know," I said, and then I broke down and began to cry again. That shocked them profoundly. I remember Judy pushing me into the library and Dick running back. Then I believe I fainted, for I recall very little until the police were in the house, and Doctor Simonds was bending over me.

They took Joseph to the hospital that night, and they extracted the bullet. He was not badly hurt, but was suffering considerable pain.

"He's strong," Doctor Simonds told me, "and he has kept himself in good condition. He's not flabby like most butlers. But he's had a shock, more of a shock than he cares to tell about."

"He won't say who did it?"

"No. He says he doesn't know. But as he was shot from in front at pretty close range, that's unlikely. Unless he was asleep."

In spite of myself I could not get Wallie out of my mind after I had learned that. Wallie with his revolver, and that odd statement of Joseph's that he did not know who shot him.

Inspector Harrison was very noncommittal. One curious thing he had found that night, ranging over that first floor while Doctor Simonds worked over Joseph in the pantry. This was that the criminal, whoever it was, had paused long enough in the library to take a glass of sherry!

A decanter had been brought in earlier in the evening with some biscuits, but none of us had touched it. Yet sherry had been poured and apparently drunk. A little had even been spilled on the top of my old desk, and as it lay for some time the desk bears the stains to this day.

"But it's incredible," I said.

"Not incredible probably if we know the answer, but it certainly argues a degree of recklessness that's unusual, to say the least. If Jock saw this person with the gun near the garage, and you heard the front door slam, it looks as though he simply walked in the back and out the front of the house."

"Stopping in the library for a little wine."

"Precisely. Stopping in the library for a little wine."

There was no weapon anywhere. True, Joseph's own revolver was in the pantry drawer where he kept it, but it had not been fired and the chambers were clean and new.

Dick had gone with the ambulance, and as Robert was not about I sent Judy home in a taxicab soon after. It was not until she had gone that the Inspector ceased his ranging over the lower floor and coming into the library planted himself in front of me.

"I'm going to ask you a few plain questions, Miss Bell, and I want plain answers. First, tell me again about young Carter going back into the house."

"He ran back for a knife. I've told you—"

"Yes. Whose idea was this 'experiment,' as you call it?"

"I think it was his. I really don't think it was Judy's. He and Judy had both been talking about it."

"But Miss Judy left the knife in the house? Are you sure of that?"

"He accused her of it. Half jokingly, of course."

"That's different. Now let's go over this. He ran in by the kitchen, through the house and into the library, and then out by the front door?"

"Yes."

"Why the front door?"

"I daresay it was nearer."

He paced the floor for a moment, and the toothpick between his strong white teeth had an aggressive tilt. I began to feel uneasy, without knowing quite why.

"How well do you know young Carter? What do you know about him?" he fired at me suddenly.

"Nothing at all, really; except that he is rather a dear boy and—Judy thinks so."

"Where does he come from? Who are his people?"

"I haven't the remotest idea. I imagine he is practically alone. I know he is an orphan."

"He's poor, I take it?"

"Poor and very proud, Inspector."

"Humph," he grunted. "Doesn't it beat the devil the way a good looking boy with nice manners can get everywhere, and no questions asked? Now understand me, Miss Bell, I'm not saying Dick Carter fired that shot tonight; but I am saying that he had an excellent chance to fire that shot. And I'm going to tell you something else. He had a revolver in that Ford of his, parked in the front drive."

I was angry and outraged, but he lifted a hand against my protest.

"Now wait a minute. I'm thinking out loud, that's all; and I have a good bit of respect for your discretion. I've got that gun here, and we have a man in the department who'll be able to tell us if it's been fired lately. Magazine's full, of course. He'd have had time to do that, and to slip it into the pocket of his car on the way back to you and Miss Judy."

"But why on earth would he shoot Joseph?" I demanded angrily. "Just because he has an automatic, and I happen to know that he has carried one in his car ever since this trouble began, it is ridiculous to suspect him."

"I told you I was only thinking out loud," he said blandly, and soon after that he went away.

It was the next day that Dick was sent for and interrogated, and Judy came around to see me with black shadows under her eyes and a look of despair in them.

"They suspect him," she said. "They've got something against him now, and they may get more. Listen. What became of that knife Dick had last night?"

"I haven't seen it since. It may be on my desk downstairs."

"It isn't," she wailed. "They've got it, and it was Wallie's. Dick found it in his room the night he and Joseph searched it, and brought it away. It had the point missing from one blade."

"Do be rational, Judy. What has that got to do with it?"

"I'm as rational as you are. That knife had the point broken off a blade, and if that point fits the piece the Inspector has, the piece he found on the step after Sarah was killed, what will they think?"

"Did Joseph see him take the knife?"

"No. He just slid it into his pocket. You see we have always been sure that it was Wallie on the stairs that night, and Dick thought the knife might prove it. He showed it to me, and I thought so too."

"You can tell them that, Judy."

"And would they believe me? They would not. How do they know I'm not mixed up in the whole rotten mess? How do they know Sarah didn't write me about the will? I came down that day, didn't I? And I telephoned Dick that night. How do they know I didn't tell him Sarah was out with that copy of the will in her pocketbook? I stood to lose a lot by that will, and so did Dick if he married me."

"You're crazy, Judy!"

"Am I? Uncle Jim saw that man on the hillside, didn't he? Saw him and recognized him. Who's he protecting? Can't they easily think he's being noble and protecting Dick for me?"

"And—Joseph?"

"They'd find a reason for Joseph, if they wanted one."

"Still I daresay that even in their wildest moments, Judy, they would not accuse Dick of knocking himself unconscious on the hill, or of trying to brain you in the garage."

She laughed a little, in spite of herself, and she went away somewhat comforted. But I myself was not so sure.

They released Dick, however, after that interrogation, and things seemed to go on much as before. But I have reason to think that he was more or less under observation from that time on.

CHAPTER TWENTY-NINE

YET THINGS were moving rapidly to the *dénouement,* although none of us suspected it. It was the next day that Inspector Harrison found, on the hillside below the garage and leading up to it, those footprints of which he was to say nothing until his case was complete. I saw him from a rear upper window, tramping about with Simmons at his heels, and every now and then he would stoop and plant a stick in the ground. Toothpicks, maybe, although they would be a trifle small.

But this was the next day. That night he left a policeman on guard in the house, and the next morning one appeared to patrol the grounds. That continued to the end.

I think it was the next day, or the day following, that Lily Sanderson called up to say that Mrs. Bassett was dead.

"She simply slept away," she said. "One of the boarders here thinks she got hold of the morphia and took an overdose, but if she did who can blame her?"

She seemed very sad and desolate. I told her to come in some time, and then what with one thing and another I am afraid I forgot them both; Lily getting her sleep now, in that meretricious bedroom of hers, and Mrs. Bassett resting at last after more trouble than most human beings are called upon to bear.

I was not well during that day or two following the shooting of Joseph. I had been profoundly shocked, and what with worry about Wallie and the long strain I almost collapsed. Doctor Simonds ordered me to bed on, I think, the second day, and Judy stayed with me as much as possible.

She was still anxious about Dick, still fearful for him. She seemed to think that because everything was quiet that that very quiet was ominous, and in her desperation she was casting about for some one, any one, on whom to throw the guilt.

Thus, I think it was on Wednesday, she said to me suddenly, after the doctor had gone:

"I don't like that man."

"Why not, Judy."

"He's oily, and he's always around!"

"Only when he's sent for."

"Is he?" She looked at me queerly. "Do you suppose he just happened to be passing the house the night Joseph was shot?"

"Was he? I didn't know that."

"Well, he was. I picked him off the street. Dick was at the telephone, and I ran down to the gate to see if I could find a policeman. He was passing by in his car then."

"Well, that was fortunate, wasn't it?"

"That depends," she said slowly. "Look back a little, Elizabeth Jane. He takes care of father when he is sick here; and he knows about the will; he knows us all, and all about us. And when you think about it, he's always around, isn't he? Somebody throws Joseph down the back stairs, and where is Doctor Simonds? He's apparently waiting in his office to be called. I get hurt in the garage, and he's at home sitting by the telephone! Joseph gets shot, and he's passing by the housc."

"Really, Judy!"

"I'm going to get rid of this if it kills me. Uncle Jim gets sick, and who is in and out of his house day and night? Simonds. It's like that nursery rhyme about the warm cot, only the answer isn't mother. It's Doctor Simonds. He could get into the garage and put that oil on the carpet of the car, and so bring Uncle Jim into it. And he's got a car of his own and drives like the devil.

"How do we know he didn't go to New York that night and see father? And he's tall and rather thin, and he's got evening clothes and wears them. What I'd like to know," she went on, her voice raised and her color high, "is where Doctor Simonds comes in in all this. We've been taking his word right along, but how do we know he isn't lying?"

"A reputable doctor—" I began.

"Oh, I'm sick of reputable doctors and reputable lawyers. I don't trust any one any more. How do we know those two didn't get together, Mr. Waite and Doctor Simonds, and cook this thing up with Wallie? Doctor Simonds dopes father, and Mr. Waite draws the will. And Sarah's suspicious. She puts on the record that father was queer that day."

"And so your Uncle Jim saw him that night on the hillside after he had killed poor Sarah, and is willing to be tried for his life to protect him? Don't be silly. Are you intimating also that Doctor Simonds did away with Wallie and shot Joseph?"

"Why not?" she said more calmly. "Wallie was coming out with the whole story on the stand, so he had to be got out of the way. And Joseph knew something, or suspected somebody, so he was shot. And don't forget this. He meant to kill Joseph. That was the big idea."

"I don't believe it. Doctor Simonds has attended me for years, and—"

She made an impatient gesture.

"Why is it," she demanded, "that all women over a certain age have a soft spot for their doctors? Doctors are human. I'm asking you to think, not to be sentimental. Wallie knows the question will come up of undue influence, or of father not being capable of making a will. So what do they do? Doctor Simonds writes him a note, that father is perfectly capable of making a will. And whose word have we that the two were as reconciled during that sickness as Wallie pretends? Doctor Simonds again! You never heard Sarah say so, did you?"

"She never talked. And she didn't like Wallie."

"Then again, come down to the night Joseph was shot. Who could walk into this house without suspicion? Suppose we'd happened in before he got Joseph? Would we have suspected him of anything? No! He'd have said he saw the door open and dropped in, or that he wanted to use the telephone, and you'd have given him a glass of the sherry he likes so much and thought nothing of it."

"Why would he have come in the back door?"

"How do we know he came in the back door? Why didn't he come in the front, take a glass of wine, and then wander back. Maybe he hadn't planned to kill Joseph just then, but there was the chance, and he took it."

I think that was on Wednesday, and Joseph had been shot on Sunday night.

It is hardly surprising that I could not sleep that night, although everything was safe enough now that crime had at last entered my very house. From the night of the shooting an officer had patrolled the grounds in the daytime, keeping out the curious crowds which would otherwise have overrun us, and another one had stayed downstairs in the house at night.

The maids left him a night supper in the pantry, and a coffee pot on the range. About two in the morning there would steal through the house the aroma of boiling coffee, and although I had begun to suffer from a chronic insomnia, that homely and domestic odor acted on me like a narcotic. Downstairs was the law, armed and substantial, and awake. I would go to sleep then.

But that night I did not. I lay in my hot bed and listened to the far-off movements below, and that theory of Judy's grew until it became a nightmare. At last I got up, put on a dressing gown and slippers, and went down the stairs.

The pantry looked very comfortable, bright with lights and with that solid square blue figure drawn up to the table before the cold roast beef, the salad, the bread and cheese and coffee which were to stay it until morning.

But the officer was taking no chances in that pantry. The shades were closely drawn, and a chair was placed against the swinging door into the kitchen.

I must have moved very silently, for when I spoke he leaped to his feet and whirled on me; none the less impressive because the only weapon in his hand was a silver fork.

"I've come for some coffee," I said.

"Come in, ma'am. Come in," he said heartily. And I gathered from the zeal with which he served me that he too had found the night long and not a little dreary.

So we sat there, the two of us, companionably supping. He recommended mustard for the cold beef and so I took mustard, which I happen to despise. All the time he carried on a running fire of conversation, like a man who is relieved to hear the sound of any voice, even his own. And when my complaisance regarding the mustard brought tears to my eyes, he even leaned over and patted my arm.

"You get that coffee down, ma'am," he said, "and you'll feel better. I guess you've been through plenty."

Here, however, he delicately decided to change the subject.

"What's happened to the red-haired girl who was here the night of the—the night you sent for us? I haven't seen her since."

"That was my niece, Judy Somers. She does not live here. But she is not red-haired."

"I don't mean Miss Somers. This girl was red-headed all right. She was running up the drive just ahead of me. When she heard me, she stopped."

I sat perfectly still. Fortunately he was busy with his coffee, into which he was putting lump after lump of sugar. I managed to steady my voice.

"A red-haired girl?" I said slowly. "Did she speak to you?"

"I'll say she did. Caught me by the arm and wanted to know what was wrong in the house. I said: 'What business is that of yours?' and she said she worked here. She had a right to know. The rest had gone on, and I was in a hurry myself, but she hung onto me, and I saw that she looked sort of sick. 'Somebody been hurt,' I said, and with that she let me go."

"You didn't see her again?"

He looked at me and smiled.

"I've been watching for her here. She was a right good looking girl. But I haven't seen her. You know who it is, I suppose?"

"Yes. But she is not in my employ any longer."

I thought he looked disappointed, but certainly not suspicious. He had however little more to tell. The precinct men had arrived before. He had come from headquarters in the side car of a motorcycle which had dropped him at the street, so that he was afoot when he overtook her.

I slept not at all that night. I was remembering a conversation I had had with the Inspector the morning after Joseph was shot, and following that examination he had made of the hillside.

"Just what do you know about Joseph, Miss Bell? His private life, I mean."

"I don't believe he had any."

"He'd never seemed in any fear, had he? For himself, I mean."

"Not that I know of."

"Never took any precautions, I suppose? Didn't act like a man with anything hanging over him?"

"Not at all. He had looked very tired lately, and I had asked him if he wanted to go away. I have never seen him show any fear, except that last night as we went through the pantry he had the windows all closed. I spoke about it, and he said it was 'safer.' Or he felt safer."

"What about women? I suppose you wouldn't know about that?"

"I am sure there was nothing of the sort."

"Well, I'm not. I'll come to that later. But there are some things about this shooting that make it just a little different from the others. In the first place, the method's different. There's no attempt to camouflage the crime, and no attempt at even ordinary care against detection. In the others care was taken. I'll go further and say that I've never seen a case where such steps were taken, during and later, to cover every possible trail.

"But look at this. You're around the corner, only fifty feet away. You've got a dog, two dogs. Except for the fact that you held the terrier that night he'd have made a row that would have awakened the neighborhood. The house is fully lighted. Joseph is awake, or was until a moment or so before the shot. If he was asleep the criminal can't know it. The shades are drawn.

"Then again, why shoot him in the house? He must have been in and out. He goes to the garage sometimes, he is not always shut up at night. Since Walter's disappearance he's been out at all hours and in all sorts of places.

"But he's shot right here, in a bright light. The psychology's different, that's all. Look at this: I've just shot Joseph back there. I've got the revolver in my pocket, and so far I've got away with it. I've been watching the place, so I know you three are outside and may come in at any moment. The front door is open; the hall is brightly lighted. You may come in that way, walk right in on me. What's my normal procedure?"

"I should think you'd get out as fast as possible."

"Absolutely. But I don't. I saunter into that library, in a full light, pour myself a glass of sherry, put down the glass and then take my departure. And if you didn't use cut glass sherry glasses I'd leave a decent fingerprint instead of what we have. It's too reckless to be normal! Unless it's a woman."

At four o'clock that morning, unwilling to disturb the Inspector until later, I called Dick and asked him what he thought of it. He was drowsy and only half awake.

"She was running up the drive, toward the house," I said. "And she didn't know what had happened. She asked the officer."

But I could hear him yawning over the telephone.

"Sorry," he said. "The old bean isn't working very well. Probably she knew a lot more than she was admitting. Maybe she was running out, and when she heard your policeman she reversed the process. It's an old dodge, you know."

I sat on the side of my bed, the telephone on my knee, and tried to think. If that casual hypothesis of Dick's was correct, then Mary Martin had shot Joseph. It would have been easy enough. She knew the house and the habits of all of us; that the two maids retired early, that Joseph sat reading until late in the pantry; if she had seen Judy and Dick and myself go out into the grounds, she knew that the lower floor outside of the pantry was unoccupied. She had only to enter by the kitchen, fire her shot, and go forward, in order to escape.

But she had not escaped. In the ten, perhaps fifteen minutes between my finding Joseph and the arrival of the police, she had had plenty of time, but she had not gone.

Had she been upstairs during that interval, on some mysterious errand of her own? In Sarah's room, perhaps, or Joseph's, and then later on in the upper hall, peering over the banister and watching that influx of blue coats and muscular bodies; still later on stealing down the stairs, step by step. Sounds from the pantry, men talking, and Mary looking over her shoulder. Then the still open front door, a run for freedom, and the sound of a motorcycle stopping and escape cut off.

Had she turned in a panic, and started back toward the house? Or had she already planned the maneuver in case of necessity? To believe that last was to believe her old in crime, infinitely cunning and desperate.

I had worked myself into a condition bordering on hysteria by seven in the morning, when I called up Inspector Harrison, but his very voice quieted me. He was angry enough, however, when I had told him the story.

"The damned blockhead!" he exploded, referring to the policeman. "I'll break him for this."

"He didn't know. She said she worked here."

"She did, did she? She's a quick thinker. But what *was* she doing there?"

"You don't think she shot Joseph?"

"Well, I don't think she's the temperament to shoot Joseph and then go in and take a glass of wine. No."

I felt relieved. I was not fond of Mary, but the picture I had drawn for myself during the night had revolted me.

"Then I'm glad I talked to you. And by the way, Mrs. Bassett is dead."

I told him of Lily Sanderson's message, and he was silent for so long when I had finished that I thought we might have been disconnected.

"Hello," I said. "Central, I've—"

"I'm still here, Miss Bell, I'm sitting on a chair thinking what a damned fool I've been. I don't belong on the force. I ought to be a paperhanger!"

And with that he hung up the receiver.

CHAPTER THIRTY

WE KNOW now of that frantic rush he made, within ten minutes of my calling, to the Halkett Street house, and of that frenzied search he made later on that day, along the highways and particularly the by-ways of the Warrenville road. Some time after midnight he found what he was after, and not too late.

That had been in his mind all that day; the fear that he would be too late. And in the meantime he had set his guards. There was to be no escape this time, not even by death.

Even then he did not know the story, of course. But he knew the criminal and his incredible cunning. Let all go on as usual. Confide in no one. Disarm him, throw him off the track, and then into that fancied security of his thrust the long arm of the law. That was his method, he has said since, and that it answered is shown by the fact that for ten days apparently nothing happened.

Ten hot July days, with Godfrey working on the appeal; with Jim growing weak from heat and strain; with Joseph in the hospital, receiving our visits with great dignity, but refusing to alter his original story that he had been asleep and had not seen his assailant; with no word whatever of Wallie, or of Mary Martin; with the flowers on Mrs. Bassett's grave shriveled in the sun, and the policemen still on duty in my house and grounds, and with Katherine still in the house on Pine Street, stubbornly refusing to accept the repudiation of her which she considered Howard's second will to be.

Some time in that ten days I made a list of possible and impossible suspects, with a notation following, and as it is before me now I reproduce it. It shows better than I can tell it the utter confusion of my mind.

This is my list:

Godfrey Lowell	(Unlikely)
Inspector Harrison	(Why?)
Doctor Simonds	(Possible)
Mr. Waite	(Possible but unlikely)
Wallie	(Improbable, and why?)
Dick Carter	(Possible but incredible)
Jim	(Possible but unlikely)
Abner	(No)
Amos	(Dead)
Joseph	(Himself shot)
Robert	(Unlikely. No reason)

In such fashion did I fill in those ten interminable days. There were apparently no new developments, and the Inspector obstinately absented himself. Judy had grown thin to the point of emaciation, and still by night our guard ranged the lower floor and by day patrolled the grounds.

Joseph had come home from the hospital that day, I remember. He took hold of the household much as usual, tottering from the silver drawer to the kitchen closets; but he was much shattered, and with that bandaged arm of his he could do very little. I arranged to send him to the country for a few weeks, and he agreed gratefully.

Then out of a clear sky, on the seventeenth of July, Katherine made her resolution and precipitated the crisis.

She was an intelligent woman, Katherine. Perhaps I have done her less than justice in this narrative. She was strange during that time, more frightened than she wanted us to know, and the result was that she withdrew herself.

I think from the time Jim took the stand at the trial, maybe even before it, she knew that he was protecting somebody.

"You say that you saw his white shirt front? What do you mean by that?"

"Just what I say. A white shirt front."

"He wore no vest?"

"I can't say. I had only an impression of evening clothes. He might have worn a dinner jacket."

"But you are sure of the cap?"

"No. I think it was a cap."

"Yet he came, according to your story, so close to you that he knocked this stick out of your hand. You could see a cap and a white shirt front, but you could not see anything more?"

And it was then that Jim hesitated. He was under oath, and an oath is a solemn matter. Then he glanced toward Katherine, and sat up a little in his chair.

"That is all I saw. I was on the ground. His face was turned down the hill."

Whom would he protect with his life but Howard? Howard with his heavy white hair, his invariable dinner dress in the evenings, and something to be kept hidden at any cost. Small wonder that Katherine thought of Margaret, or that she reverted to the will as the key to the mystery.

And so, very close to the end now, I go to the scene that afternoon, when at Katherine's request I accompanied her to Mr. Waite's office.

She had made the appointment and we were admitted at once. I was rather shocked by the change in Mr. Waite. He looked worn and not too well, and I thought there was a certain apprehension in his eyes when he greeted us.

He rose, but did not come forward.

"I am lame again," he explained, indicating a cane which stood beside him. "The old trouble. Well, I can only say that I am shocked and grieved, Mrs. Somers. Of course the appeal—"

"An appeal will do no good," said Katherine somberly.

"Still, new facts may come up. The case is of course not closed until—"

"Until they have killed an innocent man," Katherine finished for him. "And that is what they will do, Mr. Waite, unless the truth can be brought out."

He stirred uneasily in his chair.

"The truth? What is the truth? I am as much in the dark as you are." And seeing her face, he bent toward her across the desk. "I know what you mean, Mrs. Somers, and—I can understand. Nevertheless, I tell you that as surely as I sit here in this chair, Mr. Somers outlined the provisions of that will and signed it when I had prepared it. He was as rational as I am now. He discussed his family and his affairs. He even recognized that the will would be a blow to you, and said that he meant to leave an explanatory letter with it. Just why he did not do so I don't understand."

He was not acting. He was telling us facts, and I think Katherine saw it as well as I did. She sat stiffly upright, but the antagonism was gone from her voice.

"He did not explain the fund of fifty thousand dollars?"

"He did, and he did not. The son was to administer it for some purpose. He simply said that Walter would understand. He was of course still very weak, and he was not a talkative man, I understand. To be frank, I was in pain that first day, and not much better the second. I don't recall many details, although of course I have tried to since. A will is a routine matter."

"He did not appear to have been drugged?"

"Absolutely not."

"And Sarah was there? Sarah Gittings?"

"She left the room, but she came in once and gave him some medicine."

But Katherine was stubborn. Here were the facts, and she still refused to accept them. Mr. Waite saw that, and stiffened in his chair.

"The will was genuine, Mrs. Somers," he said. "If you have any doubt of it, I will go to the hotel with you, and we will repeat my own actions of those two days. I will show you that on the first day I was taken to Mr. Somers' room by the hotel manager himself, and that the floor clerk saw us and remembers this. I will show you that Walter Somers received me at the door and took me in, and that on both days Florence Gunther was with me. The floor clerk saw her there also."

"That is what she says. I know that, Mr. Waite."

He made an angry gesture.

"But she may be lying? I wonder if you realize what you are saying? If I had forged that will—and it seems to me that this is what you imply—why should I have gone there at all? Good

God, madam, what had I to gain by such a criminal proceeding? It's nonsense, insane outrageous nonsense."

Katherine, however, seemed hardly to hear him. Certainly his words had no effect on her. She looked up from that careful inspection of her gloves.

"You would be willing to go to the hotel?"

"Of course I'll go to the hotel. Do you think I am afraid to go?"

She stood up, and for the first time it apparently occurred to her that he was angry; white with anger. She looked at him with that faint childlike expression which so altered her face.

"I'm sorry. It's only that I don't understand. You see, there was no reason, no reason at all. Not if Margaret Somers was dead."

He was polite but still somewhat ruffled when we started out. None of us, I am sure, had any idea that any *dénouement* was imminent. I remember that Mr. Waite delayed a moment or two to sign some letters, and that he grunted as he got up and reached for his stick.

"I've lost four teeth and two tonsils to cure this thing," he grumbled, "and I'm just where I started."

And so we reached the hotel, Katherine silent and absorbed, Mr. Waite limping, and I trailing along and feeling absurd and in the way.

We were fortunate in one thing: the rooms Howard had occupied were empty. Unluckily the manager was out, but the floor clerk, Miss Todd, was at her desk. She greeted us with the decorous gravity the occasion seemed to demand, and bowed to Mr. Waite.

"You remember me?" he asked her.

"Oh, perfectly, Mr. Waite."

"And that I came here on two succeeding days?"

"Yes, indeed. Mr. Hendrickson brought you up the first day." And she added glibly: "The first day you had the young lady with you. The second day she came again, and the hotel notary came up later. I remember it all very clearly. Miss Gunther sat down there on that chair until you called her in."

"And why?" said Katherine suddenly, "did she wait in the hall? There was a sitting room."

Miss Todd looked slightly surprised.

"That's so," she said. "That's queer, isn't it? Do you remember why, Mr. Waite?"

Mr. Waite however did not remember. He had seen no sitting room. He had been ushered directly from the hall into the bedroom.

"I suppose the nurse was in there," he said impatiently. "If you will open the rooms, Miss Todd—"

Miss Todd was very curious, and I think rather thrilled. She led the way briskly to the sitting room of the suite, unlocked the door and threw open a window or two; but if she hoped to be asked to remain she was disappointed.

"In which room was Mr. Somers?"

"In there. I'll light the lights."

"Thanks. If you'll close the door as you go out—"

Some of Mr. Waite's irritation had returned. He limped into the bedroom Miss Todd had indicated and stood surveying it.

"I imagine your questions are answered, Mrs. Somers," he said crisply. "Here is the room. You have learned that I came here as I said. If you believe that I came for any other purpose than to draw up a will, I will remind you that I had not spoken ten words to Mr. Somers in my life until that day. I came because I was sent for, and for that reason only."

Katherine moistened her dry lips.

"And my husband was in bed?"

"In this bed. I sat down beside him, and I saw that he looked very ill. It was a dark day, but the lamp was on. I sat down here, as the lamp was on this side of the bed then. I see they have moved it."

There was a curious look in Katherine's face.

"I wonder," she said tensely, "if you mind doing again just what you did then? Can you remember? Try to remember, Mr. Waite! Everything. Every *little* thing."

I could see that her suppressed excitement had its effect on him. He glanced at her, and his voice was not so cold. He walked to the hall door and opened it.

"Let me see," he said. "Yes. Walter Somers was outside the door, in the hall. He opened the door and said: 'Father, Mr. Waite is here.' Then he stepped back and I came in alone. I think he closed the door behind me. Yes, he closed the door.

"I said: 'Well, Mr. Somers, I'm sorry to see you laid up.' He said something about his condition; that he was better, or getting better, and I put down my hat and gloves and got out some paper and my fountain pen. After that it was strictly business. He had the will pretty well thought out, and I suppose I was there only a half hour."

"And that is all?"

"All I can recall.

"He seemed perfectly normal. But he was nervous. I had propped my stick against the table, and once it slipped and fell. I remember that he jumped as though I had hit him. I picked it up and hung it on the doorknob, and—that's funny! That's damned queer."

He was staring at the wall beside the bed.

"They've taken away the door," he said.

"What door?"

"There was a door there by my right hand. It's on the other side of the bed now."

We all stood there, stupidly staring at the door. None of us, I fancy, had the remotest idea of its significance at that moment. It was Katherine who realized it first.

"Are you certain you were in this room, Mr. Waite?"

"I don't know. They all look alike. Of course they are always changing these places about."

And I think to Katherine must go the credit of that discovery, although Inspector Harrison had known it for at least a week. She was very calm, very quiet, as she went into the hall and called Miss Todd again.

"You are certain that this was my husband's bedroom?"

"Oh, yes, indeed, Mrs. Somers."

"And it has not been altered since? No changes have been made?"

"Only the new curtains at the windows."

"Thank you."

Miss Todd retired, her sharp eyes giving us a final survey as she closed the door. Not until she was gone did Katherine move, and then it was to cross the sitting room and glance into the bedroom there. Then she called to us, quietly enough.

"I think this is where you came, Mr. Waite," she said. "To Walter's bedroom, where an accomplice of Walter's impersonated his father and drew that will."

And only then was there a ring of triumph in her tired voice. "I knew it," she said. "I knew it. My poor Howard!"

CHAPTER THIRTY-ONE

Of the plot which lay behind that discovery we had no knowledge. It was enough at the moment that there had been a conspiracy.

But later on in the day, the initial shock over, our ideas began to crystallize. Who had been the man in the bed? What relation did he bear to the murders? Was he himself the murderer?

None of us, however, gathered in my library that night, believed what was the fact; that the amazing *dénouement* was even then in preparation, and that it was a matter of only a few hours until all our questions were to be answered.

We were silent but more cheerful than we had been for days on end. There was hope now for Jim, and Katherine's relief was written in her face. Jim would be saved and Howard was once again hers to mourn. The frozen look had left her.

Judy too looked better than she had looked for weeks.

She had come in with her eyes bright and her color high, to show me a very nice but extremely small diamond on her engagement finger.

"Isn't it beautiful?" she said.

"It is indeed beautiful," I told her gravely. For it seemed so to me, that symbol of Dick's pride and his essential honesty. And I was proud of Judy, that she wore that bit of stone as a queen might wear a crown.

But talking got us nowhere that night. Again and again we went back to the scene in that hotel bedroom, with no result. It was Judy, with Dick's arm around her and Katherine accepting that as she had accepted the ring, who put forth the theory that the fifty thousand dollar clause which had been put in the will was to be the payment to this unknown for his services.

And it was Dick who followed that scene to its logical conclusion, and who said that a man who could put on a wig and look enough like Howard to deceive Mr. Waite under those circumstances, could easily have fooled Jim at night on the hillside.

Nevertheless, we were as far from the identity of this man as ever.

It was a broiling July night. At ten o'clock Joseph, in his traveling clothes, brought in some lemonade—he was leaving at eleven that night for a short holiday—and I remember that he had hardly gone out when Judy drew up a window shade for air, and suddenly drew back from the window.

"There's a man out there!" she said, "Just outside the window!"

Dick ran out at once. He was gone for some time, and when he came back it was to report that nobody was in sight, but that it was about to storm and that they'd better be on their way. I thought he looked rather odd, but we were all on edge that night and so I said nothing.

I was uneasy after they had gone. I wandered back to the pantry, where Robert was talking with the policeman and waiting for Joseph to come down, and while Robert stayed in the pantry the officer made a round of the house, inside and out. He found nothing, however, and as the storm broke soon after that, Joseph departed to the car by way of the kitchen porch in such a downpour as I have seldom seen.

I did not go up to bed, although it was eleven o'clock. I had a strange feeling of uneasiness, as though something was about to happen, or had happened. And at a little after eleven Jock sat up in the hall and gave tongue to a really dreadful howl.

I do not even now pretend to explain that wail, or that when I went into the hall both dogs were standing with their neck ruffs on end, staring into the dark drawing room.

I had a picture of that, of the incredulous terror in their attitudes; then they turned and bolted into the library, and I am not ashamed to admit that I followed them, and slammed and locked the door.

No, I have no explanation. When a short time later Inspector Harrison arrived and rang the door bell, he found me locked in the library; and it was all he could do to make me open the door.

He was soaking wet, and he looked very weary. He looked dejected, too, although I did not understand that until later on.

"I'm late," he said, "but we've had to cut open a safe deposit box in a bank, and it took some time and some red tape. Then I had another little job—I'm not proud of that. Still, maybe it's all for the best. It will save Walter Somers a lot of trouble."

"Walter? He is alive?"

"He is. I've been doing a little nursing now and then, in odd moments! But he's alive. He's going to live. He's conscious, too, since yesterday. And now that you've turned up the story of the will—Waite told me—I hope the family won't prosecute. He tried to do the right thing, and it damn near cost him his life."

He sat back and bit savagely on the end of a rather soggy toothpick.

"Yes," he said, "I've bungled this thing. When I did get on the right track it was pretty late. It was the shooting of Joseph Holmes that started me straight, by the way. But I lost a lot of time, one way and another, and—well, I'll say this, our killer will never kill again."

"You've got him? The murderer?"

"Yes," he said. "Yes—and no."

I sat bolt upright in my excitement.

"Who was it, Inspector? Surely I have a right to know."

"I'm coming to that." He looked at me and smiled quizzically. "But not right off. We'll lead up to it, and then there'll be no shock."

"Shock! Then I know him?"

"You do indeed," he said gravely. "That's why I want to tell you the story first, so you'll understand. We'll call it a sort of psychological preparation. And I'm going to tell the story without telling you his name. We'll call him James C. Norton, because that's the name he used when he rented the safe deposit box. Norton. And up to a quarter to three o'clock today we hadn't a hope of landing him. We knew he was guilty, guilty as hell. We've watched him and followed him, but we hadn't a thing. Then today he went to the Commercial Bank—he had to—and he gave the show away.

"Mind you, he knew he was being watched, or he suspected it. He didn't know I'd found Walter, however. He had half killed Walter and tied him up in an abandoned farmhouse, and for a while he went back there now and then. It wasn't to his interest that Walter die. But later on it *was* to his interest that Walter Somers die. He left him where I found him, left him to die. I want you to remember that.

"Things were getting pretty hot for him, and with Walter

dead the story wasn't likely to come out. And I'll say for him, that he held on to the last minute. He knew we had nothing on him. As a matter of fact we didn't, until about seven o'clock tonight.

"I want to give you a picture of this man, Miss Bell. We knew that he was at least moderately tall and stronger than the average. After I learned the story of that little comedy at the Imperial we knew he could act, and that he was a bit of a forger. Also we knew he was quick and catlike on his feet.

"But we knew some other things.

"This man had no heart, had no bowels of compassion. He had instead a lust for money and an infinite capacity for wickedness. Also he had cunning, a cunning so devilish that he had not only covered up his tracks; he had deliberately thrown suspicion on another man by the manufacture of false evidence.

"Such, for instance was the oil in Jim Blake's car; the use of Jim Blake's name in that deadly visit to New York, and the clothing, expressly arranged to give the impression to the man Parrott that it was Blake; and there was the telephone message using Blake's name. And I say here and now that this man would have let Jim Blake go to the chair with less scruple than I break this toothpick.

"That's the picture of this assassin. I want you to remember it.

"Now I'm going to somebody else. I don't need to give you a picture of her. But she seemed to be in this thing up to the neck. She was, and my hat's off to her. Her name is Mary Martin."

"Mary! What has she done, but damage?"

He smiled again.

"She did her bit, when the truth began to drift in on her. She tried to save Howard Somers, but this—this Norton was too smart for her. She helped to find Walter. And on the night she was seen here in the drive she was running because she knew something. She knew there was going to be another murder, or an attempt at it."

"She knew Joseph was to be killed!"

"She was afraid it would be tried. We're coming to that. But she was in a bad way herself; she suspected what had happened to Walter. She was almost crazy, that girl. So she relaxed her vigilance and—you find Joseph shot."

"What possible interest had Mary Martin in Walter Somers, Inspector?" I asked, bewildered.

"She had a very real interest. She had married him last fall."

He gave me a moment to comprehend that, and then went on more briskly.

"Now let's go back. Let's go back to last summer, to the end of July.

"Walter Somers was in town, and one day he got a note to go to a house on Halkett Street. He went, and he met there this man I'm calling Norton, and a woman named Bassett. The Bassett woman claimed to have been a maid in Margaret Somers' employ in Biarritz, and that Margaret Somers had there given birth to a child."

"Howard Somers' child?" I asked sharply.

"No. I believe that was the plot at first; it was all a plot anyhow. There was no such child. This girl they were passing off was the Bassett woman's own daughter by an earlier marriage. The Bassett woman had remarried. The girl's name was Mary Martin."

"Mary! And she believed it?"

"I think she did believe it for a time. She wanted to believe it. That's natural. But when the plot failed Mrs. Bassett told her the truth. The immediate result, however, was that Walter sent for his father, and his father came here.

"Howard Somers denied the story in toto. He had had no second child by Margaret, and she had borne no child in Europe. The whole story was a lie. But he worked himself into a heart attack over it, and that was the start of the trouble.

"Norton's little plan had failed. But this sickness gave him a new idea. Queer how one criminal thought leads to another. He went to Walter with the scheme about the will, and Walter almost kicked him out. But Walter was in debt, and there was the idea. It got to 'eating him,' as he put it. Then, too, he was already interested in the girl. The girl was straight. She'd believed that story. As a matter of fact, when her mother told her the truth she tried to see Howard Somers at the Imperial, but they would not let her in.

"And there's this to say in Walter's defense; he felt that he had been badly treated, that a half of the estate should have been his. Later on, when his father was dead, he went on to New York to tell the whole story. But they alienated him there, and we have to remember that he wasn't sure his father had been murdered. Mary Martin suspected it, and told him so over the long distance telephone.

"And I'll say this for him. He went to this Norton and Norton denied it. But he laid Norton out cold on general principles, and Norton hated him from that moment. That's what I mean when I say Walter Somers had paid his price. His wife was desperately in love with him, but she loathed the whole imposture. She threatened again and again to uncover it.

"Now about this conspiracy to draw up a fake will. It wasn't Walter Somers' idea, although he helped to put it through, and the cleverness with which that will was put among his father's papers was not his idea either. It was simple enough, at that. Mr. Somers did not alter his mind or his will during that illness, but he did pay some notes of Walter's. In some ways he was a hard man, and he made Walter bring him the canceled notes.

"He meant to keep them. But Walter was afraid Mrs. Somers would find them in case his father died, so he had him endorse the envelope to be returned to him—to Walter—in that case.

"He told all this to Norton, and that was the start of the whole business. Norton suggested that a spurious will could be placed in that envelope and substituted for the notes, and that's what happened. Howard Somers himself carried back to New York and placed among his private papers that bogus will, endorsed in his own hand 'to be given to my son Walter in the event of my death.' It was neat, when you think of it."

"Neat, but wicked, Inspector!"

"Wrong, yes. Still, you must remember that no murder was contemplated. Fraud, yes, although Walter felt justifiable fraud, in a way. But murder, never.

"So the comedy was staged, with the fifty thousand dollars to be this Norton's share, his pay for that imposture, for the study he had made of Howard Somers' signature, and for that bit of comedy where he lay in a bed in a low light, on a day selected because it was dark and gray, and feebly signed that spurious document.

"I haven't been able to learn everything from Walter yet, but in that bit of comedy—and God knows it's the only comedy there is—the Bassett woman in a nurse's uniform played Sarah Gittings. Walter had prepared for that by having her give massage treatments to his father. And Norton was Mr. Somers. I imagine that Norton was the man with the box of flowers the floor clerk remembered. He had long gray hair, she said, and so

Norton probably wore into the hotel that day the wig made to resemble Howard Somers' hair.

"That flower box had flowers in it. But it had some other things, make-up and silk pyjamas, a dressing gown, a few bottles and toilet articles to dress the room. That's a guess, but it's pretty accurate.

"It was Walter's room, anyhow. But they locked off the door to the sitting room, and Walter told Sarah Gittings he was having some friends there for cocktails, and to 'stay out.'

"Yes, it looked like a water-proof scheme. The hotel manager himself brings Waite up, and Walter meets him in the hall. Nobody thinks about that door. The notary comes up on the second day and witnesses the signatures. Florence Gunther is brought in from the hall. When it is over the players go away, one at a time, by the service staircase.

"Only one thing slipped. It was Sarah Gittings' custom to go out for a breath of air, and Walter took her place. But the two gray days with rain that were the best for their purpose, the twelfth and thirteenth of August, were bad days for her. She did not go out. She read a novel aloud to Mr. Somers instead, and put that on her record.

"Now let's go on to this last spring, when Sarah met Florence Gunther. She may have remembered seeing her at the Imperial, sitting in the hall, or it may have been pure accident. It's enough for us that they met, that Sarah told her she was with you, and as your connection with the Somers family is well known, that Florence finally mentioned the will.

"Sarah Gittings was incredulous, and after learning the date of the will, she went home and examined her records. She saw then that no such will could have been drawn on those days, and she began to try to reach Mr. Blake. She also finally induced

Florence to abstract that copy from the safe, and on Monday the eighteenth of April she arranged to meet Mr. Blake at the Halkett Street house.

"She had already secreted the records in the wood cellar, but that evening she moved them to the cabinet. She had learned the terms of the will that day, and she knew well enough that there had been fraud. Also she knew about that secret compartment in the cabinet. When she took the will from Florence that afternoon she gave her the clock dial directions.

"But she felt safe enough. She had no thought of danger that night, when she left the house.

"Now, I'm going to reconstruct that night of the eighteenth of April. And you must remember that Walter Somers is still very weak, and that he himself can only guess at a part of it."

CHAPTER THIRTY-TWO

"At five minutes past seven Sarah Gittings left this house, taking the dogs with her. She had the will for safekeeping probably inside her shoe—there had been some purse-snatching in this neighborhood—and she carried in her bag the key to her room and the key to her front door; but she was excited that night, and she forgot to lock her bedroom door.

"She went out the door, and in the drive she found Walter Somers waiting for her. He knew that she frequently took the dogs out at that hour, and this night he knew something else. He knew through Norton, who had his own way of learning things, that she had met Florence that afternoon and received a longish legal envelope from her.

"It looked as though the fat was in the fire.

"After he had talked to her, Walter saw that the game was all up. He threw up his hands and told her he'd go to his father the next day and tell him the whole story. But he begged her not to tell Jim Blake. If his stepmother ever heard this story he was through. She agreed to this.

"But she would not give him the copy of the will. Said she'd left it in the house. And he didn't trust her. She had never liked him. He didn't even believe her.

"But she showed him her hand bag, and the will was not in it.

"'I'll give it back to you after you've seen your father,' she told him, and she left him standing there in the drive.

"He says, and I believe him, that he never saw her alive again.

"I'm not defending Walter for trying to get into the house and to get the will. He did get in, although he broke the point of his knife in doing so. While he was working at the putty of the door back there he says he heard her whistling and calling for Jock, who appeared to have wandered off. She was, he thought, in or near the Larimer lot, and later on, when his errand had been fruitless and Joseph had helped him to escape from the house, he thinks he still heard her.

"I imagine he is right about that. The dog had run off, and she hunted him. Then, instead of going on to the house on Halkett Street, she may have been coming back here to telephone and call off that meeting. In any event, perhaps because she was tired with the climbing she had done, on the way back she seems to have sat down on that log to rest.

"And that was where Norton found her, at or about the very time the officer had arrived and the house was being searched. He probably heard the dogs, and so located her. He struck her down from behind, so that she never saw him, and he thought she was dead. Later on, at ten o'clock, he went back to look and she was still living, although unconscious. Then he finished the job. With a knife this time, a knife with a blade approximately four and a half inches long.

"Something scared him about that time, and he ran. He didn't see Blake on the hill, coming back after waiting at the Halkett Street house for her until twenty minutes to ten. He didn't see Blake, but Blake saw him. And now remember this. He—Norton—still had that wig like Howard Somers' own hair, and he was going back to see if that job needed finishing. Also very likely he hadn't got the will that first time. I believe he put that wig on his head before he went back to the lot.

"He didn't know what had happened in the interval. She might have been found, there might be a policeman there. So he put on that disguise of his, and he fooled Jim Blake; evening clothes, longish white hair and so on. It isn't hard, when the story began to come out, to see who Jim Blake thought he saw that night.

"It put him to bed, and it damned near sent him to the chair."

"Then this Norton, or whoever he is, killed her for the will?"

"Partly. Partly, too, because, although Walter Somers was sick of the whole thing, Norton was determined that it go on. It was that determination, that the will stand, that was behind all the other murders.

"If Florence had kept quiet, she might have lived. He may have thought she would. She'd taken that will from the safe, and she might keep quiet about it. But she tried to see you, and that was fatal. Also, there was something else which marked her for death. Sarah had told Walter about her records for those two days, and when repeated searchings of this house didn't turn them up, this Norton concluded that Florence had them.

"Under the pretext of bringing her here to you, he lured her into a car.

"He killed her and searched her, and then he went to the Halkett Street house that night and examined her room. He made the Bassett woman help him. It was Mrs. Bassett the Sanderson woman heard crying.

"But I want to go back to Walter. Joseph helped him out of

the house that night, and he got away down the hill behind the garage, dressed and came back here. You were expecting him, but he had to come back anyhow. He had dropped his fountain pen into the airshaft, and it bore his initials.

"He got it, as we know. He was uneasy when Sarah didn't come back, but that's all. He was afraid she'd left the dogs somewhere and gone on to New York. That scared him; he wanted to do his own confessing, and when he went out and heard the dogs in the lot next door he thought she had tied them there. He was pretty well upset, but he went back to the club and played bridge.

"That is Walter's story, and I know that it is true in all the salient points. When Sarah was still missing the next day he was worried, especially when you found she was not in New York.

"But he still didn't believe she was dead, and he never thought of Norton.

"When her body was found, however, he went almost crazy. He went to Norton and Norton was shocked and grieved. Walter just didn't understand it, that's all. And when the swordstick disappeared he began to suspect Jim Blake.

"Only why would Blake kill her? Had she shown him that will and let him believe it was genuine? And had Blake done it, in a passion of anger or to secure the will? It was the only answer he had, and we have to admit that a good many people thought the same way.

"The only person who didn't was Mary Martin, and she suspected Norton from the start. She'd loathed the scheme from the moment she learned about it, the will and all of it.

"But Florence Gunther's death showed Walter where he stood. I'm not defending him for keeping silent, but it's easy to see how he argued. He could not bring the two women back, and how could he prove that Norton had killed them? Norton was still protesting his innocence, calling on high heaven to show that his hands were clean.

"Then you burned the carpet from the car, and Walter was all at sea. He didn't know where he was.

"But Mary knew, and Norton knew she knew, or suspected. She wasn't safe after that, so we have her taking Joseph's revolver and keeping it by her, and later on we have her going to New York to the Somers' apartment.

"She went out on the Brooklyn Bridge that night and threw the gun into the river. She felt safe, after some pretty awful weeks."

"But why go to the Somers' apartment?" I asked, bewildered.

"Because she saw this. She is quicker than Walter, and she believed what he still didn't want to accept; that Norton was the killer. She saw Norton still holding on, searching Florence's room after her death for the records, searching this house over and over. And by the way, there's your ghost! It may be helpful with your servants!

"She saw too that Mr. Somers would have to go next, before the story of that bogus will was uncovered, and that with Mr. Somers dead Jim Blake would go to the chair. Either that or Wallie would have to tell his story, and even then that mightn't save Blake. Blake mightn't have known that the will was not genuine."

"Inspector," I said gravely, "I want to know who Norton is. I must know. This is—well, it's cruel."

"I think it's kindness," he said. "I want you to realize this man first, as he is. The craft of him, using Jim Blake's name to get to Howard Somers, and even dressing like him; telling Mr. Somers the proofs of Jim's guilt, and promising for a thousand dollars to keep certain things to himself; getting Mr. Somers into his study to write that check, and putting poison into the highball while he is in that study."

"And that is what he did?"

"That is what he did. And I don't mind saying that it was that check, which we found in his box, which completed the case against him. He couldn't bring himself to destroy that check."

He looked at his watch.

"Now—I'll hurry over this—I'm going to Walter Somers again. His father's death drove him frantic. Again he had no proof, but Mary Martin was certain. She had broken the glass and raised the windows—there's an odor to cyanide—and she felt pretty sure it was murder. And if murder came out, the whole story came out. You can see why she tried to prevent that.

"She called Walter on the long distance phone and told him, and he about went crazy. But a confession then was a very grave matter; here were three deaths as a result of that conspiracy, and one of them his own father.

"He compromised with himself. He would see that Jim Blake got off; but if he was acquitted he would let things ride.

"But the verdict was a foregone conclusion. He had to come clean to save Jim, and Norton had to confess. For he knew now that Norton had got the records. He had been over this house and he knew the cabinet. When the clock dial cipher was read in court all Norton had to do was to come here and get them.

"When Walter left the club, that night before the day when he was to go on the stand, he had in his pocket a full confession of the murders. He had taken it with him to force the murderer to sign it. He had determined to get that signature, at the point of a gun if necessary. But he hoped to get it, by letting Norton have a chance to escape. It looked reasonable to him; if Walter went on the stand the next day it was all over anyhow. As to the will, I mean.

"But I ought to say this. He and Norton were definitely out. There had been furious trouble between them, and of course there was the time when Walter had knocked Norton cold. Walter hated the very sight of the other man, and he knew it.

"Walter picked him up in his car; and they drove out of town, Walter talking, the other man listening. Walter was going on the stand the next day, to tell all he knew. He was wary enough; he had his revolver. But Norton, too, was prepared for trouble that night. He was too quick for Walter.

"He knocked him out and nearly killed him, and then he took him to an abandoned farmhouse out on the Warrenville road and left him there, tied. But it wasn't to his advantage that Walter die. He drove the car over the hill where we found it, and he carried off Walter's revolver and locked him up. But he went back now and then, although Walter was in pretty poor shape when I found him.

"With Walter dead, Mary would tell the story, and he was through. He went back now and then, looked after him a bit. Not much. Just enough to keep him alive. But he had not been there for three days when we found him, and he was mighty close to death.

"Of course it's easy to say this now, but the case against Blake never had satisfied me. You know that. I gave you my reasons before. All along there have been some things that didn't quite fit. Why would Jim Blake invent a man in evening dress? Well, the answer to that is easy. He was not inventing it. He *saw* a man in evening dress. But he said this man's face was turned down the hill. Now that's not possible. A man doesn't run rapidly along a bushy hillside in the dark without looking where he is going.

"So I decided that this man, conceding that Mr. Blake saw a man, was some one he knew and wouldn't mention. And after Howard Somers' death, I began to wonder if it wasn't Somers.

"But that didn't get me very far, and to add to the confusion, Joseph is shot. Jim Blake is in jail, Mr. Somers is dead and Walter's missing. And still Joseph gets shot! I'll admit that I thought it possible at the time that Walter had done it. There was some underneath story, and Joseph either suspected or knew something. It was pretty clear to me that Joseph had had to help Walter out of the house the night he broke in.

"And I had had a theory that Walter knew a good bit about the attack on him at the top of the back stairs.

"Then there were some queer things about the shooting. Joseph was sitting in the pantry with the shades drawn, 'because it was safer,' but he tells some cock and bull story about dropping off to sleep, and that with the kitchen door standing wide open!

"It looked fishy to me, and as I say I thought of Walter Somers. He had had a revolver when he left, and of course at that time I didn't know the rest of the story. So it was for Walter's footprints that I looked the next morning, around the grounds and down the hill. But I didn't find them. I found something that I couldn't make out.

"It looked to me as though a woman had climbed that hill the night before, and gone back the same way. You'll remember that it had been raining, and the ground was soft. Certainly a woman had come up that hillside, walked past the garage and through the shrubbery toward the kitchen door. And she had gone back the same way, except that she went out the front door and around back along the opposite side of the house from where the three of you were.

"But here was the queer thing. It was a heavy-ish woman, moving slowly, and she walked on the outsides of her feet. I'd seen prints like that before.

"Well, I had two choices, and I took the wrong one. Young Carter had been in the house at the time the shot was fired, or close to it; he had a revolver in his car, and he had a knife with the point gone, and that broken blade fitted the bit I'd picked up on the steps back there. And there were other things. He had an interest in that will and he was young and strong. I don't mind saying that I gave him considerable thought.

"It was you yourself who put me on the right track. If it hadn't been for that message of yours about the Bassett woman I believe this murderer, this cold and crafty assassin, would be free tonight, and not where he is.

"But we had to move slowly. We had no proof; we had the story and the motive, but what else? Not a fingerprint, or a track, or a weapon! Nothing to hang the case on, and he knew it. We went through his belongings with a fine tooth comb, and found nothing. We could jail him for forging that will, but we wanted him for four murders!"

"Four?"

"Amos was murdered," he said. "He was shoved into the river and he couldn't swim. *Because* he couldn't swim," he amended that. "Four murders and three murderous assaults, and we had nothing.

"Nothing that we could lay our hands on, anyhow. But it came to me one day, sitting by Walter's bed, that if this man would do all he had done for fifty thousand dollars, he'd be likely to have kept that check for a thousand; that if he had, we had him.

"We watched him after that, day and night. And at last he slipped up. He slipped up today. He went today to the Commercial Bank to draw some money. He had an account there in the name of Norton. And he had a box there, too.

"We had the bank open that box tonight, and we found that check there; the check, and the duplicate copy of the will Sarah Gittings carried hidden the night she was killed.

"So we got him. We'd had his house surrounded, and he hadn't a chance. He walked out of that house tonight in a driving storm, and got into a car, the same car he had been using all along; the car he used to visit Howard Somers and the car in which he had carried Florence Gunther to her death, under pretext of bringing her here to you.

"But he was too quick for us, Miss Bell. That's why I say I bungled the job. He had some cyanide ready. He looked at the car, saw the men in and around it, said, "Well, gentlemen, I see I am not to have my holiday—"

"Holiday! You're not telling me—"

"Quietly, Miss Bell! Why should you be grieved or shocked? What pity have you for this monster, whose very wife crawled out of her deathbed to end his wickedness?"

"He is dead?"

"Yes," he said, "Joseph Holmes is dead."

And with that I believe that I fainted.

THE END

DISCUSSION QUESTIONS

- Were you able to predict any part of the solution to the case?
- After learning the solution, were there any clues you realized you had missed?
- Would the story be different if it were set in the present day? If so, how?
- Did the social context of the time play a role in the narrative? If so, how?
- What role did the geographical setting play in the narrative? Would the story have been different if it were set someplace else?
- If you were one of the main characters, would you have acted differently at any point in the story?
- Did you identify with any of the characters? If so, which?
- Did this story remind you of any other books you've read?
- If you have read other books by Mary Roberts Rinehart, how did this one compare?

MORE MARY ROBERTS RINEHART FROM
AMERICAN MYSTERY CLASSICS

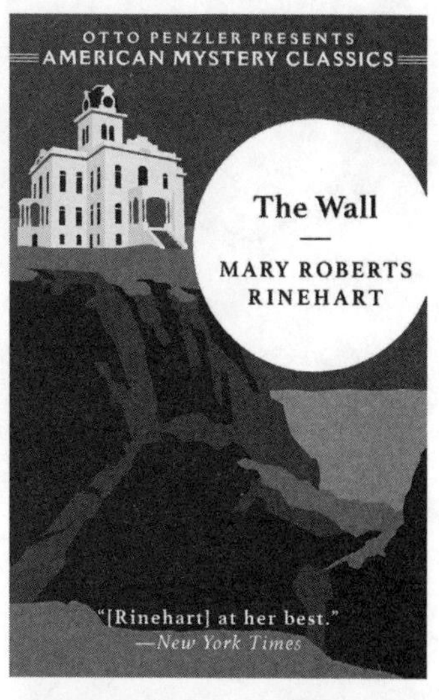

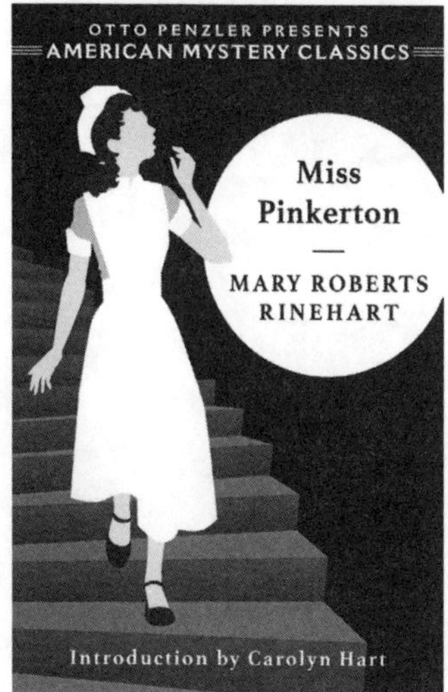

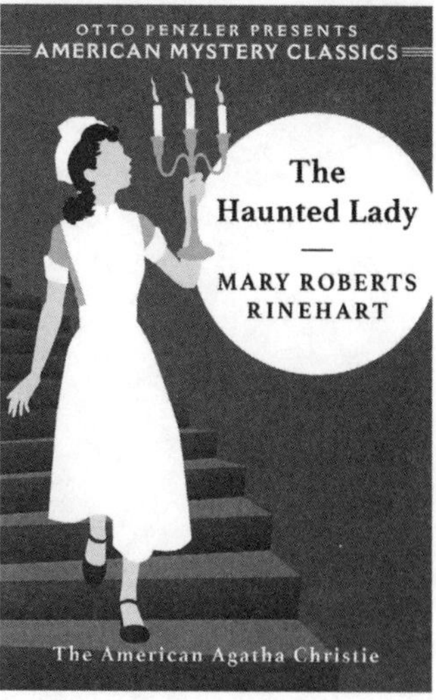